W9-ATW-439

FEB 2012

Angelina's Bachelors

**Center Point
Large Print**

**This Large Print Book carries the
Seal of Approval of N.A.V.H.**

Angelina's Bachelors

A Novel, with Food

Brian O'Reilly

Recipes by Virginia O'Reilly

CENTER POINT LARGE PRINT
THORNDIKE, MAINE

This Center Point Large Print edition is published
in the year 2012 by arrangement with Gallery Books,
a division of Simon & Schuster, Inc.

Copyright © 2011 by Brian O'Reilly.

All rights reserved.

This book is a work of fiction. Names, characters,
places, and incidents either are products of the author's
imagination or are used fictitiously. Any resemblance to
actual events or locales or persons, living or dead, is
entirely coincidental.

The text of this Large Print edition is unabridged.
In other aspects, this book may
vary from the original edition.
Printed in the United States of America
on permanent paper.
Set in 16-point Times New Roman type.

ISBN: 978-1-61173-283-2

Library of Congress Cataloging-in-Publication Data

O'Reilly, Brian, 1958–
Angelina's bachelors : a novel, with food / Brian O'Reilly ; recipes
by Virginia O'Reilly.
    p. cm.
ISBN 978-1-61173-283-2 (library binding : alk. paper)
1. Widows—Fiction. 2. Food—Fiction. 3. Large type books.
    I. Title.
PS3615.R453A85 2012
813′.6—dc22
                                                                    2011036248

Angelina's Bachelors

CONTENTS

CHAPTER ONE

Dreaming in Dark Chocolate

"Perfect," whispered Angelina.

Standing alone in the moonlit warmth of her kitchen, she stroked them each softly in turn and applied the slightest, knowing pressure to each. They were cool to the touch now, all risen to exactly the same height, the same shape and consistency, laid side by side by side on the well-worn wooden table. The dusky scent of dark chocolate lingered in the air and on her fingers.

She heard a tiny creak of expanding metal behind her. She'd left the oven on and the door halfway open, and heat was escaping into the room. She crossed the floor in her thick woolen socks and clicked off the knob. When she closed the door, a pillowy, cocoa-laced draft brushed up past her shoulders and face. She breathed in deeply, pulled back her unruly tumble of raven-black hair, and cinched the belt on her robe a little tighter.

Back to the business at hand: her Frangelico Chocolate "Dream" Cake.

As she mentally rehearsed the steps to come, as she always did when she was working out her methods for a new recipe, Angelina thought about that "dream." It was unlike her to give a recipe such an extravagant title. She preferred practical headings as a rule, which told you what was required for cooking and not much more. She always made cakes for birthdays and special occasions, but this one, for her niece Tina's twenty-first birthday party, felt special. This was going to be a cake to be remembered.

She imagined how Frank would laugh when she plunked down a big slice in front of him and called it by its whimsical name. He would laugh precisely because it was unlike her. Angelina liked to think that she could still surprise him from time to time after five years of marriage. She thought of him taking his first bite; she could hardly wait.

That would show him.

Angelina knew that she was making a point with this cake, as lovingly and in the most appetizing way possible, but making a point just the same. It had nothing to do with vanity. It was about certainty. She needed to be sure that her husband understood certain realities. Most important, she needed to be sure that he understood that cooking was not just about food. It was about character.

A few weeks earlier, she and Frank had been invited to dinner at Vince Cunio's house. Vince was a local contractor, who did well for himself and had kept both Frank and Angelina gainfully employed for the past four years—Frank as a finishing carpenter and Angelina as office manager and part-time bookkeeper.

Vince was closing in on sixty, and his wife, Amy, was busty and younger by about twenty years; you didn't have to know her long to spot the surgically enhanced chip on her shoulder. She'd left the neighborhood at seventeen for Nevada, in hot pursuit of a married man twice her age. She had returned four years ago without explanation and had wrangled Vince to the altar in short order. Amy belonged and was out of place at the same time, like a grown woman forced to move back into her teenage room, plotting a woman's schemes while lying amongst a girl's stuffed animals and high school pennants.

The four of them were friendly and familiar enough, having all grown up in the same South Philly neighborhood, though at different times and ages, but Angelina was always sure to keep in mind that it didn't pay to fool yourself into thinking that you could count too much on your close, personal friendship with your boss. One minute you're all one big happy family; the next, you've accidentally crossed some line, which was always moving, and just that quickly you're out in the cold. You can never be equals when one of you is writing the other's paycheck.

It had been a nice, genial get-together that

11

Saturday night: Vince and Amy, Angelina and Frank, and two other couples. It had started off innocently, with drinks, a couple of trays of crab puffs and cocktail wieners from the freezer section, chips and dip. Dinner had been simple enough, a big, family-style bowl of salad, good steaks, baked potatoes with sour cream and chives, and steamed broccoli "boiled in a bag," swimming in a prefabricated cheddar-cheese sauce. They opened a couple of bottles of wine that were too expensive for the occasion and passed a companionable meal talking about the rain, the Phillies' chances, and the trouble Vince was having getting an approval for the wraparound deck he was adding to his house down the shore.

Then came coffee and cake. It was a pretty cake; white frosting with a decorative swirl of chocolate sauce on top, a chocolate-covered strawberry in the center, adorned with slivers of toasted almonds on the side. Angelina knew it was going to be good before she tasted it. She recognized the style right away. It was from Tollerico's Bakery and old Mr. Tollerico knew what he was doing. The men dug right in.

"Wow, Amy," said Frank, always quick with a sincere compliment, which was one of the qualities Angelina loved about him. "What kind of cake is this?"

"It's an Italian rum cake."

12

"Did you make this yourself?" asked Frank.

"Sure did," said Amy.

There it was. *Liar,* thought Angelina.

That the cake was from Tollerico's was beyond any doubt. Angelina had recognized it as easily as if the old man had signed it. She knew the decoration, the flavors, she could probably write up the recipe in her sleep. In fact, she could write a better recipe in her sleep.

Angelina felt the heat rising at the back of her neck. She couldn't just let it pass, on principle, but calling Amy on it in front of the others was out of the question. Maybe she just needed a little nudge toward confession. Without taking her eyes off her cake, Angelina said, "The butter cream is really nice. Did you poach the eggs in the syrup or make the custard first?"

Any baker capable of making this cake would know which was the more stable emulsion method, the one that keeps in the refrigerator longer if you're making it a day or two ahead for guests. She was pretty sure Amy wouldn't.

Angelina had dark, penetrating eyes. She had been told more than once that she often unnerved people she hardly knew by looking at them too intently, so she looked purposefully down at her plate and listened for her answer.

"I just did it the regular way," said Amy, after a noticeable hesitation.

"Oh," said Angelina. *Busted,* she thought.

Taking credit for a cake you couldn't bake if your life depended on it, that you'd bought instead, was so like Amy. She would have told the same lie to the first person who'd asked; it just happened to be Frank. But the way she'd said it, preening, flirtatious, almost as if she'd been making a play for her husband right in front of her, and under false pretenses no less . . . it was like stroking a cat's fur backward; it rubbed Angelina the wrong way.

Or, maybe, Angelina thought, if she were going to be completely honest, *maybe she was just jealous.* Not jealous of Amy; that would be beyond ridiculous and beyond unfair to a man like Frank. But maybe she was jealous that her husband might possibly like somebody else's cake just a little too much. Maybe the fact that it was Lying Amy's cake was just the icing.

As they drove home after the party, she'd told Frank about the deception, and he had treated it lightly, as she knew he would.

"So, if you needed a heart transplant, and Amy was your doctor and told you she could do it, but she was really a *podiatrist,* that would be okay with you?" Angelina had argued.

"Honey, telling me Amy isn't a baker is like telling me Amy isn't a doctor. It doesn't really come as a surprise," said Frank.

Angelina rolled her eyes in mock exasperation. "Boys don't know anything!"

She was enjoying her over-the-top sense of moral outrage and so was Frank. She loved the way it made her feel whenever she could make him laugh.

She was going to show him, though. Because she loved him, she had to make sure he'd never again forget the difference between a store-bought and a homemade cake, especially hers. This cake would be irresistible.

When she'd come down to the kitchen after her shower, she'd deliberately left the lights off. She liked the way the cake looked in the bright light of the full moon that was streaming in through the windows. On the kitchen table a wooden spoon sat in a small saucepot, which held crushed hazelnuts that had been soaked and heated in Frangelico, next to the bowl of thick, velvety pastry cream she had prepared earlier. She released one of the layers from its baking pan and settled it onto the cake plate. She had sprinkled them while they were still warm with the same infused brandy, so they were now redolent with a harmonious perfume of filberts and chocolate. She deftly spread some of the pastry cream on the first layer and sprinkled a tablespoon of the crushed nuts on top of it. She added the second layer of cake, more buttery cream, and a dusting of nuts.

Angelina always aimed for an extra shading of flavor when she created a recipe, something to complement and enhance the most prominent flavor in a dish, something that tickled the palate and the imagination. Here, she had chosen aromatic, earthy hazelnuts to add an extra dimension of texture and taste. She'd heard someplace that some musical composers said that it was the spaces between the notes that made all of the difference; when you were cooking, it was the little details, too.

Each layer of the dense cake covered the one beneath it as she laid them on, like dark disks of chocolate eclipsing moons made of crème anglaise instead of green cheese. In short order, the sixth and final layer had efficiently been fixed into place. She took a half step back to check for symmetry and balance, then moved on to the frosting.

She poured the mixture of butter, milk, and chocolate that had been resting on the stove top into a mixing bowl, added a pinch of salt, a dash of real vanilla extract, and began whisking it all together with powdered sugar, which she sifted in stages to make sure that it combined thoroughly.

She took the bowl to the counter and plugged in the electric hand mixer.

Stiff peaks, she thought, as the blades purred to life in her hand.

The first time her mother, Emmaline, had let her use the mixer on her own was when she was seven. . . .

"Swirl it around gently, all the way in, until you get stiff peaks," her mother said.

As a little girl, Angelina had no idea what that meant, but soldiered ahead and started vigorously whipping the cream, assuming that her mother would tell her right when to stop, as she always did.

"Ma, is it 'stiff peaks' yet?" she had asked after a minute or two.

Her mother glanced over casually and said, "Not yet."

Half a minute later: "How about now?"

"Not yet."

Then the oven timer dinged. When Emmaline went to pull that day's cake out of the oven, she failed to completely cover the heel of her hand with her towel and gave herself a little burn. She rinsed it quickly under cold water, no harm done, as Angelina kept mixing. A moment too long later, Emmaline reached in and turned off the beaters.

They leaned over the bowl together. Emmaline dipped in a finger and tasted. "Oops. You made butter."

Angelina poked in a finger and tasted, too. It was sweet, but it wasn't whipped cream. She had miraculously *made* butter.

As they prepared a second batch, Emmaline explained the mystical relationship between cream and butter, in a way that was easy for a seven-year-old to understand and remember.

Emmaline was French, having been courted and swept away to America by Angelina's father after the war, and she was a wonderful cook. She had a deep, abiding appreciation for all things culinary that she had passed on to her daughter like her eye color and thoughtful turn of mind.

While she'd been lost in memories of her mother, Angelina's frosting had come together nicely. She dragged a high wooden stool over to the bowl on the table and lithely perched on it cross-legged, her habit since she was a teenager. She had an artist's touch with a frosting knife, and soon the cake stood royally resplendent in a smooth, russet-colored coating.

She reached for a block of white chocolate and started whittling thin, blond strips off it with a vegetable peeler. When she had a generous pile in front of her, she put down the peeler, scooped up a double handful of shavings, and paused for a beat as she considered the top of the cake, the way a golfer coolly considers a fairway. With a single, graceful movement, she passed her hands over the top and a curtain of white curls settled like magic on the cake's surface, each shaving falling precisely where she had meant it to.

Only then did she let out a satisfied breath and start cleaning up. Of all life's rich rewards, Angelina felt that the creation of cake must be one of the most gratifying, if you knew what you were doing.

Once she had everything back in its proper place, she opened her recipe diary.

When she was fifteen, her mother had given her a copy of *Mastering the Art of French Cooking* by Julia Child and a volume of *Larousse Gastronomique*. Angelina had studied them systematically and completely, and she had started making her own notes in a recipe diary soon after she'd graduated from high school, a practice she kept up diligently to this day. The crushed hazelnuts were a new invention and she wanted to make sure that she made note of it on the day she first thought of it, as was her longtime practice.

She placed the glass cover over the cake stand and put the cake in the refrigerator. She tipped a little Frangelico into two tiny aperitif glasses and took them with her as she headed back upstairs.

Frangelico Chocolate "Dream" Cake

Serves 16

INGREDIENTS FOR PASTRY CREAM
  3 cups whole milk
  9 tablespoons cornstarch, sifted
  ¾ cup sugar
  5 eggs
  5 tablespoons cold butter, cubed
  1⅛ teaspoons vanilla extract

INGREDIENTS FOR THE SIX-LAYER CHOCOLATE CAKE

1⅛ cups flour

1 cup Ghirardelli sweet ground chocolate powder

3 teaspoons baking powder

2 ¼ cups sugar

15 eggs, room temperature

6 tablespoons butter, room temperature

¾ cup milk, room temperature

INGREDIENTS FOR HAZELNUT FILLING

2½ cups sugar

1 teaspoon cream of tartar

½ cup Frangelico brandy

1 ¼ cups hazelnuts (coarsely crushed in a plastic bag with the side of a meat mallet)

INGREDIENTS FOR CHOCOLATE FROSTING AND GARNISH

⅛ teaspoon salt

2 tablespoons Frangelico brandy

½ teaspoon vanilla extract

2 cups butter

1 cup heavy cream

1 cup Hershey's Special Dark cocoa

6 cups sifted confectioners' sugar

1 two-ounce bar white chocolate for shaving curls (such as Perugina) or ½ cup white chocolate chips (such as Ghirardelli)

METHOD FOR THE PASTRY CREAM

Pour ⅜ cup of the milk into a large mixing bowl. Gradually sift in the cornstarch, whisking it into the milk as you go to create a slurry. Add half the sugar (⅜ cup) and the eggs and whisk to completely combine.

In a medium heavy-bottomed saucepan, combine the remaining 2⅝ cups of the milk with the remaining ⅜ cup sugar and stir to dissolve, about 2 to 3 minutes. Continue to stir constantly over medium-low heat, until the temperature reaches between 160° and 165°F as measured with a candy thermometer, then remove from the heat. Temper the egg mixture with 1 tablespoon at a time of half of the hot milk mixture (about 21 to 24 tablespoons) whisking the egg mixture constantly as you do so. (This is done to equalize temperatures without cooking the eggs.) Return all the liquids to the pot and bring again up to 160°F over medium-low heat (be vigilant because at 170°F the eggs will begin to curdle), stirring frequently with a wooden spoon until you feel a drag on the spoon as the mixture begins to thicken. Cook for one minute. Remove the custard from the stove and whisk in the butter and vanilla extract. Pour into a mixing bowl and allow to cool to room temperature, then chill in the refrigerator for at least 4 hours.

METHOD FOR THE CAKE

Preheat the oven to 400°F and arrange two of the oven racks on the middle-most levels. So the batter will cling to the sides, line only the bottoms of six 9-inch round cake pans with parchment paper.

Sift together the flour, chocolate powder, and baking powder multiple times to remove clumps and to aerate. In a large mixing bowl, use an electric mixer set on high speed and very gradually let the sugar flow into the mixer blades as you beat the eggs until they become light lemony yellow in color and hold soft peaks, about 5 to 10 minutes, depending on the power of your mixer. Sift ⅓ of the flour mixture onto the whipped egg mixture and fold it in. Repeat twice, folding in each addition before adding the next. Over medium-low heat, melt the butter in the milk in a heavy-bottomed saucepot. Immediately fold the hot milk/butter mixture into the egg/flour mixture, combining well but taking care not to overmix. Spoon the batter in even amounts into the six prepared cake tins, spreading as evenly as possible.

Bake until the top of the cake springs back when lightly prodded, and a toothpick inserted into the center comes out clean, about 10 to 15 minutes. Remove the cakes from the oven and use a thin knife to loosen the sides. Let cool 10 minutes in the pan, then flip each one onto a plate and peel off the parchment paper, transferring each to a cooling rack as you do so. Let the cakes cool completely before attempting to fill and frost.

METHOD FOR THE HAZELNUT FILLING IN SYRUP

Preheat the oven to 350°F.

Combine the sugar and cream of tartar in a heavy-bottomed saucepot. Add the Frangelico and ½ cup water, stirring constantly over medium-low heat only until the sugar is dissolved, about 10 minutes. Stop stirring and cook over very low heat until the syrup is hot and has the consistency of thick maple syrup, about 5 minutes. Meanwhile, spread the hazelnuts on a baking sheet and toast them for about 5 minutes. Sprinkle the hazelnuts over the surface of the syrup, remove it from the heat, and let it cool slightly, about 5 minutes.

To keep the cake plate clean while you are filling and frosting the cake, tear off about six 12-inch squares of waxed paper and fold them corner to corner twice to form wedges. Spoon a small amount of the hazelnut syrup in the center of the cake plate to act as an anchor for the bottom layer. Place the waxed-paper wedges daisy-petal style around the cake plate with the pointed end of each at the center of the plate. (The waxed paper wedges will be held in place by the dollop of syrup.) Then, place the bottom layer of the cake onto the plate and spoon a fifth of the hazelnut filling (about 2 or 3 tablespoons) in dollops onto

5 of the 6 layers (reserving the nicest layer for the top frosted layer), spreading it out evenly with a flat spatula. Let the layers stand with the hazelnut syrup while you prepare the frosting.

METHOD FOR THE FROSTING
In a large, heavy-bottomed saucepot, dissolve the salt in the Frangelico and vanilla. Add the butter and half the cream and sift in the cocoa over low heat, stirring continuously until the butter melts, about 3 minutes. Remove from the heat and transfer to a large mixing bowl. Gradually sift in the confectioners' sugar, mixing well with an electric mixer as you go and combining thoroughly before each addition of confectioners' sugar until smooth and soft peaks form. Let the frosting cool to room temperature.

ASSEMBLY
Divide the chilled pastry cream into 5 even shares and drop each ⅓- to ½-cup portion in dollops over the nut-topped base layer using an offset spatula to evenly spread it to within 1 inch of the edge. Layer the other nut-topped cake layers in turn, filling each the same way, and frost the sides and top of the assembled cake. Use a cheese plane or vegetable peeler to shave curls of white chocolate evenly onto the top of the cake. Keep refrigerated until ready to serve.

Frank walked into the bedroom pulling on a clean white T-shirt. Angelina liked watching him dress, liked the way his chest and shoulders moved as he stretched his way into or, better yet, out of his T-shirts. He ran his fingers through his slightly graying hair, still damp from the shower. He was older than Angelina by about half a dozen years. He'd worn his good looks well over time and seemed to grow into them as he got older, as he became more comfortable with himself. He worked hard for a living, but the work never seemed to wear him down. It tempered him, kept him trim, taught him the value of being able to concentrate on life one step, one board, one nail, at a time, and it had taught him that steadiness paid off over time. He had no really bad habits, though he used to smoke before they were married and she'd made him quit.

He was the least vain man she had ever met. Tonight, though, he made sure she was watching, then made a little show of turning to look at himself in profile in the bedroom mirror and patting his belly.

"Uh-oh," he said, "I think I'm gaining weight."

Angelina laughed and played along. "You could use a little weight on you, you worry so much."

She reached over and handed him his glass from the night table. They clinked and sipped. He came over and sat on the edge of the bed. "I can't keep eating the way I ate at dinner tonight," he said. "But I couldn't stop. It was too good. I'm going to weigh five hundred pounds if I keep eating like that. You're gonna have to come and visit me when I'm the fat man in the circus."

She got up on her knees and slid across the bed in his direction. "Oh, don't worry, honey, I'll grow a beard and we can still be together."

He laughed and she hugged him from behind.

"You haven't gained five pounds in the five years we've been married," she said. "Besides, I know what I'm doing. You think I'd risk messing up your good looks?"

"Wow, a good cook and a sweet talker, too? How did I get so lucky to get you to marry me?"

"*I* got lucky."

"We both did."

They kissed, and as happened more often than not, Frank held it an extra moment or two and let her be the one to decide when the kiss was over.

She sighed. It had been one of the things early on that made her fall madly for him. Angelina clambered back over to her pillows. Frank stretched out full length on his back on the bed and rubbed his chest thoughtfully.

"I picked up a weird phone call at work today," said Angelina.

"Weird how?"

"It was a lady from the bank, looking for Vince. When I asked what it was regarding

26

before I transferred her over, she said that a 'deposit' had bounced in the company account."

"So?" said Frank. "He probably didn't move all that money he's got to the right account in time."

"It wasn't a check that bounced—at least, I don't think so. She said deposit. That means it could have been a direct deposit from a builder. That would be bad."

"How come?"

"If Vince has a builder who's defaulting on a *deposit,* or God forbid more than one, he could go out of business. Seriously. I see the books once a quarter, he runs that business right on the edge. He likes buying shore houses and vacations for Amy too much."

"Maybe she meant to say *check.*"

"Maybe. I'd feel better, though, if we had more money saved up in case something happened."

"If you're really worried, maybe we should skip the party."

She looked at him and could see his sincere concern for her feelings. He was so easy for her to read.

"No, you have one niece," she gently chided him. "You're like a second father to her, she adores you. Tina's only going to turn twenty-one once, you know. I'm doing all of the cooking, so it's not costing that much. Plus, I already bought all of the food."

"Still, if you're feeling kind of tense about it,

27

maybe I can help with that." He reached back, fluffed his pillows, and grinned.

"I don't know, maybe you better call Amy. Maybe she'll drive right over with a nice piece of cake for you."

He laughed. "I don't want a piece of Amy's cake. I want a piece of—"

Angelina's eyes went wide. "Don't be rude!"

She ran her fingers through his hair. Frank reached past her and turned off the table lamp. He slid in under the covers and they leaned into each other eagerly and melted together, the way they always did.

2:00 a.m.

Frank had been tossing and turning for an hour or more. Now he lay staring at the ceiling. His wife was curled up next to him with her back turned, sleeping peacefully, her feet lightly touching the side of his calf under the blankets.

"Angelina," he whispered.

She rolled over and bunched the covers in her fist under her chin. "Hmmph?"

"I can't sleep."

"I'll make you some warm milk."

"No, don't wake up, I'll go do it. You go back to sleep, okay?"

" 'Kay. Don't touch the cake, it's for the party," she said. "Love you."

"Love you, too."

Angelina nestled deeper into the warmth he left behind in their bed. As she drifted back toward dreaming again, she knew, sure as morning comes, that he was going to try for a piece of cake, and the thought of it made her smile. As she fell back to sleep, she forgave him in advance. He'd never stand a chance with a cake like that.

Frank winced a little as he made his way down the hall. His left arm had fallen asleep, and he opened and closed his hand to get the blood flowing again. He'd been nursing a pain in his lower back and one in his shoulder all day, which was odd, since he didn't remember pulling anything lately. *Once you break forty, it's all over,* he thought.

He made his way down the hall in his robe and slippers and down the stairs without turning on any lights. He knew from experience that the bright light in the hallway would do more to wake Angelina up than a whisper in the dark had.

Frank was a light sleeper, a condition that he felt had been getting worse in the last few months. His father had always had trouble sleeping later in his life, and Frank could remember as a kid hearing him padding around the house at night when everyone else was in bed. The apple never fell far from the tree, he supposed.

Frank entered the kitchen and a remnant of moon was still shining in the window, so there was enough light without having to turn on the kitchen switch. Something about lighting up the house in the middle of the night worked against ever getting back to sleep. Once he started turning on lights, it was only a matter of time before he'd turn on the TV, and then he was done for—he'd wake up achy and cold on the sofa the next morning, which was a mighty lonesome feeling.

He opened the refrigerator door and poised silently, motionlessly when he saw it, standing foursquare on the brightly lit top shelf on its pedestal, in all of its majesty. He caught the peripheral scent of chocolate in the air, taunting him, enticing him. He swung the door open and reverently lifted the cake in his hands.

He placed it on the table and removed the lid, setting it down ever so softly, so that it made no noise at all, even to his own ears. He leaned over, spread his palms on the tabletop, and inhaled. If there had been any hope of self-denial left, that incredible aroma finished it off.

Frank had a technique that he used on Angelina's cakes, and he had only gotten caught once (or so he thought), so he felt pretty confident in its effectiveness. He would take the big cake knife, cut out a sliver for himself, ever so thin, then skillfully close the gap and cover it over as seamlessly as possible with the leftover frosting Angelina always kept in the fridge for touch-ups.

He moved to the cupboard, silent as a jungle cat, then slid a small plate and a glass onto the table. He fetched the glass pitcher of milk and plunked it down clumsily beside the cake with a loud thump. He had nearly dropped it; his hand was still half-asleep. He had to be more careful or he'd wake up the whole house. He went to the drawer for the big knife and fork. The fork slipped out of his hand and he cringed as it clattered to the floor.

"This is ridiculous," he muttered to himself. He bent over to pick it up.

That's when the hot, granite shards exploded and slammed into his chest.

The room dimmed to black, like the closing of the iris of a camera. The pain, a blazing iron spike in his ribs, knocked him over and he hit the ground hard, fighting to stay up on his hands and knees. As his sight seeped back slowly, his only thought was to get to his feet.

He was in trouble. He had an overwhelming feeling that if he stayed down, he might not ever get up again. Frank made it as far as one of the kitchen chairs, one that was still tucked under the big table. He tried to raise his arms, to grab for the top of the chair, but could only lift his right arm as far as the seat. He attempted to push himself up, into a standing position.

The second shocking wave snapped his head back and he whacked it with stunning force against the unyielding underside of the table with a crack. Flashing lights burst through the haze and he would have cried out, but he couldn't catch a breath.

Some fierce and unexpected reflex suddenly kicked in and shoved him upright onto his two legs. He was groggy and insensible from lack of oxygen, from the grinding, shutting-down pains in his chest, and now, from a fresh concussion. Nothing looked familiar, nothing looked real to him, and he staggered and tried desperately to find something he could hold on to.

He focused on the cake.

Angelina's cake, framed in a halo of moonlight with a radiant mist around it, beckoned, its icing glistening, calling to him. Frank reeled unsteadily, his knees buckled, and by providence, came to rest in a chair within arm's length of it.

Like a child in a high chair, he stretched and extended two fingers the whole long way across the table, scooped out a crumbly, nutty, succulent morsel, and by instinct guided it into his mouth. He smiled a sweet smile.

Sheer chocolaty pleasure.

His last breath was a sigh of pure delight.

CHAPTER TWO

Life Goes On

Angelina was awakened suddenly by the empty place in their bed, as if she'd been elbowed hard in the ribs. It was dark outside; the moon had moved on. Her first thought had been that she would find him on the couch with the TV volume turned down low. She'd have to sneak down and put a blanket on him, which he always forgot to do for himself. When she saw the empty couch, her next thought was to head straight for the kitchen. From the doorway, she saw the cake out on the table and felt a flash of annoyance, which worsened when she looked closer and saw the gash in its side.

What had he been thinking? When she stepped into the kitchen and saw the outline of her husband in the gloom, head nodded off to one side, sleeping beside the cake, she softened. He looked so peaceful. He must have dozed off in the chair, which meant that she'd have to coax him awake just enough to lean on her, so she could lead him back upstairs.

Somewhere in the blur of panic that occurred over the next few minutes, she broke a small drinking glass in the sink and cut her hand. She somehow managed to call 911 and say something about "my husband"; she would never be able to recall exactly what. She was able to clean up the remains of the broken glass, but she was shaking so badly that it took longer than it should have. The cut wasn't serious at all and stopped bleeding on its own.

Nothing about the time she waited with him was real; it could have been twenty minutes or twenty hours, for all she knew. She knew that at one point she cried so hard that she was afraid she might have broken something in her chest. She stopped crying and thought she might vomit.

The feeling subsided by the time she made it to the bathroom. She threw hot water on her face, but couldn't bear to look at herself in the mirror.

She returned to the kitchen. She wanted to touch him, not to say good-bye, really, but to make sure . . . she tenderly wiped the cake crumbs from his lips and felt the fine morning stubble on his chin as she did it. She brushed her fingers against his hair; it felt the way it always had. She rested her hand on his shoulder for a moment, then moved to the sink and numbly looked out the kitchen window. She didn't want to leave him alone.

Soon after, the ambulance arrived. A cop named

Kenny Devine, who'd heard the call and who had gone to school with Frank, came to the house. At first glance, Kenny looked too heavy and slow to be a cop, but anybody who'd played football with him in high school knew he was sneaky quick and as tough as a two-dollar steak. He took Angelina gently by the hand and led her out of the room while they moved the body. He made her a cup of tea she didn't drink and stayed with her until the sun came up. Kenny knew the family and made the call to Frank's mother and brother and broke the news. He waited until Angelina put on some clothes and then drove her over to her mother-in-law's in his squad car, and that's where she stayed until the night of the viewing.

Mamma Gia, Frank's mother, shielded Angelina from having too many visitors once word of Frank's death got out. The only people she allowed into the house were her other son, Joe; Father DiTucci; the funeral director from DiGregorio's; and a couple of close, old family friends, women who were Gia's age, who knew instinctively when to keep their voices low, when to be in the room and when to stay out. Joe and his wife, Maria, stepped up and had made all of the funeral arrangements. Word spread through the neighborhood quickly, and the expressions of sympathy and offers of food and help were managed by Gia.

Being kept busy helped Gia work through her

own feelings of grief and loss. She counted on her inner strength, on her faith, and on her life experience to carry her through the unimaginable sadness of losing a child. She worried more about Angelina than about herself, who was so withdrawn and silent. She was afraid that the Angelina who could sit and talk with her about practically anything over a bowl of minestra on a Sunday afternoon after mass was gone and might not be coming back.

The following evening, Angelina felt gaunt and frail as she sat, dressed and veiled in black, waiting for the car to take her and Gia to DiGregorio's Funeral Home, as though there were less of her now than there was supposed to be.

Life comes at you, she thought. *Life comes at you and it has earthquakes, floods, fire, and sudden death on its side. You can do whatever you like to try and hold it back, but it doesn't matter.* But if she'd known that her husband was going to go downstairs in the middle of the night and never come back up the steps to her again, she'd have gotten down on her knees and tried with all of her might and prayed until her heart burst for the earthquakes, floods, or fire instead.

Life had dealt her dirty blows before. Just after she had been accepted into cooking school, her mother had fallen ill, and Angelina had to change her plans and nurse her for three years until Emmaline had finally, peacefully, mercifully, passed away in her sleep. Within six months, her father, Ralph, had begun to suffer from a kind of heartbroken dementia, and a stroke took him two years later. She never regretted the time she gave to their care because she loved her parents and she cherished her memories of them—in good health and in bad. But by the time they were gone, she'd lost the thread of her ambition and desire. Then she met Frank and settled into their life together, and that had been more than enough.

At the wake, Gregory DiGregorio Sr., the director of the funeral home, drew near to Angelina deferentially, then sat down on a wooden chair beside her. He was closing in on his ninetieth birthday, but he approached it with a straight spine, a clear eye, and all of his own hair, neatly trimmed and combed back in the same parted style he had favored as a young man. His sons, Gregory Jr. and David, always unfailingly courteous and efficient, had seated Angelina in a small alcove with her mother-in-law and one of the younger parish priests. Mr. DiGregorio had a knack for holding the strands of the different stories of families who passed through the doors of his funeral home in his memory.

"Mrs. D'Angelo, may I sit with you for a minute?"

Angelina pulled the black shawl she was wearing a bit tighter around her shoulders when she turned to face him.

"Sure, Mr. DiGregorio. Thank you, by the way. Everything looks beautiful."

"Thank you for saying so. I'm very sorry for your loss. Your husband was a fine man, and I knew his family well. He will be missed by everyone."

Angelina noted, not for the first or last time, that nobody used Frank's name when they spoke to her. It was as if they all knew instinctively how much it hurt her to hear it.

"I lost my wife, Florence, at a young age," he said. "I have been on my own for forty years. I never remarried. When I'm missing her, I say a prayer and I feel better right away. I can't say if she hears it, but I think she has a hand in that feeling somehow. Those we love never leave our hearts, but life goes on. Life goes on. If you need anything at all, Mrs. D'Angelo, will you please let me or one of my sons know?"

"Yes. I will. Thank you."

Angelina felt grateful in that moment to Mr. DiGregorio. By telling her about his wife and his life after her loss, he had taken her out of herself for a moment, which had clearly been his intention.

Mr. DiGregorio nodded and walked back to his post near the door. She wanted to call to him then and tell him, yes, she did need something. Could he or one of his sons possibly arrange to send her back in time about a week? That way, she could maybe get Frank to the doctor for a checkup, maybe follow him downstairs and call an ambulance in time, change something.

She felt as if she were drifting outside herself, the way she'd heard people describe near-death experiences. She was still alive, but she thought that if Frank and she were truly married, if they had truly been joined as one, that maybe what she was feeling was what death felt like for him, felt like for him right now, this second. If so, then death was cold, dark, and lonely.

From where she sat, Angelina could see Mr. DiGregorio shaking hands with Frank's brother, Joe, his wife, Maria, and their daughter, Tina. Tina was a pretty girl with long black hair and long lashes that framed dark brown eyes, which normally sparkled vivaciously and took everything in. Angelina and Tina had always been close, even when Tina was a little girl. Angelina hadn't seen Tina at the house and got up and went into the front parlor to greet her and her parents. As soon as their eyes met, Tina rushed into Angelina's arms.

"Oh, my God, Aunt Angelina . . ." Fresh tears spilled out of Tina's already red-rimmed eyes.

"I know, sweetie."

Maria was quiet and dabbed at her eyes with a handkerchief. Joe came up and put his arms around both Angelina and Tina. Angelina thought he looked pale and tired. She held Tina a little closer and then brushed the hair back out of her eyes.

"I just can't believe he's not here anymore."

"I know, Tina, honey, I know."

Joe stood back and put his hands in his pockets. "How you holding up, Ange?"

"Okay." Angelina looked away. She was afraid that if he started crying, she'd go, too. She concentrated on consoling Tina, who was already crying enough for both of them.

"She's been like this since she heard," said Joe.

Angelina hugged Tina a little closer. "She loved him," said Angelina and kissed her hair.

"We all did. He was the best brother you could have." Joe's voice quivered slightly.

"Tina just wanted to make sure she saw you, is all, but we should probably get back home," Maria said with tears in her eyes. "We'll see you in the morning at the mass?"

"Sure, let me walk you out."

Angelina took Maria's arm and walked them as far as the foyer. She took Tina's face in both of her hands and kissed her on the cheek good-night. After seeing them off, Angelina turned back toward the main parlor. Off to her right, on the wall in a little nook, she noticed a portrait of old Mr. DiGregorio and his wife, Florence. She walked over and stood in front of it.

They looked so young in the picture, maybe around her age now, and happy. Mrs. DiGregorio had a big, beaming smile on her face, and Angelina imagined Mr. DiGregorio might have said something to make his wife laugh just before the picture was taken, something that he knew only she'd find funny, and Angelina thought, what a lovely moment to capture for all time.

She and Frank used to write each other little notes. One time, as they were getting ready to go out, she laid out a selection of sweaters in different colors for him to pick from and left a note on top that said, "Your choice." He'd flipped over the note and written: "I think you're choice, too!" She kept that note in her bedside table drawer. Now, she wished she'd kept them all. A warm tide of tears started at the back of her throat and welled up toward her eyes.

Just then, two younger women from the neighborhood, Anna and Natalie, drifted to a stop near the door, which obscured Angelina from their view. Something in their tone stopped her tears before they fell, and she couldn't help but over-hear.

"I am dying for a cigarette," said Anna.

"We're going in a minute," said Natalie. "My Danny's just talking to Mike DeNicholas, he'll only be a minute or two. I told him to hurry it up."

"I hate coming to these things. They make me too sad."

"Yeah, but you got to show up," said Natalie.

"So sad that a guy like him had to go so young. He was so handsome and she's so pretty."

"Pretty? I'd say she's cute, not pretty. But he

was a doll." Natalie lowered her voice conspiratorially. "And lookit, what does she have now?"

"What do you mean?" asked Anna.

"Think about it. Five years married and no kids?"

"They just didn't get lucky, maybe."

"Yeah, well, maybe he was gettin' lucky somewhere's else . . . you know what I'm saying? He sure could have done better . . ." Natalie spoke softly, but not low enough that Angelina couldn't still hear. "You know what? I know my Danny, he's no saint. But one thing I got in my house, that's the love of my kids."

"You're their mother."

"Now that Frank's gone," said Natalie, "what's Angelina got? Nothing."

Anna glanced vacantly over Natalie's shoulder and her jaw suddenly went slack. She grabbed Natalie's arm to silence her, but it was too late.

"*Saccente . . . donnaccia!*"

Angelina wasn't the only one eavesdropping. A strongly built, imposing older woman, Gia's friend Mary, stood in the foyer glaring at Natalie and Anna like God's own judgment, her stance wide and threatening, her hands clenched into stony fists on her redoubtable hips.

"Angelina," said Mary as she held out her hand.

Angelina came out from behind the door. Anna's cheeks blushed a fiery crimson and Natalie's hand flew to her open mouth as she gasped in horror.

42

"Oh, my God," said Natalie.

Angelina strode toward her, eyes blazing, just barely resisting the urge to slap Natalie hard across the face. The room went deathly quiet.

When Angelina finally spoke, her voice was level and cold, but hard as ice. "Why are you here?" she asked Natalie.

Natalie stood frozen. Even if she'd harbored thoughts of escape, she had no hope of making it past Mary.

Angelina moved a step closer. Her emotions were shoved back down in her throat now, but her voice never wavered. "Why would you even come here if you have it in you to talk about me and my husband that way? Who do you think you are?"

Natalie looked down and away.

"Answer me," said Angelina.

"I dunno' . . . I . . . I'm sorry," Natalie said in a dull, small voice.

Mourners had begun to gather around them, and Natalie's face had turned ashen. Word would circulate for days, maybe years, about what Natalie had said at the funeral. Angelina felt sure that Natalie's "best friend" Anna would somehow see to that; for some girls, having a nasty story to tell trumps loyalty every time. Secure in that knowledge, Angelina let her anger begin to subside, but not before she'd had the final say.

"Look at me," she said.

Natalie met her eyes as best she could.

"You think my husband and I didn't want to have a baby?" Her mind involuntarily flickered to an image of Frank with a baby bundled in white, held safely in his strong arms. "More than life on this earth, but now he's gone . . ." Angelina's voice broke. She pushed through it, allowing herself a slow, calming breath. "But you know what we did have? Love for each other. That's something you'll *never* have, Natalie."

Gia's friends, the older women in black, had instinctively gathered at Angelina's back and escorted her inside. Satisfied that Angelina'd had the last word, Mary shifted into action and herded Natalie toward the door.

"*Sparisci*," Mary growled. "Move it."

Once Natalie had slunk through the double doors, Mary turned her attention to Anna.

"What did *I* do?" asked Anna.

Mary pushed her right sleeve back from her balled fist, and Anna knew enough about Italian grandmothers straight off the boat from Palermo to make a break for the exit.

As Angelina walked away, she knew that by stating the simple truth about her life with Frank, though she'd never understand, she had given her something even Natalie would have to think about for a long time.

Her husband would have approved. Angelina was dying to tell him about it.

But he was gone.

CHAPTER THREE

Stracciatella
and Storm Clouds

The funeral went by as if it were happening to someone else. Joe and Tina did the readings, and Father DiTucci gave a beautiful homily, about which Angelina could remember little or nothing. A military honor guard was at the cemetery, since Frank had been honorably discharged as a corporal in the Army. At the end of the graveside ceremony, Angelina started to shake when one of the young soldiers handed her the flag from the coffin, which he and his fellow guard had folded with such intense reverence, precision, and discipline. When the youngest soldier, hardly more than a boy, played taps so mournfully on his bugle, Angelina was afraid, for the first time since she found Frank in the kitchen, that she'd lose it completely. Fortunately, and at Mamma Gia's direction, the family doctor, Dr. Vitale, gave Angelina a mild muscle relaxer as they walked back to the car, which, combined with the stress and her profound fatigue, made the rest of the day drift by in a cottony fog.

Lunch was served afterward at Gia's, but Angelina hardly ate. She lay down and slept for most of the afternoon and into the evening. When she awoke, she picked at some cold pasta salad, nursed a glass of ginger ale, and watched old movies on television without interest. Joe waited until she was ready and took her back to her house well after midnight. He and Tina waited to make sure she got securely into bed, then locked up and left her to slip into a tranquilized, blank, and impenetrable sleep.

In the morning, Angelina sat alone in her nightgown, robe, and slippers, staring blankly into a steaming cup of coffee. It was a bright, sunny day but she couldn't seem to get warm. It was eleven o'clock and it had taken a lot out of her to get even this far into the day and down to the kitchen. She had managed the coffee by habit, but sat down heavily and became lost in thought when she realized she had automatically made enough for two.

Frank had been a heavy coffee drinker. His habit had always been two strong cups in the morning before he went out the door with his big thermos in hand, which Angelina knew that he finished off at lunch; then he'd get a big take-out cup in the afternoon at whatever job site he was on. If he was working around the house on a

Saturday, he'd make a big pot after lunch and work his way through it before the sun went down. When she got to Sunday, Angelina stopped herself. She couldn't take thinking about him in the past tense, about the way he used to be.

After a soft knock at the back door, a key turned in the lock and Mamma Gia came in with two canvas shopping bags folded neatly under her arm. Gia never came to the front door—the front door was reserved for guests and visiting clergy; not family, and the back door put her right where she usually wanted to be, in the kitchen, where the action is. Without a word, Gia went to the windows and raised the shades, letting some sunshine into the room. She was a pleasantly stout woman, with dark hair shot through with advancing gray, and gold-rimmed glasses that pinched her nose. She waddled a bit when she walked, since her hips had started bothering her a couple of years ago. Her sons had encouraged her to consider getting a hip replacement, but the thought of it seemed outlandish and completely impractical to her, when all she had to do to get around was to walk a little differently than she was used to.

Whoever heard of getting old without having to make a few adjustments? She had a little bit of pain when it was wet or cold, and even she thought that maybe she had slowed down a step or two, but she proudly wielded the strength and determination of a woman half her age.

"Come on, honey," said Gia. "How come you're not dressed?"

She and Angelina had made a practice of shopping together on Saturday mornings, in good weather and in bad, practically every Saturday for the last four years.

"I don't know, Ma. I'm tired, I guess. You want some coffee?" Angelina spoke softly. Speaking out loud seemed to be taking a lot out of her.

"Don't get up." Gia poured herself a cup of coffee, took a seat, and administered her customary three teaspoons of sugar. "So, you coming shopping, or what?"

Angelina picked at the handle of her cup with her thumb. "No."

"Why not?"

"I don't feel like it."

"Why not?"

Angelina let go of her cup and sat up straight in her chair. The rush of irritation she felt at the question . . . no, at the question's being *repeated* . . . cleared the fog. She was suddenly feeling a little picked on.

Gia knew what she was starting, but she was determined. Angelina clenched and unclenched her teeth before she spoke.

"Why not? I don't know, maybe because my husband just died. Maybe that's why."

"For you a husband, for me a son."

Angelina sank down in her chair again. Had she told Gia she was sorry that her son, her beautiful eldest son, had died? She wasn't sure that she had.

"I know, Ma. I'm sorry, I don't mean to be mad."

Gia took off her glasses and placed them on the table. She rubbed at the red indentations they left behind.

"Frankie's father, he died young. And my father, his grandfather, he died too young, too. You cry, you pray a little, and you keep them in your heart, and you move on with your life."

Angelina could hardly believe what she was hearing from Gia, in those calm, measured, and world-weary tones. Was this what she had to look forward to, tired resignation at life's calamities, just "say a prayer" and move on? Move on to what? Was she supposed to accept it all with a quiet nod, accept her loss graciously, get up and dust the house? Where was she supposed to keep him in her heart if it was broken? Her hand to God, she couldn't even tell whether she was going to make it through today or not, let alone move on to next week or next year, or *whenever*. Angelina had felt sorry for Gia. Now she felt sorrier for herself.

"What, I should be over the death of my husband already?" said Angelina, tight-lipped. "We just buried him for God's sake. And I'm not going shopping because I have all of this food in the house for the party, which obviously is not going to happen now, so I have enough food to feed an army."

Gia stirred her coffee.

"I mean, tell me, Gia, am I being punished? What did I do? Was I too happy? Is it because nobody's supposed to be that happy? *Why* did this happen?"

Gia took a sip and slid her glasses back on.

"Why?" said Angelina.

"Hey, you don't have to go shopping if you don't want to."

Angelina quieted down. She knew that Gia had only been trying to do her some good. She wasn't sure she would have had it in her to make the effort if their roles had been reversed.

"I don't care, Ma," said Angelina wearily. "I don't care if I never cook again."

"You have your breakfast?"

"I'm having coffee."

"I'm going to cook for you." Gia pushed up from the table and her chair scraped back noisily.

"I'm not hungry."

Gia went to the sideboard, found an apron, and tied it around her waist as she headed for the stove. "You're hungry, you just don't know it. Just some soup, a little *brodo*."

At the mention of soup, a perceptible growl escaped from Angelina's tummy. "All right."

Gia turned on the burner and reached for a

saucepan. She lightly crushed two cloves of garlic with the side of a knife, then minced and sautéed them in olive oil and a knob of butter. She whisked in a little flour, toasting it in the oil, added a pinch of salt, then raised the heat and whisked in a cup of homemade chicken broth from the fridge until the soup began to thicken. She beat two eggs together in a bowl with some grated Parmesan and added them gently to the soup, where they poached into gold and white strands of savory-soft egg and cheese.

Gia selected a big earthenware bowl, ladled in her soup, ground in some fresh black pepper, and placed it in front of Angelina with a napkin and a spoon.

"*Stracciatella.* For you."

Angelina leaned over the bowl with her eyes closed and let the delicious wisps of steam rise up to her face. She picked up the spoon and sulkily nicked off a piece of egg. Gia returned to her cup of coffee, with an experienced parent's complete indifference as to whether the meal she'd prepared was eaten or not.

Angelina stole a glance at her and dipped into the bowl, seduced by the aroma of toast laced with sweet and savory garlic, mingled with the soothing sustenance of good chicken broth. She sipped and felt warm comfort spread into her belly, across the bridge of her nose and the back of her neck.

Gia added yet another sugar to her coffee. "I

don't know if you know this about me, but I was married once before Frankie's father."

Angelina's eyes opened wide. "You were married before Jack?"

Gia smiled as she settled into her story. "Yes, I was. I guess you could say I was a war bride. His name was Danny. He wasn't as good-looking as my Giacomo. He kind of looked like Ernest Borgnine, to tell you the truth, but he was such a nice man. He had a big heart. And he was some kind of dancer, too. One thing I could never get Jack to do was take me dancing."

"So, what happened?"

"He went to war and didn't come back. He died at Anzio Beach. They buried him over there, so I never saw him again."

"How come you never said anything?"

"That was the way it was at that time," said Gia matter-of-factly. "So many of the boys didn't come back. It was common. Girls handled it two ways, you either talked about it all the time or you never did."

"Gia, I'm so sorry."

"Don't be sorry. We had almost eight months before he shipped out, and that's more than most. Then when I met Jack, I fell in love all over again. It was different, but I have to say, it was just as good. We had the boys, and he saw them grow up to be men. Then Maria came for Joey, Tina came along, you came for Frankie. It may not seem like it right now, but the good things aren't over forever. My point is, I've been widowed twice, you see. So, if you want to talk to somebody who's been there, you can talk to me."

"Thanks, Gia. I just can't think about it right now."

"I get what you're saying, honey. But that doesn't mean you don't get dressed."

There was something about Gia's story that made Angelina feel that she might actually be able to face the day. Maybe her story meant that tomorrow, however dim a prospect, was a possibility after all.

Angelina nodded as she sipped. "Okay, I'll get dressed. I promise. But I'll have my soup first."

Gia sat placidly and folded her hands on the table. One of her true pleasures in life was watching someone else eat. "Good?"

"So good."

"I can't come and do this every day," said Gia. "You're not gonna starve to death, are you?"

"I'll be fine. It's just been a couple of days."

Angelina meticulously cupped the last of the rich broth onto her spoon. "I promise I'll come with you next week, okay?"

"Okay. I'm going home. You don't need anything?"

"I have everything. Thanks for coming over." Angelina reached over and gave Gia's hand a squeeze.

Gia got up, cupped Angelina's cheeks, and kissed them both. "*Mi raccomando.* Get dressed and get moving. Don't lay around."

Stracciatella (*Roman Egg Drop Soup*)
....

Serves 2

INGREDIENTS
- 1 tablespoon olive oil
- 1 tablespoon butter
- 2 large garlic cloves, lightly crushed and minced
- 2 tablespoons flour
- 1 pint chicken broth
- 2 eggs
- ¼ cup grated Parmesan cheese
- Salt and freshly ground black pepper, to taste

METHOD
In a heavy-bottomed saucepot, heat the olive oil over medium heat until it begins to slightly shimmer. Melt the butter in the oil, add the garlic cloves, and cook them for 2 minutes, stirring frequently. Gradually whisk in the flour to make a roux and cook—stirring frequently—until the flour begins to toast. Whisk in the chicken broth a little at a time and bring to a boil. Beat the eggs and Parmesan in a small bowl and gradually add

this mixture to the boiling soup where the liquid is breaking the surface so as to encourage the egg mixture to disperse in strands.

Remove from heat and season to taste with salt and pepper.

Angelina showered and dressed, though it took her a while. She chose a pleated navy linen skirt and crisp pin-tucked white blouse, too nice, really, for bumming around on a Saturday. It was the kind of outfit she would put on for work, if someone serious was coming into the office. *Clothes make the woman,* she thought. She didn't want to risk being accused of hedging if and when Gia came back.

When she passed the phone on the little table at the bottom of the steps, she noticed that the message light was on. She was surprised to hear Vince's voice when she played back the message. He and Amy had been out of touch on one of their innumerable getaways and had missed the funeral completely. Maybe he was calling to apologize.

"Angelina, I know it's Saturday, but can you come over to the office as soon as you get this?" said the raspy voice on the speaker. "I need to see you right away. And I've got some money for you, so please come right over. Thanks."

Well, that's as strange as it gets, she thought.

She hadn't given a thought to work since Frank's death. Father DiTucci had called Vince's secretary, Susan, to explain Angelina's absence; Susan was holding down the fort while Vince and Amy were in St. Bart's. They weren't due back until late last night, so calling in again hadn't even occurred to her.

Angelina caught the bus over to the office on Oregon Avenue, found a window seat, and leaned her throbbing head against the cool glass as they drove. Storm clouds were moving in.

Philadelphia is a city of neighborhoods. Some of them have names, like Jewelers' Row, Fishtown, Brewerytown, and Old City, that explain themselves. For others, such as Devil's Pocket and Kingsessing, who knows? South Philadelphia has places like Bella Vista, Marconi Plaza, and Italian Market where you don't really need a word of English to do your grocery shopping. In South Philly, the organizing principles were family, church, and neighborhood, in that order. It was a good place to be from, Angelina had always thought.

The bus wandered its circuitous, bumpy way down Passyunk Avenue toward the stadiums. If you were from South Philly, as Angelina had often explained to people who weren't, you said "Pashunk" Avenue, not "Passy-unk," to describe that sprawling, winding insult to proper road planning that seemed determined to cut and

56

swerve at least once across every street in every neighborhood. As she passed Geno's and Pat's Steaks, site of the longest-standing turf war in the history of fast food, it crossed Angelina's mind that people around here took cheesesteaks as seriously as some people took the West Bank. Everybody who lived here had to have an opinion about everything and know yours. Her mother came from the French countryside and never quite got used to it, even after all those years.

"*Petite*," she used to say to Angelina, "in South Philly, you have to know who you are, or somebody will be only too happy to tell you."

She got off the bus and into the building, made her way up the ancient elevator, and through the old-fashioned glass door, inscribed CUNIO CONSTRUCTION, LTD. It always reminded her of Sam Spade's office door in the movies.

The room was a mess. The four desks and the big worktable were buried in boxes, files, and paperwork. A stack of manila folders had fallen to the floor and had spilled all over the place. She heard the toilet flush, and the bathroom door over in the corner opened. Vince walked out, drying his hands on a paper towel.

One thing stood out above everything else: he looked like hell.

"Sorry to have to call you in like this, Angelina. I've been up all night. I couldn't find the receivables, which is why I called, but I found them. I tried Frank's pager but he didn't answer. I've been up all night and I guess I'm not thinking straight. We're going out of business."

Angelina found it impossible to move. "What?" she said quietly.

"I got in late last night. Twenty messages from my lawyer waiting. So much for getting away from it all."

Angelina took a tentative step into the room. "What happened?"

"I've been hung out to dry. I'm not getting paid for the last half of the biggest job we ever did. And, according to my genius attorney, there's pretty much nothing I can do about it."

"I don't understand. Why aren't they paying?"

"That bastard's leveraging all his cash into a new project in Atlantic City. I can spend the next fifty years suing him, and there's still no guarantee we'll ever get paid."

He picked up a white envelope and handed it to her.

"What's this?"

"Severance. I'm sorry, it's all I can give you. Frank's a union guy, he'll land on his feet. You two'll be fine."

She took the envelope automatically and looked Vince quietly in his bloodshot eyes.

"Vince, Frank's dead."

Vince had his defenses up. His shoulders were hunched and he had been fully prepared for her to yell at him or accuse him or to get upset, so what she said didn't register at first.

"Huh? He's what?"

Angelina felt alone and exposed in the middle of the floor. "He died. He had a heart attack in the middle of the night. We buried him yesterday. Nobody got in touch with you?"

Vince sat down heavily in his squeaky swivel chair.

"I . . . we've been having trouble, Amy and me. I wanted us to get away from everything, just the two of us. The place we were staying at didn't even have a phone. He's dead?"

"Yes."

There was nothing else to say.

Vince sat stiffly and stared at the floor, so Angelina opened the envelope. A hundred dollars was inside, in well-worn tens and twenties, which must have come straight out of Vince's pants pockets.

"A hundred dollars? Vince, after four years, what am I supposed to think when you hand me a hundred dollars in cash?"

Amy had entered unnoticed through the open office door, and all she had heard was the last question Angelina had asked.

"That's not *good enough* for you?" said Amy.

Angelina turned and looked at her. She was wearing a powder-blue, sleeveless top and sporting a deep, Hawaiian Tropic tan, which was peeling off her cheeks and freckled shoulders.

Vince looked up tiredly. "Knock it off, Amy."

Amy went on as if she hadn't heard him say a thing. "My life is ruined. Our business is over, my marriage is over, and you're worried about a hundred dollars? You can get another *job,* Angelina—"

Vince heaved up to his feet. "Amy, I said knock it off!"

He went to her, grabbed her by the shoulders, and steered her across the room. He looked back at Angelina, then spoke to his wife in an urgent whisper. When he let go, yellow-and-white finger marks dotted her chestnut-brown upper arms.

Amy looked at Angelina, choked once loudly, and ran out of the room, the heels of her expensive strappy sandals clacking and echoing as she diminished down the hallway.

Vince stood immobile, head down, the very picture of defeat.

Angelina wanted nothing more at that moment than to be anywhere else. She tucked the envelope in her purse, touched Vince gently on the arm as she passed, then left without a backward glance.

By the time she returned home, Angelina was totally drained. Dark clouds drifted overhead, but the coming storm was still holding off. It left the neighborhood feeling airless and tensed in anticipation. The sour aftertaste of what had just happened still lay in the back of her mouth. She dropped her purse on the couch with a heavy sigh and headed straight up the stairs. She felt disoriented, as if she had come into someone else's house by mistake.

If she had been worried about money last week, there was no question that her situation this week was much, much worse. She vaguely remembered something about a small insurance policy and a union benefits package and had decided on the ride back that she had no choice but to force herself to go through their papers, the sooner the better. She stood at the door to Frank's closet for a moment with her hand on the knob, took a deep breath, opened it, and turned on the light.

All of their records and personal papers were stashed in shoe boxes, some in her closet, some in his. She rummaged in the back on her hands and knees and found five boxes. The smell of leather, the feel and smell of the cloth of his jackets and pants on her skin as they brushed against her in her search, were all a warning to her heart not to spend too much time in there.

The first box held nothing of real interest, except that they were things that had belonged to Frank: old ticket stubs to ball games, coins neatly loaded into paper wrappers, a Swiss army knife, the collar that the dog he'd owned as a kid used to wear. She found a receipt in the corner of the box from Fratto's Jewelers for her engagement ring. It was handwritten and the ring was listed as "1 carat eng. ring."

After they were married, Frank had told her the story of once overhearing two secretaries talking about their rings in an office. One girl had said that hers was "three-quarters of a carat," and he explained how that had struck him as being the wrong way to go about it, how it sounded like cutting corners. He thought there shouldn't be any fractions involved in the one thing his wife was going to wear her whole life.

The second box offered up a cache of the papers she was looking for—the mortgage papers, their marriage certificate, a small life insurance policy connected with the union that looked to be worth about $8,000. She sorted out every paper that looked legal, official, or otherwise potentially important and made a stack that she would go through more methodically later.

Is this what it all comes down to? Five shoe boxes and a stack of papers?

Angelina peeked into the last box and found a pile of photographs. She leaned back against the bedstead and began leafing through them. She started from the bottom and turned each one over from the blank side, as if she wanted a moment's rest between each one. There were family photos, pictures of birthdays and Christmases long past. There was a picture of Frank's first car. On the back he had written, "My first car," which made her smile. He stood beside it proudly in jeans and a white T-shirt, and she thought he looked lean and cool, but nice, and she could spot the beginnings of the man he became. When she got to the middle of the pile, she found another photo with his handwritten caption on the back: "The girl I'm going to marry!"

She turned it over. There they were, Frank and Angelina, more than half a dozen years ago, in bathing suits on the beach in Avalon. She remembered that day because it was the first time they had gone away together on a day trip, back when they first started seriously dating. They had corralled a couple of teenage girls to take the picture, so they could both be in it. They ate clams and spaghetti and drank Beaujolais later that night at some seafood shack whose name she couldn't remember. She couldn't take her eyes off him then and she couldn't now. In the picture, their heads were together and he had his arm around her shoulders and she could practically feel the warmth of the sun on their skin where they were leaning together and touching. He had written the date on the back, too, which he always did to mark a certain day in his memory.

She only breathed again when she realized the front doorbell was ringing. With a huff of exasperation, she got up and charged down the steps to answer the door. When she flung it open, she was surprised to see Dottie from down the street standing there, smiling sweetly, holding a small pot in her hands with two homemade pot holders.

"Hi, Angie. I brought you something to eat, hon. Are you busy?"

Dottie was plump and kindly, a bit older, as evidenced by the white that flecked her strawberry-blond hair. She was a widow, had no children, and was generally thought of as a good-hearted soul who never gossiped and would give you the shirt off her back if you asked. *I'm a widow, too,* thought Angelina. *Two widows standing in a doorway.*

"No, I'm not busy, Dottie, come on in."

Dottie bustled in across the threshold and indicated the pot with a shrug. "Can I bring this into the kitchen? It's still a little hot."

"Sure, go right in."

In the kitchen, Dottie put the pot on the stove and turned the burner on low, so that the blue flame barely flickered. Angelina slid onto a chair noiselessly.

"I'm just going to leave it on low, so's you have it warm for later."

Dottie joined Angelina at the table and pulled her chair close. Angelina was looking at the picture again, which was still in her hand, and turned it facedown when Dottie sat down because she didn't really want to have to talk about it.

Dottie reached over and touched her arm gently. "How you feeling, hon?"

For five full seconds, nothing.

Then the dam burst, and Angelina started sobbing uncontrollably.

"Oh, my God, you poor thing, come here." Dottie came up halfway out of her chair and pulled Angelina's head onto her shoulder, then pulled her chair even closer and sat back down, knee to knee. Dottie pulled a crumpled hankie out of her pocket and handed it to Angelina.

"You go ahead and cry. Let it all out. That's it."

Dottie was talking to her the way you would talk to a little girl, but that was just what Angelina needed right now and she was thankful for it, and she cried and cried.

"Oh, Dottie, I'm just so sad. I'm so sad! I can't even miss him yet, 'cause I think he's going to come in the door any minute." The words came out of Angelina in spurts in between tearful gasps. "Am I going to be this sad for the rest of my life? Because I don't feel like . . . it's ever going to stop. I'm just saying . . . if I have to feel like this forever, I'm gonna take the bridge . . ."

"Aw, jeez."

"I might as well walk into the ocean . . ."

"Oh, my goodness."

"I'll just stick my head in the oven . . ."

"Blow," said Dottie. She took the handkerchief out of Angelina's hands and pinched it on her nose. Angelina honked into it loudly, then had to laugh as they both sat there trying to figure out what to do with it next.

Angelina started crying again, but softer, without all of the racking sobs. "Oh, God."

Dottie fetched a handful of tissues. Angelina took them and mopped her eyes.

"There you go," said Dottie. "Do you feel a little better now?"

"Yes. I think so."

Dottie took her by the hand and led her back toward the front room.

"Listen, sweetie," said Dottie. "I'm going to give you three aspirins and a warm washcloth for your eyes, and you're going to lay down on the sofa."

Angelina shuffled after her compliantly and nodded.

"I'm going to stay here until you fall asleep. I'll leave the soup on the stove with the lid on, and when you wake up, you can have some and you won't have to cook."

"Okay."

Dottie arranged Angelina on the sofa, found an afghan, and wrapped her up tight. Dottie drew the front curtains, gave Angelina the aspirins and the wet cloth, and waited while she swallowed the pills and drank her water.

"I know it's hard, but don't you worry about a thing, you'll be back on your feet in no time."

Dottie fluffed a pillow under Angelina's head and placed the cloth over her eyes.

"What kind is it?" asked Angelina.

"What's that, dear?"

"The soup. What kind of soup did you bring?"

"Escarole."

"Thanks, Dottie."

In a few short minutes, Angelina was out like a light. Dottie quietly put down her *Good Housekeeping* and picked the washcloth up off the floor where it had dropped when Angelina had rolled over. Dottie turned on the small lamp on the table in the little hall that led to the kitchen, so there was no chance that Angelina would wake up alone in the dark. A good cry and a good sleep were just what she needed.

Dottie snuck on her tiptoes to the front door, turned the lock on the knob so it locked behind her, and left Angelina slumbering soundly.

CHAPTER FOUR

In the Wee Hours of the Mourning

By the time Angelina awoke, night had fallen. Her blanket was tucked tightly under her chin and her feet were cold. She came out of her exhausted sleep slowly, piecing together the events that had led her to the couch. It was nighttime. It was Saturday. Had she slept the whole day away? She was hungry. What was she making for dinner again? Where was Frank?

She pulled the blanket tighter. Her head was throbbing, her eyes felt swollen, and her mouth was dry. Nothing to do but get up. She wrapped the afghan around her shoulders and dragged herself into the kitchen.

Dottie's soup was still on the stove. Angelina turned up the heat, filled herself a big glass of water out of the tap, then went upstairs and brushed her teeth. She threw on an old sweater and sweatpants and turned up the thermostat when she got back downstairs. When the soup was ready, Angelina filled her bowl and sat down. She took a sip.

"Oh."

Angelina bent low over the bowl and sniffed. She took the pepper shaker in hand and doused the soup liberally. She tried it again. If possible, the pepper made it even worse. She had a sudden urge to scrape her tongue with the spoon.

"Oh, Dottie. Bless your heart, but, oh, my God."

She rinsed out her bowl in the sink. The remains of the soup in the pot followed close behind. Angelina built herself a sandwich instead—rye bread, thin slices of *soppressata*, tomato, and a little mayonnaise. It was the most silent supper she could ever remember.

She spent a long time in the shower; the hot water, as hot as she could possibly stand it, felt good pounding down on the back of her neck. When the water heater finally ran out, she shut the knobs off with a squeak, climbed out of the old cast-iron, claw-foot tub, and wrapped herself in a big white cotton towel.

Sometimes, if Frank was taking a shower after her, she would draw a smiley face on the mirror in the steam. She ran her finger across the mirror as she left the bathroom, just a slash for no one to see.

She felt weak but warm and relaxed as she sat in her robe brushing her hair on the bench at the foot of the bed. She was completely aware that this was her first real night in the house alone and was preparing herself to face the fact that everything she looked at or touched or thought about tonight was going to remind her of him.

Angelina turned off the lamp and got fully under the covers. As she lay there with her eyes open, nothing came to her. Not sleep, not tears, not sadness, not relief, not memories of her childhood or of her life with Frank, no ideas for getting a new job or worries about when the money would run out, not even an idea for a new dish or recipe.

She listened to the alarm clock tick, then got up and drew the curtains closed to block the moonlight. After another round of straightening covers that hardly needed it, she tried closing her eyes.

Ticking. Ticking.

She grabbed the alarm clock and marched it into the bathroom, where she left it under a stack of towels on top of the hamper. Back in bed, even with the bathroom door closed, she could still hear it. Angelina threw off the covers and sat up. Then it came to her.

She jumped out of bed, went down to the kitchen without her slippers, flicked on the lights, and there it was. It had been moved to the counter but was still sitting there, glistening around the edges, listing and abandoned, with an ugly gash in its side. That stupid, beautiful, treacherous cake, for which she'd had such big plans. She removed the glass cover and picked up the cake stand by the base.

She kicked open the back screen door and marched angrily out to the concrete slab where they kept the trash cans. She yanked the metal lid off of the first one she came to. The unhappy remains of that Frangelico Chocolate Dream, minus one big fingerful of cake and frosting, plummeted to the bottom of the can. Angelina slammed the lid into place with all of the force she could bring to bear and stormed back through the screen door.

She looked around. The back of her neck was blazing hot.

It was starting to come into focus for her now, the sheer weight of all of the food in the house: the peppers, eggplant, tomatoes, prosciutto, the chicken, *baccalà*, fresh produce, the greens, the cheeses—all for the party, the party that wasn't ever going to happen now.

Canceled. No more parties. It was all going in the garbage.

Angelina raided the fridge. She grabbed a packet of fish, fresh cod, and slammed it down on the table. She rolled five eggplants onto the table, catching the last one as it nearly tumbled off the edge. They were followed by packages of beef, pork, and sausages, a whole roasting chicken, all wrapped in crisp white butcher paper. She slammed each one down as hard as she could. She pulled out both crisper drawers and upended their contents. An avalanche of bell peppers, onions, carrots with their fluffy greens still attached, zucchini, tomatoes, celery, pinkish-white cloves of garlic, bunches of parsley—all spilled out in a colorful cascade.

Angelina searched in the pantry until she found a big green plastic trash bag. It snapped like a whip crack when she shook it open with a flick of her wrist. She began furiously shoving food into the bag; she wanted it all out of her life forever.

She heard a soft bump. A big sack of flour in the pantry had been jostled and it slumped over tiredly. The lazy, insolent way it had fallen over irritated her. She grabbed it and hefted it onto the table with the rest of the food. The flap at the top of the bag was slightly open, and when she slammed it down, a great powdery, white puff exploded into her eyes, face, and hair.

Surprised, she coughed and waved until the cloud of flour dispersed.

Angelina caught sight of herself in the shiny stainless-steel door of the refrigerator, which she kept meticulously polished to a high gloss shine.

And she laughed.

Laughing that laugh was like pulling the rip cord on a parachute. She laughed down deep, down in her belly and her back, a laugh that shook her shoulders and filled her up till tears formed in her eyes and she slumped over in gentle surrender on the countertop. She'd forgotten she knew how.

She picked up a clean dish towel, dabbed her eyes and dusted herself off as best she could. Still laughing, she emptied the food from the plastic bag carefully back onto the counter.

It was going on midnight, but Angelina knew one thing. She wasn't going back to bed.

She wanted to cook.

She fetched a big metal mixing bowl and an oversize Pyrex measuring cup, used it to pour warm water into the bowl, then added a scoop of sugar and stirred in a packet of yeast.

Minutes later, Angelina returned to the kitchen, dressed in jeans and a sweatshirt, sleeves pushed up, sneakers on, hair pulled back, ready to go to work. She dipped her finger into the yeasty mixture in the bowl and tasted. Satisfied, she weighed out a large measure of flour from the bag with a metal scoop and combined it with a bit of salt and the yeast and water. She started mixing with both hands, reveling in the warm, bready scent of the dough as it came together. She kneaded it, pounded it with that familiar satisfying rhythm she'd learned as a child, until a slight glistening of sweat formed on her forehead.

Every time she squeezed the dough, she used all of her strength to push away the memories of Frank that pressed in on her. She would remember them all and cherish them all later, but right now they were just too painful.

Soon, she had shaped a softball-size round of dough, which she nestled back into the bowl. She draped a dry dish towel over the top of it and set it aside. Angelina stood back and coolly appraised the stove, walking through the steps in her mind that would fill up the six burners and dual ovens.

Down came the big gravy pot. Out came the knives. Stove flame on.

She called her massive stove "Old Reliable." Her father, Ralph, had found and installed this mammoth, cast-iron-and-white-ceramic creation of the Reliable Stove Company in her mother's kitchen thirty some years ago, just before Angelina was born, when he and Emmaline had first moved into their house to begin their married life together. It had six powerful gas burners, two full-size ovens, a grill, a stand-alone broiler, and a separate warming oven. The Reliable Stove Company stopped making cooking equipment in the thirties, but the ones they built, they built to last. Old Reliable never failed. It inspired confidence.

The stove, the only real legacy left to her when her parents died, had moved into this house from storage when she and Frank had. If only her parents had had the chance to know Frank. He was so wonderful, the way he had brought her into his family, the way he'd made sure that they knew how much he loved her and respected her, the way he'd given her the chance to get to know them on her own terms. She remembered the first time she'd cooked for them and how nervous she'd been, making the red gravy for an Italian man's Italian mother . . .

Focus.

The red gravy was the starting point—sauce *tomate* to her mom, the mother sauce. She grabbed a big yellow onion, two ribs of celery, a fat carrot, and a handful of parsley, the *quattro evangelistas*, the "four saints," of Italian cooking.

She diced the onion, celery, and carrot first, then cut a sweet red pepper and parsley even finer, like grains of wet sand, running the knife through them again and again. She picked off five cloves of garlic, smashed, peeled, and gave them a rough dice, so that they'd flavor the sauce but not overwhelm it.

Three big glugs of olive oil went into the heated pot, followed by the *evangelistas*, salt and pepper, and only then by the garlic, so it wouldn't burn. She folded in a dollop of tomato paste. While they simmered, she stripped a handful of dried herbs from the collection she kept hanging—rosemary, basil, thyme, oregano—then rubbed her hands together over the pot and watched the flecks drift down like tiny green snowflakes.

She inhaled the perfume they left behind on her fingers. The smell reminded her of her parents: helping her mom with the sauce when she was a little girl, hugging her daddy when he walked in from work, the scent of the fresh herbs mingled with his aftershave.

Angelina splashed in red wine, which made a satisfying sizzle when it hit the pot, added a tomatoey waterfall of crushed *pomodoros*, reseasoned, brought the sauce up to a near boil, then lowered it way down to a simmer.

Her grandmother Nonna, her father's mother, used to preserve her own tomatoes straight off the vines in her garden. She used to bring jars and jars of them to Emmaline, and they would sit together for hours eating cornichons with Edam cheese and drinking beer. Nonna was the only person Emmaline would ever drink beer with.

Angelina was getting loose. She started a pot of cannellini for her classic Tuscan white bean soup, then grabbed the red and green peppers, halved them, deseeded and lightly oiled them, then set them into the oven to roast. She could have blackened them right on the gas burners, but slow-roasting coaxed out every last ounce of flavor, and she felt as if she had all the time in the world.

Might as well cook the chicken now, too. She had a big, fat roaster that she had gone all the way up to the Amish market to buy. She carefully worked butter cubes dusted with pulverized parsley, sage, thyme and peppercorns under the chicken skin. As the bird cooked, the butter would baste and infuse the meat, allowing the essences of the herbs to penetrate deeply to the bone. She rinsed the cavity of the chicken with white vermouth and spilled some into the roasting pan.

When Emmaline had taught Angelina the mysteries of how to roast a chicken that was achingly moist and tender inside with skin as brown as a walnut shell and crisp as a potato chip, she had, only half-jokingly, said, "A good roasted chicken, no man can resist. When you grow up, if you decide you want a husband, you can get one with a good chicken." Sure enough, three weeks after the first time Angelina made a roast chicken for Frank, he proposed.

Once the bird was in the oven, Angelina poured herself a glass of wine.

"It's too quiet in here," she said out loud, just to hear her own voice. "Too quiet!" she shouted.

She shoved open the swinging dining-room door and marched into the corner where the old hi-fi stood. She rummaged and pulled out an LP in a tattered sleeve, an old favorite of her father's, the one he used to love to dance to with her when she was knee-high: *Louis Prima's Collected Hits.*

She put the record on the turntable, set the needle in the groove, and turned it up loud so she could hear it in the kitchen.

"Angelina, I adore you . . . ," crooned Louis. Then the New Orleans Gang picked up the beat and King Louis sang, *"I eat antipasto twice, just because she is so nice, Angelina . . ."*

Fresh pasta time. Angelina cracked three eggs

into the center of a mound of 00 flour, in time to the music, and began teasing the flour into the sticky center. With a hand-cranked pasta maker, she rolled out the dough into long, silky-thin sheets, laid them out until they covered the entire table, then used a *mezza luna* to carefully slice wide strips of pasta for a new dish she wanted to try that she called Lasagna Provençal, a combination of Italian and French cheeses, Roma and sun-dried tomatoes, Herbes de Provence, and fresh basil. It was a recipe for which she had very high hopes.

Angelina started assembling her lasagna. She mixed creamy Neufchâtel, ricotta, and a sharp, grated Parmigiano-Reggiano in with a whole egg to bind it together. She layered fresh pasta sheets in a lasagna dish, coated them with the cheesy mixture, ripped in some fresh basil and oregano and sun-dried tomatoes. She worked quickly, but with iron concentration.

"I'm-a just a gigolo, everywhere I go . . . ," sang King Louie.

For the second layer, she used more pasta topped with Gruyère and herbed Boursin cheese. The third layer was the same as the first. For the fourth layer, she used the rest of the Boursin and dollops of crème fraîche, then ladled the thick, rich tomato sauce from the stove on top and finished it with a sprinkling of shredded Gruyère. She set it aside for baking later and felt a flush of craftswomanly pride in the way it had all come together.

It wasn't enough.

Angelina cubed, floured, and seared big hunks of chuck roast until they were perfectly caramelized on all sides. She had purposely had the smoke alarm removed from the kitchen for times like these, when the fat hit the pan. In no time, she had her braise going, dousing the beef in a bottle of burgundy, à la bourguignonne, another salute to Emmaline.

Angelina was fired up now, pacing the kitchen. The Prima record was over, but she didn't need it anymore. She started on the braided bread.

Angelina pulled the dish towel off the bowl with the bread dough in it. It had risen and tripled in size. She pounded it down with whack after gratifying whack, then cut it into sections and began twisting and braiding. Braiding was one of the earliest skills she remembered learning from her mom, because she always had long hair as a girl. Soon, she had wrestled the dough into three immense braided loaves. When she was finished, the spectacular presentation was worthy of a Paris *boulangerie*. She would give the loaves some time to proof, then slip them into the oven just before dawn, when any self-respecting *boulanger* would.

She made her aubergine napoleons, a beautifully layered dish of smoked mozzarella paired with a nutty, millet flour–coated, sautéed eggplant, finished lightly crispy on the outside and velvety smooth on the inside. She peeled her roasted peppers and laid them out with fresh balls of salty mozzarella, cherry tomatoes, fresh basil, and a sprinkle of balsamic vinaigrette. She broke out a mixture of ground beef, veal, and pork for the rosemary and garlic meatballs, fried up in a cast-iron skillet and set swimming in her red-gravy cauldron.

Frank was generally helpless in the kitchen, but for some reason he always insisted on helping her roll the meatballs. Then he'd brag that he'd made them when company arrived and sat down at the table.

Angelina realized that for the rest of her life she would think of Frank every time she made meatballs, and she was surprised to find that, at least in that moment, she was glad of it.

Next, *baccalà marechiara*, codfish with a sauce of tomatoes, capers, olives, garlic, and parsley, a lighter version of her puttanesca. She laid out fresh cod in a baking dish, ladled the *marechiara* sauce over it, and set it in the oven until the cod was cooked through and flaky. She would serve it on a platter over linguine dressed with the good olive oil and cracked black pepper.

As the sun came up, she set out the fresh-baked bread, and its aroma enveloped the room. She'd made platters of salads, melon balls wrapped with prosciutto, a huge antipasto with cuts of cured meats, cheeses, and olives, and a fresh-fruit tray that exploded with color. She pulled the chicken out to rest, sampled the bourguignonne, set the lasagna to bubble and cool on the big table, stirred her soup and turned down the heat on it.

For the next forty minutes, she plated. By the time her banquet table was complete forty-five minutes later, the display looked like a culinary fantasy worthy of a center spread for *Bon Appétit*.

When she had finished the washing up, she stopped and took a long, last lingering look at what she had wrought. With a sigh, she wrapped herself in her trusty blanket, drank the end of her wine, and dropped into a peaceful and contented sleep on the sofa, with a smudge of flour on her cheek and the comforting fragrance of a night of good home cooking laced in her hair.

For a single second, just before she slipped away, she felt like herself again.

Angelina had finally fallen into a profoundly deep sleep, and she had been out no more than an hour when Mamma Gia and Tina came calling. Tina had celebrated her birthday quietly the night before with her parents and a few close friends, then picked Gia up this morning to go to mass. Now they'd come to see Angelina.

Gia was resolved to help her daughter-in-law get back into the regular rhythms and routines of her life. Todays were more important than yesterdays; it just wasn't practical to sit around thinking about the past all the time. The past was gone, like last week's groceries.

Gia found the back door unlocked and stepped into the kitchen with Tina following close behind. As the screen door softly clicked closed behind them, the stunning sight of the feast laid on the table stopped them both dead in their tracks. Tina gasped. Gia stood in the middle of the floor with her hands on her hips.

"*Cos'e tutto questo?*" she whispered. "What's all this?"

"Oh my gosh," said Tina.

They approached the table the way tourists approach a national monument, slowly, taking everything in.

Gia took the lid off of the Tuscan cannellini soup and sniffed approvingly. "Smells pretty good."

"Are you kidding? It smells incredible in here," said Tina.

"*Lasagna . . . melanzane . . . pappardelle . . . baccalà . . .* this is a lot of food."

Tina leaned over the big wicker basket with the twisted bread in it. "Oh, my God. The bread's still warm."

"Red gravy and meatballs . . . ," Gia continued her checklist.

"Look at that chicken. It's beautiful. Who's going to eat all of this?"

"I don't know. Where's Angelina?"

Tina pushed open the door to the dining room and peeked through. "Mamma Gia, look in here." They looked in on Angelina, snoring peacefully, and quietly eased the kitchen door closed. Gia shrugged off her coat and rolled up her sleeves. "Come on, honey," she said. "You and me are gonna put all of this food away. Then we'll make some coffee and wait for Angelina to wake up."

By two o'clock, the three of them, Angelina, Tina, and Gia, were seated around the kitchen table. Gia was drinking her usual cup with three sugars and had just put a midday breakfast of scrambled eggs, fried bread, sausages, and broiled tomatoes on the table in front of Angelina and Tina. They dug in hungrily.

"I'm starving," said Angelina, a little guiltily, "I guess I worked up an appetite."

"I guess I have to come and cook for you every day so you don't starve," said Gia.

Tina got the joke and laughed. "I've never seen so much food," she said. "We could hardly close the refrigerator door. You must have been cooking all night."

Gia sat with them at the table. "What happened, you forget you're not having a party anymore?"

Angelina smiled sheepishly. "I couldn't sleep. I needed something to do and I had all of this food, so I just started cooking."

"You can't read a magazine?" said Gia.

"I guess I got carried away."

"Carried away?" said Gia. "They didn't have this much food at the loaves and fishes."

"Aunt Angelina, what are you going to do with all of this food?" asked Tina. "It's going to go bad."

Gia's head came up with a start. "Don't waste food!"

She had spoken.

"I don't want to waste any food, Gia," said Angelina, "but what should I do? Can you take some?"

"I can take some home," offered Tina.

Gia pushed her coffee aside and rose to her feet. "We're going to pass it out around the neighborhood. I'm going to take that big chicken down to little Mrs. Santaguida. That poor girl, she's got five kids and a new baby."

"You want me to take the soup to the rectory?" Tina asked.

"Good idea," said Gia. "But put some in a jar for me to take home. That smells really good."

Angelina got up, opened the fridge, put her hands on her hips, and coolly appraised the tightly packed shelves, like a general scanning her battlefield before launching a major offensive.

"Okay, finish up, girls," she said. "We've got a lot of work to do."

Aubergine Napoleons

Serves 6 to 8

INGREDIENTS
  2 one-pound eggplants (aubergines)
  Salt, to taste
  1 cup milk
  1 cup white-rice flour or all-purpose flour
  1 teaspoon marjoram
  1 teaspoon dried basil
  ¼ teaspoon ground black pepper plus a pinch
    for the dredging flour
  2 to 3 eggs beaten with 1 tablespoon water,
    approximately, as needed for egg wash
  1 cup millet flour or panko bread crumbs
  1 tablespoon dried rosemary, ground to a
    powder with a mortar and pestle
  ⅛ teaspoon salt
  6 to 8 portobello mushrooms, cleaned,
    trimmed, and bitter gills scraped away with
    the tip of a teaspoon
  1 cup olive oil (*not* extra-virgin),
    approximately, 2 to 3 tablespoons to oil the
    portobellos, 1 tablespoon to sauté the
    portobellos, 1 tablespoon to sauté the
    mushrooms, and 2 to 3 tablespoons to
    sauté each side of eggplant in 2 to 3
    batches
  1 tablespoon butter

2 shallot cloves, minced
2 garlic cloves, lightly crushed and minced
6 ounces (about 3 cups) large white
  mushrooms, cleaned, trimmed, and sliced
  into ¼-inch-thick slices
½ cup tomato paste (a 6-ounce can)
½ teaspoon allspice
1 pound smoked fresh mozzarella,
  in ½-inch-thick slices
6 to 8 tablespoons sour cream
½ pound Gruyère cheese, sliced with a
  cheese plane
½ cup crème fraîche
6 to 8 small sprigs fresh basil

METHOD
Slice the eggplants crosswise into ½-inch-thick slices and sprinkle a smidgen of salt on each side as you do so, laying them on top of a double thickness of paper towels. Place a second layer of paper towels on the top of the salted pieces. Weigh them down with a heavy bowl or some canned goods set on a large cutting board and let them sit for 30 minutes. (This will remove any bitterness from the flesh and compress the slices so that they will not absorb too much oil during sautéing.)

Set up your breading station. Pour the milk into a shallow container such as a pie plate. Mix the flour with the marjoram, basil, and a pinch (¹⁄₁₆ teaspoon) ground black pepper and spread the mixture on a plate or flat work surface. Pour the egg wash into a separate shallow container. Have a large sheet of waxed paper spread out nearby on which to lay the coated eggplant. Dip each slice of eggplant into the milk and then into the flour. Allow any excess flour to fall away, then dip into the beaten eggs and into the millet flour or crumbs, and place the coated eggplant on the waxed paper. Repeat for each slice of eggplant. Let the coated slices air dry for 30 minutes.

While the eggplant is air drying, mix the pulverized rosemary, salt and ¼ teaspoon black pepper in a small bowl. Rub the portobello mushrooms with 2 to 3 tablespoons of the oil, and rub some of the rosemary mixture into all surfaces of them. Melt the butter in 1 tablespoon of the oil over medium heat in a large sauté pan, reserving the rest of the oil. When the oil begins to shimmer, sauté each side of the rubbed portobellos, curved side down first, until they release their juices, about 3 to 4 minutes per side. Transfer the portobellos to a utility platter and pour the juices into a small heatproof bowl.

To the same pan add another tablespoon of oil and sauté the shallots, garlic, and white mushrooms over medium heat, stirring frequently to prevent burning, until the mushrooms begin to give up their juices but are still retaining their shape, about 5 to 8 minutes. Then, using tongs or a slotted spoon, transfer the white mushrooms to a small plate (to let cool to room temperature) and transfer the garlic, shallots, and pan juices to the bowl that contains the juices from the portobellos.

When the coated eggplant has air dried, clean out the sauté pan and heat enough oil to coat the bottom of the pan to a depth of about $\frac{1}{16}$ of an inch (about 2 to 3 tablespoons) over medium-high heat. When the oil begins to shimmer, add the slices of coated eggplant, leaving undisturbed for the first 2 minutes or so to let the coating integrate into the surface of the eggplant and to prevent "crusting off" of the breading. Flip the eggplant slices and cook the other side undisturbed in the same way, adding oil as needed, then transfer to paper towels to drain. Cook the eggplant this way in batches, wiping out the sauté pan between batches and replenishing with fresh oil for each new batch (about 3 batches in a 14-inch pan).

Preheat the oven to 350°F.

Mix the tomato paste and allspice into the bowl that contains the mushroom juices, garlic, and shallots.

Assemble each napoleon in a wide CorningWare or Pyrex baking dish such as a 10-inch-by-12-inch-by-2-inch-deep lasagna dish, greased with butter. The layering sequence from bottom to top for each napoleon is one portobello, a slice of mozzarella, and a slice of eggplant, topped by a tablespoon of tomato-paste mixture, 4 or 5 slices of white mushrooms, a second slice of eggplant, a tablespoon of sour cream, then 1 teaspoon more of the tomato-paste mixture and two 2-by-4-inch pieces of Gruyère. (If you have additional eggplant, place it on a baking sheet.) Cover the dish with foil and bake until the eggplant is cooked through, the cheese is heated through, and the napoleons are set, about 30 minutes, then remove the foil and bake for 5 more minutes. (Bake the extra eggplant at the same time.)

Remove from the oven and let the napoleons rest for 5 minutes.

PRESENTATION
Carefully place a napoleon in the center of each serving dish. Top with a dollop of crème fraîche and garnish with a sprig of basil. Serve extra eggplant on a platter as a supplement to the meal. This is delicious with a crisp chardonnay.

CHAPTER FIVE

Mr. Cupertino's Proposal

Tina walked up the block past the school and the church and made the right through the skinny iron gate of the tiny yard of the rectory of Saint Joseph's, bumping the latch with her hip to click it open because her hands were filled with a big pot of soup. She thought that the lawn could use a good weeding. When she was back at school, in the springtime, the nuns picked the good girls in the fifth grade to help out with the gardening and the good boys picked the weeds.

She hit the buzzer with her elbow and peeked inside through the lacy curtains as Father DiTucci in his heavy-knit, black sweater and slippers shuffled his way down the hall to the door. He opened his hands wide when he saw her and beamed when she handed him the pot. He blessed her as she made the sign of the cross, then she rushed off to make her next delivery.

Over at the Santaguidas', Jeanie, the lady of the house and a mere slip of a girl to be mother to six children ranging in age from ten months to twelve and a half, was beside herself when Gia arrived unannounced, carrying a big tray with the roasted chicken, a Tupperware of gravy, mounds of risotto and green beans—enough for the whole family and then some, and just as the deadline for getting dinner started was looming. After Gia's few words of explanation, Jeanie started laughing like she'd hit a number and invited Gia in for coffee while she tented the chicken with a big sheet of foil and set it to warming in the oven.

Gia scooped the baby, Rosie, out of her high chair and snuggled her onto her ample lap. Two of the littler boys tussled at her feet, and the three-year-old pulled at her skirt and reached out her arms to be lifted up next to the baby. She told Jeanie to take her time with the coffee; Gia was in her glory.

Tina was on her second stop. She carried a deep, oven-ready dish up the stoop to the Cappuccios' front door and rang the bell. Mrs. Cappuccio was a nice old lady who lived in the house with her grandson, Johnny, whose mother and father had passed away some years back.

Johnny opened the door. He was slim, on the tall side with gentle blue eyes, was a little quiet, but handsome, at least Tina thought so. The ball game was playing in the background.

"Hi, Johnny."

"Hi, Tina."

Tina shyly offered him the dish. "This is for

you and your grandmom. It's a beef stew my aunt Angelina made. She's a really good cook. You just have to stick it in the oven and it's ready to go."

"Really. Wow. Thanks. It looks great. Tell Mrs. D'Angelo thanks, okay?"

"Okay."

Tina turned slowly and went down the steps. "Bye, Johnny."

Tina liked saying Johnny's name; Johnny liked hearing her say it.

"Bye."

Johnny backed in the door as Tina backed down the street and they managed to keep their eyes on each other until Tina slipped around the corner.

Over the next couple of hours, Angelina's food spread around the neighborhood like electricity, until all that was left was the lasagna. Angelina recalled Dottie's kindness from the day before and had it in mind for her specially. She put on her coat, cradled the lasagna dish, and headed across the street.

"Angelina, what are you bringing?" Dottie asked as she opened the door.

Angelina thrust the dish into her hands and smiled. "Dottie, you were so nice to bring me over that escarole and everything yesterday, so I baked you a little lasagna."

"Oh my gosh, that's so nice. You didn't have to do that. How was the soup?"

"It's gone already."

"Oh, good. You want to come in?"

"No, I got to get going, but thanks again, Dottie, so much."

"Okay, hon." She looked out over Angelina's shoulder. "Oh, Angelina, wait, come here. I have to introduce you," Dottie said as she hurried down the steps, dish in hand.

Angelina turned and saw an older man making his way down the street, reading a folded newspaper. He was gracefully balding, of average height and build, dressed plainly but tastefully, from brown leather wing-tip shoes to a pale blue Pima polo shirt and perfectly pressed herringbone trousers. He was tilting his reading glasses up and down as he walked, as if trying to find the perfect point of compromise between his desire to read the paper and his need to navigate the sidewalk without tripping or bumping into anything. He was so absorbed that he nearly overshot the stoop, then sensed he was being watched and looked up in time to notice the two ladies waiting to greet him.

"Basil," said Dottie. "I'd like to introduce you to someone."

Basil looked past Dottie to Angelina. "Oh, hello," he said to her.

"Angelina, this is my brother, Basil Cupertino. He just retired and is coming to live with me. This is Angelina, from across the street, the one I was telling you about."

Angelina stuck out her hand. "How are you, Mr. Cupertino? Welcome to the neighborhood."

"I'm very charmed to meet you, young lady. Very sorry, too, to hear about the loss of your husband."

Angelina looked away for a moment. The mention of the word husband made her flinch. For a moment, and against her better nature, she regretted having come over. Then she looked back at Mr. Cupertino and found that she had no trouble looking him in the eye, and the fleeting feeling passed as quickly as it came. He seemed like a nice man.

"Thank you," she said. "He was a great guy."

Mr. Cupertino smiled the slightest of smiles. "And a wise man, to marry such a beautiful girl. What's in the dish?"

"Angelina's brought a lasagna," said Dottie.

Mr. Cupertino regarded the dish and Angelina in turn. "That's very nice of you," he said.

"It's nothing," Angelina replied. "I hope you like it."

"Will you stay for a cup of coffee?" he asked.

"I have to get going. But thank you. Some other time?"

"Very good," he said with a courteous nod, as he tucked his reading glasses into his pocket.

"Well," said Dottie, "I'll go and get this in the oven. Thanks, Ange."

Basil followed Dottie inside and turned to give

94

Angelina a last genial wave with his paper before shutting the door. As she turned toward home, Angelina thought how pleased Dottie must be to be able to count on having company for dinner.

A few days later, after her first relatively restful night's sleep, Angelina was catching up on her chores. She took pride in always keeping her kitchen floor clean enough to eat off of; she stayed on top of it and made sure that dirt never got a chance to take hold. She was down on her hands and knees practicing that philosophy with a stiff brush and a bucket of hot, soapy water when the doorbell rang.

She took a few extra seconds to finish a stubborn spot, and the bell rang again. She got up, dropped the brush into the bucket, and opened the door abruptly, in her apron and yellow rubber gloves.

Basil Cupertino stood there, with an empty lasagna pan in his hands.

"Oh, hi, Mr. Cupertino."

She stripped off the gloves and tucked them into her apron pocket. Mr. Cupertino stood silently. Angelina couldn't help the sudden feeling that he was sizing her up somehow.

"Hello, Angelina. My sister sent me over with this." He indicated the dish with his eyes, but didn't actually offer it to her.

"To return it," he said, after a long pause.

Angelina was unsure whether she should reach

for it or not. He seemed disinclined to let it go.

"Here it is," he said at last, then reluctantly handed it over.

"Thanks, Mr. Cupertino. You didn't have to do that. I would have stopped by for it."

"Well, now there's no need."

He put his hands into his pockets, like a man waiting for a bus; or just waiting.

"Believe me, it's not a problem."

Angelina put her hand on the side of the door. "Well, thanks again . . ."

"It was my pleasure."

"Okay, then."

"Glad to do it," he replied.

He showed not even the smallest perceptible signal of going and exhibited every sign of a man with something on his mind. Angelina, under the lasting influence of a polite upbringing, was left no choice but to temporarily abandon her intention to get back to scrubbing the floor.

"Would you like to come in for a cup of coffee, Mr. Cupertino?"

He inclined his head diffidently at the invitation. "Yes," he said as he scrupulously wiped his feet on the mat. "Yes, I would. Thank you very much."

He walked past her and into the living room. Angelina clicked the door shut and followed.

"I was just finishing cleaning up in the kitchen."

"Oh, are you making anything?" Basil asked eagerly. He sounded hopeful.

"No. But I have a fresh pot of coffee brewing if you'd like . . ."

"That would be wonderful."

Basil made a beeline for the kitchen. The tightly spaced row homes up and down Angelina's street were virtually the same in layout, so he knew precisely where he was going. Frank had made some home improvements; he had built a bow window in the front and expanded the kitchen by a few feet to give Angelina space for a walk-in pantry and to make room for Old Reliable and a big, old wooden farm table. But so alike were Dottie's and Angelina's that Mr. Cupertino was able to immediately make himself right at home.

As Angelina put away her cleaning supplies, he paced, not nervously, but like a man in the market for a new house taking the measure of the kitchen in a model home. He ran his hand along the counters, commented appreciatively on the cornucopia of herbs she had hanging and drying, and asked some intelligent questions about her undeniably impressive stove, about its provenance, BTU output, and the like. Once he had taken a seat at the kitchen table, Angelina placed a steaming china mug in front of him.

"How do you take it?" she asked.

"Black is fine."

She sat down facing him from across the table.

He suddenly tapped the cup with his forefinger.

"On second thought, is there a drop of milk for the coffee?"

"Sure."

Before she could even move to get up, Basil was on his feet and heading for the refrigerator, begging her, "Please, allow me." He opened the refrigerator door and his head disappeared under its top edge.

Seconds passed. Angelina tilted her head quizzically and said, "It's on the top shelf."

More seconds later Basil replied, "Yes. Yes, I see. My goodness."

His head reappeared. He seemed pleased.

He returned with the quart bottle of milk in his hand and tipped a little into his cup. He took a sip before he said, "Your kitchen is very clean." It was more of a verdict than an opinion or a compliment.

Angelina drank from her cup and smiled. "My mother always said it was easier to cook good food in a clean kitchen."

The sentiment behind that remark seemed to put him even more at his ease. He sighed appreciatively. "I have lived my entire working career in just such an orderly fashion," said Basil.

"What did you do? If you don't mind me prying," she added with a touch of irony.

He folded his hands and looked at her evenly, with a businesslike mien. "I was an actuary for forty years, nearly to the day. Head of the department for the last ten. My job was to calculate and assess risk for a large insurance company. I could often tell to within a month how long a man might live after he retired. Or if he would make it to retirement."

"Really?" Angelina nodded, impressed.

"Yes. I always had very good information to work with, but I think I had an instinct for it, too. Actuarial tables can only tell you so much. The human element is very important. If a man was an avid hobbyist of some kind, or had grandchildren, if he had a clearly stated proposition for living longer, I would add time to my assessments, always. There's no question, having something to live for counts, from a practical point of view."

"That makes a lot of sense."

Basil looked down. "And now I'm retired. And I've come to live with my sister."

Angelina was about to tell him how much she liked Dottie and what a good neighbor she'd been over the years, but he preempted her and spoke first, finally coming to his point.

"Would you mind if I told you what I want to live for now, Angelina?"

"What's that, Mr. Cupertino?"

He pushed his cup aside and leaned forward. "Passion."

"Passion?"

"That's right, Angelina. Passion."

Angelina shifted in her chair, caught somewhat

off-guard, but captivated by his sudden intensity.

"For forty years," he said, "almost to the day, I have diligently applied myself to numbers. I read—mostly newspapers and the like, I saw the occasional film—but never anything that really stirred the soul. But now, I am determined to experience the artistic side of life. I want to read poetry—epic poetry, poetry that has stood the test of time. I want to go to museums and see paintings—Picassos and van Goghs, to see beyond mere paint and canvas to the soul underneath them. I want to hear a symphony orchestra and go to an opera and listen to Miles Davis and Louis Armstrong and buy a Beatles record. All these things that I've missed, these are the things I want to experience now, if I can. I want to experience the passion of the senses."

He waited, gauging her reaction. Angelina's eyes had gone wider and wider as he spoke.

"Really?" was all she could manage to say.

"Yes." Basil leaned in even farther. "Yes, and I needed to talk to you, Angelina, because I believe that I've begun to experience my passion, thanks to you."

"Mr. Cupertino, I'm not completely sure what you're talking about here, but don't you think I'm too young for you?"

He laughed, a deep, affable laugh, filled with easy amusement. "It's not you, dear. It's your *lasagna*."

"My lasagna?"

Basil closed his eyes. "*Lasagna.* I never realized what a beautiful word it was until now. *Laa-sahn-yah.* Just saying the word, I swear I can taste it again. I've been eating your lasagna for three days. Three rapturous days. Each bite gets my senses going all over again, and the more I eat, the better it gets. Angelina, eating that lasagna you made was one of the most moving experiences of my life."

"I'm glad you liked it."

Basil took his glasses out of his shirt pocket and put them on. "I did. So, let's get down to business. Angelina, how are you fixed since your late husband passed away?"

She hadn't seen that one coming at all, but she matched his professional manner.

"I'm not sure that is your business."

"Forgive me," said Basil. "That was indelicate. Please, allow me to start over. In actual fact, I came here to make you a proposal."

"I'm not sure what to make of all this, Mr. Cupertino, but, frankly, you intrigue me."

"I was hoping you'd feel that way." He peered over his glasses. "Here it is: I would like to pay you to cook for me. My sister, Dottie, is a wonderful, companionable person, but she is a god-awful cook."

Angelina looked at him sympathetically. "I'm so sorry."

"It would be worse for you if you ate her *pasta e fagioli.* To continue, I would like to commission you to cook breakfasts and dinners for me, six days a week, with a day off of your choosing. I would come to you, so there wouldn't be any transportation of goods required. The menus will also be entirely of your choosing."

"You'd come to me?"

"Of course. If that would be acceptable?"

"Sounds reasonable."

"In exchange, I will pay you, on a monthly basis, in advance, the amount I have written on this piece of paper."

He took a folded, lined sheet of paper out of his pocket and slid it across the table. Angelina opened it, read it, refolded it, and placed it in front of her.

"I can't argue the fact that I could use some help making ends meet, Mr. Cupertino. And I could feed you extremely well for the number written on this piece of paper. But how does Dottie feel about the idea? I don't want to step on anybody's toes."

Basil nodded, clearly having anticipated the question.

"She's started working the night shift at the store, so I'd be on my own for most of my meals, anyway. I have discussed it with her and she's all for it."

Angelina sat still, taking a moment to let the idea sink in. Basil waited her out patiently, then, when he felt the time was right, said, "Do we have a deal?"

"Yes. We have a deal."

Mr. Cupertino stood and they shook on it.

Their business successfully transacted, Mr. Cupertino took his jacket from the back of the chair and put it on, then Angelina saw him to the door. He stopped when he reached the sidewalk and called back to her jauntily. "See you for breakfast tomorrow? Eight o'clock?"

"Eight it is. Don't be late."

"I never am."

Angelina smiled in spite of herself as she leaned against the closed front door lost in thought. Had she agreed too quickly? The number that Mr. Cupertino had written on that piece of paper was extremely generous. Even if she hadn't lost her job, it might have been impossible to refuse. She felt a tingle of pride and excitement. He certainly liked her cooking, didn't he?

Too late to turn back now, she thought. *A deal's a deal.* She had to go shopping. As she got ready to go out, picture after picture of ideas for breakfasts and dinners riffled rapidly through her mind like a culinary flip book. She would have to start him off with something a little bit special, something classic, for breakfast.

And she might have to go and buy a frame for that lasagna recipe.

Lasagna Provençal

....

Serves 12

INGREDIENTS
  2 tablespoons olive oil (1 to sauté and 1 to
    toss with the noodles)
  2 shallot cloves, diced small
  2 cloves garlic, lightly crushed and minced
  One 16-ounce can diced tomatoes
  1 teaspoon fresh rosemary leaves, very finely
    minced (from about 1 large sprig)
  1 tablespoon fresh thyme leaves minced
    (from about 6 to 12 sprigs depending on
    how densely the leaves have grown on the
    stems)
  1 tablespoon fresh flat-leaf parsley leaves,
    minced (from about 12 sprigs)
  2 fresh sage leaves, finely minced
  ½ teaspoon salt
  ¼ teaspoon ground black pepper
  One 16-ounce package lasagna noodles
    (which contains approximately 16 to 20
    noodles)
  2 cups ricotta cheese
  4 ounces Parmigiano-Reggiano cheese, 2
    ounces grated to yield 1 cup and 2 ounces
    cut into 24 two-inch-long, ¼-inch batonnets
  8 ounces Neufchâtel cheese, cut into ½-inch
    cubes

2 large eggs, beaten

½ cup fresh chopped basil leaves, ¼ cup to layer over the tomato fresca (sauce) and ¼ cup for the top plus 12 tiny sprigs to garnish

2 tablespoons fresh oregano leaves, minced (from about 6 to 12 sprigs depending on density of leaves)

1½ cups oil-packed, sun-dried tomatoes, julienne cut, about an 8-ounce jar

2 cups shredded Gruyère cheese (about 8 ounces)

5-ounce package herbed Boursin cheese

½ cup crème fraîche

METHOD

Bring a large pot of salted water to a boil for the lasagna noodles.

To make the tomato fresca, heat one tablespoon of the olive oil over medium high heat in a medium saucepot, and sauté the shallots and garlic until they become translucent. Add the diced tomatoes, rosemary, thyme, parsley, sage, and salt and pepper, and stir to combine. Bring to a boil, then reduce the heat to low and simmer uncovered just until the flavors are integrated but before the tomatoes begin to break down, about 20 minutes, checking periodically to make sure the sauce doesn't burn.

Boil the lasagna noodles until al dente, about

10 to 15 minutes. Drain and transfer to a large bowl. Toss with the remaining tablespoon of olive oil so the noodles don't stick together. Let cool so you can handle them.

This lasagna will have 4 layers but two different types of cheese layers. One type of cheese layer will consist of ricotta, grated Parmesan, Neufchâtel, and egg to bind. Combine the ricotta and Parmesan in a mixing bowl, stir in half of the cubed Neufchâtel (reserving half of the cubes until assembly), whisk in the eggs, and set aside briefly. Preheat the oven to 350°F.

Layer 4 to 5 lasagna noodles lengthwise side by side with edges overlapping in an ovenproof lasagna dish. Top with half of the cheese/egg mixture and arrange 12 of the Parmesan strips and half of the reserved cubed Neufchâtel evenly over it, reserving the rest of the Parmesan and Neufchâtel for the other layer. (It is easiest to drop evenly spaced spoonfuls of the cheese/egg mixture over the noodles, then spread it out.) Distribute 2 tablespoons of the fresh basil, half of the fresh oregano, and ½ cup of the sun-dried tomatoes over the cheese, then layer another 4 or 5 lasagna noodles over the cheese in the same fashion as the first layer of noodles.

The second type of cheese layer will consist of Gruyère and Boursin. Spread half of the Gruyère over the second layer of noodles and drop dollops of half of the Boursin cheese over the Gruyère.

Distribute another ½ cup of the sun-dried tomatoes over the cheese. For the third layer, repeat the process with the noodles, remaining cheese/egg mixture, the remaining 12 Parmesan strips, remaining half of the reserved cubed Neufchâtel, 2 tablespoons basil, remaining oregano, and remaining sun-dried tomatoes. For the last (top) layer, spread out the final course of noodles, top with dollops of the remaining Boursin and dollops of the crème fraîche, and then ladle the tomato sauce over the top and finish with the remaining Gruyère.

Bake covered (with foil) in the oven for 30 minutes, remove the foil, and bake for 10 more minutes. Remove from the oven and let rest for 10 minutes before slicing into 12 squares. Sprinkle the surface with ¼ cup fresh-minced basil. Arrange a basil sprig next to the lasagna on each serving plate.

CHAPTER SIX

Eggs Benedict with Basil

Basil Cupertino was a man of fastidious habits, possessed of a methodical way of approaching his life. He had planned financially for his retirement, meticulously so, but he knew that taking full advantage of his newfound free time required planning of an entirely different sort. He had considered that he might travel in the coming years, maybe to Italy, to Florence or Rome, but quickly enough decided that those kinds of adventures might come only sporadically at best. He knew himself well enough to know that he didn't travel especially well, and that he never looked forward to the disruption of a reliable, daily routine that came with packing up and shuffling off to some undiscovered country. He wouldn't rule it out, but wouldn't commit to making it a mainstay of his plans. With admirable efficiency, he'd concluded that he would satisfy himself instead with adventures of the mind.

Philadelphia had a world-class museum, a symphony orchestra, a great library, and he was within easy striking distance of New York and Washington, which meant the Met, the National Gallery, Lincoln Center, the Smithsonian. There would be time to sample and take pleasure in experiencing it all—starting now with what he had every reason to believe would most likely be the best food he had ever eaten in his life, and, even better, served on a regular schedule, twice a day, six times a week.

As for the rest, there was no time like the present. He would start in on his reading with the Western Canon. He'd gone to the Free Library straightaway after he'd left Angelina, filled out an application for a library card, and begun his organized research and exploration into its vast literary collection. He wanted nothing too esoteric to start. He would work his way up to more challenging works such as Dante's *Inferno* or *The Iliad* as his literary and aesthetic muscles grew stronger. Shakespeare wasn't going anywhere. He wanted something substantial but exciting to start with, a book with real emotion, definitely poetry, but a little action, too. In the end, he decided on Cervantes. So, when he left the house the next day, at three minutes to eight for the trip across the street, he carried a Penguin Classics edition of *Don Quixote* in his pocket. He made his first trip in two and a half minutes and knocked on the door with a comfortable cushion of thirty seconds to spare.

"Hi, Mr. Cupertino," Angelina said, opening the front door. "Wow, you're right on time. Come on in."

Basil entered the warmth of the parlor and was immediately encouraged by the smells wafting in from the kitchen. He followed Angelina into the dining room and saw that a place had been set for him along the side of the table, which was covered with a fresh linen tablecloth. A small flowerpot with African violets was set in the center of the table, and a glass of fresh-squeezed orange juice was by his place setting.

"Take a seat," said Angelina. She left and returned with a carafe of hot coffee in her hand.

"You want the TV on, or some music or something?" she asked as she went back into the kitchen.

"No, thanks, I've got my book."

"Oh, what are you reading?"

"*Don Quixote.* You know, the *Man of La Mancha.*"

Angelina reappeared in the doorway, whipping with a whisk in a steel mixing bowl with practiced dexterity. "Oh, God, I love that show. Isn't that the one with 'The Impossible Dream'?"

"Oh, sure," he said.

The egg timer dinged and Angelina disappeared. Basil sampled the coffee, which alone was worth the price of admission. Angelina had laid out a small porcelain pitcher of milk and a sugar bowl, but today Basil drank it black.

Angelina had been up since four-thirty and felt shaky. Despite that she hadn't been getting much rest, sleep never came to her easily when she had something serious on for the next day, and this was serious business. She'd seldom, if ever, doubted herself in the realm of food, especially in her own kitchen, but today was different. This time, she was getting paid to cook for someone she really didn't know very well, which was far different from cooking for friends or for her family, who would compliment her whatever the circumstances; this time, she had no idea what to expect. She'd spent the whole morning pacing and drinking coffee, started cooking at seven-thirty, and by ten minutes to eight, when it was too late to turn back, she was kicking herself.

Why in heaven's name was she making a breakfast dish for a man she didn't know that had *spinach* in it? What if he hated spinach? What if her hollandaise broke? What, she couldn't have just started him off with bacon, scrambled eggs, and toast?

She dipped a clean pinkie into the hollandaise in the bowl. It coated her finger like a sheath of yellow velvet. Despite her nerves, she plated swiftly and surely. She lifted the poached eggs clear from the shimmering, hot water with a safecracker's touch, laying each one with infinite care in place on top of its foundation of English muffin and Canadian bacon. Silky drizzle of hollandaise, sprinkle of fresh parsley, grind of black pepper, framed with creamed spinach, dusted with paprika. Done.

Basil hadn't achieved more than a page of his book when Angelina swept in with his breakfast. Wisps of fragrant steam wafted up as the plate landed before him.

"Oh, my Lord," Basil said. "Is that spinach? What is this?"

Angelina's heart skipped a beat. "It's eggs Benedict Florentine."

He bowed down and took in the aromas more deeply.

"Don't you like eggs Benedict?" she asked.

"I don't know. I've never had it. What's in it?"

Angelina took a quick breath. "It's poached eggs on an English muffin with Canadian bacon and hollandaise sauce. And I creamed a little spinach with nutmeg and Parmesan cheese. My mother taught me how to make it. She used to make it for my father every Easter Sunday. I hope you like it."

"It smells good. Thank you."

"Enjoy," she said, and left the room.

A little mirror hung on the dining room wall, a tchotchke with a curlicue frame she'd picked up for a song in New Hope, which Angelina suddenly realized had been placed in the perfect position for spying on Mr. Cupertino from right where she stood in the kitchen.

Basil picked up his knife and fork and cut into the egg and bacon, down through the crispy, perfectly browned muffin. The golden yolk, not too firm or too runny, trickled sinuously into the rich hollandaise, which was delicately speckled with smoked paprika. He speared egg, ham, and bread, pushed a little of the creamed spinach that surrounded it onto the fork with his knife, and raised the artfully composed bite to his lips.

He tasted for a full twelve seconds before he breathed out with an audible moan.

Angelina had heard that sound before. Her daddy used to make that sound on Easter, and Frank had made it the first time he tasted that dish.

"Magnificent!" called Basil. "Is every day going to be like this?"

Angelina looked straight into the glare of the sun shining through the kitchen window. It was a trick she'd always used to keep from crying as a little girl. She couldn't start crying; she'd never be able to explain to him why.

"You want some more coffee?" she called back.

"Yes, please."

Angelina checked herself in the little mirror, returned to the table, and refilled his cup. "I'm so glad you like it," she said, her confidence almost fully restored. "And, no, if you eat like this every day, you'll get spoiled. And fat. Tomorrow, you get steel-cut oatmeal. With a little fresh cranberry conserve."

"I cannot wait." His eyes crinkled with gustatory bliss.

Angelina left him alone with his meal and busied herself in the kitchen. Basil abandoned any pretense of reading because he found it impossible to concentrate on anything but the meal in front of him. He savored it and took his time, but in a few all-too-brief minutes, it was over and gone.

It took Angelina two shakes to finish the washing up as Basil lingered over the last of the coffee. She declared her intention to go and do a bit of food shopping, but not before Basil, as good as his word, handed her a check for the first month's installment of what, he now felt more certain than ever, would be a long-standing and happy arrangement. They left the house together.

Eggs Benedict Florentine

Serves 4

INGREDIENTS FOR CANADIAN BACON
  1 teaspoon canola or olive oil
  4 half-inch-thick slices Canadian bacon

INGREDIENTS FOR CREAMED SPINACH
  ½ cup heavy cream
  ¼ teaspoon grated nutmeg
  1 pound fresh spinach, soaked in salt water

to remove grit and dried in a salad spinner
Salt, if needed, and freshly ground black
  pepper, to taste
1 cup finely grated Parmigiano-Reggiano
  cheese, freshly grated from about a
  2-ounce piece

INGREDIENTS FOR POACHED EGGS
  4 eggs
  1 tablespoon vinegar
  2 English muffins, fork split
  Butter, as needed, for the English muffins
  ⅛ teaspoon paprika

INGREDIENTS FOR HOLLANDAISE
  2 large egg yolks
  1 tablespoon chilled white wine
  1/16 teaspoon salt (a pinch)
  ½ cup butter (see note in method about this
    amount), fully melted but no longer
    steaming hot
  Juice of ½ a fresh lemon

METHOD FOR CANADIAN BACON
Heat the oil in a skillet over medium-high heat.
Lightly brown each side of the Canadian bacon.
Remove it from the heat and cover it to keep it
warm until needed.

METHOD FOR CREAMED SPINACH

Heat the cream and nutmeg over medium to medium-low heat in a heavy-bottomed saucepot, and reduce by three-fourths, about 5 minutes, monitoring to prevent burning.

Steam the spinach until it's tender but still bright green.

Remove the cream from the heat and mix well with the Parmesan, then fold in the spinach. Adjust the seasoning to taste with salt, if needed, and black pepper. Cover to keep warm, and set aside.

METHOD FOR THE POACHED EGGS

Poach the eggs before you begin the hollandaise, as hollandaise cannot sit long before it is served and will reheat the eggs it tops.

Add 1 tablespoon vinegar to a medium saucepan of gently boiling water over medium-high heat. Add the eggs one at a time so they don't cook into one mass.

The eggs should be cooked until the whites are set but the centers are still soft. Ideally, the eggs will float freely and independently without sinking to the bottom. But if an egg sinks to the bottom, wait until it's nearly set before attempting to work it loose, or the yolk will surely break. For food-safety reasons, remove the eggs from the pot with a slotted wooden or plastic spoon and place in another pot or bowl filled with water that has been heated to 150°F (hot enough to kill microorganisms without further cooking the eggs), cover, and let sit about 5 minutes, while you make the hollandaise, then drain them on a paper towel and pat them dry.

Toast and butter the English muffins.

METHOD FOR THE HOLLANDAISE

Combine the egg yolks, wine, and salt in a double boiler set over simmering water (in classical cooking, a simmer is *just below* a boil, a temperature that should be maintained to keep the eggs from curdling), and whisk constantly for about 2 minutes, then gradually begin adding melted butter in a slow, thin stream, continuing to whisk constantly until the mixture is emulsified and the sauce begins to thicken. (Important: If you achieve a pleasantly thickened sauce before all the butter has been added, don't feel compelled to use it all because attempting to do so may cause the sauce to break.) Whisk in the lemon juice, and remove the double boiler from the heat. Cover and keep the sauce in the double boiler (but not for long).

PRESENTATION

Make a circle of creamed spinach around the perimeter of each serving plate. Place a toasted and buttered English muffin in the center of each plate and top with a slice of Canadian bacon and a poached egg. Spoon some hollandaise sauce over the egg and sprinkle with paprika.

––––––––

They had barely descended to the pavement when a five-year-old boy, Dominic, ran up to them breathlessly. He had been sent on a courier's mission by his mother, who was in close conversation with the mailman down the street and who waved to Angelina and pointed to the little boy as he jumped to a stop in front of them with both feet.

"Hi, Mrs. D'Angelo!"

"Hi, Dominic. Boy, you're getting big."

"I know. Is that your dad?" He indicated Basil with an accusatory forefinger.

"No, sweetie, he's not my dad. This is my friend Mr. Cupertino from down the street."

"Okay," said Dominic, "my mom says to tell you that Mrs. Cappuccio wants you to come and see her."

"Right now?" asked Angelina.

"Yes."

"Okay, tell her I'm coming over. But don't run."

He ran off to deliver the message to his mom, and Angelina turned to Basil. "So, Mr. Cupertino, do you want anything special for your dinner?"

"You think I ever in a million years would have come up with eggs Benedict?"

Angelina laughed and gave him a pat on the back. "See you at seven o'clock," she called as Basil headed for home.

A minute later, she knocked on the Cappuccios' door. Johnny answered and let her in. He took her coat and handbag and conscientiously hung them up in the hall closet. Johnny had always been a little shy with Angelina. He was a sweet kid and she liked to tease him, but she usually waited until after he'd had a few minutes to warm up to her actually being in the same room.

"You working today, Johnny?" she asked.

"Yeah. I mean, yes, I'm going in a minute. Can I get you anything?"

"No thanks, honey. Little Dominic said your grandma wanted to see me?"

"You can go ahead upstairs, she's in her room," said Johnny. "I'll tell her you're here."

He took one step toward the foot of the steps and yelled, "Grandmom! Mrs. D'Angelo's here!"

A distant, reedy female voice called back from the dark at the top of the stairs, "Do you think they heard you in Sicily?"

Johnny turned to Angelina with the beginnings of a blush forming. "Sorry," he said quietly. Then he called out at the top of his lungs, "I'm going to work!"

His grandmother called out, "Good-bye!"—with a playful tone of and good riddance! that made Angelina smile.

"Angelina, are you coming up to see me?"

"Hi, Mrs. Cappuccio, I'll be up in a minute."

Johnny shrugged into his jacket and headed for the door. "Thanks for coming over, Mrs. D'Angelo. Um, I gotta' go . . ."

119

"You go. I'll lock up after. Go and have a nice day."

Johnny dashed out the door. Angelina closed it behind him and headed up the steps. She'd been in the house plenty of times, but had never been up to Mrs. Cappuccio's bedroom. She knew that the dear was getting up in age and had been having more and more trouble making the trip all the way down to the first floor. One of the drawbacks of South Philly row homes was the precipitous climb up and down the stairs, which wore on a soul as the years rolled by.

Mrs. Cappuccio's room had that unmistakable little-old-lady smell of stale perfume with a dash of camphor laced with potpourri that came together in a comforting musk, especially when the heat was turned up high all of the time. There were religious icons and pictures all over the room, of the Sacred Heart of Jesus, Our Lady of Fatima, of Mary and Joseph leaning in wonder over baby Jesus in the manger, thumbtacked to the walls and arranged on tiny shelves.

Mrs. Cappuccio sat upright in bed. She looked old and too thin, but her hair was still nearly black, with vivid streaks of gray, and was knotted in a long, beautiful braid that showed outside her black-and-orange quilt. She smiled at Angelina with strong, white teeth and patted the covers beside her.

"Hello, Angelina. Come sit by me."

Angelina walked over, perched on the edge of the mattress, and asked, "How are you doing, Mrs. Cappuccio?"

"I'm doing okay, honey. Sorry I couldn't get to the funeral."

"That's okay. You haven't been feeling well. It was nice that Johnny came."

Mrs. Cappuccio leaned back, settling herself in for a nice visit. Angelina could see that the very mention of her grandson's name made her happy. "If your Tina was there, my Johnny's gonna be there," she said knowingly.

"Yeah, I kind of think you're right."

"It's a bad time," said Mrs. Cappuccio, "but it's good to have a nice funeral. Everybody comes, you see them, they make you feel better. When my Bill died, the funeral was three days. The full boat."

"Three days. Wow."

"My Bill, he just thought the church was the big thing. See alla' this junk in the room, with the crosses and the statues? That's all him. He was a nut for Jesus Christ and His Mother. Me, I like pictures of dogs and birds."

"Dogs and birds are nice," said Angelina. "So, what did you want to talk to me about?"

Mrs. Cappuccio snuggled in comfortably and savored having Angelina's full attention before she spoke.

"So, you're cooking the meals for Dottie's brother?"

Angelina enjoyed seeing the look of small triumph that crossed Mrs. Cappuccio's face, a look that said, despite her age and confinement, she still knew what was what in the neighborhood.

Angelina replied with friendly astonishment, "How'd you know that? I just started this morning."

Mrs. Cappuccio continued with a casual air, as if this kind of thing happened every day, "Dottie brings me some of her chicken noodle soup, once a week, or twice. She told me about it. She thinks it's a good idea. She don't like to cook, except for soup."

"How was the chicken noodle anyway?"

"I gotta eat it, she comes right up to the room, I can't get away. So, anyhow, if you're taking in some cooking, I want you to maybe take in my Gianni. He's got a good job; it's no problem for him to pay you."

Angelina did a little double take. This was the last thing she'd expected, but she saw the appeal of the idea right away, given her present circumstances. Mrs. Cappuccio was prepared for Angelina's next question even before she asked it.

"But how about you?"

"Oh, don't worry about me. I'm moving over to the Heaven Hotel. I can't take the steps no more, so I'm going to the Sacred Heart Home. I got it all arranged."

"Oh, I'm sorry."

"Don't be sorry. The mother superior over there, she used to be Margaret O'Healy. We were best friends all through school. We used to chase all the boys, but only I could catch them. That's probably why she become a nun." The old woman laughed merrily at a snippet of memory from her girlhood. "Now she's 'Sister Bartholomew of the Flaming Sword.' Scares the hell out of everybody, but Maggie'll make sure they take good care of me."

There it was, all wrapped up as neat as a pin.

"Sure, I'll take care of Johnny," said Angelina. "Send him over and I'll set him up."

Mrs. Cappuccio grinned, and the accord was struck. Johnny would come for dinner that very evening, at seven sharp.

"You're a good girl, Angelina. Could you do me a favor before you go, hon?"

"Sure, what?"

"Make me a sandwich and a cup a tea? And throw out that goddamn soup for me?"

Downstairs, Angelina rummaged through Mrs. Cappuccio's refrigerator and found some pumpernickel bread, the end of a smoked pork roast, and a half a pound of Swiss cheese. She started thinking of the kinds of food she'd miss making most if she were stuck in bed most of the day, and she immediately thought *deli*. She cruised the refrigerator shelves and found some India relish, which she mixed together with a bit of ketchup and mayonnaise to make an improvised Thousand Island dressing. When she found a little can of sauerkraut in the cupboard, she knew she had a winner. She cooked up a Reuben sandwich in a cast-iron skillet, brewed a strong cup of tea with two sugars and a drop of milk, and brought it up to the room on a tray with some dill pickle slices on the side.

They whiled away the next hour chatting like old girlfriends, and Angelina used the opportunity to find out about the kinds of dinners Johnny liked to eat. When Angelina noticed that Mrs. Cappuccio was getting tired, she said good-bye and promised to visit her again later in the week, to see how she was getting on. She left Mrs. Cappuccio napping contentedly, gave the kitchen a once-over before she left, and locked the door securely behind her.

Angelina headed off in the direction of the bank, fingering Mr. Cupertino's check in her pocket as she walked. She could hardly believe that it had only been yesterday that she'd agreed to cook for Mr. Cupertino, and it had hit her forcefully this morning just what a leap of faith it had been. The money he had agreed to pay her was generous, would allow for the purchase of quality ingredients, and allow her to make some excellent meals for him and still turn a profit, but as far as supporting her, that was quite another matter.

Even with Frank's small life insurance policy, she wouldn't be able to survive on that kind of money alone for long. When she thought about it, she felt a little sick to her stomach.

It had crossed her mind as early as last night that things might be a lot better if she were cooking for more than one person. She would have had a tough time saying no to Mrs. Cappuccio regardless, and Johnny was a sweetheart, but she also realized that this latest wrinkle definitely helped her financial cause.

Then it occurred to her that, before she'd gone ahead and signed on another "client," it might have been a good idea to have consulted with Mr. Cupertino, her first and, let's face it, most important paying customer, to make sure that it was okay by him.

What if he balked at the idea? She made herself a mental promise not to put it off and to bring it up with him as soon as possible.

It was cool outside, but the sun was shining, so after Angelina made the deposit at the bank, she wandered over in the direction of Sacco's Italian Deli. As she walked those familiar sidewalks, she let her mind wander and thought, *Sardines in the can have more elbow room than the houses on Tasker Street.*

She remembered back to her friend in eighth grade Linda Spinelli, who used to live on Tasker. She and Angelina used to butter white bread on the outside, heat up a pan and make toasted chocolate sandwiches with Hershey's bars, then share them while they pressed their ears to the electric socket on the common kitchen wall with Linda's neighbors and listened to them argue after dinner. Everyone in South Philly wanted to know everyone else's business, but, for the most part, they took pride in being part of a respectable community, too. Every front stoop Angelina passed was as clean as a dinner plate. In this neighborhood, the lady of the house regarded her front steps as the first steps into her home.

The bell over the door tinkled as Angelina walked into Sacco's. The family-owned place had great cheeses and *salumi*, fresh pasta and bread made every day; it had been on this corner for as long as she could remember. The old man and his wife stayed in the back, making soups and salads, pastries and gelato, and their son, who was in his sixties and who almost everybody knew as Mr. Sack (though they never said it to his face), tended the counter and made sandwiches with his two sons, Donnie and Sal. Angelina took a number and looked around at a display of olive oils on the shelf while she waited. Soon, Donnie called out her number and she placed it in a tiny wicker basket on the counter.

"Hi, Donnie."

"How ya' doin', Mrs. D'Angelo?"

They went straight into their familiar rhythm of

ordering. Donnie could remember up to about fourteen items before he had to write anything down, but kept the stub of a pencil behind his ear at all times, just in case. He started cutting with the slicer as she recited her list.

"I need some cheese, give me half a pound of provolone . . ."

"Okay, what else?"

". . . half a pound *bufala* mozarell' . . ."

"Okay, what else?"

"*Capicol'*, a pound, prosciut', half a pound . . ."

"Okay, what else?"

". . . olives, the Calabrese, some of those cherry peppers . . . your mom make them?"

"Absolutely. 'Zat it?"

"And a loaf of that big bread," she said, pointing. "That's it, thanks, Donnie."

"You got it." The first packet of cheese, wrapped in white butcher paper, hit the counter as he spoke, and he went off to put together the rest of her order.

Angelina gave a little wave to Mr. Sacco, who was glaring out from behind the counter. "Hi, Mr. Sacco."

He glared at her, but in a nice way, not the way he generally glared at everybody else. "Hey, honey, how you doin'?" he grumbled.

The bell rang on the door behind her and, to her surprise, Jerry Mancini walked in. Angelina saw him before he saw her and she smiled in spite of herself. Jerry and she went way back—back to grade school at Saint Teresa's before they tore it down and everybody went over to Saint Joe. He was one year ahead of her, one of those guys you never dated but was always around, always funny, always made you laugh. He was a few inches taller than Angelina all through school, still was, with dark hair, brown eyes; he had a nice build but never played sports; never tucked in his shirt, never really combed his hair, but it worked for him and he got away with it because the teachers all liked him. He had an opinion of himself, for sure, at least he did back in the day. Angelina couldn't put a day to the last time she'd seen him around. He looked good, though.

Jerry headed toward the counter. "Hey, Donnie."

Donnie looked up long enough to barely acknowledge the greeting as he worked.

Jerry grinned. "Hey, Mr. Sack."

If looks could kill, Mr. Sacco could have gone up for murder one. Jerry knew exactly what he was doing when he said it and was clearly basking in the older man's disdain when he turned and spotted Angelina.

"Oh, my God, Angelina!"

"Hi, Jerry."

He came right over and gave her a hug. "Hey, how are you doing?" The simple, genuine compassion in his voice told her that he had heard the news about Frank.

"I'm doing . . . okay."

"I only heard yesterday; I couldn't believe it. I'm so sorry. How are you holding up?"

"I'm doing okay. Sad."

"Frank," Jerry said, "he was one of those guys that we all looked up to, you know what I mean?"

Angelina nodded.

"And not just because he got you to marry him."

Angelina smiled and looked down. Jerry saw that it was probably best to leave it alone for a minute, so he called over his shoulder, "Hey, Donnie, remember that number?"

"Yeah. So what about it?" Donnie plopped another packet on the counter.

"Yeah, I hit that number."

"You got lucky," said Donnie.

Jerry left Angelina and grabbed a bag of chips off the rack. He popped them open and started munching.

Mr. Sacco growled, "Hey. Big shot. You gonna buy something, or just advertise?"

"Oh, I'm going to buy something, Mr. Sacco," said Jerry. "But first you gotta serve Mrs. D'Angelo here."

Angelina came alongside and started gathering her order into her shopping basket. "I ordered already. You go."

Jerry munched and thought for a second or two.

"Okay, um . . . can I get a pound of salami, and a loaf of bread? And a Coke?"

Mr. Sacco shook his head as if Jerry had just asked for his daughter's phone number and started slicing lunch meat.

"Is that for breakfast, lunch, or dinner?" Angelina asked.

"All three. Depends on what time I'm eating it."

Angelina put the last of her goods into the basket. "A grown man, and you don't know how to cook for yourself after all these years?"

"Hey," said Jerry. "I know how to cook, I just don't know anything about makin' food."

Mr. Sacco slapped down the last of the salami like he was slapping a fly.

Angelina suddenly got a picture in her head, of Jerry slumped in a chair, lit only by the mournful glow of the TV, in his stocking feet, munching pathetically on a sad-looking, plain salami sandwich, sucking on a Coke, watching *Wheel of Fortune*, all alone.

"You need a woman to cook for you," said Angelina, surprising herself as she headed for the register.

Now Jerry trailed close behind her. "I do?"

"Yes."

"Really . . . ?"

"Yes, really."

Jerry was suddenly beaming.

"Don't get too excited," Angelina chided him.

"I'm taking in some cooking, that's all. I'm just saying, you could think about coming and eating your meals at my house."

"Angelina Cuccinata, are you inviting me over for dinner?"

"And breakfast. I serve two meals a day, but it'll cost you. This is a paying proposition."

Jerry was now seriously intrigued. "Every day?"

"Every day but Saturday."

Jerry leaned against the countertop. He meant it to be coy, but Angelina could see that she had him hooked.

"What's it gonna cost me?"

Angelina reeled him in. "I'll tell you what. Come tonight, see if you like the food, then I'll tell you what it's going to cost."

"Hear that, Mr. Sacco?" said Jerry. "Free sample, that's a pretty good idea . . ."

Mr. Sacco had finished ringing up Angelina's order and was stuffing it in a bag. He would have stuffed Jerry if he'd had a bigger bag.

"Well?" said Angelina.

"Well, if you're actually inviting me over for dinner, after all these years, what can I say but yes?"

Jerry threw a triumphant look at Donnie, who rolled his eyes as he gave Angelina her change.

"So, I'll see you tonight at seven?" she said, collecting her bag from the counter.

"It's a date," Jerry said.

"See you guys," said Angelina.

As she headed for the door, Angelina felt an unexpected twinge of guilt, as if she'd been flirting with another man behind her husband's back. Jerry must have sensed it because he made sure to walk her to the door and respectfully opened it for her. He touched her reassuringly on the shoulder as she passed him and said, "I'm really glad I ran into you, Angelina. And I'm really sorry about Frank."

"Thanks, Jerry. I'll see you later."

She teared up a little on the other side of the door, but by the time she made it halfway down the block, she felt better. She felt as if she had just made her first independent marketing decision.

Jerry closed the door behind her. He looked at Mr. Sacco.

"Whaddya think of *that,* Mr. Sack?"

Mr. Sacco stuck out his palm.

"Shut up and gimme your money."

CHAPTER SEVEN

Hunger Is the Best Sauce

Angelina was a little behind.

She had spent the rest of her morning going over her cooking diary, updating recipes, looking back for good ideas that might have slipped her mind, making notes in the margins and then transcribing them on her old Correcting Selectric. Angelina would often draw pencil sketches or diagrams of dishes that she was particularly proud of and clip them into her book, too. She enjoyed drawing and had even taken a few commercial art courses at the community college. Sketching in the fine details of the ridges on a lasagna noodle or capturing the shiny surface of an eggplant on paper helped her to think about them in a different way. More than once, her drawings had inspired new approaches or recipes that she might not have thought of otherwise.

She'd decided on a recipe for that evening's dinner that her father used to love—veal *braciole* with a *piccata* sauce. It was thinly sliced veal rolled around a little Parmigiano, parsley, and ham, then lightly browned in olive oil. Angelina had bought that nice prosciutto from Sacco's and this seemed like the perfect way to showcase it. She wanted to add some extra zing, so in addition to a squeeze of lemon juice and capers, she was planning to enrich the sauce with dry vermouth and top it with a garnish of fresh-grated lemon zest. She'd serve the veal over linguine dressed in extra-virgin olive oil and butter with lots of cracked pepper, and a side of baby asparagus.

Veal Braciole *with* Piccata *Sauce*

Serves 6

INGREDIENTS

  3 pounds sliced boneless veal

  Freshly ground black pepper, to taste

  ¼ pound prosciutto, cut into 24 pieces, each about 2 inches square

  ½ cup fresh flat-leaf parsley, minced

  4 ounces Parmigiano-Reggiano cheese, 1½ cups finely grated from about a 2- or 3-ounce piece, and the rest cut medium brunoise (¼-inch julienne, then crosswise) into ½-inch lengths

  3 tablespoons to ½ cup canola oil, as needed

  2 shallot cloves, minced (or one clove if they're large)

½ cup dry vermouth

2 cups chicken stock

½ teaspoon organic beef base (such as Better Than Bouillon brand, sold in an 8-ounce jar)

2 tablespoons white-rice flour or all-purpose flour

1 fresh lemon, zest grated off then juiced

¼ cup capers, about half of a 3-ounce jar

1 pound cooked linguine dressed with extra-virgin olive oil, freshly ground black pepper, and minced parsley (as an accompaniment)

1 pound steamed asparagus spears (as an accompaniment)

METHOD

Spread sheets of plastic wrap over the surface of a large cutting board, tucking the edges under to secure them. Lay the veal on the plastic wrap and season it with black pepper. Cover the meat with a second layer of plastic wrap to keep the mess down, and pound it down to an even thickness of ⅛ inch with a meat mallet. Slice the veal into 4-inch-by-6-inch sections to yield about 24 pieces. Lay a piece of prosciutto on each piece of veal, sprinkling each with a teaspoon of parsley and a tablespoon of the grated cheese. Top each with a few chunks of the cheese. Roll up the slices of meat, folding in the sides as you go and secure with toothpicks. (Keep count of the toothpicks so you can be sure to retrieve them all.) The veal will probably have to be seared in batches. For each batch, heat 2 tablespoons of the oil in a large sauté pan over medium heat. When it begins to shimmer, place the veal rolls in the pan, seam-side down first, and sear for 1 minute undisturbed before flipping and searing the other side the same way. Transfer the seared rolled meat seam-side down to a baking dish and remove all the toothpicks. Cover with foil to let rest.

Preheat the oven to 300°F.

In the same sauté pan, heat 1 tablespoon of oil over medium heat and sauté the shallots until they turn translucent, stirring frequently to prevent burning, about 2 minutes. Deglaze the pan with the vermouth and let most of the alcohol evaporate. Then add the chicken stock and heat to a gentle boil. Whisk in the beef base to blend, then gradually whisk in the flour. Lower the heat to medium and let cook about 5 to 10 minutes to allow the flavors to integrate and the sauce to thicken. Reduce the heat to low and whisk in the lemon juice. Pour the sauce over the meat. Cover and place in the oven until the veal is infused with the sauce and very tender, about 50 minutes to 1 hour.

PRESENTATION

Place a bed of linguine in the center of each serving plate. Use two large spoons to carefully transfer 3 to 4 veal rolls to each plate, arranging them around the linguine. Spoon about 3 to 4 tablespoons of sauce over the veal and the pasta. Sprinkle one teaspoon of capers and a pinch of lemon zest on each piece of veal. Arrange several asparagus spears around the perimeter of the plate.

—————

Angelina wanted to start them off with a soup, one that would contrast nicely with the veal. She decided on her Mint Sweet Potato Bisque, a wonderful puréed soup, slightly thickened with rice, accented with golden raisins, brightened by fresh mint. And dessert called for pie. This was the first time she was having Johnny and Jerry to the table, and in Jerry's case it was almost a sales pitch, so everything had to be great. She jotted "pears, black cherries, whole allspice, airplane bottle of Old Overholt Rye" down on her shopping list. The pie would bring it across the finish line.

Tracking down fresh mint and black cherries proved problematic. After four stops and no luck, she ended up taking the bus all the way to the Reading Terminal Market. Compromising on dried mint and canned cherries was out of the question. It worked out well enough in the end because she found what she was looking for and even managed to duck into the Spice Terminal and score whole allspice for the pie, some Spanish saffron (because it was on sale), cardamom pods (impossible to find anywhere else), and mace blades (because she'd never tried them before).

By the time she had made her way home and gotten the soup started, Angelina was behind. She assembled the pie and put it in the oven in time, then started in on the braciola, pounding it extra-thin to make it melt-in-your-mouth tender. She worked efficiently, as always, and by the time Mr. Cupertino had arrived she was in pretty good shape, except that she hadn't had time to set the table.

"Mr. Cupertino," she said, as she rushed to let him in. "I'm glad you're here. There's something I have to ask you. Come in."

Basil marched in lockstep behind her into the kitchen as she hurried to take the pie out of the oven.

"Here's the thing," she said, setting the pie down to cool. "What would you think of the idea of having some company for dinner?"

Basil paused and looked at Angelina, then at the pie, then back at her again, as if giving the notion his most serious consideration.

"Company as in guests?" he asked shrewdly. "Or company as in, how should I put it, expanding your customer base?"

"As in, a couple more paying customers. Bachelors, like you. Expanding my, you know, what you said."

Basil looked delighted. "Terrific!"

"Really?" said Angelina, relieved.

"Sure. Nobody likes to eat alone. The more the merrier."

Angelina laughed. "Oh, thank God, because they're coming tonight." She began stacking dishes to set the table.

"Who've you got coming?" he asked.

"Well, Johnny from down the street and Jerry Mancini, a really good guy from the neighborhood. We went to grade school together."

"Dottie introduced me to Johnny the other day," said Basil. "Nice kid. I'm sure we'll all get along famously. And I'll have somebody to talk to about your food. Speaking of which, what're you making?"

"Sweet Potato Bisque," said Angelina, pointing to the stove. "Veal Piccata with Linguine, and a Cherry Pear Pie for dessert." She paused. "You do eat veal, don't you?"

"Veal—be still my heart!" said Basil.

A knock sounded on the door.

"That's probably Jerry. . . ," said Angelina.

"I'll get it," Basil said, heading out of the kitchen. "And don't worry about me, I'm eating anything you're cooking. I'm starving. And, as Cervantes says, 'The best sauce in the world is hunger.' "

"Good, because I made a ton of everything!"

Basil let Jerry in and Angelina made the

introductions on the run. She opened a bottle of Chianti and left them chatting amiably in the living room. She stirred the soup and assembled plates, glasses, and utensils on the sideboard ready to take out to the table. The *braciole* was finished and resting in the oven. She still had to boil the pasta and plate the food, but she was almost there.

She called out to the living room, "Is Johnny here yet?"

Jerry jumped up and looked out the window. "Not yet. No, wait a minute, he's making a liar out of me."

Johnny's shadow appeared at the outside door. Basil opened it and ushered him in. "Come on in there, Johnny."

"Thanks, Mr. Cupertino."

"Oh, hey, Jerry," said Johnny.

Johnny took off his jacket, folded it over once, and laid it over the arm of one of the living room chairs.

"You made it just in time, young man," said Basil.

Jerry clapped Johnny on the back. "Dinner's almost ready. Did you wash your hands for supper?"

"Yeah, I washed them at my house," Johnny replied earnestly.

"You get behind the ears?"

Johnny thought about it for a second longer than he should have, and Jerry grinned.

"Shut up, Jerry," said Johnny, smiling gamely.

"He's just ribbing you, kid," said Basil. "Get ready for a treat."

Angelina bustled into the dining room with a beautiful antipasto platter of cold meats, cheese, olives, and peppers, which she laid on the table.

"Hi, Johnny," she said. "If you guys want to sit down, I'll set the table."

"Angelina, everything smells unbelievable," said Jerry.

Basil took his now usual seat and Jerry pulled out the chair opposite him.

Johnny was about to sit at the head of the table, but Jerry touched his arm gently and said, "Hey, John, don't take that chair. That's Frank's chair. Come sit by me, pal."

"Oh, sorry."

Johnny pushed the chair reverently back into its proper place and sat beside Jerry. Angelina set their places around them, and in no time they had started in on the appetizers.

The doorbell rang. Angelina called in from the other room, "Now who could that be? Would you mind getting that, Mr. Cupertino?"

Basil pushed back from the table, placed his folded napkin beside his plate, and went to the door. When he opened it, he found a young man of enormous size, with his hands folded in front of him like an oversize choirboy, clean shaven, dressed in a neat but inexpensive-looking black suit and tie. He was so large that he blotted out most of the background and waited politely to be addressed before he spoke.

"May I help you?" asked Basil.

"Good evening, sir. My name is Philip Rosetti. Is this the home of Mrs. D'Angelo?"

"Yes, it is."

Phil nodded and looked back over his shoulder at a long, black Cadillac double-parked in the street. He smiled and gave a little thumbs-up to a man barely visible through the back window, who waved genially back at him.

The young man cleared his throat and shifted back and forth on his substantial feet. "The gentleman in the car, my uncle, Don Eddie Frangipani, requests that he would like to speak with Mrs. D'Angelo if she wouldn't mind joining him out in the car for just a moment?"

Basil listened, then said solemnly, "If you don't mind waiting, I will inquire."

"I can wait. Thank you."

Basil closed the door. Philip never moved, not even an inch. By now, both Jerry and Johnny had left the table and were peering through the curtains out the front window.

Angelina came in wiping her hands on her apron. "Who was that, Mr. Cupertino?"

"You have a visitor," said Basil with a trace of amusement.

"Holy smokes. Do you know who that is?" said Jerry. "That's Don Eddie."

"What are you talking about?" Angelina said, slightly annoyed. "Who's coming to the house at dinnertime like this?"

"You've never heard of Don Eddie?" asked Jerry. "How long have you been living here, Angelina?"

"Are you kidding me? The soup is ready. Who is this guy?"

"Well," Jerry said, "he's a very special guy."

"When you say *guy*," Basil chimed in, "you don't mean one of *those* guys?" He pushed his nose out flat to one side.

Jerry took his meaning. "No, not really. He's not one of those guys, per se, but he's sort of an honorary guy, in the sense that those guys, they love this guy, that's why they call him 'the Don,' even though he isn't."

"Isn't what?" asked Johnny.

"One of those guys," Jerry replied.

Angelina's patience was running onion-skin thin. "What in the name of God are you talking about?"

"Listen," said Jerry. "This guy outside, Eddie, he grew up with, you know, the Head Guy, and you know who I mean."

Johnny and Angelina, even Basil, all nodded knowingly.

"All right," said Jerry. "Apparently, Eddie saved

the guy's life one time when they were kids, or so the story goes. So, the Head Guy always looked out for Eddie. Now, Eddie never wanted to get into any trouble, you see, he always kept his nose clean; but they all love him anyway—he listens, he picks stuff up, he gives good advice, and they just like having him around. They trust him. He's . . . special."

"So . . . what does he want with me?" Angelina asked with a hint of concern in her voice.

"He wants to talk to you," said Basil.

"You gotta go," said Jerry urgently.

"Go where?" she said.

"He wants you to go out to the car and talk to him," said Basil.

"You gotta go," Jerry said with conviction. "This is very unusual. This is an opportunity."

"Opportunity for what?" asked Angelina.

"That's it. You don't know," said Jerry. "That's why you have to go."

Angelina looked worriedly toward the front door, then worriedly toward the kitchen where her dinner was waiting to be served.

Jerry placed a reassuring hand on her shoulder. "Just go. I'll be watching from the window."

Johnny and Basil looked at her expectantly. Angelina rolled her eyes in utter exasperation. She tore off her apron and handed it to Jerry.

"All right, fine! I'll go," she said finally. "Mr. Cupertino, could you please turn down the soup?"

"You can count on me," said Basil.

Basil opened the door and Philip was still standing there motionless in the same exact spot, the door inches from his nose. He nodded once he saw Angelina approaching and preceded her down the steps.

"Good luck," whispered Basil as Angelina walked outside.

Angelina followed Phil out to the car and climbed in when he courteously opened the door for her. She slid across the plush blue leather seat and found herself sitting face-to-face with the Don. He looked to Angelina to be well on the high side of eighty. His smooth white hair was so perfectly barbered, he looked as if he had just climbed out of the barber's chair. He wore a beautiful camel-hair coat with a white gardenia in the lapel. His eyes, Angelina noticed, were an ideal shade of cloudless blue sky.

When he spoke, his tone was soothing and confidential, "Hello, Angelina. How you doing, dear?"

"Hi."

She wasn't nearly ready to let him off the hook for interrupting dinner.

"My name is Ed Frangipani, and I'm quite pleased to finally meet you."

"Hello, Mr. Frangipani," she said, just barely shaking his outstretched hand.

"Please, Angelina, call me Don Eddie. Everybody does."

"Excuse me, Mr. Frangipani, I don't mean to rush you, but I've got a house full of people and I'm trying to get a meal on the table. So . . ."

"Ah. I heard you are a good cook."

"You heard that, did you?" She crossed her arms.

"Yes, I did. I hear things. Irregardless of which, I've been meaning to come and see you for a while."

For the first time, Angelina was curious. "Come and see me, why?"

"About your husband, Frankie."

"What about my husband?" she asked suspiciously. Angelina tried to keep the tension out of her voice, but there it was.

Don Eddie shifted slightly in his seat to face her a little more squarely. "I knew him a little. I liked him very much. He was a hard worker, good union guy. I hang around, you know? Talk to the men, after work or when they're eating lunch. They talk to me about things."

The comfortable warmth of the car, the intoxicating scent of gardenia, and the mellifluous sound of his voice were drawing her in.

"What things?" she asked softly.

"I wanted to share a story Frank told me about you one time."

"A story about me?"

Those Sinatra-blue eyes looked right into hers. "You were in a little car accident one time, a couple years ago?"

Angelina shook her head, just a little. "Not really. A bus accident. I went to the emergency room, but I didn't get hurt, just a little shaken up. Nobody really got hurt. Why would Frank ever mention that?"

Don Eddie smiled. "I like to hear stories about the men's families, you know? I never got married, I've got no kids. We were all talking one time, about bad days, the kind of a bad day you never forget. 'What was your worst day?' One guy said this, another guy said that. And Frankie, he got very quiet, which I noticed. So, before I go, I got him aside, and he told me this story:

"When he got the call that you were in an accident and went looking for you in the hospital that day, he saw a woman who looked like you; she had your kind of coat on, she was bleeding, the doctors were working on her, as she was hurt very badly. At first, he thought that it was you, that you were the one that was hurt so bad. And the thought that he was losing you, that day, that made it his worst day ever."

Angelina could hardly whisper, "He never told me that."

The Don got quiet, too. "The thing is, he shed a tear when he told me that story. And when I heard that he passed away, I felt I should come over and tell you that you had a husband who loved you so much, he shed a tear in front of an old man, telling me that story."

Don Eddie took her hand as the tears welled up in her eyes. He offered her a clean white handkerchief and she cried quietly for a minute on the shoulder of his impeccable coat as he patted her arm.

She sniffled, pulled herself together, and looked at him gratefully. "Do you want to come in for dinner? I made plenty."

Don Eddie chuckled, and Angelina could see that when Jerry called this guy "special," he knew what he was talking about.

"I'm glad you asked. Me and Phil, we had a guy who cooked for us, pretty good, but he's not going to be around for the next three to five years. And I heard you are a good cook, so we thought we might also give your operation a try. I heard good things. That is, if you go for it?"

Angelina laughed and Don Eddie tapped on the window. Phil, who had waited patiently outside and given them their privacy, circled around and opened Angelina's door for her. He escorted her up the steps, then did the same for the Don.

Chairs and place settings were arranged in no time, and Don Eddie and Phil got in on the last of the antipasto. The soup was served piping hot. As everyone tucked in, at first sipping gingerly to avoid mouth-burn, the room was quiet save for the gentle clinking of the soup spoons on the bowls. Angelina stopped and savored the moment, the sound and the sight of them all eating her food, as her guests savored the soup.

Jerry, who had neatly managed to have Don Eddie seated next to him, struck up a conversation with him as if they were old friends, and the sentiment seemed to be fully returned. Even Johnny got into the act. Big Phil never said a word before his final "Thank you, Mrs. D'Angelo, and good night," but Angelina could tell that he liked his meal. In the end, the Cherry Pear Pie was the clincher. Angelina saw them all to the door as they left, and they thanked her one by one. Jerry helped her to clear and was the last to leave. As she walked him to the door, she reached into her apron and pulled out a $100 bill.

"Look what I found under Don Eddie's plate when I was cleaning up."

Jerry whistled. "Nice."

"I can't take it. It's too much. I have to give it back to him," she insisted.

"No! Angelina, you can't do that, ever. Listen, that's how he's going to pay you. He's not the kind of a guy that you hand him a tab. And don't worry, he's not going to leave you a hundred dollars every time. Just let him do it his own way. Believe me, it'll work out."

Angelina was unconvinced. "Are you sure?"

"Yes. I promise. And don't ever, *ever* give it back to him. Please. Promise me."

She laughed at how seriously Jerry was taking it. "Okay, okay. Actually, he's a very sweet man. So, are you coming back tomorrow?"

"Absolutely."

She opened the door for him. "Hey, Jerry. It's nice to see you again. Thanks for coming over."

"Thanks for having me." Jerry shoved his hands into the pockets of his brown leather jacket and sauntered down the steps. He ran a hand through his hair, then waved and walked up the street. "Good night, Angelina!"

As she watched him go, she felt a tug inside, a pull, and it took her the whole way back to the kitchen until she finally put her finger on it.

She was probably just hungry. She hadn't eaten a single thing herself all day.

Mint Sweet Potato Bisque

Serves 6 to 8

INGREDIENTS
   1 tablespoon canola oil
   2 garlic cloves, lightly crushed and minced
   2 shallot cloves, minced
   1 quart vegetable stock
   2½ pounds sweet potatoes peeled and cut
      into 1-inch chunks
   ½ cup dry white rice
   1 tablespoon chili powder
   1 teaspoon cinnamon

2 teaspoons salt
1 teaspoon ground black pepper
1 cup golden raisins, rinsed, drained, and
   chopped
½ cup packed fresh mint leaves, finely
   minced, plus 8 small mint sprigs
½ cup walnuts
1 fresh lime, zest micro-grated off and juiced
½ cup sour cream

METHOD

Heat the canola oil over medium heat in a large stockpot. When it begins to shimmer, sauté the garlic and shallots until they soften, stirring frequently to prevent burning, about 1 or 2 minutes. Pour the vegetable stock and 4 cups water into the pot, bring to a boil, and add the rice, sweet potatoes, chili powder, cinnamon, and salt and pepper to taste. Return to a boil, reduce the heat to low, cover and let cook undisturbed for 20 minutes. Remove the soup pot from the heat and let stand for 5 minutes before removing the lid.

Meanwhile preheat the oven to 350°F.

Use a hand masher to break up the sweet potatoes, then blend right in the pot with an immersion blender. Add the raisins and return to medium heat to soften the raisins, about 5 minutes. Remove from the heat and stir in the minced mint.

Spread the walnuts on a baking sheet and toast them in the oven for about 3 to 5 minutes, then crush them in a plastic bag using a rolling pin.

PRESENTATION
Ladle the soup into crocks and drizzle about 1 teaspoon of the lime juice over the surface of the soup in each. Spoon a tablespoon of sour cream into the center of each and top with a pinch of lime zest. Encircle the sour cream with a tablespoon of grated walnuts. Arrange a mint sprig in the sour cream.

––––––––

Cherry Pear Pie

Serves 6

INGREDIENTS FOR THE PIE FILLING
  ½ fresh lemon, micro-zested and juiced
  3 large, firm Bartlett pears
  ⅔ cup sugar
  ¼ teaspoon salt (⅛ teaspoon for the pears and ⅛ teaspoon for the cherries)
  ⅛ cup whiskey
  1 pint (about 1 pound) fresh black cherries, pitted with a cherry stoner and halved (cherry-pitting gadgets such as those made by OXO and Bialetti can be found at Fantes.com)

1 teaspoon ground cinnamon (½ teaspoon for the pears and ½ teaspoon for the cherries)

6 small cardamom pods ground in a spice mill and chaff removed

½ cup walnuts, coarsely crushed in a plastic bag with a rolling pin

1 tablespoon brown sugar

1 tablespoon butter

INGREDIENTS FOR THE PIE CRUST

3 cups all-purpose flour, plus some to flour the pastry cloth

⅛ teaspoon salt

4 tablespoons cold butter

4 tablespoons cold shortening

¼ to ½ cup water as needed to moisten dough (have a glass of ice water handy)

1 egg, beaten for an egg wash

TOPPINGS

2 ounces yellow or white mild cheddar cheese, thinly sliced with a cheese plane

1 pint vanilla ice cream

Fresh mint leaves

METHOD FOR THE PIE FILLING

Pour half the lemon juice into a large bowl. Slice the pears lengthwise into quarters (leaving the skin on because it is pretty and provides roughage) and remove the fibrous cores, seeds, and stems. Then further slice the pears into ¼-inch-thick wedges and cut the wedges crosswise into 1-inch lengths into the bowl of lemon juice, coating the pears as you go to prevent oxidation. Add ⅓ cup of the sugar, ⅛ teaspoon of the salt, and 1 tablespoon of the whiskey, mixing gently, but well.

In a separate bowl, combine the cherries with the remaining ⅓ cup sugar, ⅛ teaspoon of the salt, a tablespoon of the whiskey, ½ teaspoon of the cinnamon, and the cardamom.

METHOD FOR THE PIE CRUST
Place the flour and salt in the bowl of a food processor fitted with a dough blade. Add the butter and shortening and use the pulse button on the food processor to combine just until the mixture resembles coarse crumbs. Then, through the feed tube, add ice water a little at a time, pulsing until the dough just comes together in a cohesive mass and using only the amount of water needed to make that happen. It is important to avoid overworking the dough so that it will remain as flaky and delicate as possible. If you use too much water you also run the risk of the dough becoming too sticky. Transfer the dough to a bowl and gently form into a ball. Slice the dough ball in half. Keep the bowl covered with a damp kitchen towel while you roll out the dough.

Flour a scrupulously clean pastry cloth or a large non-terry cloth kitchen towel (that has been laundered in chlorine bleach and allowed to air dry) and allow any excess flour to fall away. (For a two-crust pie such as this, it would be handy to have two cloths, one each for the top and bottom crusts.) Fold the towel crosswise in half and place half of the dough ball within the folded towel, pressing it into a mostly flattened disk. Use a rolling pin to roll the dough into a circle of about 11 inches in diameter, rolling from the center outward and turning the pastry cloth as you go to ensure an even shape.

Invert a 9-inch CorningWare or Pyrex pie plate on the rolled-out dough to use as a template, centering the dough to the plate and using a pizza cutter or butter knife to cut a clean-edged circle about one-inch larger all around than the pie plate. Set aside briefly to be used as the top crust.

Flour another pastry cloth, letting any excess flour fall away. Place the second half of the dough ball into the folded cloth as before, flatten into a disk, and roll into an 11-inch circle using the same technique. Trim the edges of the dough circle for neatness. Ever so gingerly slip your hand under the pastry cloth (so as not to tear the dough) and flip the dough circle into the pie plate, gently easing the dough into it.

METHOD FOR FILLING AND BAKING THE PIE

Preheat the oven to 400°F. Mix the walnuts with the brown sugar and spread over the base of the bottom crust. Spoon the pear filling into the pie crust, sprinkle with the remaining cinnamon, and spoon the cherry filling over it. Distribute the lemon zest over the top of the cherries. Divide the tablespoon of butter into quarters and dot the top of the filling with it. In a smooth motion, flip the second dough circle onto the top of the pie, fold the edges of the top circle of dough under the edges of the bottom circle of dough, and crimp the edges between your fingers by pinching every inch or so. Brush the crust with beaten egg and use a knife to slice six vents in a starburst pattern in the top crust. Place in the oven over a sheet of foil to catch drips. Bake until the fruit is soft and the crust is golden, about 45 to 55 minutes.

Let cool to room temperature before serving.

PRESENTATION

Cut the pie into approximately six wedges. Place each wedge on a dessert plate and garnish with 1 scoop of vanilla ice cream or with 1 or 2 small slices of cheddar, which has been melted by placing the cheese-topped wedge of pie briefly into a 250°F oven. Add small sprigs of mint.

———

CHAPTER EIGHT

Nothing Beats a Box of Steaks

The next few weeks kept Angelina as busy as she could remember having been in quite a while, and she was surprised at how completely her newfound responsibilities filled her days. She now had five men coming to her six days a week for their dinners, and most of them for their breakfasts as well. Basil was as reliable as her old stove—eight on the dot for breakfast, seven on the button for dinner. He had taken it as his informal charge to squire Johnny to and from since they were only five doors apart, and Johnny fell right in to adopting Basil's punctual habits. Jerry claimed that he was mostly a "coffee and Colgate" kind of guy when it came to breakfast, but he would always discreetly inquire and show up if some-thing special was on. It was funny how he managed to conveniently be in the neighbor-hood on Belgian Waffle Day. Don Eddie and Big Phil started coming for breakfast, too, and soon never missed a meal.

Breakfast turned out to be more of a challenge than Angelina had expected, mainly because she had decided early on to take it on herself to cater to the individual needs of her "customers." She always had a big pot of oatmeal going on the stove and was happy to whip up a short stack of pancakes at the drop of a hat, but she pretty much made the rest of the plates to order. After the first week she had a good handle not only on what each man liked for his morning meal, but what he needed. Mr. Cupertino still loved the occasional inspired omelet and once she had made him Eggs *Meurette*, poached eggs in a red wine sauce, served with a chunk of crusty French bread, which was a big hit. She balanced him out other mornings with hot cereal, and fresh fruit with yogurt or cottage cheese. Johnny mostly went for bowls of cereal washed down with an ocean of cold milk, so Angelina kept a nice variety on hand, though nothing too sugary. The Don would happily eat a soft-boiled egg with buttered toast every day for the rest of his life, but she inevitably got him to eat a little bowl of oatmeal just before or after with his coffee. Big Phil was on the receiving end of her supersize, stick-to-your-ribs special—sometimes scrambled eggs, toast, potatoes, and bacon, other times maybe a pile of French toast and a slice of ham. Angelina decided to start loading up his plate on her own when she realized he was bashful about asking for seconds.

On Sundays, she put on a big spread at ten o'clock, after they had all been to church, which variously included such items as smoked salmon and bagels, sausages, broiled tomatoes with a Parmesan crust, scrapple (the only day she'd serve it), bacon, fresh, hot biscuits and fruit muffins, or a homemade fruit strudel. She made omelets to order for Jerry and Mr. Cupertino. Then they'd all reconvene at five for the Sunday roast with all the trimmings.

She kept up a breakneck pace of creativity at weekday dinners and took pride in having never served the same entrée twice, at least so far, though she had been getting requests from Mr. Cupertino for repeat performances of a few of his personal favorites. The money at the end of each week had been a godsend. Johnny and Jerry paid her in cash and she dutifully handed them a receipt at the end of each week. The Don more than paid his way for both himself and Phil, and Angelina kept a tally of everything he paid her, too, but on the sly, just in case he asked.

Angelina was beginning to think that, if she had a couple more regulars, she wouldn't be in half-bad financial shape at all. She had the extra leaves for the dining room table down in the basement, and she had straight-back chairs up in the spare room she could press into service easily enough, and cooking for two or three more would hardly make a difference, except to her pocketbook.

The days were getting shorter, but she still had a nice supply of thyme, sage, oregano, lavender, and other herbs growing in her kitchen garden in the yard; she'd brought her basil plants inside the week before, and the rosemary would soon follow. The yard had a good southern exposure and most everything she planted thrived there. Her sweet bay laurel plant was not supposed to be hardy in the Philadelphia climate, but it had remained healthy and vibrant through every winter since she planted it and was now as big as a small shrub. For tonight's meal, Angelina had pur-chased two nice-size legs of lamb, boned, which she was going to roll and rub with allspice, salt, and pepper, then roast with fresh herbs, lavender foremost among them. To go with, she planned a Ratatouille Frittata, a dish of yellow and green zucchini sautéed with shallots, coriander, and savory, baked with scrambled eggs, like a giant open omelet, and decorated with squash blossoms.

The room was filled with the intoxicating aroma of allspice when she finished grinding the last of it in the big mortar and pestle. She took her shears, buttoned on a cardigan sweater over her apron, and went out to the garden. Angelina ran her hands over the plants. She loved the way they sprang back and gave up their fragrance when she did it. She had clipped healthy sprigs of lavender, winter savory, and the end of some coriander when a loud crash echoed into the yard from out in the street.

"Judas Priest!" a man shouted.

Angelina stuffed the herbs into her apron pocket and rushed out front. On the street was a man with blond hair standing beside a good-size, old-fashioned steamer trunk sprawled open on the sidewalk. Pants, shirts, and sundries were scattered everywhere, and loose sheets of paper were starting to make their bid for freedom down the street in the breeze. It looked as if the trunk had literally exploded.

The poor fellow looked bewildered, as if he didn't know where to turn or what to try to chase down or pick up first. As she headed across the street to help him, Angelina couldn't help but notice that he was uncommonly good-looking. The wind gusted and a few more sheets took off. Angelina set off in pursuit, but spotted a slighter man, nattily dressed in tweeds, deftly and efficiently nabbing the sheets of paper as they tumbled down the sidewalk in his direction. He was as quick as a cat. It was quite a performance. Angelina stood spellbound for a moment as she watched him stab the last one with the tip of his umbrella.

The blond-haired man let out a grunt as he tried stuffing clothes back into his broken luggage.

"What happened?" Angelina asked as he looked up at her in dismay.

"It's a disaster."

"No kidding. What did you do, throw this thing off the roof?"

The man indicated the door of Dottie's house. "I'm a day early. I was looking for the hide-a-key and I propped my trunk up for a second. Then it slid down the railing and kind of *launched* into space. When it hit the hydrant, it just exploded!"

He grinned and spread his hands wide in wonder and disbelief. They stood and looked at each other. For a moment, it felt strangely like two people meeting at the beginning of a blind date. Angelina broke the spell when she stooped to pick up a black sweater and a couple of socks and tossed them into the trunk.

The well-dressed gentleman from down the street now approached them, organizing a rebellious sheaf of papers as he walked. "Sir," he said with an air of formality, "I believe I have retrieved all of your papers."

"Thank you," said the blond man. Taking the stack, he put them in the trunk and weighted them down with a black leather shaving kit. Within minutes, the three of them had gathered everything into a pile in the center of the two halves of his luggage.

"Thank you both, so much, for helping me. I really appreciate it," the blond man said as the other gentleman helped him snap the clasps shut.

"You sure have a lot of black sweaters," said Angelina.

"Well, they're very slimming." He smiled. "I'm Guy Mariano." He extended his hand.

She reached out to shake it. "I'm Angelina."

He was slightly taller than she, square shoulders, meticulously clean-shaven. Her earlier impression that this was a nice-looking man was more than confirmed up close; he might even have been too good-looking but for a nose that had probably been broken a time or two when he was a kid. He had pleasant laugh lines at the corners of his eyes and an awkward, engaging smile.

"Nice to meet you," Guy replied, then extended his hand to the other man.

"My name's Pettibone. Pleased to meet you." He shook both of their hands, then two business cards appeared from nowhere, one for each of them. Angelina read D. WINSTON PETTIBONE, HEAD BUYER, JOHN WANAMAKER'S.

"So why are you trying to get into Dottie's house?" Angelina said to Guy. "I mean, if you don't mind my asking."

He stuck his hands into the pockets of his black pea coat. "Dottie's my aunt. I'm staying with her for a while."

"That's unusual," said Mr. Pettibone.

Guy and Angelina both looked at him. He sniffed at the crisp autumn air just once, like an alert retriever, then looked over at them and quickly explained, "Oh, sorry. I didn't mean that it's unusual for you to be staying with family. I was thinking aloud. I smell fresh lavender. And coriander, and, I believe, a hint of allspice?"

After a bemused few seconds, Angelina pulled the bunch of herbs she'd cut earlier from her apron pocket. "You can smell all of that?"

"Indeed. Looks like I missed the winter savory."

"You didn't miss much. I just cut these herbs, but the allspice is back in the kitchen."

"Kitchen?" said Pettibone. "Are you cooking with fresh lavender?"

"I was about to."

Pettibone tapped his umbrella lightly on the pavement. The pencil-thin mustache under his prominent, aquiline nose twitched curiously, and his storm-gray eyes came to life under dark, aristocratic brows.

"My word. I'm a bit of an amateur gourmand myself. I would be quite interested to know what you plan on making with that lavender."

Angelina saw a glimmer of a prospect in this elegant-looking gentleman. "If you've got a few minutes, I can show you the recipe now."

"I will make the time," said Mr. Pettibone.

She turned to Guy then. "Why don't you take your trunk to my house? Mr. Cupertino comes to me for dinner, so, worst case, he can let you in then."

"Okay," said Guy. "Are you sure we're not imposing?"

"Not at all."

Mr. Pettibone tucked his umbrella under his arm. "Take sides?" he said to Guy.

"Pardon?"

"The trunk. You take one side and I'll take the other."

"Oh, right."

They balanced the load between them like stretcher bearers and followed Angelina in procession back across the road.

Soon, Guy sat at the kitchen table nursing a cup of coffee. Mr. Pettibone had taken a post by Angelina's side with his hands clasped behind his back as she was skillfully dressing the second leg of lamb.

"I like to use an aromatic herb," she explained, "like rosemary or lavender, especially with lamb, because it infuses the meat and the aroma gives it a whole new level of flavor just before you bite into it."

"It smells wonderful already," Pettibone said, rapt in admiration. "It's French-countryside cooking all the way. Beautifully done."

Guy cocked his head to one side. "Hey, did you hear something?"

"Like what?" asked Angelina.

"A thump?"

"No."

"Okay." Guy got up and joined them at the counter. "So, Mr. Pettibone, how did you know what Angelina was carrying in her pockets, anyway?"

"Oh, I'm not a mentalist or anything," said Pettibone. "I'm a *parfumeur*, amongst other interests. I'm a perfume buyer. I have an extremely sensitive olfactory instrument." He tapped the side of his nose. "You know, a good sniffer."

Angelina smiled appreciatively. "I haven't seen you around the neighborhood before, Mr. Pettibone."

"Funny thing, that. They changed the buses and my transfer takes me right up this street now. I'm glad they did."

Guy saluted him with his coffee cup. "Lucky thing for me today, anyway. I'd have hated to lose those papers."

Angelina finished bundling the herbs into the lamb and trussing the meat, then washed her hands. "What were they?" she asked Guy.

"I'm working on a book, sort of."

"Oh, you're a writer?" she asked.

Guy looked down and scuffed a foot on the floor. "Not really. I'm sort of between jobs."

"I know the feeling," said Angelina, since, technically, she was between jobs, too, even though she was actually doing all right, at least for the time being. She pulled a knife out of the holder. "How long are you staying?"

"Not sure yet," said Guy. "A while, I think."

Angelina started cutting up zucchini, first

lengthwise, then thinly across on a bias. "You know, Mr. Mariano—"

"Guy."

Angelina nodded. "Guy. Speaking of dinners, you should think about eating here."

"Really?"

"Now that your aunt Dottie works nights, your uncle, Mr. Cupertino, has his breakfast and dinner over here, six days a week."

Guy laughed in sudden realization. "Have you tasted Aunt Dottie's minestrone?"

Angelina laughed, too, a little guiltily. "*Anyway,* it's very affordable. I've been cooking for some of the gentlemen in the neighborhood—you know, to make ends meet, since my husband . . . he . . . passed away. He died."

"I'm sorry to hear that," said Guy.

Angelina flashed to a time a couple of years earlier, when Frank had arrived home unexpectedly for dinner with two guests in tow, his cousin Nick and an older man named Carlos, who was one of Nick's bosses, in an office or something. Frank left to pick up a couple of bottles of wine, and Angelina remembered having a lovely chat with Nick and Carlos in the kitchen over coffee while she made . . . what had she made? Caesar salad, manicotti, and . . . raspberry parfaits.

She imagined for a moment that Frank had unexpectedly brought Guy and Mr. Pettibone home for dinner and had only gone around the corner to the state store for a couple of bottles of wine. These would be just the kind of guys he wouldn't at all have minded having over for dinner.

"My condolences," said Mr. Pettibone.

"Thanks," said Angelina quietly. Then she pointed the tip of her knife at him. "While I'm on the subject, Mr. Pettibone . . . ," she said playfully.

"A supper club?" he said without a second's hesitation. "Splendid! I'd love to join you."

"Good." She turned toward Guy. "How about you?"

Guy swirled the end of his coffee. "I'd like that," he said with a tip of his cup. "If it's good enough for Uncle Basil . . ."

"Perfect," said Angelina, then half to herself, "now I've got a full table."

There was a heavy knock on the back door.

Through the screen, Angelina saw a beefy guy in a deliveryman's shirt standing on the step, next to four large, white boxes on a hand truck.

"How ya doin', ma'am? Meat delivery."

Angelina put down her knife and opened the screen door. He wheeled the boxes straight into the kitchen and consulted the clipboard in his oversize paws.

"What's all this?" she asked.

"I just need you to sign for your meat, miss," he said matter-of-factly.

168

"What meat?" Angelina leaned over the clipboard to get a peek.

The delivery guy read down the list. "I got some pork roasts, beef roasts, a couple of hams, sausages, some bacon, ground beef, pork chops, some veal shanks, veal chops, some whole chickens. And he said to get ya' a nice box of steaks."

"You've got the wrong address. I didn't order any meat." Angelina double-checked his list. "And even if I did, where on earth would I put it?"

The screen door slammed open and two more guys struggled through the door at either end of an enormous cardboard box. They had a lot of forward momentum and were nearly all the way in before Angelina could say a word. They dropped the box with a *whump!*

"Sorry, didn't mean to bang your door, ma'am," said the sweaty, littler guy bringing up the rear. "Meat locker in the basement?"

The blood started to rise into Angelina's cheeks. "The what?" she cried.

"Put your meat in the basement, miss?" asked the beefy guy.

The front doorbell rang.

"Oh, my God, now what?" said Angelina.

She turned, then stopped and spread her arms wide, like a boxing referee holding back two fighters at the end of a round.

"Please. Nobody move."

She marched through the living room with Guy close behind and flung open the door.

Don Eddie stood on the front stoop, glowing. He jauntily whipped off his fedora and handed it to Phil, who was standing just behind him. The Don strutted in past Angelina, rubbing his kid-gloved hands together in gleeful anticipation.

"Everything get here okay?" he called to Angelina, clearly delighted to have arrived in time for the big reveal.

By the time Angelina had closed the door behind Phil, Don Eddie was in the kitchen, greeting the meat guys like long-lost buddies who'd just gotten back from the war. As he was shaking hands with Guy and Pettibone as if he were running for mayor, Angelina appeared in the kitchen doorway, arms crossed, tapping her foot, and fixed Don Eddie with as icy a stare as she could manufacture on such short notice.

A scene flickered in Angelina's mind of a big box marked "APPLIANCE," falling off of the back of a truck.

"What did you do?" she demanded, her voice tinged with mild accusation.

The Don looked to all of his comrades-in-arms assembled around him now, confident in their support.

"What?" he said, the picture of earthly innocence. "I got you some free meat, is all."

"And the freezer?"

"Hey, where you going to keep all this meat? Angelina, this is a lot of meat," he said as if she might not have noticed.

Angelina's foot stopped tapping, but her arms remained sternly folded.

The Don threw himself on the mercy of the court. "Please, accept it as my gift, Angelina, bought and paid for, I promise. A gift for your new business. Okay?"

She pursed her lips, then gave in and gave him a daughterly hug. "Okay. Thank you."

"All rii-ight," said the Don, "now we're talking. How about a cup of coffee?"

Making himself right at home, Mr. Pettibone fetched some cups and the pot and starting pouring coffee for Eddie, while Phil obligingly offered to take the deliverymen down to the basement to find a place for the freezer.

Angelina turned and noticed Guy leaning against the refrigerator with a big grin on his face.

"Well? What?" she asked, ready to take him on, too.

He shrugged and she had no choice but to grin back.

"Hey," said Guy philosophically, "you never turn down a box of steaks."

Lavender-Spiced Leg of Lamb
and Ratatouille Frittata

Serves 6

INGREDIENTS FOR THE LAMB
  3-to-4-pound boneless leg of lamb, silver
    membrane removed
  1 teaspoon salt
  ¼ teaspoon freshly ground black pepper
  1 teaspoon ground allspice
  1 tablespoon fresh culinary lavender or
    rosemary, very finely minced
  2 tablespoons canola or olive oil

SPECIAL EQUIPMENT FOR THE LAMB
  2 yards of butcher's string or natural-fiber
    kitchen twine
  2 to 3 disposable thin bamboo skewers
    (to secure the meat)

INGREDIENTS FOR THE RATATOUILLE
  FRITTATA
  3 tablespoons canola or olive oil
    (1 tablespoon to sauté the onion and garlic
    and 2 tablespoons for the squash)
  1 large red onion, diced medium
  2 large garlic cloves, lightly crushed and
    minced
  1 small zucchini squash, sliced into
    ⅛-inch-thick pieces

172

1 small yellow squash, sliced into
⅛-inch-thick pieces
1 tablespoon fresh cilantro, minced
1 teaspoon dried savory, ground to a powder
with a mortar and pestle
12 eggs, beaten
Salt and freshly ground black pepper, to taste
2 ounces Gruyère cheese, thinly sliced with a
cheese plane
6 tablespoons crème fraîche or sour cream
6 small fresh basil sprigs
6 squash blossoms (optional)

INGREDIENTS FOR THE WHITE SHALLOT SAUCE

4 shallot cloves, peeled and quartered
¼ teaspoon salt
¼ teaspoon ground black pepper
1 teaspoon fresh thyme leaves
⅛ cup dry white rice
1 cup beef stock
¼ teaspoon poultry seasoning
¾ cup small-curd cottage cheese

METHOD FOR THE LAMB

Soak the lamb for 15 minutes in a bowl of cold water mixed with 1 tablespoon salt to remove residue, and pat it dry with paper towels. Combine the salt, pepper, and allspice and rub the mixture well into the outside surface of the lamb leg.

Refrigerate for at least 2 hours.

Preheat the oven to 350°F. Distribute the lavender evenly over the inside surface of the meat, rubbing it well into the flesh. Tie the leg meat back together with the butcher's string, and, if needed, use skewers to secure any errant flaps of meat. Keep count of the number of skewers you use so you are sure to retrieve them all before service, breaking them flush with the outside of the roast so you can easily sear the lamb.

Heat the oil over medium-high heat in a large sauté pan with an oven-safe handle. When the oil begins to shimmer, brown the exterior of the rubbed meat on all sides, leaving each side undisturbed for 2 to 4 minutes to let the seasonings integrate into the surface of the meat.

Transfer the lamb to the oven to finish. If you wish the meat to be rare, roast to an internal temperature of 130°F, about 25 minutes per pound. For medium, roast to an internal temperature of 145°F, about 30 minutes per pound. For well-done, roast until an internal temperature of 160°F is reached, approximately 35 minutes per pound.

(Begin the frittata about 45 minutes before you expect the lamb to be finished. Begin the sauce about 30 minutes before service.)

Remove the lamb from the oven and let rest 5 minutes. Cut away the string and remove all the skewers before slicing.

METHOD FOR THE FRITTATA

Heat 1 tablespoon of the oil over medium heat in a 10-inch skillet with a lid, reserving the rest of the oil for the vegetables. When it begins to shimmer, add the onion and garlic and sauté until the onion turns translucent, about 2 to 3 minutes, stirring frequently to prevent burning. Transfer the cooked onion and garlic briefly to a small plate.

In the same pan, heat the remaining 2 table-spoons of the oil over low heat, making sure the entire inside surface of the pan is coated. Quickly layer alternating slices of zucchini and yellow squash, in concentric circles with the edges overlapping. Distribute the sautéed onion and garlic over the surface of the squash and sprinkle with cilantro and savory. Cover the pan and increase the heat to medium. Cook until the squash begins to soften, about 10 minutes. (Be careful not to disturb the arrangement of the squash when checking on its progress.)

Pour the beaten eggs over the squash and season the surface of the eggs with salt and pepper. Cover and let cook undisturbed for about 5 to 10 minutes to allow the eggs to set up. Then, remove the lid and loosen the edges of the frittata carefully with a thin spatula. Place the uncovered skillet of eggs and squash in the oven (with the lamb) for about 10 minutes to allow the eggs to tighten up.

Remove the pan from the oven and top with the sliced Gruyère. Cover to keep warm and to melt the cheese a bit.

METHOD FOR THE WHITE SHALLOT SAUCE
Bring the shallots, salt, pepper, thyme, rice, beef stock, and ¾ cup water to a boil in a heavy-bottomed saucepan. Reduce the heat to low and let simmer covered for 25 minutes. Pour into a blender with the cap to the feed opening removed and, while holding a clean kitchen towel firmly over the opening to allow the steam to vent, purée the sauce with the poultry seasoning and cottage cheese.

Reheat the sauce over low heat before service.

PRESENTATION
Slice the lamb into uniform ½-inch- or ¾-inch-thick slices. Cut the frittata into 6 wedges. Arrange slices of lamb and frittata on serving plates. Spoon 1 to 2 tablespoons of sauce over the lamb. Top each wedge of the frittata with a tablespoon of crème fraîche and sprinkle with fresh basil. Garnish with squash blossoms.

———

Chapter Nine

Fortune's Fool

As time and cleaned plates went by, and as the men grew more comfortable with each other, Angelina's supper club started to feel more like a family. The daily routine loosened up, and not all of them made it to the table every single night (though none of them would ever miss without giving her notice, so that Angelina always knew how many she'd be cooking for). Guy and Mr. Pettibone fit in seamlessly. Basil not only enjoyed spending time with his nephew and having another man around the house, but clearly relished hearing Pettibone's dissertations on Angelina's cooking, a subject upon which the gentleman spoke with great authority and in knowledgeable detail.

When November arrived, Angelina steeled herself for the coming wave of holidays—Thanksgiving, Christmas, New Year's, Frank's birthday, her own. All firsts without Frank. All of which she looked forward to with premonitions of depression and dread. There was no help for it but to pray and hope for the best. And cook. Angelina's kitchen became a culinary workshop. She'd started making her own stocks, usually a daylong process, and spent her free time developing and testing new sauces and recipes in small batches before serving them for dinner. She'd ask Pettibone or Basil to taste the day before, then adjust the seasoning to perfect the flavor in time for dinner the following evening.

Sometimes it felt as if she were cooking around the clock. She liked it that way. Angelina moved like a shark in a tank in her kitchen—stirring, chopping, tasting, washing; keeping her recipe book up-to-date, meticulously recording the results of her experiments with scientific precision; darting busily from stove to sink to table. Keeping busy helped distract her from the lingering ghost of grief, the shadow of which was never far from her mind.

November and the impending arrival of winter meant braising for Angelina, the long, unhurried, soul-satisfying cooking of tough but beautifully marbled cuts in flavorful broths and stocks until the meat finally surrendered and slipped off the bone to mingle luxuriously in its own penetrating liquids.

Osso buco had been one of Frank's favorites, but was too expensive for them to have had often. Sure, she was making it now for a tableful of paying guests, but cooking one of Frank's favorites when he couldn't be there to enjoy it, she couldn't help feeling a little disloyal.

She dismissed the thought, though, when she reminded herself that Frank would never have begrudged anyone the kind of meal she was planning. He would have liked these guys and would have wanted them to taste all of Angelina's best dishes. She decided that she would put on the best spread she could tonight, in Frank's honor.

But since he couldn't be there to have any, she wouldn't either, in solidarity.

Angelina simmered the veal shanks all afternoon in homemade chicken stock and vermouth, with shallots, garlic, and dried herbs. She made fresh egg noodles and an antipasto of spicy pickled vegetables she had put up herself the week before. When the veal had fully imparted its subtle but unmistakable flavor to the braising liquid, and the meat was beginning to bid a fond farewell to the bones, Angelina retrieved and strained the pan juices, reducing them before carefully adding eggs and cream for a thick and lustrous sauce that she brightened with a squeeze of lemon before she ladled it all over big platters of egg noodles and garnished the dishes generously with parsley and capers.

Osso Buco with
Egg Noodles and Capers

Serves 8

INGREDIENTS

Eight 6-to-8-ounce pieces osso-buco-cut veal (cross section of shank cut into 1½-inch-thick pieces)

Salt and freshly ground black pepper, to taste

½ teaspoon nutmeg, approximately, as needed to sprinkle on veal

3 tablespoons canola or olive oil (not extra-virgin)

2 shallot cloves, minced

1 large garlic clove, lightly crushed and minced

1 cup dry vermouth

1 quart chicken stock

12 peppercorns

4 large sprigs fresh thyme

2 bay leaves

2 fresh sage leaves

1 large carrot, peeled and diced small

2 tablespoons butter

4 egg yolks

1 pound egg noodles or fettuccine

½ cup heavy cream

1 fresh lemon, zested and juiced

2 tablespoons capers

1 tablespoon minced fresh dill leaves
2 tablespoons fresh flat-leaf parsley leaves, minced

METHOD

Rinse the veal to remove residue and pat the meat dry with paper towels. Season each piece on both sides with salt, pepper, and nutmeg. Heat 1 table-spoon of the oil over medium-high heat in a large sauté pan, and sear the veal leaving undisturbed for about 2 to 4 minutes to allow the seasonings to integrate into the surface of the meat and to prevent tearing of the flesh. Add a second table-spoon of oil to the pan, flip the veal, and sear the other side in the same way, then remove to a utility platter. To the same pan, add the remaining tablespoon of oil and, over medium heat, cook the shallot cloves and garlic until the shallots turn translucent, stirring frequently to prevent burning, about 1 to 2 minutes. Deglaze the pan with the vermouth and allow most of the liquid to evaporate, about 5 minutes. Add the chicken stock and return the veal to the pan. Reduce the heat to low and add the peppercorns, thyme, bay leaves, and sage leaves. Cover the pan and let cook over low heat until fork tender, about 2 hours.

Sauté the carrots over medium low heat in the butter until tender, stirring frequently to prevent burning. Transfer the mixture to a small bowl, cover, and set aside until needed.

When the veal is tender, begin boiling the water for the egg noodles.

Carefully remove the veal to a platter keeping the osso buco pieces intact, and cover to keep warm. Strain the cooking liquids into a small bowl, wipe out the pan, and return the liquid to the pan to make the sauce. Increase the heat to medium high and allow the liquids to reduce to 1 cup, about 10 minutes.

In a small bowl, whisk the egg yolks until no streaks remain and they turn light yellow in color.

Meanwhile begin boiling the egg noodles until al dente.

When the pan juices have reduced, reduce the heat to medium low and whisk in the heavy cream to heat through. Remove the pan from the heat and, 1 tablespoon at a time, add the liquid to the bowl of egg yolks, whisking between additions. (This liaison will equalize the temperatures so the eggs don't coagulate.) When half of the cream mixture from the pan has been added to the egg yolks, pour the entire contents of the small bowl into the pan and whisk thoroughly to combine well. Add the lemon juice and capers, set the heat to medium low, and stir constantly until the mixture begins to thicken slightly and it reaches a temperature of 165°F as measured with a candy thermometer, 5 to 7 minutes.

Drain the egg noodles and toss with the butter/ carrot mixture and fresh dill. Cover to keep warm.

PRESENTATION

Arrange a piece of veal alongside some egg noodles on each serving plate. Spoon about ¼-cup sauce over the veal and top with 1 teaspoon minced parsley and a pinch of lemon zest. Delicious served with steamed green beans that have been tossed with butter and sautéed minced garlic.

For dessert, Angelina served an apple tarte tatin and coffee.

"Angelina," asked Mr. Pettibone as she poured his decaf, "if you don't mind my asking, how did you make the sauce? Did you make a liaison?"

"Yes, I did," said Angelina, impressed.

"A liaison? Really, Mr. Pettibone?" said Basil. "I thought that's what I was doing when I snuck behind the schoolhouse with Louise O'Donnell when I was fifteen."

Jerry nearly choked on his coffee. Angelina laughed and punched him playfully in the arm.

"Oh, be quiet," Angelina said. "Mr. Pettibone is exactly right. If you're not careful and bring everything up to temperature nice and slow, you get a sauce full of scrambled eggs."

"Yes," said Pettibone. "And the acid in the lemon and capers—a magnificent choice, by the way—balanced the creaminess, so that it didn't taste too rich. It was fantastic."

"As usual," said Guy.

Jerry led them all in light applause.

"Mr. Pettibone," said Basil, "you could be a food critic or something. How did you come by your appreciation of food? Very erudite, I must say."

"I've taken some courses of study. And, happily, I grew up in a household where great food was celebrated," said Pettibone. "My father was a psychologist and had his office in our house. My mother was often unwell, unfortunately, so my father did most of the cooking and developed quite a passion for it after a while. He was an inspiration to the avid cook, especially skilled at Asian cuisine, funnily enough."

"Chinese food?" said Johnny. "I didn't know you could make it, I thought you had to get takeout."

That got a laugh from everyone, though some lively discussion followed about whether he was actually right about that.

For the last week or so, Johnny had insisted on staying after and helping out with the dishes. He hadn't said a word about it, he just disappeared into the kitchen one night and started washing up. Angelina knew better than to call attention to this new development, realizing that it would make him uncomfortable. She appreciated the help but felt a little guilty about letting him take on the extra chore.

Johnny started clearing after everyone had gone except Don Eddie and Phil.

"Angelina," asked Eddie, "would you mind making me a couple pieces of toast and putting those marrowbones on a plate for me, dear?"

Angelina understood what he wanted at once and returned with two pieces of toast and some of the veal bones, slightly warmed on the plate. Eddie rubbed his hands together and began scraping the succulent marrow from them onto the plate with the wrong end of his fork. He spread the marrow onto the points of the toast and savored every bite. Phil was patiently settled in nearby in a living room chair with the *Daily News*.

"You know," Eddie said to Angelina as he ate, "when I was a boy, my mother, Rose, Philly's grandmother, used to make the veal bones and always saved them for me at the end of dinner. I was the littlest, and my brother and sister usually got to the food faster than I did, so she always made me a treat after. I don't think I've had this since she died."

"How'd she die?" asked Angelina.

"Cancer. Phil was her only grandkid. He lived with her through school and all after his mother and father passed away. My mother thought the sun rose and set on that little guy."

Angelina noticed, as Eddie said that, that Phil's paper had lowered an inch or two. She was sure she saw him wipe a tear away. She returned to the kitchen for a moment, then went into the parlor and came up behind him unannounced.

"Phil? Would you like to try some?"

He was startled, but Angelina just put a napkin on his lap and handed him a fork and his own plate of toast and marrowbones.

"Thank you, Mrs. D'Angelo. Very much."

"Okay, enjoy."

Angelina glanced back and watched him dig in with just as much enthusiasm as Eddie had, and the sight of it warmed her heart. She hadn't realized until tonight that, as quiet as he was, Phil listened to and thought about everything.

When Phil and the Don had gone, Angelina washed while Johnny stacked and dried.

"You know, Johnny, you really don't have to help out with the dishes. It's all part of the deal."

Johnny kept drying diligently. "I couldn't just walk out of the house and leave you with all the dishes, Mrs. D'Angelo. Besides, if my grand-mother found out I'd been doing that, she'd hunt me down. And she'd be right."

"How's she doing at the home?"

Johnny smiled. "Real good. She's like the queen bee over there."

"Since you're so nice, I'm going to bake some cookies, so you can bring some over to her and the sisters."

"Aw, she'd love it."

He went silent for three plates. Angelina tried to

catch a glance at his face. She decided he was trying to get up his nerve to say something.

"Actually," Johnny started, "and besides that, I've been trying to get a chance to talk to you alone."

Angelina made sure to concentrate on her dishes and give him room to speak his mind.

"Really?" she said casually. "What about?"

"Romance."

He had obviously searched long and hard for the right word and he said it quickly, like pulling off a Band-Aid.

Angelina knew immediately where he was heading, but she couldn't help herself; she batted her eyes at him when she handed him the next dish. "Johnny, don't you think I'm too old for you?"

That scored a big, red blush on both cheeks. Angelina nudged him playfully with her hip.

"That—that's not what I mean . . . ," Johnny stammered.

"Oh, no, look at that face!" she said merrily. "I know, sweetie, I'm sorry, I was just teasing you. I know exactly what you're talking about."

"Yeah, yes . . . about Tina."

"Of course, about Tina. So, what did you want to know?"

Johnny put the last dry dish on the stack and looked at Angelina with the most serious expression and said confidentially, "I'm really nuts about Tina."

Angelina took the towel from his hands and dried her own. "I think the secret's out, Johnny." She laughed. "You two have been making eyes at each other since the day you met."

"But, here's my question. We've been going out and I feel like Tina's just the right girl for me, and I think we have an understanding and all, but, what's the right time for . . . for a . . ."

"A proposal?"

Johnny looked relieved that she had said the word for him. "Yeah."

Angelina folded her arms and leaned against the counter. Her thoughts wandered of their own accord back to the soft-focus, shiny days of her own courtship. "The answer is, it's its own answer. You'll know when the time is right. It'll jump right out at you."

"Really?"

"Before Frank proposed to me, he told me he carried the ring around in his pocket for three weeks."

"No kidding."

"He waited, until he knew the time was right."

"When was the time?" asked Johnny.

When she caught the sweet, earnest look on his face, Angelina saw in Johnny notes of the qualities that Tina must have just loved to death.

"Well," said Angelina, "that's personal. He got it right, though. So will you. Trust me."

Johnny unfolded the towel and spread it on the rack to dry.

"Okay, I'll take your advice," he said. "I'll just know."

She could almost see his plans coming together in his head. Johnny and Tina seemed so right; what luck, that they had found one another. No matter what, if and when they got married, no matter the ups and downs, the good times and sad, it would be the adventure of their lives. *What I wouldn't give to have one more day married to Frank.*

She gave Johnny a quick hug.

"You will. Trust me. You're still going to help out with the dishes though, right?"

"Oh, absolutely."

The next day, thankfully, was Saturday, and Angelina slept until eleven o'clock. She awoke feeling deeply groggy with a dragging heaviness in her arms and legs and took a full half hour to climb out of her nice, warm bed.

She hardly ever slept in, especially this late, but she put her sluggishness down to stress and overwork—she'd been going nonstop, day in, day out, and after so many years of just cooking for two. Angelina felt tired all the way through the middle of the day and hoped she wasn't coming down with anything. She decided to take it easy, put on a pot of potato-and-leek soup, and curled up on the couch for most of the afternoon.

At about a quarter past four, there was a knock at the door, and Angelina found Guy standing on the front steps.

"Hello," he said, smiling.

"Hi. You know it's Saturday, right?"

"Sure," said Guy, reasonably confident in his facts.

"I'm not cooking tonight. Saturday's our day off."

"Right," he said in full agreement.

Angelina had resigned herself long ago to the phenomenon that the men in her life seldom, if ever, came to the point quickly.

"So," she said finally, "see you tomorrow?"

The next pause lasted long enough to approach awkwardness, and she nearly had the door closed when he spoke up.

"Hey."

She opened the door again and said politely, "Yes?"

"Um, I wanted to know, are you busy tonight?"

"Me?"

"There's a function at the church hall tonight. Basil told me about it. I was wondering if you would like to go. To it."

"With you?"

"Not like a date or anything. But I . . . we could definitely walk over together."

She thought about it. It might be nice to get out

of the house for a change and see some people.

"Yeah, okay," she said finally.

"Great."

Answer received, mission accomplished, Guy made it halfway down the steps, then came back up all in a rush.

"Okay. What time?"

"Don't you have to tell me?" said Angelina.

He checked for the watch on his wrist, realized he wasn't wearing it, and said, "Seven o'clock?"

"Okay. See you then. Bye."

She closed the door and through the curtains watched Guy hurry back across the street. She stopped and took a minute to think things through. As long as it wasn't a date, she supposed it was fine, but now she was feeling a twinge of buyer's remorse. Maybe she should have taken some time to mull it over. But, then again, what harm could there be in getting out of the kitchen for a change? None, she decided, and went back in to ladle herself a cup of hot soup.

The basement rec hall at Saint Joseph's was paneled in plywood, and the green carpet had seen its best days more than a few years back. But it was warm and cozy with a few homey touches, such as comfortable overstuffed armchairs donated from local living rooms. With some festive bunting, it became a perfectly lovely place to hold a dance or a raffle to raise money for whatever the latest worthy cause might be.

Angelina and Guy walked over together, chatting easily as they made their way through the double doors and down the stairs to the party. A lot of the folks from the neighborhood were there, old-timers who had been church supporters forever, their kids and grandkids, housewives manning the soft drinks and sandwiches, men from the Knights of Columbus handing out long-neck beers and selling chances. Danny DeFino was spinning records, the same ones and in practically the same order as he did whenever his PA system and vintage collection of vinyl LPs were pressed into service.

Basil spotted them right away and greeted Angelina with a big hug.

"Angelina, you made it." He then clapped Guy on the back. "Good job, Guy. I didn't know if you had it in you, boy."

Angelina shot Basil a piercing look as a fleetingly guilty expression flitted across his face. "What's that supposed to mean?" she asked.

"It just seemed to me that you were staying in too much on a Saturday night," Basil said. "Don't look at us, it was Dottie's idea—and a good one at that. I'm very glad you came." Basil gave her arm a warm squeeze.

"Why don't I get us something to drink— Angelina, punch okay?" Guy asked.

"I'll take a 7UP. Thanks."

Guy walked off, neatly making his way through the handful of couples on the dance floor.

Angelina took a step closer to Basil. "You know," she said quietly, "you don't seem to remember that I just lost my husband. I'm not interested in being set up on any dates, Mr. Cupertino—and especially not with any of your dining companions."

Basil was bobbing in time to the music. "It's not a date, it's an outing."

"Outing, *schmouting*."

"Ethical problem?" asked Basil, amused.

"In a way, yes," Angelina said, raising her voice a touch to emphasize her point.

Basil never broke his rhythm and said, "Ethical implications aside, I don't think he's interested in you, anyhow."

"What's that supposed to mean? Why not?" she asked, feeling a prickle of wounded pride, even though Basil had just told her what she wanted to hear.

"Not that he might *not* be interested. It's just that I've known him since he was a kid and he is not someone who rushes into anything. In fact, uncertainty may be his defining characteristic. Not sure about playing ball, what school to go to, wasn't sure about going in the service, wasn't sure about staying in the service. One thing I'm sure about is that he's not sure."

"What are you talking about?"

"That's why he's here," said Basil. "He's not sure."

"About what?"

Basil leaned in and spoke a little softer. "About the seminary."

Angelina's eyes opened wide. "He's a priest?" she whispered.

"Not yet he isn't. He was studying to be a priest, out at St. Charles Seminary on City Line. Two months from graduation, then he left it and came to us."

"Why'd he leave?"

"I'm curious myself. I guess he's not sure he wants to be a priest."

Just then Guy appeared with a beer and a bottle of soda with a bendy straw in it. "The meatballs look pretty good. You two want to get something to eat?" asked Guy, handing Angelina her drink.

"You go," said Basil. "I already had three meat-ball sandwiches. On Saturdays, I eat to live. Every other day, I live to eat." He saluted Angelina with a nifty little bow. "I'm going to find someone to dance with. You know, live a little."

He danced away from them with a surprisingly graceful two-step.

Angelina relaxed a little now that Basil had confirmed that Guy's intentions toward her were not romantic. She ate and drank and listened to the old men tell bad jokes and talked to a couple of girlfriends she felt as if she hadn't seen in ages.

Guy stayed close to her most of the time, though he seemed to be attracting a lot of female attention.

Angelina wasn't sure what to make of it when she saw some of the women chattering and glancing their way. Maybe she'd come out too soon. She wasn't emotionally braced for the possibility of having unnecessarily subjected herself to gossip. Angelina tensed visibly when Teri D'Orazio, whom God knew liked to talk about everybody, started making her way toward them.

"Hi, Angelina. I'm surprised to see you here," said Teri, nodding a hello to Guy. "I wanted to ask you something." Angelina caught her breath. "Do you think you could make us one of your cherry cheesecakes for the next fund-raiser?"

Angelina exhaled. "Oh, well, yes, I mean, for a fund-raiser, of course."

"Oh, good. You're a doll," said Teri.

Teri gave Angelina a half hug, smiled curiously at Guy, then turned and walked away.

"You look pale, are you all right?" asked Guy.

"Yes. Sorry. It's just . . . I think I've had my fill of socializing. Do you feel like getting out of here?"

"Sure, let's roll."

They strolled out into the fresh night air. It wasn't late at all, hardly past nine thirty, and a lot of people were out and about, couples and groups of kids walking to their next destination or to no place special. It occurred to Angelina that she hadn't gone anywhere except grocery shopping since Frank died—it felt as if she'd hardly ever left the stove.

She looked at Guy. They were walking perfectly in step with one another. He had a really nice profile.

"I guess I should thank you for getting me out of the house," she said.

"It was Basil's idea, but, really, it was my pleasure."

"So, is it weird for you, being at the church and all?" Angelina asked tentatively.

Guy looked up, momentarily unsure of her meaning until he realized Basil must have let the cat out of the bag. "Because I left the seminary?"

"Yeah. I mean, once you get there, I don't imagine a lot of guys quit."

"You'd be surprised."

"So, why did you leave?"

He looked thoughtful, as if he were hoping that he might reach out and find an easy answer this time to a question he'd been pondering for a while. "Hard to say. I'm old for the seminary, you know. I went through college, went into the Marines, and I had a couple of jobs before I went in."

"So what was it that made you pack up your steamer trunk and come to Dottie? Did something happen?"

He shook his head. "You'll laugh."

"No, I won't. I promise."

"Well," said Guy as they walked, "they keep you pretty busy in the seminary, studying Latin and doctrine and so forth. It's pretty rigorous and I felt like I needed a break, so I took the train down to Washington for the day. I just wanted to be on my own, take in the Air and Space Museum, walk around and clear my head."

"That's at the Smithsonian, right?"

"Right. So, it was a sunny day and I was walking near the National Mall, and a woman drove by in a blue Corvette convertible. I never really even got a good look at her face, but she was young and pretty and her long hair was blowing in the wind. It was over in a few seconds, she sped up and drove away, but that picture of her got kind of stuck in my head. I kept thinking about it; it intruded on my thoughts, even at prayers. Then I started questioning myself, wondering if I was really ready to make the kind of commitment you have to make when you take your vows. It was as if I was feeling the weight of the years ahead of me and I hadn't even started yet."

"Guess what? You're only human."

Guy gave her a thoughtful grin. "I think that the Church might be hoping for a little bit more. So, I guess you could say I'm still trying to figure it out."

"Figure what out?"

"If maybe there isn't more to life than I'd be letting myself in for."

"Honestly?" said Angelina. "I've been wondering if there's more to life, too."

They had slowed to a stop. Guy looked over her shoulder, then smiled like a man struck with a sudden inspiration.

"Maybe we can find out." He took a theatrical pause. "Look."

Up across the street, on the opposite corner in the front window of a row house, was a hand-painted sign with Christmas lights around it:

Palms—Cards—Psychic Readings
Madame Sousatska.

To somebody who wasn't from the neighborhood, it would have been hard for Angelina to explain her hesitation. From South Street on down, the farther you went, the more handmade window signs you saw for fortune-tellers, often set up right in people's houses. Most folks saw it as a harmless way for usually single older women to make a little extra cash, but when she'd been in her early twenties, a woman that her mother used to consult, a woman with snow-white hair named Leila, did a reading for Angelina and, when it was finished, handed her a note with just two words written on it: "Dream delayed."

The next year, Emmaline fell ill, and Angelina

had to stay home to care for her, then for her father, and so the story went. Angelina wasn't a believer exactly, but she didn't take these things lightly. But Guy looked so eager and amused . . . so, in they went.

The inside layout of Madame Sousatska's house mirrored the familiar design of most of the houses in the neighborhood. The parlor might not have been dusted as often as most, and swatches of colorful fabrics, some tie-dyed, some that shimmered like silk dipped in glitter, were draped haphazardly across the sofa and chairs. An impressive collection of scented candles of various brands and sizes flickered on top of the radiator and on the side tables, and the combined effluvium of patchouli, Jasmine Rain, Balsam & Pine, and Pumpkin Pie lent the room an air that managed to be both mysterious and chintzy. In the middle of the room sat a large card table, the kind with the folding legs that stowed away quickly. A fringy shawl dotted with moons and stars was draped over it.

The lady of the house bustled into the room carrying two mismatched mugs of hot tea. One had Garfield on it and the other a *Far Side* cartoon. She was well past middle age, compact, wearing a floral housecoat over blue jeans and fluffy bedroom slippers. Her hair was frizzy, the color of balsa wood, and caught the light in a funny way. She wore heavy green eye shadow but no other visible makeup and sported two large, dangly earrings that looked as if they had been filched from a dining room chandelier. A fat dog waddled in behind her and flopped down sloppily on a knotted rug.

"Here you go, kids," she said kindly in a deep, cigarette-raspy voice, "a nice cup of tea helps set the mood. What are your names?"

"This is Angelina, and I'm Guy."

The woman took her seat with a flourish, as if summoning up her psychic forces before she sat.

"You can call me Claire. *Claire Voyent.*"

She took in the disbelieving looks on their faces and cracked up.

"I'm kidding!" she cackled. "Just like to lighten the mood. If we're all in a good mood, I can focus in on the beam a little better. I'm Sandra. Oh, you're so pretty, the two of you."

Angelina sniffed suspiciously at her cup. "What is this?"

"Herbal tea, hon. It's motherwort and chamomile. It'll help you feel better."

"About what?" Angelina asked apprehensively.

"You just lost someone, didn't you?" said Sandra serenely. "I can see that you have a little cloud"—she tapped her own chest lightly—"right here, over your heart."

Angelina felt a chilly wave of goose bumps race up her arms. That *was* the spot where she felt it most.

"So," Sandra continued, "the reading is five dollars each, or eight for the two of you as a couple."

Angelina recovered and piped up quickly, "Oh, we're not a couple."

Sandra fixed her with an icy-cold and all-knowing stare. "I'll be the judge of that, honey." She slapped a deck of tarots down in front of Guy, hard.

"Cut the cards."

More than an hour later, empty teacups and half-finished Cokes sat ignored in front of Guy and Angelina, who both now sat looking nervously at their hostess.

Sandra turned over the Queen of Wands and looked at Angelina. "You a cook, honey? Or a gardener?"

Angelina, who was still more than a little spooked, just nodded.

Sandra sighed, shook her head. "You might want to think about loosening up some. Maybe you shouldn't spend all your time doing just the one thing. All work and no play makes Jill a dull girl!"

She laughed loudly. Neither Guy nor Angelina joined in.

Cards covered the table, laid out in star patterns, in columns, in crosses, Kings and Queens on horseback, Knights with golden cups, a dark-cloaked Mr. Death, and one poor guy eternally stuck hanging upside down, who kept coming up again and again.

Sandra flipped over The Fool and looked squarely at Guy. "You're at a crossroads, aren't you, handsome?"

She hadn't said anything in a while so Guy was startled. "I guess you could say that."

"You're trying to make up your mind?"

"I guess I am."

"Well, *don't*. You're not ready."

"Yes, ma'am."

Soon, Sandra's legal pad, which was covered with scribbled notes and what appeared to be a long series of intricate numerological notations, had a visible coating of eraser bits, pencil shavings, and cigarette ash. "This is something," said Sandra, muttering to herself. "There is definitely something going on here."

She erased some more and tore a little hole in the paper. She licked her finger and stuck the tiny flap back into place.

"What is it?" said Angelina, whose nerves were starting to fray around the edges.

Sandra scratched her head, and Guy was sure he noticed a few flecks of glitter flutter down from her hair. Sandra suddenly turned to a fresh page and wrote at frantic speed, like a student trying to finish under the wire at the SATs.

"I'd tell you that you were going to meet a handsome stranger," she said as she scribbled, "but you've obviously done that already."

She glanced up and gave Guy a wink and a toothy smile. She finished writing and ripped the page from the pad so hard that it made Angelina jump.

"Here's how I'm going to work this," said Sandra, shoulders hunched, brows knitted, eyes narrowed to unreadable slits. "Usually, I would write out a page of notes each about your life, which I would urge you to take seriously. That's why I can charge money, get it? Because I am not kidding around. Don't fool with Sister Sandra. You understand?"

Guy swallowed hard.

"I think so," he said.

"Good. Good boy," said Sandra. "This is what I got for the both of you. Take this, sweetie." She folded the sheet of paper in half, in half again, and once again, then handed it to Angelina. "Do me a favor, read it together just before you get home."

The absolutely last thing Angelina wanted out of this experience was to be handed a little note.

"Can't you just tell me—?"

"No. Please, indulge an old lady. Be brave. That'll be eight bucks."

The entire rest of the walk home, that folded piece of paper burned a hole in Angelina's pocket. It was much worse than carrying a note home from the principal the time she'd cut school to get her book signed by Julia Child at the library. At least *that* had been totally worth it.

By the time Guy and Angelina had covered the few remaining blocks to their shared street without saying a word, she could hardly stand the suspense. They arrived from the top of the street, so they came to the front of Angelina's house first. She marched them to a full stop.

"Okay. We're home. Should we read it or not?"

"We have to," said Guy. "Or we're out eight dollars."

"Okay, but we have to read it together. All right? This is serious."

"Deal. Fire when ready."

Angelina took the note out of her pocket.

"I'm shaking," said Angelina, who was trembling partly from the cold, but partly from the unexpected import of the moment.

"Don't worry. I've got you," said Guy.

She unfolded it, and held it at arm's length for dramatic effect. "Here goes," she said breath-lessly. Guy moved in closer to her under the streetlight and they read the note together. The single line was written in Sandra's flowery and distinctive scrawl:

You may hold a new life in your hands.

They both realized at the same time that, as they were reading, they were holding hands. They looked at each other, then let go, quickly putting about four feet of distance between them. The nuns at school would have been proud.

"Well, that was a really fun night," said Guy.

"Me, too. I mean, it was. Fun."

"So, see you tomorrow?"

"Yeah, I'm going to do a roast," she said.

Angelina put her hand on the railing and her foot on the first step.

Guy half-turned back toward Dottie's. "Well, good night."

"Night."

When he got to his front door, Guy looked back. Angelina was waiting at the top of her stoop and waved. The night breeze brushed a wisp of hair across her cheek. He felt as though he were still standing right next to her.

She thought she saw him lean in her direction, as if he were about to come down the steps and back across the street. She waited an extra breath or two.

Guy waved and in they both went.

Don't fool with Sister Sandra.

CHAPTER TEN

◈——————◈

A Seven Fishes to Remember

Angelina walked through the door of Napolito's Seafood, which was bustling with ladies, young and old, ordering and gossiping and jostling for position. Outside, Napolito's looked like any one of a hundred other little shops in the neighborhood. Inside, it was plainer than plain, and no thought was given to advertising or amenities of any kind. It had no tables, no chairs, no take-out counter, no menus, no pictures on the walls, no fishing nets hanging overhead adorned with fake starfish and seashells; just whitewashed walls, cement floors, and glass cases filled with nothing but ice and the freshest fish imaginable.

It was December and Angelina had worn her warm, lined boots with the flat soles for the trip because she had been getting footsore and experiencing some lower-back pain lately, caused by all of the standing in the kitchen during the week, she had decided. She attacked the problem with flats and the occasional footbath with Epsom salts before bedtime. The most practical solutions were always the best, Emmaline always said.

Angelina stopped just inside the door and inhaled deeply, as she did every time; that was her pleasure and part of the experience. Napolito's stock-in-trade was fish, but she had never, ever caught a trace of a fishy smell of any kind. She never smelled disinfectants or detergents, either; the place just smelled clean, with maybe a hint of sea spray in the air.

Guy had offered to accompany her and help with all of the packages, but she had her pull cart and decided she'd go it alone. There hadn't been much of fallout to speak of after the encounter with Sandra the fortune-teller. She and Guy treated the whole thing with good humor, and it was easier to make light of it in the cold light of day. It preyed on Angelina's mind, though. She kept that slip of paper in her bedside table and found herself pulling it out and looking at it every few nights.

She shook her head. Thank God she was able to keep busy.

It was closing in on Christmas Eve, and she had the Feast of the Seven Fishes to plan.

The Seven Fishes had been a tradition in her house growing up. Angelina's father had been blessed in his life in many ways, one being that his wife and his mother enjoyed each other's company. They both loved to cook, and rather than compete in the kitchen, they complemented and learned from one another. So, Angelina had the benefit not only of their twinned knowledge and skills, since they were both natural teachers, but of their good examples. Nonna introduced the practice of celebrating Christmas Eve with a meal that consisted entirely of classical Italian seafood dishes, a custom she'd inherited from her mother, who had grown up in the south of Italy. Abstinence from meat on Fridays and on Catholic holidays had been the rule back then, and given seven sacraments, seven fish dishes had long ago been chosen as the proper number.

Angelina and Frank had always spent Christmas Eve at Mamma Gia's with his brother, Joe; Joe's wife, Maria; and Tina. Gia had been the architect of the feast, and Angelina and Maria willingly pitched in, but there was never any question who was the boss in Gia's kitchen.

Frank and Angelina would always arrive first. She and Gia would ensconce themselves in the kitchen, and Frank would get ready for his session with his brother, Joe. It was the only time of year that they would set up a chessboard. Frank could never just sit and watch TV, so while they were playing and plotting their next moves, he and Joe would trade off spinning records on the old hi-fi. They'd program a nice selection of Christmas records, of course, Sinatra, Johnny Mathis, and Gia's favorite, Perry Como; but they'd also slip in some Everly Brothers, Otis Redding, even a little

Elton John, which set Maria and Tina to dancing in the kitchen.

Angelina and Frank would always save Nat King Cole for Christmas Day together. Once the games wound down, Frank would magically appear at her side while she was cooking, to "supervise," kiss her on the neck and swipe some olives from the antipasto tray. She could practically feel the tickle of his beard and the soft smell of good wine on his breath. The anticipation of his sudden arrival next to her in the kitchen might be the thing she'd miss most of all on Christmas Eve.

This year, Angelina had proposed that everybody come to her house for the festive supper: her family, "the bachelors' club," Dottie, Mrs. Cappuccio. She wanted as full a house and as busy a day as possible, since she had no idea how she was going to handle waking up in her bed alone on Christmas morning.

She let Mrs. Scarduzzo go ahead of her in line. Angelina always timed it to make sure that she'd be waited on by Angelo, the dwarvish and ancient fishmonger who had been an institution at Napolito's since before Angelina was high enough to see over the counter.

One time, a few years back, she had called ahead for a whole side of salmon. A new kid at the shop had it wrapped and ready to go when she arrived, but when she opened it at home, shockingly, it had a noticeable, day-old fish odor; not rank, but not as fresh as she was used to from Napolito's, for sure. As she stood in her kitchen contemplating what she should do next, there was a rap at the door. It was Angelo—holding a new side of salmon, which he pressed into her hands with a gentlemanly, old-world bow, along with a full refund and his most sincere apologies that a piece of fish that he had intended for no more than cat food had made its way, through the carelessness of an ignorant boy, into the hands of any of his customers, let alone one he knew to be such a fine and careful cook. She thanked him profusely and tried to press the money on him, but he simply raised his hand, bowed again, and was off. From that day to this and forever, there was no other man for her when it came to seafood than Angelo.

She let one more customer go ahead of her, then saw that he was free.

"Hey, Angelo, merry Christmas!" she said brightly, dropping her paper number in the basket on the counter.

He looked up, and his weathered, deeply lined face split in a big grin. "*Buon Natale, Angelina, buon Natale.*"

She had called her order in ahead of time to him, so he had it pulled and cut and all ready, but his custom was to wait and wrap each item as his customers watched. Angelo liked to have one last chance to inspect every piece of fish he sold before it walked out the door.

"You have my *baccalà*?" asked Angelina.

"*Baccalà*, that's the salt fish, 'cause God's Word gives a flavor to the world."

Each of the fishes traditionally had a special religious reason for being served at the feast, and Angelina ran through the checklist with Angelo as if reciting a liturgical call and response at mass.

"Clams and oysters?" asked Angelina.

" 'Cause God is your armor from trouble," said Angelo.

"Calamari?"

" 'Cause God can reach out his arms and find you everywhere you go."

"Got my eels?"

" 'Cause God's Word goes so quick like a flash to your ears." Big, white paper packets of wrapped fish landed on the counter with each benediction.

"The smelts?"

"Even the smallest will be as the biggest when Kingdom comes."

"And the flounder?"

Angelo looked at her and playfully tapped one eye. "God's eyes are always open."

She reached over and shook his hand and put all of the packages into her basket. "Thanks, Angelo, merry Christmas!"

The old man blew her a couple of kisses as he looked for his next customer. "*Ciao,* baby. *Buon Natale.*"

Marinated Unagi
over Arborio Rice Patties

Serves 6

INGREDIENTS FOR THE MARINATED EEL
  ¼ cup soy sauce
  ¼ cup balsamic vinegar
  ¼ teaspoon cayenne pepper
  ¼ cup olive oil
  1 pound freshwater eel fillets cut into
    1-inch-by-2-inch pieces

INGREDIENTS FOR THE RICE PATTIES
  1 quart beef stock
  3 tablespoons olive oil
  1 medium onion, minced
  2 cups arborio rice
  1 cup tawny port, such as Sandeman
  2 cups grated Asiago cheese (from a piece
    that is about 4 ounces)
  ¾ teaspoon ground black pepper
  ½ teaspoon dried oregano
  Salt, to taste
  1 fresh lemon, zested with a micro-grater and
    juiced
  1½ teaspoons Frank's Red Hot Original
    cayenne pepper sauce (use more if you like
    it hot)
  2 tablespoons minced fresh basil leaves

METHOD FOR THE EEL FILLETS

Combine the soy sauce and balsamic vinegar in a mixing bowl. In a separate small bowl, whisk the cayenne pepper gradually into the olive oil. Then, whisking constantly, gradually pour the olive oil mixture in a slow thin stream into the soy sauce/vinegar mixture to create an emulsion. Place the eel fillets into a nonreactive container to be used for marinating the eel and coat each of them with the mixture. Cover and refrigerate overnight (at least 8 hours). (If the fillets do not fit in a single layer or are not immersed, flip them and recoat them periodically during the marinating.)

Shortly before service, brush a grill pan with a small amount of oil, and get it hot over medium-high heat, about 3 to 5 minutes.

Grill the marinated eel, until cooked through, about 3 minutes per side.

METHOD FOR THE ARBORIO RICE PATTIES

Begin cooking the rice about 40 minutes before service. Heat the beef stock and 2 cups water to boiling in a large pot, then reduce the heat to low so it will simmer. In a large pot, heat the olive oil over medium-high heat until it shimmers. Sauté the onion until it turns translucent, about 2 to 3 minutes. Add the dry arborio rice to the pot and stir to coat with the olive oil. Toast the grains of rice until they are just golden, about 3 minutes,

213

stirring frequently to prevent burning. Add the port and stir until the rice absorbs it. Begin adding the hot beef stock about ½ cup at a time, allowing each addition of stock to become absorbed in the rice before adding the next, stirring constantly so the rice doesn't stick to the bottom of the pot. When half the stock has been added this way, add the balance of it all at once and continue to stir until all of the liquid is absorbed into the rice and the rice is al dente. Do not allow the rice to become gummy. Total stirring time for the rice will be approximately 22 minutes; it is labor-intensive, but time well spent. When all the stock has been absorbed, and the rice is cooked but firm "to the bite," stir in the grated cheese, the black pepper, and the oregano. Add salt to taste, cover the pot, and remove from the heat.

(Begin grilling the eel only after the rice has been cooked.)

PRESENTATION
Using a 2½-inch circle cutter as a mold, firmly press even amounts of the rice (4 to 6 tablespoons) into 6 patties, one on each serving plate. Top with one or 2 slices of grilled eel, drizzle with 1 teaspoon lemon juice and ¼ teaspoon hot sauce, and garnish with minced basil and a pinch of lemon zest.

———

Caesar Salad
with Batter-Dipped Smelts

Serves 6

INGREDIENTS FOR CROUTONS
½ baguette loaf (or any small loaf of crispy
French or Italian bread), cut into
½-inch cubes
¼ cup olive oil
1 teaspoon garlic powder
Salt and freshly ground black pepper to taste

INGREDIENTS FOR BATTER-DIPPED SMELTS
⅜ cup white rice flour or all-purpose flour
½ teaspoon baking powder
Pinch salt (1/16 teaspoon)
¾ teaspoon canola oil
1 egg
⅜ cup milk
¼ teaspoon ground black pepper
1 liter canola oil (or 2 to 4 liters if you are
using a deep fryer)
1 pound boneless smelts, halved lengthwise
(a pound will yield about 3 dozen halves)

INGREDIENTS FOR SALAD AND DRESSING
1 large head romaine lettuce, soaked in salt
water to remove grit and dried in a salad
spinner

2 large garlic cloves, peeled and quartered
1 pasteurized egg (these are identified in stores as "pasteurized" and although not cooked have been sufficiently heated for food safety)
½ teaspoon Worcestershire sauce
½ fresh lemon, micro-zested and juiced
½ cup extra-virgin olive oil
1 cup finely grated Parmigiano-Reggiano cheese (from about a ¼-pound chunk), plus some to shave over the salad
Freshly ground black pepper, to taste
Salt to taste

METHOD FOR THE CROUTONS

Preheat the oven to 250°F. In a mixing bowl, toss the bread cubes with olive oil, sprinkle with garlic powder, salt, and pepper, and toss again to coat thoroughly. Place the bread cubes on a baking sheet and toast them until lightly browned, about 5 minutes. Remove from the oven and let cool.

METHOD FOR THE SMELTS

In a small bowl, combine the flour, baking powder, and salt and mix well. Whisk in the canola oil, egg, and milk, and season with black pepper. Heat the oil over medium-high heat in a large sauté pan until it shimmers or, if using a deep fryer, to 375°F (or according to the manu-facturer's instructions for similar foods). Dip the smelts in the batter to coat, allowing excess to drip away, and add them to the hot oil, cooking until golden brown, turning with tongs to brown both sides, about 20 seconds for the first side and 10 seconds for the other side (or in the deep-fryer basket, if applicable). Drain on paper toweling and let cool to room temperature.

METHOD FOR THE SALAD AND DRESSING

Remove the large "spines" from the lettuce leaves and tear the tender portions of the leaves into bite-size pieces.

One at a time through the feed opening of a running blender, mix the garlic cloves, egg, Worcestershire sauce, and the lemon juice. Add extra-virgin olive oil in a slow, thin stream to emulsify. Transfer the dressing to a small bowl and mix in the grated cheese. Season with black pepper (and salt only if necessary since the cheese lends saltiness).

Just before service, toss the romaine lettuce and lemon zest in a mixing bowl with only enough dressing to coat.

PRESENTATION

Place some salad in the center of salad-size serving dishes and sprinkle with croutons. Garnish with shaved cheese and arrange 5 or 6 fried smelts around the perimeter of the plate.

On Christmas Eve, Angelina spent the better part of the day prepping, and Gia and Tina arrived to help with the cooking around five o'clock; Mr. Cupertino came at five-thirty to set up the bar; and by the time seven o'clock rolled around, nearly everyone had arrived: Jerry, Mr. Pettibone, Dottie, Joe and Maria, Phil and Don Eddie.

Guy and Johnny arrived last and carried Mrs. Cappuccio up the steps in a wheelchair they had borrowed from the home. She had been having more and more trouble getting around, but she looked healthy otherwise and well cared for and thrilled as punch to be there with them all.

Angelina and Tina met them at the door.

"How did the pick-up go?" Angelina asked Guy, as Tina navigated Mrs. Cappuccio into the warmth of the living room.

"Well, to tell you the truth, Johnny and I did have a little trouble, actually, lifting her into the chair. Um, you know, as to . . . where to get a grip on her," said Guy.

Angelina was amused, but also mildly appalled. "Are you kidding me?" she said.

"No, I'm afraid not," said Guy. "Not our finest hour. Then Sister Bartholomew shows up and she smacks me with her cane, bends me over, Mrs. Cappuccio grabs me around the neck and I ended up carrying her all the way out to the cab. The two of them were laughing at Johnny and me the whole time."

Angelina's eyes went wide.

"You met Sister Bartholomew? What was she like?" she asked breathlessly.

Guy rubbed his arm and thought for a minute.

"Formidable," he said, and they closed the door and went inside.

Soon, things were heating up in the kitchen. The first course was a variation on a French recipe that had been around since Escoffier, *Baccalà Brandade.* Angelina created a silky forcemeat with milk, codfish, olive oil, pepper, and freshly grated nutmeg. She squeezed in a couple of heads of slow-roasted garlic, a drizzle of lemon juice, and a shower of fresh parsley, then served it as a dip with sliced sourdough and warmed pita-bread wedges, paired with glasses of bubbly Prosecco.

The second course had been a favorite of her mother's, called Angels on Horseback—freshly shucked oysters, wrapped in thin slices of prosciutto, then broiled on slices of herb-buttered bread. When the oysters cooked, they curled up to resemble tiny angels' wings. Angelina accented the freshness of the oyster with a dab of anchovy paste and wasabi on each hors d'oeuvre. She'd loved the Angels since she was a little girl; they were a heavenly mouthful.

The third course was grilled Marinated *Unagi*, or freshwater eel, over Arborio Rice Patties. Angelina had marinated the eels all day and flash-grilled them just before serving on rice patties laced with Asiago cheese.

This was followed by a Caesar salad topped with hot, batter-dipped, deep-fried smelts. Angelina's father used to crunch his way through the small, silvery fish like French fries. Tonight, Angelina arranged them artfully around mounds of Caesar salad on each plate and ushered them out the door.

For the fifth course, Angelina had prepared a big pot of her Mediterranean Clam Soup the night before, a lighter version of Manhattan clam chowder. The last two courses were Parmesan-Stuffed Poached Calamari over Linguine in Red Sauce, and the pièce de résistance, Broiled Flounder with a Coriander Reduction.

The atmosphere was like backstage at the dinner rush at a good restaurant.

"Tina, honey," called Angelina, "can you bring in the dishes from the salad?"

"I got 'em already, they're stacked over there," said Tina.

Gia grabbed a big pot off the stove and muscled it over to the sink. "I'm pulling the macaroni for the calamar' and linguine."

"Pull it," said Angelina. "Tina, get the two big bowls and get ready to dish out the linguine. I'm bringing the calamari."

"Got it," called Tina as she grabbed the second bowl.

Gia tossed and dressed the linguine in extra-virgin and black pepper, while Angelina doled out the calamari and sauce.

The kitchen seemed hotter than usual to Angelina, probably because Old Reliable was working overtime. While Gia and Tina served the soup, Angelina poured herself a glass of ice water, held the glass against her temple for a minute, then drank it down in one go.

"Angelina, you and me can carry in the bowls, okay?" said Gia. "Tina, you have to go and sit next to Johnny and get something to eat."

"And take off your apron," said Angelina. "And put on your pretty white sweater."

Tina wiped her hands and gave Angelina a quick kiss on the cheek, then said, "Here I go," and dashed out of the door.

Gia came over to help with dividing the calamari and linguine into two bowls. "Angelina, you going to sit and eat something?"

"No, Ma, my stomach's a little flippy from doing all of this seafood. Are you?"

Gia finished and picked up the bowl. "I never sit."

In the dining room, the wine and food and Christmas carols playing had cast a wonderful yuletide spell on the table. Everybody talked and laughed and applauded each course as it arrived. Tina kissed Johnny on the cheek and sat next to him at the table as Mr. Pettibone came around and poured wine into her glass.

When Angelina and Gia made their grand entrance, each carrying a big pasta bowl filled with calamari and linguine, more cheers erupted— "He-ey!" from Don Eddie and "Bravo!" from Mr. Pettibone, and more scattered applause. Angelina bowed playfully, then went back into the kitchen as Gia and Dottie started dishing out the pasta.

What happened next became the stuff of family legend.

Dottie was diligently working her way down the left side of the table and, when she reached Johnny and Tina, Johnny helpfully scooched his chair to one side so that Tina could be served first. Dottie scooped and, as the linguine hit Tina's plate, an errant drop of red *pomodoro* sauce took off like a tiny spark from struck flint, flew, and splattered on her white cashmere sweater.

Tina gasped.

Without a second's thought, acting on instinct, Johnny pulled his hankie out of his jacket pocket. As it came free, the engagement ring that it had been wrapped around went spinning into the air.

They all followed its flight in sudden silence. The ring arced and landed, whirling like a coin to a stop on the tablecloth, the small diamond flickering with light before it finally quivered and lay still.

As if in a dream, Johnny delicately picked up the ring and looked into Tina's eyes.

With lightning speed, Gia poked her head into

the kitchen and hissed urgently to Angelina, "Come quick, Johnny's gonna propose!"

Angelina dropped her towel, rushed into the room, and stood next to Gia, their eyes riveted on the young couple frozen in time across the room.

Johnny turned and looked from face to expectant face around the table, as if searching for any last-minute instructions. Jerry caught his eye and made a slow downward gesture with the palm of his hand. Johnny dropped slowly to one knee.

Gia looked at Jerry with a firm nod of approval.

"Tina," said Johnny in a clear, unwavering voice that she would never forget, "I promise to love you for the rest of our days, if you will do me the honor of becoming my wife."

With tears in her eyes and not a moment's hesitation, Tina said:

"Yes, Johnny, I will."

Johnny slipped the ring onto her finger and she threw herself into his arms. Thunderous applause erupted, hugs and backslaps and handshakes were exchanged around the room. Wine was poured, toasts were offered, and glasses rang in a chorus of spontaneous celebration.

Angelina's eyes rolled back in her head and she dropped to the floor in a dead faint and did not move.

Angelina's eyes fluttered once or twice, but she never fully regained consciousness until Dr.

Vitale arrived about twenty minutes later, as soon as Gia called him. He only lived a few blocks away and had been the family doctor for so many years that Gia knew she could rely on Doctor Al to drop everything and come right away, even on Christmas Eve.

The men had moved Angelina as gently as possible from the floor to the couch in the living room, put a pillow under her head, and layered blankets over her to keep her warm. Everyone was tensely gathered into the front room while Dr. Vitale checked her pulse, gently opened her eyelids one at a time and flashed his light into her pupils, then reached into his black bag and found an ammonia capsule. He broke it under her nose and her eyes immediately opened as she tried to sit up.

"Somebody turn down the oven," she said.

Jerry laughed, not only because she was awake, but because she was picking up right where she left off. Johnny put his hand on Tina's shoulder and Don Eddie let out an audible "whew."

"I got the oven, honey," said Gia. "How you feeling?"

Angelina was still disoriented and took them all in at a glance, trying to get her bearings. "I'm so dizzy. I got dizzy and I . . . what happened?"

"You fainted," said Basil, who still looked a little washed-out himself.

"Scared me half to death," said Guy, who had been the first to her side.

Some color came back into Angelina's cheeks and her gaze alighted on Johnny and Tina. "Tina," she said, reaching for her hand, "did you get engaged?"

Tina stretched out her hand and Angelina elbowed up to a sitting position to get her first proper look at the ring.

"The two of you, get over here right now and give me a hug."

Tina bent down and embraced her tightly, and Johnny followed. Angelina gave his hand an extra-hard squeeze, to let him know that he had gotten it right.

Dr. Vitale reached down into his bag and came up with a stethoscope. "Angelina, can you lean forward a little bit?"

"I think so." She sat up and leaned forward, which made her feel breathless. Dr. Vitale listened intently for a minute, then took the stethoscope off and tossed it back into his black bag. He straightened his tie, stepped away from Angelina and over to Gia. They conferred in low tones for a moment or two, and Angelina overheard Gia say, "Sure, okay."

Gia turned to the assembled and waved her apron in the direction of the dining room. "*Tutti a tavola*," she said, clapping her hands once sharply. "Back to the table, let's go. Everything's getting cold."

When Gia spoke in that tone of voice, people

generally listened. They all moved along quickly back into the dining room, but everyone understood without having to be told that the doctor wanted a moment or two with Angelina alone.

Dr. Vitale retook his seat and patted her shoulder kindly. "Angelina, when's the last time you came to see me?"

Angelina had to stop and think. It was like being asked when your last confession had been. It was hard to remember exactly unless you had really sinned or really been sick.

"I don't know, I guess last year when I had the flu?"

Dr. Vitale reached into his vest pocket, checked his watch, then tucked it back in place. "Were you planning on coming to see me anytime soon?"

For a moment, Angelina nearly lost track of what they were talking about. Dr. Vitale always had a way of slowing things down for her and making her relax. It felt as though they were chatting about the weather and he was hinting around for lemonade and chocolate chip cookies.

"No. I've just been tired, is all," she said.

He didn't reply.

Angelina suddenly grew suspicious, a little frightened, and more than a little worried.

Dr. Vitale was unreadable.

"Is something wrong?"

Dr. Vitale leaned back in the chair and placed

his hands on his knees. "I wouldn't say wrong, really."

"What is it?" Angelina asked, steeling herself now against the news.

He smiled. "Well, unless you usually have two heartbeats, you're going to have a baby."

"What?"

Dr. Vitale waited patiently and only spoke again when he could see that the idea was beginning to take hold. In a better world, he might have won the Nobel Prize in bedside manner.

"Not only that," he said, "you've got to be nearly five months along."

There was a rushing sound in her ears, then Angelina could hear the clinking of silverware in the other room. She was thankful that Dr. Vitale had sent everyone back into the dining room so that now it was just the two of them.

She lay back and her hands moved hesitantly to her belly. Her mind raced back in a flash over the past few months and the dots connected and the stars aligned and she knew suddenly in her heart, he was right. *Oh, my God.*

It wasn't just the two of them, after all.

"Oh, my God," she said softly. "I'm having Frank's baby."

CHAPTER ELEVEN

The Pie's the Thing

Angelina used to experience the oddest sensation when she was a little girl. Her father and mother would take her down the shore every summer for two weeks to a little bungalow near the ocean. The place belonged to an elderly maiden aunt of her father's, who rented it out for a week at a time to beachgoers, but who also conscientiously reserved time for members of her family to vacation for free. For two weeks, they would sun and splash in the surf, eat crabs and fried bluefish and saltwater taffy, and Angelina would return home brown as a berry. That's when she would hold her breath: the moment when her father turned the key in the door.

After two weeks away, it always felt to her as though she were seeing her own house again for the first time. It was exhilarating. As her parents brought in the bags, she'd run from room to room noticing everything: the pictures on the wall she never paid attention to, the fresh smell of the carpet her mother had vacuumed twice before they'd left home, the enormous size of their reliable, old kitchen stove, until she'd finally run upstairs and rediscover her own room, bounce on the bed, and hug the old, threadbare stuffed lion she slept with. Nothing had really changed, but in those precious few moments her familiar, everyday world looked completely new and different.

She'd stopped having that feeling after she was about thirteen, and soon after that, her great-aunt died and the house went out of the family's hands, but she felt that same sensation now, so strongly that she could hardly speak. Everything was the same, and everything had changed.

She asked for Gia, whose hands flew to her cheeks when she heard the news. She hugged Angelina so fast and hard that they both almost fell off the couch. They cried, just for a few seconds, and Gia said a quick prayer of thanks to God, while Angelina and Dr. Vitale blessed themselves and bowed their heads.

"Who should I tell?" said Gia suddenly. "I have to let Tina know. And I have to tell Joey and Maria."

Angelina smiled gamely and nodded, but she still looked pale and weak. "Sure, Ma, please let everyone know, but I feel like I better go and lie down for a while."

Gia helped her up and draped the blanket around her shoulders. "Come on, honey, I'll take you up. I'll take care of everything, don't you worry about anything."

Dr. Vitale rose to his feet.

"Doctor Al, are you going to stay for some food?" asked Gia.

"No, thank you, Gia. I have to get back home to my wife. You'll bring Angelina to see me the day after tomorrow?"

"We'll be there," said Gia.

"Thanks, Doctor, for coming over," said Angelina, still rattled and unsteady on her feet.

Dr. Vitale put on his hat and coat and picked up his bag. "Don't worry, Angelina, everything seems to be fine. Get some rest. Good night."

He tipped his hat and let himself out, and Gia gingerly escorted Angelina up the steps.

Angelina was asleep on her bed, still in her clothes, under a heavy down comforter. It was dark, but there was light in the room from the moon outside. Her eyes opened when she heard loud laughter from downstairs, followed by a smattering of applause. Sounded like a big celebration was going on. She wasn't sure how long she'd been sleeping. She took the knitted blanket draped over the back of her vanity chair, wrapped herself up in it, and, barefoot, headed downstairs.

As she reached the bottom step, another peal of laughter came from the dining room; Jerry must have said something funny, with his usual perfect timing and delivery.

As Angelina rounded the corner, she saw someone with his back to her sitting at the head of the table. That had never happened before. As she approached, he turned and smiled.

It was Frank, dressed in a shirt and tie with a large slice of chocolate cake in front of him. No one else at the table looked at her when she walked in, they just continued chattering amiably among themselves.

"What are you doing here?" she asked.

Frank laughed and cocked his head to one side, the way he did when he was about to tease her. She could always see it coming.

"How could you not know you were having a *baby?*" Frank's tone was gently mocking, but his face was full of love—not to mention concern. For Angelina, it was like chatting with a trusted part of herself.

"You didn't notice all the changes in your . . . you know," said Frank.

"My what? You don't know what you're talking about. I've been working my backside off, I wasn't eating regular meals, and besides, in case you hadn't noticed, I've been sleeping alone lately. So, you know, I put it down to a lack of . . ."

"Lack of what?"

She liked that glint in his eye, in spite of herself. She looked up to the ceiling, then narrowed her eyes at him and said, "I've . . . been . . . busy."

Frank knew when to get off a subject. "You've been so busy cooking for everybody else, but now you have to remember to eat. You're eating for two, you know." Frank got up and headed for the kitchen. She followed him and waited as he pulled his chair out, gesturing for her to have a seat. "Sit down. I'll fix you something to eat. You've got to eat."

Back in bed, Angelina's eyes flickered open.

"Hi." Jerry had pulled a chair up beside the bed and had turned on a small lamp across the room. "You've got to eat," he said again.

"What did you say?" Angelina shifted under the comforter, then sat up against the pillows.

"I brought you something to eat."

Jerry got up and came back across the room with a bed tray. On it was a bowl of soup, a dish with some saltines, and a glass of ginger ale. One of the pillows slipped off the bed to the floor. Jerry set the tray down on the night table.

"I got it. Try some of that."

"What is it?"

"Nothing fancy. Some chicken broth, a little pepper and *acini de pepe*. I used to make this for my little brother whenever he had to stay home from school."

"I didn't know you had a brother," said Angelina, settling in beneath the tray.

"Sure, I did. He had MS when he was a kid. He died when he was thirteen."

"Oh, my God. I never knew that. I'm so sorry."

"Yeah, thanks. He was a great kid. You should have seen him hit a baseball before he got sick. Man, he was great." Jerry sat back down in the chair beside the bed.

"What was his name?" Angelina blew on the broth in her spoon.

"Kevin. How's the soup?"

"Hot. Perfect," she said gratefully.

"I should have put a little ice cube in it to cool it off. So, everybody except Gia went home, but they all send their congratulations. How are you feeling?"

"I'm okay. Surprised."

"You got that right. Welcome to the club. We're getting shirts made."

Angelina felt comfortable and warm as the piping hot liquid traveled down into her chest, penetrating deeply as it went. She felt herself drifting into a mood that seemed warm and familiar at first, like snuggling into a comfy, old sweater, but then unsettling somehow. It was a strange and intimate feeling when she realized that there was a man in her bedroom.

She sat up a little straighter in bed. "Thank you for this, Jerry."

Jerry sat up a little straighter in the chair. "Enjoy it. I'm going back downstairs. Gia will be up, she's going to sleep over. I'm going to stick around for a while, help clean up. Call down if you want something."

He got up and went to the door.

"Thanks again," said Angelina.

"No problem. Merry Christmas, Angelina."

Guy was sitting alone in the dining room when Jerry got back downstairs. Gia had set out three coffee cups, three small crystal glasses, and a bottle of anisette.

"I thought you left," said Jerry, taking his usual seat at the table.

"Gia invited me to stay for a drink," said Guy as he poured a clear dram of the viscous licorice aperitif for each of them. "Cheers."

They clinked glasses and sipped.

"*Salute*," said Jerry.

"How is she?" asked Guy.

"She's good," said Jerry with a smile.

"I mean, how is she feeling? Did you ask her?"

"Yeah, of course I did. She's fine."

"I'll stop by in the morning," said Guy, almost to himself. "I'm sure she's going to want somebody to talk to."

Jerry's jaw set in a way that was hard to read. "Pretty sure the kitchen's closed tomorrow."

Guy met Jerry's gaze evenly. "What's that supposed to mean?"

"I'm just saying, she seems fine, is all. I don't

234

think she needs any early-morning visits."

"Hey, all I want is what's best for Angelina," said Guy.

"So do I."

"Coffee's ready," said Gia. She stood framed by the light in the doorway with a fresh pot in hand and eyed them both intently before she came slowly to the table and started filling their cups.

Gia settled into a chair opposite the two of them. Guy passed her a glass of anisette and Jerry added sugar to his coffee, which gave them both a moment to be occupied with something besides each other. Gia blew gently on her coffee and waited until she had their complete attention.

"I grew up around two brothers and all of their friends," she said, "so let me tell you, I know it when I see the signs, okay?"

The two men sat still—a little guiltily, both slightly sulky—and listened.

"I know Angelina," said Gia. "And if anybody can get through this kind of a thing, she can. But it's a shock to the body, in more ways than one. My job, and your job, is to make sure she knows she's not gonna have to do it by herself. But she needs friends right now, not boyfriends. *Capisci*?"

"We just want to help," said Guy.

"We all do. Nothing to worry about, Gia," said Jerry.

"I'm not worried," she said. "But I am going up to bed."

They cleared the cups and glasses away and Gia saw them to the door. She hugged them both, said the last *Buon Natale*, and locked up for the night. As she drew the front curtains, she saw Guy and Jerry talking for a minute, then shaking hands under the streetlight before heading off in opposite directions.

They were young enough to be her sons, but Gia knew she was dealing with two grown men, both with experiences in their lives that she knew nothing about. She had no way of knowing whether their handshake had been a truce or a signal, "may the best man win." She felt that she knew them well enough, though, to tell that they were gentlemen and hoped, most of all, deep down, that that they had agreed to treat the situation and Angelina with the one thing that counted above everything else—respect.

Weeks passed by as Angelina acclimated to the new shape of her world. Breakfasts and dinners continued right on schedule, although they became simpler, less adventurous, and more wholesome—and she got lots more help in the kitchen. Her gentleman diners, always deferential and polite, had all become positively solicitous overnight. The meals were mostly served family-style now, and she had a fight on her hands if she ever tried to clear and do the dishes.

Tina and Gia stopped by much more regularly,

ostensibly to make sure that Angelina had all of the help she needed, but Angelina could see subtle undertones. Gia was practically bursting at the seams with pride and anticipation—between Angelina's pregnancy and Tina's pending nuptials, Gia was in her element, ready to dispense advice and lend a hand at the drop of a hat. Tina, who clearly had it in mind to dazzle her new husband in the kitchen, wanted desperately to learn the secrets of Angelina's red gravy.

So they picked a Sunday afternoon soon after New Year's and Angelina hauled out her mother's old sausage grinder and stuffer. Gia had volunteered to make the trip to the butcher's shop and brought back good hog casings, a few pounds of beautifully marbled pork butt and shoulder glistening with clean, white fat, and a four-pound beef chuck roast. It wasn't every day that the grinder came out for fresh homemade sausages and meatballs, but it wasn't every day that Gia and Angelina teamed up to pass on the Mother Recipe to the next generation.

Gia patiently instructed Tina on the proper technique for flushing and preparing the casings, then set them aside while Angelina showed her how to build the sauce: start with white onion, and a fine mince of celery, fresh flat-leaf parsley, and deep red, extra-sweet frying peppers; add copious amounts of garlic (chopped not so finely); season with sea salt, crushed red pepper, and freshly ground black pepper; simmer and sweat on a medium flame in good olive oil; generously sprinkle with dried herbs from the garden (palmfuls of oregano, rosemary, and basil); follow with a big dollop of thick, rich tomato paste; cook down some more until all of the ingredients were completely combined; pour in big cans of fresh-packed crushed tomatoes and a cup of red wine (preferably a Sangiovese or a Barolo); reseason, finish with fresh herbs; bring to a high simmer, then down to a low flame; walk away.

"That's it?" said Tina in a hushed tone when it was finished.

"That's it. Do it just like that for maybe . . . ten years or so," said Gia.

"Later, once you have it down, you can switch it up and make it your own," said Angelina.

Gia and Tina ground the pork for the sausages, then Angelina instructed Tina on the order and proportions for her spice mix. The cold weather was settled into Gia's two arthritic knuckles, so Angelina and Tina started in on stuffing the sausages and pinching them into uniform links. They were about halfway through the second casing when Angelina unexpectedly turned a shade of pale green reminiscent of the color of half-ripened bananas.

"Uh-oh," said Angelina, and rushed out of the room with a towel clamped over her lips.

Tina and Gia heard the powder-room door

slam, then the bellowing sounds of her reversal of lunch. Minutes later, looking pale, wrung-out, and worn, Angelina returned tentatively to the kitchen, drying her hands on a towel.

She was crying. "I can't do this."

Gia took her by the shoulders as Tina hurriedly washed her hands clean in the sink behind them.

"Don't worry, honey," said Gia soothingly. "Everything's going to be okay."

Angelina turned to face her and her eyes were teary and despairing. "What if I can't do this, Gia? The baby. How am I going to do it without Frank?" She choked a little when she said his name.

Angelina sobbed a loud, heartbroken sob and collapsed into a chair. Tina handed her a wad of tissues and hugged her from behind. They stayed there together while Gia ran some cool tap water into a glass, added a pinch of salt and a squeeze of lemon juice, then took it to the table and had Angelina sip it slowly.

Gia waited patiently until Angelina had composed herself and looked as though she felt a little better. Then Gia leaned in and said quietly, "You can do it. We're all here to help you with anything you need. All of us. You know that, way down deep in your bones, right?"

"Yeah, I know it." Angelina put her hand over her heart.

Gia smiled and patted Angelina on the shoulder.

Gia's voice took on an extra gravity when she said, "And there's just one more thing you can never forget."

"What's that?" said Angelina, and blew her nose.

"Those poor men. Not one of them with a woman. You stop cooking for them, they all starve to death and *die*."

Angelina laughed then; so did Tina.

Gia smiled in unspoken satisfaction. She had a few surprises left up her sleeve. Nobody knew it, but she could be pretty damn funny, when she wanted to be.

Once or twice a week, Basil began making it his habit to stop by Angelina's mid-afternoon with a treat for them to share. They would sit and talk for a while, usually about some record he had listened to or painting he had seen or the latest book he had been reading. Angelina began to think of it as the Cupertino Culture Hour and looked forward to his company even more than she did the sweet treats he brought along. He appeared at the door on a nippy Tuesday in his topcoat and tweed cap, cradling a brown bag. He tipped his hat and she ushered him into the kitchen.

"What did you bring?" she asked, smiling broadly.

"Butter Brickle," he said proudly, as he yanked the surprise out of the bag. "It's my favorite kind of ice cream."

"Oh, I love it. I haven't had it in ages—good call."

"I love the name. *Butter,* of course, which you can't go wrong with, and *brickle* . . . whatever that is. What is brickle, anyway?"

"Nobody knows," said Angelina. "I'll get the bowls."

She furnished two big spoons, a scoop, and dishes, and they hunkered down over the carton as Basil introduced his topic of the day.

"I've just finished reading *Cyrano de Bergerac.* Ho, boy, what a story. And what an ending. Do you know it?"

"The guy with the big nose? Sure."

"The guy with the big nose, right. And, though he's in love with a beautiful woman, Roxanne, the love of his life, he can never bring himself to approach her or get together with her, because he feels the weight of his nose. I mean, he feels that she will reject him because of the way he looks. Or worse, for him, not take him seriously."

"So he doesn't have confidence, because he's self-conscious about his looks?"

"No. Not at all. Just the opposite. As it turns out, he's the most confident man on the face of the earth. He fights with a sword, he knows about food . . ."

"Really?" she said.

"Yep. His best friend is a baker."

"Never go wrong that way," said Angelina.

"And Cyrano is a great writer; I'm telling you, the poetry just flies out of him. So, because he doesn't want Roxanne to be alone, he writes all the best lines for this handsome young guy, Christian, to woo her. And, boy, does he woo."

"She marries Christian?" asked Angelina.

"No," said Basil. "Christian gets killed in the war. And Roxanne chooses to mourn him for twenty years, until, in the end, she finds out that it was Cyrano who loved her all along, and that she loved him. But of course, it's too late, because he dies."

"Oh, no. Sad."

"Sad is right. The girl had this great love right in front of her, she could have reached out and had it anytime. But she chose not to see it. So, by not choosing, she made her choice. Very powerful stuff."

They scooped in silence.

"So, how are you doing with the pregnancy?" Basil asked.

"Great," she said, but he could see that her mind was still on Cyrano.

"This is a very different situation you find yourself in, isn't it?"

"You have no idea," she said.

"Hard to be alone."

"I'm not alone," said Angelina, and touched the back of Basil's hand.

"You know what I mean. I never knew your

husband, but I've been told by everybody that he was a wonderful man."

"He was."

"I'm just saying, when this beautiful baby is born, and you're settled in, maybe you could afford to start thinking about that part of your life again."

"What part?" she asked warily.

"It just crossed my mind if you're leaving yourself open to the idea of suitors."

Angelina sat back in her chair and crossed her arms; she did not want to talk about this, she was still just barely used to the idea of being pregnant. But when she saw how heartfelt Basil was being, she realized that he would only have suggested it because he cared. He was talking to her the way her father might have, if he were still around, and she was smart enough to appreciate that. She picked up her spoon again.

"You could have suitors. You might already have suitors," Basil pressed on.

"I don't think so." She chuckled and patted her tummy.

"I'm just saying that every man in your life is not old like me and Eddie, or a kid like Johnny."

Her mind flashed on Guy, whom she figured Basil most likely meant, and then, funnily, on Guy running around, bending over trying to pick up all his clothes off the street, which was a pretty cute picture. Then she purposely swept the image out of her head with a giant mound of Butter Brickle and a shot of brain freeze.

"Mr. Cupertino, I appreciate the sentiment, but, believe me, that's the furthest thing from my mind right now."

"Right now, sure. Look, all I'm saying is, sometimes the best things in life are right under your nose if you just open yourself up to the possibility."

"Maybe," she said, "someday."

"Someday never comes. Roxanne and Cyrano. I'm just saying."

"Maybe those things have a way of taking care of themselves."

Now Basil smiled and sagely shook his head. "Angelina, do you expect that the perfect man will just show up and knock on your door someday?"

She bit into a big chunk of brickle and laughed. "You did."

The next day, Angelina was tending a fresh pot of red gravy on the stove. She was going to make Veal Parmigiana for dinner, to be accompanied by pasta, fresh bread, and salad. She left the sauce on low and went to put the finishing touches on the pie she had planned. Earlier, she had made a *vol-au-vent*—the word means "windblown" in French—a pastry that was as light and feathery as a summer breeze, that Angelina had adapted to serve as a fluffy, delicately crispy pie crust.

The crust had cooled and formed a burnished auburn crown around the rim of the pie plate. She took a bowl of custardy crème anglaise out of the refrigerator and began loading it into a pie-filling gadget that looked like a big plastic syringe. With it, she then injected copious amounts of the glossy crème into the interior of the pie without disturbing the perfect, golden-crusty dome. That done, she heated chocolate and cream on the stove top to create a chocolate ganache, which she would use as icing on the pie, just to take it completely over the top.

Boston Custard Puff-Pastry Pie

Serves 6 to 8

INGREDIENTS FOR PASTRY CREAM FILLING
   1½ cups whole milk
   9 tablespoons sifted cornstarch
   ¾ cup sugar
   6 eggs
   1½ cups heavy cream
   2 vanilla beans or 3 tablespoons vanilla
     extract
   6 tablespoons cold butter, cubed

INGREDIENTS FOR VOL-AU-VENT (PASTRY SHELL)

- 2 sheets of puff pastry dough, completely defrosted to prevent cracking (these are often sold in 17- or 18-ounce packages containing two 9- or 10-inch-square sheets of puff pastry)
- 1 egg, beaten (for egg wash)

INGREDIENTS FOR WHIPPED-CREAM FILLING

- 2 cups heavy cream
- 2 tablespoons sugar
- 2 teaspoons vanilla extract

INGREDIENTS FOR GANACHE (CHOCOLATE ICING)

- ½ cup (about 4 ounces) semisweet dark-chocolate pieces or finely chopped chocolate squares
- ⅓ cup heavy cream

SPECIAL EQUIPMENT

- A pastry brush
- A pastry bag or syringe fitted with a medium star tip (such as the Wilton Dessert Decorator Pro with star tip #1M)

METHOD FOR THE PASTRY CREAM FILLING

Pour ⅜ cup of the milk into a large mixing bowl and gradually sift in the cornstarch, whisking as you go to make a slurry, and ensuring that all the lumps are whisked out. Add half the sugar (⅜ cup) and the eggs to the slurry, and further whisk to completely combine.

In a medium-heavy-bottomed saucepan, over medium-low heat, combine the rest of the milk with the remaining ⅜ cup of the sugar and stir constantly to dissolve the sugar, about 2 to 3 minutes. Add the heavy cream and scrape the seeds from the vanilla bean into the pot (or add vanilla extract). (If using vanilla beans, put the vanilla pods in the pot as well.) Stirring frequently, bring to a temperature between 160°F and 165°F as measured with a candy thermometer. Create a liaison to temper the eggs by adding 1 tablespoon at a time of the heated milk mixture to the bowl while whisking constantly, until half of the milk mixture (about 24 tablespoons) is incorporated. (This will equalize the temperatures of the liquids in the mixture to avoid making them into scrambled eggs!) Pour the liaison into the milk already in the pot, and bring the temperature up again to 160°F over medium-low heat (use care in maintaining the temperature because at 170°F the eggs will begin to curdle), stirring frequently with a wooden spoon until you feel a drag on the spoon as the mixture begins to thicken. Then, cook for one minute. Remove the custard from the stove and gradually whisk in the cold butter, incorporating each addition before adding the next. Allow the custard to cool to room temperature, about 15 minutes, then refrigerate until it is well chilled, for at least 4 hours, but preferably 8 hours or overnight.

Remove the vanilla pod, if any, and discard it.

METHOD FOR THE VOL-AU-VENT

Make the *vol-au-vent* (tart pastry) early in the same day you will be serving it, leaving enough time for it to cool completely. Before beginning, completely defrost the puff pastry so it won't crack, about 45 minutes. Arrange the oven rack in the middle of the oven and preheat the temperature to 400°F. Grease the bottom only of a 9-inch Pyrex or CorningWare pie plate.

Unfold the sheets of puff pastry dough on a lightly floured pastry cloth or floured board and stretch them out so you will be able to cut two circles, using the inverted pie plate as a template.

With a pizza cutter, make a dough circle about 11½ inches in diameter (cut it 1 inch larger than the template dish all the way around).

From the other sheet of pastry, cut a second dough circle exactly along the edge of the pie plate so that the diameter will measure 9 inches plus whatever the width of the lip is, usually ½ inch to ¾ inch. Then, create a circular band of dough from this piece that is exactly the width of the lip of the pie plate (usually ½ to ¾ inch in width). Do this by cutting a concentric circle within this smaller dough round and removing the 9-inch diameter piece from the center. (Reserve the center circle as well as all the dough scraps in the refrigerator or freezer for another recipe.)

Ease the larger (11½-inch) circle into the greased pie plate so that the edge lies flat on the rim. Brush the entire surface with egg wash. Carefully place the half-inch-wide band of dough on top of the large dough circle, matching up the edges at the perimeter. Brush egg wash over the surface of this ½-inch-wide band as well. Then press the edges of the two dough pieces together and use a fork to prick *through* the dough band and *into* the accompanying round beneath it. Place in the oven and bake until golden brown, about 20 to 25 minutes. The bottom round will rise to form a dome.

Remove the pastry from the oven and place it on a cooling rack to let cool completely.

METHOD FOR THE WHIPPED-CREAM FILLING

In a large mixing bowl, combine the heavy cream, sugar, and vanilla. Use an electric beater to beat until stiff peaks form, then chill well.

METHOD FOR FILLING THE PIE

Use a thin bamboo skewer to poke small holes in 8 evenly spaced places around the dome of the cooled pastry shell and 1 hole in the center top. Fill the pastry syringe with the chilled pastry cream and pipe the custard into the shell.

Wash and dry the pastry syringe, and use it to pipe the whipped cream into the pie in the same way.

METHOD FOR APPLYING THE GANACHE
Place the chocolate in a small heatproof bowl. Bring the cream to just under a boil in a small saucepan. Pour the cream over the chocolate and let sit for a few seconds. Stir gently with a rubber spatula until the chocolate is melted and smooth. If the chocolate is not melting readily, nest the bowl in another bowl of hot tap water.

Spoon the icing as a glaze over the surface of the filled pastry (pie).

Let the icing cool on the surface of the pastry for about 10 minutes, then chill the completed pie well before serving, at least 4 hours.

PRESENTATION
Use a sharp, finely serrated knife to cut wedges of the pie so as not to crush the layers of puff pastry. Serve with coffee or espresso.

––––––––

As she was dipping her fingers and licking the chocolate out of the bottom of the bowl, she heard a tapping on the back door. It was Guy, who came bearing a small, wrapped gift. Angelina waved him inside.

"Hey," he said, "I was just passing by."

He was immediately stopped in his tracks when he caught sight of the finished pie. "What are you making?" he asked, with a detectable undertone of awe.

"Oh, that?" said Angelina, obviously pleased by his reaction. "It's a pie. I call it Boston Custard Puff-Pastry Pie."

"Oh . . . my. That looks incredible."

Guy stood transfixed for a moment longer, then remembered why he had stopped by in the first place. He took his coat off and handed her the package. "I got something for you."

"You didn't have to do that." She wiped her hands on her apron and took the package. She sat down and peeled back the paper. It was a book, *What to Expect the First Year*, by Heidi Murkoff. "Aw, you're so nice." She held it up and showed off the cover, as if they were both seeing it for the first time.

"It's supposed to be the best one," said Guy. "The gift for the woman who has everything."

She hugged the book to her chest for a second, the way she would whenever Frank gave her a new cookbook. She loved the smell and feel of a brand-new book before she cracked the spine. Sitting felt good, and Angelina reached her hands way back over her head and stretched like a cat, until her neck gave a tiny pop. She smiled and let her hands settle on her widening belly.

251

"Let's face it," she said, "I don't have every-thing. I have a baby coming, but I have no husband."

Guy pulled out the chair closest to her and reversed it, then sat with his forearms resting on its back. "That's not your fault, or the baby's."

"Who do I see about it, then? Your old boss?"

Guy shrugged. "God? He's a funny guy. 'He works in mysterious ways.' "

"That's not very helpful. Whatever made you decide to become a priest anyway?"

As soon as the words were out of her mouth, Angelina was afraid they'd come out wrong. She didn't want to make Guy feel as if she were jumping on him or prying. But she suddenly realized, she wanted an answer to her question.

"I mean," she continued quickly, "after being in the service and everything you've done, why think about the priesthood?"

Guy paused inscrutably for a moment. After he concluded one of his private conversations with himself, he started his story.

"I was an RP when I was in the service. A 'religious programs' specialist. I worked under a chaplain named Commander Stanton. He was a Catholic priest and a really impressive guy. I traveled with him overseas a few times, and you could see right away what it meant to guys who were far away from home, who were going through things that nothing can really prepare you for, how something as simple as saying mass could mean so much. 'When a chaplain shows up, it's Sunday,' he used to say.

"I was with him at a service for a marine lieutenant who was killed in action; his men had set up a field memorial with the man's rifle, his boots, his helmet, and his dog tags. Commander Stanton talked to every man in that unit afterwards, and believe me, they had some pretty serious questions for him. Somehow, he almost always came up with the right thing to say, and if he couldn't, he prayed with them and that seemed to be enough. He made a difference, I could see it. So, when I left the Marines and was trying to figure out what the heck I was going to do next, I kept thinking back to Commander Stanton. The Church has a lot of problems, but it's one of the few organizations you can join where the actual stated mission is to do some good. So, I thought, maybe I should give that a try. Maybe I can do some good."

"But you have doubts," said Angelina.

"I have doubts. I'm sure it will all work out in the end, though."

"God will take care of it?"

"He knows what he's doing," said Guy. "I like to think He does anyway."

Angelina crossed her ankles and took a deep breath. "If that's true, why would He take Frank in the middle of the night like that when the baby he wanted so much is on the way? Doesn't seem right, if you ask me."

Guy was quiet for a moment as he thought about his answer. "Maybe it was Frank's time. And now you'll have a part of him with you forever. Not just in your heart, but here, in this kitchen, or at the table, eating spaghetti with the rest of us."

She smiled at the thought of the room full of uncles her baby would be inheriting.

"So, maybe that's His gift to you," said Guy. "Outside of that, maybe the best thing we have going for us is just believing, having faith that somebody really is looking out for us, out there somewhere."

"Well, I'm glad he sent me you guys. I don't know what I'd be doing if he didn't."

Guy smiled. "Maybe God likes your cooking."

"Maybe." She got up and put the pie in the refrigerator to chill.

Guy checked his watch. "It's early. Why don't you go up and lie down for an hour? I'll watch the sauce and clean up a little. I promise not to burn the place down."

"Okay, thanks. I think I will." Angelina untied the apron that was doing a poor job of hiding her bump and handed it to him.

She was about to leave, then stopped. "Guy?"

"Yes?"

"You're a nice man to talk to. Thanks again for the book."

Angelina headed out toward the parlor, thinking that that might have been as close as she was going to get to a baby shower. If that had been it, it had been lovely.

Guy had just started water running in the sink when Angelina let out a little scream and ran back into the kitchen. Guy rushed over to her.

"What is it?"

"Oh, my God," she said.

"What? What?"

"I . . . he looks like . . . I think he's dead," she hissed in a loud whisper.

"Who?"

She grabbed Guy by the arm, dragged him into the dining room and pointed to the living room, darkening in the gathering late afternoon dusk.

The still, unmoving form of Don Eddie was propped awkwardly against the arm of the sofa. His thin and aged hands were at his sides, unnaturally stiff. His skin looked ashen and gray in the shadows, his slackened jaw drooped slightly and his body had listed at a cruel angle to one side, but he remained utterly, utterly still. Angelina was close to tears.

He was so much older and he'd looked so frail the last time she'd seen him, hadn't he, only last night? How long had he been here? She hadn't even heard him come in. *Oh, God, this can't be.* She'd failed him, too.

"Oh, no," said Guy.

Guy left her side and moved slowly across the living room. Her hand went to her mouth.

Guy looked back at her helplessly, then in dread at the silent and motionless form of their friend.

Angelina let out a heartbroken sob.

Don Eddie awoke with a lurch, Angelina screamed and Guy fell back and over the coffee table.

"Oh, my Lord!" cried Guy.

"Jesus Mary and Joseph!" cried Angelina.

"What happened?" said Don Eddie.

Overcome with frustration and relief, Angelina slammed her new book down on the dining room table.

"When the *hell* did you get in here?" said Angelina.

Don Eddie straightened his tie and wiggled up into a proper sitting position on the sofa, struggling to recover some small modicum of his absented dignity.

"Phil had to go to the dentist and he dropped me off at the curb. I come in the front door and nobody was here, so I sat down. Looks like I grabbed forty winks."

"I must have been out back when you came in," said Angelina.

Guy picked himself up off of the floor and replaced the magazines he'd knocked over when he went sprawling.

"You all right?" asked the Don.

"Yeah, thanks," said Guy.

Angelina came into the room as Don Eddie levered himself up onto his feet. He came over and took her by the hand.

"I see what happened, dear," he said. "You ain't the first. I take a nap and sometimes I look like I'm dead when I'm doing it."

"You almost gave me a coronary," said Angelina.

Her heart was slowly making the trip back down from her throat. Eddie looked forlorn and grave and badly in need of a hug. She gave him one and it helped them both feel better.

Guy stuck his hands in his pockets. Angelina started up the steps slowly and looked at them both with a weird sense of fascination.

How did I let all of these men get into my house?

Though, in point of fact, at that moment they looked more like naughty little boys who were no doubt going to get back into some sort of mischief as soon as she left the room.

"Okay. I don't want any more trouble," said Angelina. "You're in charge of each other. Come and wake me up in an hour."

When she was out of sight and they'd heard the bedroom door close, Guy and Eddie looked at one another.

"Cup of joe?"

"Sure."

Later, the men were finishing up the evening meal. The conversation had flowed easily and casually and, as it usually did when they were all in attendance, it inevitably circled back to the food. Mr. Cupertino stabbed his last bite of veal, swirled some pasta around his fork, took a last artistic swipe of the sauce on his plate and put it into his mouth.

"I swear," he said as he finished chewing, "I have never had food like this before. In my life. This woman, she makes the veal sit up and beg for you to eat it. Always, perfecto."

He made a little kissing gesture with his fingers and lips.

"And the interplay of flavors," said Mr. Pettibone, "so delicate, yet so bold at the same time. Her touch with spices . . . I'm telling you, she's a poet."

"Yeah," said Jerry, "and there's always so much of it."

That got a big laugh from Johnny.

Guy leaned in conspiratorially.

"You know," he said in a tone of cool confidence, "there's a pie coming for dessert. A custard pie."

"Don't toy with me, please," said Basil, with a little tremor in his voice.

"Yes. I saw it with my own eyes. She calls it her Boston Custard Puff-Pastry Pie."

Basil touched his napkin to his brow. He took his glass in hand and raised it to his fellows.

"Gentlemen, I am sure that this will be the greatest pie you ever have tasted or ever will taste again in your life."

"Hear, hear," said Pettibone.

"*Salute!*" said Jerry and glasses clinked.

Only seconds later, Angelina poked her head through the kitchen door.

"Everybody ready for dessert?" she asked.

The murmured assent was mixed with tangible excitement and a thrill of anticipation. Angelina disappeared for hardly a moment and returned bearing a big wooden tray filled with cut-glass dishes of Jell-O. In the weighty silence that followed, she efficiently began placing a small dish at each place.

"What's this?" said Basil.

"Strawberry Jell-O," said Angelina.

Phil and Don Eddie picked up their spoons and started eating, completely unperturbed.

It was Guy who finally gathered up the nerve to ask, "What happened to the pie?"

"What pie?" said Angelina.

Guy felt like a man trapped in a world he no longer understood.

"The pie. The Puffy Boston Cream Puffy Custard Pie," he stammered.

"Oh," she said. "I ate it for dinner."

Basil was crestfallen.

"Why?" was all he could manage to say.

"I was hungry," said Angelina.

She put down the last dish and smiled.

"Coffee, anyone?" she asked

"You ate the whole pie?" asked Guy.

Her dark eyes flashed dangerously.

"It's for the baby," she said coldly.

"Is there any left?" asked Basil.

"One piece."

"Can I have it?"

"No."

"Please?"

He'd asked politely, but she came that close to completely losing her patience with him.

"Mr. Cupertino, how can I give it to you and nobody else? Besides, I'm having it for dessert."

And she was gone.

Basil and Guy solemnly regarded the wobbly dessert in their dishes.

"The thing I'm wondering is, who's gonna' be named godfather?" said Don Eddie between spoonfuls.

They all sat and thought about that to a tinkling chorus of Jell-O spoons.

CHAPTER TWELVE

High Tea and Sympathy

The middle of February felt like the middle of the ocean to Angelina, and she pined to sight the distant shores of Springtime. It was frigid outside and had been for the past two weeks solid. The arctic cold and her condition had forced her indoors, so she hadn't even left the house for five days. She recalled a book she'd read for school by Jane Austen in which one of the characters had been in the family way, and they all referred to her "confinement." Angelina finally knew what they meant.

Things were coming along nicely, she supposed. The baby was growing beautifully, kicking her just to say "hi" any old time, day or night. She was great "with child," as any look into any mirror or reflective surface in the house could tell her, but today, she didn't feel that great. She felt cranky and huge, as if she were lugging a bowling ball around under her sweater.

She had counted every crack and every loose edge of wallpaper on every set of four walls in every room of the house. To top it all off, it was Saturday, which meant that nobody was coming over and nothing was on TV, which she didn't like watching anyway, and she was hungry and didn't know what she wanted to eat. She was burning up with cabin fever.

Angelina went into the kitchen, her only hope of sanctuary, and started building a couple of sandwiches. She toasted some Italian sandwich bread, cooked up half a pound of thick-cut bacon, sliced some tomato, diced up a hard-boiled egg, cut some razor-thin slices of red onion, laid on a couple of sardines, topped the stack with lettuce, and schmeared generous swirls of mayo on the bread. Then she made herself a big, hot cup of peppermint tea and sat down at the table for her lunch.

Just as Angelina was finishing up the last bite of her second sandwich, she heard a knock on the door. She brushed her hands together to chase off the crumbs and rushed to answer it. Even if it was the mailman, he was coming in for a cup of coffee and a piece of crumb cake, whether he wanted to or not.

"Jerry!" she said as she threw open the door.

"Hi . . ."

She pulled him by the wrist in out of the cold and slammed the door. "Brrr, oh my gosh, it's cold." She thrust her hands under her arms. "When is it ever going to end? I'm so glad you showed up. I was just having a cup of tea, but how about I make you some coffee and give you a piece of cake? I just made it for breakfast this morning, but—"

"Hold it," said Jerry, grinning. "I don't want any cake."

"You have to have some cake." Angelina took him by the arm and pulled him toward the kitchen.

Jerry laughed. "No, wait! Are you busy?"

"I am *so* not busy, it's not even funny."

"Good. Get your coat."

The sparkle returned to her eyes. "My coat? What for?" she asked eagerly.

"We're going out, you and me."

"Out where?" said Angelina, hardly able to contain her growing excitement.

Jerry stuck his hands deep into the pockets of his jacket and tucked his nose down into his thick scarf before he answered. "Well, we took up a collection, the gents and me, and I got elected as delegate."

Angelina shifted back and forth on her feet with tingling expectation. "Delegate for what?"

"We're going baby shopping."

It took her all of fifty-seven seconds to reappear in front of him, dressed snug and warm in her boots, coat, scarf, hat, and gloves. She'd even had time left over to grab a stack of oatmeal-raisin cookies from the pantry and handed him one as they sailed out the door. Just outside, a yellow cab was waiting, running the heater to keep it nice and toasty inside.

Angelina was thrilled. Her dreary day of confinement had magically been transformed into an expedition.

A short drive up Broad Street into Center City and past the showy, ornate balustrades of City Hall left them at the doorstep of the Wanamaker Building. They stepped out of the cab, rushed through the doors into the main lobby, past the great golden eagle and monumental pipe organ, but only when they were headed toward the escalator toward Infants & Toddlers did Angelina begin to fully realize that she was only two months away from her due date and hopelessly unprepared.

She had nibbled around the edges of buying baby clothes and had picked up a few insubstantial stuffed animals for the nursery, but now Angelina was abruptly faced with the unavoidable fact that she, of all people, had neglected to properly plan for everything she'd need to clothe an infant and fill up a baby's room. It was an inexcusable failure of *mise en place.*

The baby was due in April and she had decided that she was going to wait until the birth to find out whether it was a boy or a girl. As she perused the shelves for gender-neutral clothing (no monster trucks or fairy princesses), she was pleased to find that lots of the cutest items were on sale, and in no time she had collected an impressive ensemble of diminutive pants, shirts, sweatpants, sweatshirts, undershirts, tiny overalls, baby socks with tassels, turtlenecks, and T-shirts and had piled them all into Jerry's arms as they went.

"Oh, Jerry, look." She held up an adorable pair of Dr. Denton's footsy pajamas in fire-engine red with a bunny on the front.

"You think they have that in my size?" said Jerry, nodding for her to throw it on his pile.

They settled up at the register and moved on to Bedroom Furniture, where Angelina immediately made a beeline to a beautiful wood-carved crib. An unmistakable look of recognition of its utter perfection passed over her face . . . until she saw the price.

"That's the one," said Jerry.

She fingered the price tag and sighed. "No, it's too much money," she said wistfully.

Jerry came over and gently took the tag from her hand and flipped it over. "I'll tell you when we get to too much money," he said firmly. "I got orders to spend every last cent. We're getting it."

Angelina squealed before she could stop herself and gripped the railing of the crib, her head swimming with the thrill of ownership. They found a saleswoman, gave her the delivery information, and soldiered on.

Once they made it to Toys, Jerry felt that he was on more solid ground. Angelina spent twenty minutes in the educational-toys aisle, shopping carefully for early-learning toys and board books. She picked *Goodnight Moon*, of course, and a book of Mother Goose with gorgeous pen-and-ink illustrations, and her heart skipped a beat when she saw a classic reprint of *The Little Prince* by Antoine de Saint-Exupéry, a book that her mother must have read to her a thousand times. She was caught in a memory of Emmaline when Jerry came around the corner with a baseball bat, a catcher's mitt, a football, and a toy rifle, wearing a little cowboy hat.

"I'm taking a stand. It's a boy," he said.

Angelina laughed out loud. "In that case, we'd better get out of here before you find the golf clubs."

Jerry carried all of the shopping bags filled with clothes and arranged for delivery the following week of the crib, high chair, changing table, playpen, bassinet, baby swing, Winnie-the-Pooh rug, sheets, pillowcases, blankets, and comforters. Their last purchase was a dazzlingly white stuffed polar bear, nearly actual size, with a red ribbon tied around its neck that rode on Jerry's shoulders, like the MVP after a big game, as they paraded toward the exit.

"Angelina," called a voice.

They turned around and saw a familiar figure walking briskly toward them, unimpeachably turned out in a three-piece suit, complete with watch chain and a white-rosebud boutonniere.

"Mr. Pettibone," said Angelina. "I forgot that you worked here."

"I do, indeed. I'm the head buyer for the cosmetics department. What are you two up to?"

Jerry suddenly spoke up and took Mr. Pettibone by the arm. "Hey, Pettibone, good to see you. I actually need to ask you something. Could you wait here a second, Ange?"

"Sure," said Angelina.

Jerry pulled Mr. Pettibone a short way off, just out of earshot. Jerry did most of the talking as Pettibone nodded, then they both returned to Angelina.

"I didn't realize you were coming today," said Pettibone, "or I would have been certain to have met you at the door. Angelina, do you have your receipts for everything?"

Angelina patted her purse. "Yes. Jerry told me to hold on to them in case anything had to go back."

"May I have them, please? I want to apply my twenty percent management discount. I'll just run up to customer service and get you all squared away."

"You can do that?" asked Angelina.

"I certainly can. And that goes for anything else you buy, young lady. Now, where were you two planning to have lunch?"

"Hoagie shop around the corner?" said Jerry helpfully.

"Not today."

In moments, Pettibone had marched them to the elevators and escorted them up to the ninth floor, to the Crystal Tea Room. The breathtaking dining room was housed in an enormous space, with miles of tables draped in immaculate white linen, each set with a magnificent floral centerpiece, with flawless silver and glassware, surrounded by golden, high-backed chairs. The room bustled with efficient, black-jacketed waiters moving with faultless, old-world precision, ferrying dishes to and from tables, all shielded by shiny plate covers that, when swept away with a flourish, revealed sumptuous portions of tempting-looking entrées. The clink of forks and knives and tinkle of china and goblets blended together with strains of classical music played by a live string quartet on a small raised stage off to one side. The space, grand as it was, was dominated by the biggest, most magnificent cut-glass chandelier Angelina had ever seen—just looking up at it made her feel light-headed.

Pettibone took them over to the tuxedoed maître d' and said, "Gary, please meet Angelina and Jerry. Can you seat them right away? They're my guests."

Gary smiled and, with a nearly imperceptible bow, said, "Sure, I can seat you right now. Are you here for lunch or afternoon tea?"

Angelina's eyes saucered wide and Jerry laughed.

"I have a feeling, and correct me if I'm wrong," he said, "that we're here . . ."

". . . for afternoon tea, please," chirped Angelina.

As Gary was gathering their menus and checking his seating chart, Angelina hugged and kissed Mr. Pettibone.

"Mr. Pettibone, thank you so much for everything."

"Angelina, I think it's high time you started calling me Douglas."

"Douglas, thank you," she said sincerely.

He extended his hand toward the dining room. "In you go. Enjoy."

"Thanks, Dougie," said Jerry. "You're the best."

"Dougie?" said Angelina.

"Maybe you and I should stick to *Pettibone*?" said Mr. Pettibone.

"Probably a good idea," agreed Jerry as they shook hands and said good-bye.

By the time he and Angelina reached their table near the center of the room and the maître d' had held her chair and unfolded her napkin and placed the leather-bound menu by her plate, Angelina was beside herself.

"Jerry, this is so special. You guys are the greatest."

A busboy came by and poured water into their glasses. Jerry watched Angelina as she took her first sip. She was radiant.

"You deserve it," he said, "and so does that little guy."

"How do you know it's a little guy? She might be a little ballerina."

"Go ahead and paint everything blue, it's a lock. I got the feeling."

She laughed. "Oh, then it must be true."

"I'm telling you, when I get the feeling, I'm never wrong."

Their waiter came and took their order, and Angelina settled back into her satin-covered chair. "So, Jerry, you're in the construction business, right? I used to work in a construction office, you know."

Jerry leaned forward and shifted the centerpiece so that he had a clear view of Angelina as they talked. "Really? Yeah, I've been rehabbing houses. The idea is, I get them for cheap, fix them up, and sell them at a profit. At least, that's the idea. I've done three in the last year, so it's going pretty well."

"Wow. I'm impressed."

Their Earl Grey arrived, and Angelina spent some time twirling the spoon in her cup before she broached the next subject. "Let me ask you a question," she said, looking Jerry in the eye. "You've been so sweet today, when are you planning to find a girl and get married?"

Jerry chuckled as he heaped two sugars into his cup. "Nah, that's not for me. I like being a bachelor too much."

"You have something against being married?"

Jerry drained his elegant but slight china cup in one go and reached over to pour some more. "Not really, not as an institution. But . . . you know, my parents broke up right after my brother died."

"I'm sorry," said Angelina sympathetically.

"To be honest, they never got along very well."

"That's a shame."

"Yeah, it was. But, you know what always got to me? That tie."

Angelina was at a loss for a moment. "What tie?"

"My father's tie. He was a salesman, and he wore a skinny black tie to work every single day. Put it on when he got up and took it off when he went to sleep. He even wore it on weekends. And as far back as I can remember, he woke up every day and did exactly what everybody else wanted him to do—he took the whole world on his shoulders, and it wore him down, you could see it, and to me the tie was like his leash."

Jerry paused and Angelina could hear a mix of both admiration and disappointment in his voice.

"After he died a couple of years back, I was looking at old pictures of my mom and dad before they got married. No ties. I don't have one picture of my father in a tie when he was a younger guy. That spoke to me."

Angelina thought it was a funny idea, but she

could see that Jerry took it seriously. "So, you don't like ties."

"I just don't know if I'm ready to put on a tie for the rest of my life."

Angelina could see that he had given this notion a lot of thought, but couldn't help wondering if he was as certain about it as he tried to sound. "Nobody says you gotta wear a tie," she said agreeably.

"Good." He took a sip of tea.

"Except the day you get married. Then you better wear a tie."

He laughed. "Maybe. I'll put on a tie for the right girl, maybe. That's how you'll know, right?"

"Good." Angelina raised her cup to her lips to hide her smile.

Just then, the waiter arrived, wheeling a wooden cart that carried an elaborate silver tray that was resplendent with assorted tea sandwiches of every shape and size, filled with savory fish and chicken salads, smoked salmon, pastel creams and little wisps of sprouts and cress, intermingled with tiny scones, colorful tarts, and petits fours. The waiter placed a bowl of clotted cream on the table, fresh butter, and a bowl of chocolate-covered straw-berries.

"Please, enjoy," he said, and hustled away.

"My goodness," said Angelina. "Oh, aren't they pretty?"

Jerry looked pleasantly confused. "I thought we were getting a tray of sandwiches?"

"They're tea sandwiches." She picked up a miniature salmon-mousse-and-cucumber sandwich on pumpernickel and tasted it. "Ooh. That is yummy."

"I don't see any pickles or chips, either," said Jerry.

Angelina reached over for a petite wedge of rye bread with curried chicken salad. "Boys don't know anything. Eat this."

He ate it and nodded approvingly. "Wow. That's good. Eighty-three more of those and we won't have to stop for cheesesteaks on the way home."

Angelina laughed. Then she thought, maybe cheesesteaks on the way home wasn't such a bad idea.

After all, we're eating for three.

Philadelphia Tea Sandwiches

Serves 4 to 6

RULES FOR MAKING THE PLEASING
PLATTER OF TEA SANDWICHES
- Use really fresh bread.
- Provide for variety in color and taste of the fillings, and make them fine in texture.
- Use a good fine-tooth knife (which won't squash the bread) to slice off the crusts of the sandwiches after they're assembled.

BREAD COMPONENTS

1 loaf fresh white bread (every two slices of bread yield 4 tea sandwiches)

1 loaf fresh pumpernickel bread (every two slices of bread yield 4 to 6 tea sandwiches)

12 to 18 small parsley sprigs for garnish

INGREDIENTS FOR WATERCRESS/CREAM CHEESE FILLING

(*green in color with bitter finish to the sweet cheese*)

4 ounces whipped cream cheese

½ cup fresh watercress, finely minced

Pinch salt

Dash ground black pepper

INGREDIENTS FOR THE EGG SALAD FILLING

(*yellow in color with a mustardy/salty finish*)

2 hard-boiled eggs, peeled while still warm, and chilled

½ teaspoon Colman's dry mustard

1 tablespoon mayonnaise

Salt and freshly ground black pepper, to taste

Dash paprika

INGREDIENTS FOR THE BEET/MASCARPONE SALAD

(*pink with a sweet quality*)

2 ounces mascarpone cheese

One 4-ounce can beets, drained, patted dry
with paper towels, and cut fine brunoise
(tiny cubes)
Pinch salt
Dash ground black pepper

INGREDIENTS FOR THE CURRIED CHICKEN
SALAD
(*yellowish hue with a pungent quality*)
Two 6-ounce chicken breasts
1 teaspoon curry powder
2 tablespoons mayonnaise
1 tablespoon fresh flat-leaf parsley leaves,
minced
1 stalk celery, minced
Salt and freshly ground black pepper to taste

INGREDIENTS FOR THE TUNA WALDORF
SALAD
(*bits of red from the apple and a sweet flavor*)
Two 6-ounce cans water-packed albacore
tuna, well drained and finely minced
1 red apple, skin on, stem and seeds
removed, and cut fine brunoise into a bowl
of lemon juice
2 tablespoons mayonnaise
1 tablespoon walnut meats, finely chopped
Salt, to taste
Dash black pepper
½ cup white seedless grapes, quartered
lengthwise and thinly sliced

METHOD FOR THE WATERCRESS/CREAM CHEESE SANDWICHES

Mix the cream cheese and watercress in a small bowl. Season with salt and pepper to taste.

METHOD FOR THE EGG SALAD FILLING

Slice the eggs crosswise into ¼-inch-thick slices, then chop finely. Mix in a small bowl with dry mustard, mayonnaise, salt and pepper. Sprinkle the paprika over the surface of the egg salad after spreading it on the bread.

METHOD FOR THE BEET/MASCARPONE SALAD

In a small bowl soften the cheese with a fork, then use a wooden spoon or rubber spatula to thoroughly and gently mix in the cubed beets. Season to taste with salt and pepper.

METHOD FOR THE CURRIED CHICKEN SALAD

Season both sides of the chicken breasts with the curry powder, rubbing the seasoning well into the flesh. Place the chicken into a shallow pan and fill with enough water to cover, being careful not to disturb the seasoning too much. Poach over medium heat until the chicken is cooked through (the juices run clear and it is fork tender), then transfer to a utility platter to let cool to room temperature. Chop the cooled chicken finely and refrigerate to chill, about 1 to 2 hours. Mix with mayonnaise, parsley, and celery, and season with salt and pepper.

METHOD FOR THE TUNA WALDORF SALAD
Mix the tuna, apple, mayonnaise, walnuts, salt, and pepper in a small bowl. Layer the sliced grapes on top of the layer of tuna salad after spreading it on the bread as directed below.

ASSEMBLY OF TEA SANDWICHES
Spread the filling on a slice of white or pumpernickel bread in an even ¼-inch thickness, and cover with a second slice of bread (repeating as desired for each group of tea sandwiches) and cut off the crusts. If the bread has a generally square cross section, cut the sandwiches into four 2-inch triangles by making perpendicular diagonal cuts. Some bread, such as pumpernickel, may be oblong in cross section. For sandwiches made with such bread, you can cut them into approximately 6 uniform squares rather than triangles.

CHAPTER THIRTEEN

Snowbound and Determined

The sand felt warm and clean between Angelina's toes, and the heat of the sun on the back of her neck stung, but in a delicious kind of a way, the way a sip of ice-cold gin with a squeeze of fresh key lime stings on your tongue. She was sitting on a tiny spit of land, barely as wide as the street in front of her house; a crystal clear lagoon was on her left, and a broad, cerulean ocean on her right. The whitecaps danced and vied for her attention with the gulls that drifted lazily overhead. Frank's head broke through the wavelets lapping the shore and he strode powerfully out of the water, stripped to the waist in drenched, rolled-up khakis, with a bright red lobster thrashing and snapping in his hands. He dropped it on the ground; it scuttled over to a cast-iron pot that hung over the fire crackling nearby and was pulled into the pot by two other lobsters.

Frank sat down next to her. He was tan and smelled like salt and sea breezes and coconut oil. "We should have done this sooner, babe," he said as he threw his head back and winnowed the water out of his dark hair. "You wait too long on the things you're supposed to do and you miss out."

"You are so right," said Angelina.

He leaned in to kiss her.

The alarm was shrill and the sound it made was a cross between a boat horn and a conch shell being scraped across a blackboard. Angelina woke up all alone. She dragged herself out of bed with a sigh, dragging a keen sense of disappointment and of missing Frank with her, yet again. It was time to get the oatmeal going on the stove. She'd feel better when the guys showed up and she had somebody to talk to.

Once Angelina had sailed well into her third trimester, it was collectively decided that she needed to wind down, then cut back completely on cooking to rest and prepare for the impending birth of her child. The idea was announced by Gia, seconded by Tina, and passed unanimously by both sides of the table. The gentlemen would be responsible for their own care and feeding until the christening, and God willing, Angelina would resume her culinary duties after her "maternity leave."

After the big Wanamaker shopping trip, Jerry had urged her not to make a big fuss about thanking them all individually or by making a big speech or anything of the sort, because some of them had given more than others and he felt strongly that nobody should be made to feel self-conscious about it. Apparently, it was a "guy thing," according to Jerry. Although the concept of not universally expressing her gratitude went against her grain, Angelina promised to keep it all low-key and to respect his wishes. The way men related to each other was baffling beyond belief.

Angelina had been seeing an ob-gyn, recommended by Dr. Vitale, named LeAnn Fitzpatrick, an energetic, petite woman of Asian descent who'd married an Irish radiologist. She had the gift of dispensing calm, sensible, and reassuring medical wisdom laced with a generous and good-natured sense of humor. She had particular empathy for Angelina's situation, having raised a daughter on her own before her second marriage, and Angelina soon found herself relying on the doctor's advice and understanding. Angelina faithfully attended Lamaze classes for a few weeks, starting out with Gia as her coach, who was soon replaced by Tina when the exercises proved to be too hard on Gia's knees.

For the past month, the seventh of her pregnancy, Angelina had been plagued at all hours by recurring Braxton Hicks contractions, pangs of cramping and sudden tremors that mimicked labor pains, which afflicted her to the point of anxiety. She'd been assured that they were no cause for alarm, but one scary episode of false labor that had dragged her and Dr. Fitzpatrick screeching out to the emergency room at Hahnemann Hospital at three o'clock in the morning on an icy-cold winter's night had left her shaken and upset. Her doctor laughed it off and swore that she had been planning to go out jogging anyway, but after the incident Angelina felt like the jittery expectant mother who had cried wolf.

Late one morning, Angelina was working on "feathering her nest" with Gia's help, cleaning and organizing and preparing for her last full week of cooking, when Basil Cupertino unexpectedly rang her doorbell. Angelina opened the door, and she failed at first to see why he had a look of such melancholy chagrin on his face.

"Hi," she said.

"Hi," he repeated dully.

"Everything okay?"

He indicated his hands, which held a small, familiar-looking pot with a lid on it.

"What's that?"

"Soup."

"You better come in."

They proceeded silently into the kitchen and Basil placed the pot, which was still quite warm, onto a burner and Angelina turned on the flame.

"What happened?" she asked.

"Well," said Basil as he sat, "lately I've been talking a lot about the food you've been making over here. Maybe too much. You know how I get."

"How'd that go over?"

"Not so good. So, this morning, my sister made this . . . this soup. And she wants to know what you think of it."

They looked over at the pot, which let out a little *blurp* as it came up to temperature.

"What kind is it?" asked Angelina.

"Split pea with ham."

Angelina rose warily, went to the cupboard, picked out two very small soup bowls, two spoons, and ladled some of Dottie's split pea into each one. She placed the bowls at the table gently, as though they might accidentally explode if handled carelessly, and sat down.

"You don't have to do this," said Basil. "I'll just tell her that you thought it was fine."

"I don't want you to have to lie."

"I don't want to hurt the baby."

"Oh, don't be ridiculous."

Angelina made ready with her spoon. Basil got up and began nervously filling two glasses with water and ice, for emergency palate cleansing.

Gia, who had been dusting upstairs, came into the room and saw an empty chair and a little bowl of soup, so she sat right down and picked up a spoon.

"Ah, *zuppa*." She scooped up a little and blew on it.

"Wait," said Basil from behind her.

"Oh, hello, Mr. Cupertino, when did you get here?" said Gia, then she slurped hungrily.

Angelina and Basil could only stare. Gia took a

second sip. And a third, before they recovered their wits.

"Ma?" said Angelina.

"What?"

"How's the soup?"

"It's good."

Angelina took a sip.

"What's it taste like?" Basil asked her.

"Tastes like split-pea soup," said Angelina.

Basil sat and tried some. "You're right."

"What did you think it was?" asked Gia finally.

"Dottie made the soup," said Basil.

Gia eyed her bowl with fresh suspicion.

"You know," said Basil helpfully, "I watched her when she was starting to make it, and she was actually looking at the recipe on the bag that the split peas came in. I've never seen her do that before."

"Maybe she just needed some encouragement," said Gia. "You know, I thought Dottie might start feeling bad about the way you're always going on and on about another woman's cooking, Mr. Cupertino."

"Who, me?" asked Basil with a twinkle in his eye. "I'm the poster boy for diplomacy."

"Ha!" said Gia. "You talk about Angelina like she invented spaghetti or something."

"I just have trouble restraining my enthusiasm sometimes, that's all."

"Yeah, well, every woman in every man's life

wants to think that nobody else can cook for him the way that she can," Gia went on. "Angelina knows what I'm talking about."

Leaning forward, hands folded, Angelina authoritatively replied, "The power of food is second only to sex."

"That's a bold statement," said Basil.

"You should be honored that Gia and I are letting you in on it. This is something every woman knows without being told and no man suspects. Until it's too late."

"I am feeling a little surrounded behind enemy lines," said Basil.

"Think about it," said Angelina. "What if you met a woman and fell in love? Don't you think she'd want to cook for you? Maybe you'd leave us for her. Maybe she'd *make* you leave us for her. I bet I would."

"Me, too," said Gia.

"I never thought about it that way," said Basil.

"Yeah, well, I pray for you, Mr. Cupertino," said Gia. "Of all people, I think you might crack up if you had to choose between a woman and a lasagna."

The night of their last supper came soon enough. Angelina dubbed it the "Thank You Dinner" and assumed that they all knew what she meant. She served them homemade chicken and pork sausages, with fingerling potatoes and braised cabbage in individual fresh-baked bread boules. She made the skinless sausages from scratch, flavored with caraway and sage, and finished the boules by lining them with provolone. It was profoundly comforting comfort food. The meal was a big hit, and she even sent Mr. Cupertino back across the street with a pan of her lasagna, whose siren song had first called him to her table, to help ease his transition, or, as he put it, "going cold turkey."

Caraway-Sage Chicken-Pork Sausages with Braised Cabbage in Individual Boules

Serves 8

INGREDIENTS FOR THE INDIVIDUAL *BOULES*
  2 tablespoons sugar
  2 quarter-ounce packets fresh fast-acting
    yeast
  8 cups all-purpose flour, plus some extra to
    knead the dough
  2 tablespoons salt
  ½ cup melted butter plus some to grease the
    crocks
  1 pound sliced provolone cheese

SPECIAL EQUIPMENT FOR THE *BOULES*
  8 individual ovenproof crocks, such as
    8-ounce onion-soup bowls

INGREDIENTS FOR THE SKINLESS SAUSAGES

¼ cup canola oil (1 tablespoon to sauté the vegetables and 3 tablespoons as needed to sauté the sausages)

1 red bell pepper, stem and seeds removed and cut small brunoise

4 fresh sage leaves, minced

3 shallot cloves, minced

1 large apple, a firm variety such as Cortland or Braeburn, skin left on but cored and cut small brunoise

1 pound ground chicken, chopped in a food processor until smooth

1 pound ground pork, chopped in a food processor until smooth

2 teaspoons salt

½ teaspoon ground black pepper

2 teaspoons caraway seeds, 1 teaspoon left whole and 1 teaspoon ground to a powder with a spice mill or a mortar and pestle

½ cup sorghum or millet flour

¼ teaspoon cayenne pepper

INGREDIENTS FOR THE BRAISED CABBAGE

1 tablespoon canola oil

1 tablespoon butter

3 large cloves garlic, lightly crushed and minced

16 fingerling potatoes (about ¾ to 1 pound), scrubbed

1 large head green cabbage, cored and cut into ¾-inch-thick wedges
3 large carrots, peeled and cut small brunoise
1 teaspoon crushed red pepper
1 teaspoon salt
⅛ teaspoon freshly ground black pepper
⅜ cup minced fresh dill

METHOD FOR THE *BOULES*

Dissolve the sugar and the yeast in 3 cups of warm water between 100°F to 115°F, as measured with a candy thermometer (any hotter than this will kill the yeast; any cooler than this will prevent the yeast from being activated). Allow the yeast to proof. If it is viable, in about 15 minutes it will develop a foam that looks like the head of a beer. If it doesn't proof after 30 minutes, the yeast is dead and should be discarded and replaced with a fresh batch. Place the flour in a food processor fitted with a dough blade and add the salt. (This may have to be done in two batches depending on the capacity of the food processor.) Through the feed tube with the food processor running, slowly pour the proofed yeast mixture in a thin, constant stream, until the dough comes together and is a cohesive mass. Transfer the dough to a large bowl, cover with plastic wrap, and allow the dough to rise, so that it roughly doubles in volume. (This will take about 30 minutes to an hour. The dough has risen enough if you can make an indentation with your finger and it does not spring back.)

(Meanwhile, begin the sausages.)

Punch the dough down and allow it to rise again. (Allowing the dough to rise a second time gives it a finer texture. Note that it will not rise as much the second time.)

Preheat the oven to 400°F.

Grease a crock for each loaf. Divide the dough into 8 even portions, and transfer each portion in turn to a lightly floured board while keeping the balance covered. Shape each dough portion into a circle by pulling from the side and pushing the dough under and up from the bottom to form a dome, rotating to make it circular, and transfer the dough balls to their respective crocks. Repeat for each section of dough. Brush the loaves with melted butter and bake until the crust is golden brown and crispy and until the bread sounds hollow when tapped, approximately 30 to 35 minutes. Remove the loaves from oven and let cool 5 to 10 minutes (in the crocks).

While the bread is still warm, slice the tops off the *boules* and remove a sufficient amount of the interior bread to make a large enough cavity to hold some braised cabbage, potatoes, and sausages. (Reserve this interior bread for use as bread crumbs in another recipe.)

Line the inside of the *boules* with several slices of provolone cheese. This cheese will be melted to provide a tasty barrier between the bread and the braising juice so that the bread does not get completely saturated.

METHOD FOR THE SKINLESS SAUSAGES

Heat 1 tablespoon of the oil in a skillet over medium heat. Sauté the bell pepper, sage, shallots, and apple until the peppers are tender and the shallots turn translucent, stirring frequently to prevent burning, about 5 minutes. Transfer to a large bowl and let cool.

(Begin the braised cabbage.)

Add the ground chicken, pork, salt, pepper, and whole caraway seeds (reserving the ground caraway) to the cooled bell-pepper mixture and mix well.

Combine the sorghum flour thoroughly with the ground caraway and cayenne and spread onto a flat surface.

Form the meat into 1-inch spheres or patties or 2-inch-long, uniformly sized 1-inch diameter cylinders and coat these sausages with the flour mixture.

Heat the remaining oil over medium heat in a large skillet, and when it begins to shimmer, sauté the coated sausages on all sides, leaving each side undisturbed for a minute or so to allow the flour and seasonings to integrate into the surface of the meat. As the sausages finish searing, use a slotted spoon to transfer them to the pot of braising cabbage.

METHOD FOR THE BRAISED CABBAGE AND
  FINGERLING POTATOES

In a 6-quart sauté pan with a lid, heat the oil over medium heat and melt the butter in it. Add the garlic and cook until it becomes tender, stirring frequently to prevent burning, about 2 or 3 minutes. Stir in the fingerling potatoes to coat with the butter/garlic mixture. Add the cabbage, carrots, and 4 cups water. Season with crushed red pepper, salt, and pepper. Reduce heat to low and let slowly come to a simmer.

(Return to the sausages.)

Cook covered over medium-low heat until the potatoes and cabbage are tender and the sausages are cooked through, about 45 minutes to one hour.

PRESENTATION

Place each crock containing a cheese-lined *boule* onto a dinner plate. Ladle some braised cabbage, 1 or 2 potatoes, and 1 or 2 sausages into each *boule*. Sprinkle with minced fresh dill and place the top piece of bread back on each like a "lid." Arrange any additional sausages and fingerlings around the perimeter of the dinner plate. Serve the rest of the sausages, potatoes, and cabbage in the broth in a large soup tureen.

––––––––––

Every few years, March went out like a lion and dumped an avalanche of snow on the city. With its narrow streets and rows of houses so close together, South Philly was typically brought to a standstill after a blizzard, but this year's snowfall was bigger and deeper than anybody could remember having witnessed in twenty years. It started drifting down around noon, continued into the evening hours, took a couple of hours off until the next front came in about midnight, then fell in shovelfuls until the sun came up.

Angelina had been awake all night. She'd again been bothered by irregular contractions practically from the time her head hit the pillow at one o'clock. She'd spent an hour in a warm bath from four to five, trickling in hot water all the while, which gave her some relief and helped relax her enough to barely manage a catnap around six. By the time she arose at seven o'clock, the entire surrounding area was socked in. She looked out of the second-story window and the drifts were up to the roofs of most of the parked cars buried in the street. The stoops of practically every house looked more like lumpy, marshmallow easy chairs than concrete steps.

She cranked the heat up, got dressed, and breakfasted on a couple of soft-boiled eggs and toast. She had planned to work on the baby's room all day, and Guy had kindly offered to stop by to lend her a hand.

Angelina was converting her workroom into a nursery. She'd painted one wall and had even assembled the crib the day before, which was now pushed against the lone dry, finished wall. She'd put down a drop cloth, retrieved the stepladder from the upstairs closet, and had the remains of the first can of paint open at her feet.

The room was noisy because she had a fan going full blast to direct the fumes of paint out the partially open top sash of the window. Angelina was bundled in layers, two T-shirts and a thermal, topped by one of Frank's heaviest old sweatshirts to keep warm. She heard a thumping as the front door opened and closed. She had told Guy not to stand on ceremony and to come right in, to save her the trip down steps.

"Hello!" he called. "Anybody home?" She could hear his feet clomping the snow off his boots in the entryway.

"I'm up in the baby's bedroom!"

Guy came into the room, dressed in a heavy ski sweater, his face still red from the cold. "Holy cow. I just came from across the street and I lost two dogs from my sled team."

Angelina was on the second step of a short stepladder with a roller in her hand. "Thanks for coming over. I could really use the help. I have to get this room done or the baby's going to be sleeping in my dresser drawer."

"I'm glad you called me." Guy stood for a moment flexing his fingers. "Let me get some feeling back in these things and I'll grab a paintbrush."

Angelina climbed down and handed him the roller. "I'll make some tea."

"No, you stay off the stairs. I'll make it and bring it up."

He carefully dropped the roller in the paint tray on the floor and left. Angelina pressed her hands on her rear and stretched backward, momentarily taking the strain off her lower back, which was hurting her. She called after Guy, "Bring the cookie jar, too."

The kettle on the stove whistled brightly a few minutes later, and Guy was about to pour the hot water when he heard a crash and a thump on the second floor. He dashed out of the kitchen and bolted up the stairs to the nursery. The nearly empty can of paint had been tipped over by the fallen stepladder and was oozing onto the drop cloth. Angelina was on the floor with one hand on the bars of the crib, trying unsuccessfully to get to her feet.

Guy rushed to help her. "What happened?"

Angelina seemed unhurt, but kneeling beside her, Guy could see that her hands were trembling.

"I knocked over the ladder," she said. Instinctively, she ran her hands over her belly, and she shivered. Her palms came to rest on her thighs, and Angelina realized that she was partially soaked.

"Oh, my God, my water broke. I think the baby's coming."

Guy definitely did not like the sound of that. "No, it isn't time. The baby isn't supposed to come for a couple of weeks, is it?"

She winced with a shock of pain that took her breath away. "I've been having contractions all night. I thought it was another false labor, but it looks like it's the real thing."

"Okay. Okay, let's get you up and get you to the hospital."

Angelina looked at him and a feeling of perfect dread came over her, which started in her nostrils and was propelled down into her chest with her next terrified breath, like the wicked, scary feeling of walking down a dark alley in the wrong part of town.

"Oh, no," she whispered. "We're in trouble."

"What's the matter?"

"You haven't lived in this neighborhood your whole life," said Angelina, struggling to keep her voice level and calm. "With snow like this, no taxi is going to be able to even get close to the house until they plow the streets."

Guy felt the cold touch of panic rising now. "What if I call an ambulance?"

"Unless it's a flying ambulance, we're stuck here until the street gets plowed." Angelina rocked herself into a sitting position and held out her hand.

"Can you make it to your bed?"

"Yeah, help me up."

They made it to the side of Angelina's bed before the next contraction hit. It was so strong, Angelina crumpled like a candy bar wrapper and grabbed hold of Guy hard to keep from falling.

Guy's knees bent from the sudden weight of her and her fierce grip on his arms. He didn't know what to do, whether to help her straighten up or lie down on the bed or to let her sink to the floor. He was shocked by how strong she was. He felt a spasm travel through her.

When she looked up at him, her face was flushed red and tears were flowing freely. "Guy, I'm scared," she said, though so softly he could barely hear the words.

Guy's response was instantaneous and nakedly honest: "So am I."

The way he said it almost made Angelina laugh. He *really* looked scared. She suddenly couldn't help feeling brave by comparison. She sagged against him and put her head on his shoulder. He felt her warm tears seep into his shirt.

"I can't breathe. I need a tissue," said Angelina.

Guy leaned over and snagged six tissues in fast succession out of the pop-up box by her bedside like a blackjack dealer. She swabbed her nose and he helped her to sit on the edge of the bed.

"I know what I'll do," said Guy. "I'll boil water and get some newspapers."

In an effort to encourage him and make him feel better, Angelina joked, "Oh, good, the baby can read the funnies and have a cup of tea."

She had gone a sickly shade of pale while they had been talking, as if somebody had pulled a plug and drained all of the blood out of her face. Guy now stood frozen, helpless to leave without the word from her, awaiting instructions like a runner on first looking for the sign to steal.

"Call Dr. Fitzpatrick," said Angelina. "The number's on the phone stand at the bottom of the stairs."

"Good idea. You stay here."

Angelina slipped off her sneakers. *Really? Where else would I go?*

Without another word, Guy disappeared into the hallway, leaving Angelina alone in the room with the inescapable knowledge that she was about to give birth in the same bed where she had conceived. For a moment, she felt dizzy and disoriented, as if this must all be happening to someone else. She shook her head angrily and tried to focus.

This is it, Angelina, she told herself harshly, *this is as real as it gets.*

"Okay, baby," she said aloud. "It's you and me. Let's not screw this up."

She felt the baby move at the sound of her voice, and the fear snapped back at her like a rattlesnake. If things went wrong, this would be the terrible moment just before it happened that she would remember for the rest of her life.

A sheen of sweat broke out at her hairline and she felt it trickle down the nape of her neck, under her shirt, and down her back. Then, another terrifying thought struck her: Guy was going to see her without her pants on.

She gritted her teeth. Too bad, there was no way around it. *The only way to get to the other side of anything is to go through it,* she thought. And she wasn't going to do it flat on her back. Angelina stripped off her sweatshirt and suddenly felt a stabbing pain in her lower back that doubled her over. She slid down and knelt on the floor hoping to take the pressure off her spine. It didn't work.

Since she was on the floor anyway, Angelina got down on all fours next to the bed and rocked her pelvis forward with her arms stretched out like a cat's and her butt in the air—a technique she learned in Lamaze. She breathed out hard through her nose, then weathered another contraction that way, and it gave her at least some sense of control.

Guy seemed as if he had been gone for ages, but he finally returned carrying a basin filled with steaming-hot water, yesterday's *Inquirer* under his arm, a roll of gauze, and a collection of items, scissors and the like, that he'd grabbed from the medicine chest.

"Angelina!" he cried when he saw her on the floor. Guy placed the basin on the chest at the foot of the bed and piled the supplies next to it in a jumbled heap. "Why are you on the floor?"

"Please . . . don't ask questions," she gasped.

"Are you all right?"

"No!" She opened her mouth and heard herself make a sound, a loud, long animal sound of anguish. The pain was blinding, crippling. She felt as if her insides were being pried open with a crowbar. "Help me," she gasped. "I need help."

She tried to think. It was all about breathing now, wasn't it? That's all they ever talked about, the breathing, but she couldn't catch her breath. The pain was so bad.

It sliced through her again. When it finally stopped, after lasting forever, she felt something warm and wet on her chin. Guy was wiping blood off her mouth with a damp washcloth where she'd bitten her lip.

Guy peeled back the covers and helped her up onto the bed. She curled up and laid her sweaty head on the pillows. "Get clean towels . . . from the closet . . . in the hall."

At the end of the next contraction, Angelina slipped off her sweatpants under the covers before Guy returned with the stack of towels.

"Did you get the doctor?" she asked.

"No. I mean, yes. I had Dr. Fitzpatrick paged, but I got through to Dr. Vitale. His wife gave me his number at the hospital. He called 911 and he's going to try and get here as soon as he can. I told him about the contractions you had last night;

he said it sounds like you're fully effaced and it's almost time to push. Don't worry, he told me what to do."

"Oh, God . . ." Angelina tensed reflexively, grimly anticipating the next spasm.

Guy bent over and looked her straight in the eye. "The doctor told me to try and feel where the baby is. That's what I'm doing, okay?"

She nodded. Guy pulled back the covers and put his hand on her belly. His touch felt warm and confident. She didn't feel a shred of embarrassment. They were in this together.

"Know what?" said Guy.

"What?" She started panting vigorously, in and out, in and out.

"Everything's going to be fine."

"I know—"

The "know" turned into a "noooo!" and the worst contraction yet. When it passed, Angelina looked at Guy desperately as she choked out vicious, staccato breaths. "I'm not going to make it!" she cried.

"Yes, you are."

"I can't!"

"You can. Listen to me. You have to wait, then push. If you're not pushing, you're waiting and breathing, okay? Wait and breathe. I know how tough you are. You can do this. You hear me?"

"Yes. Okay," she panted.

"Can you feel when to push?"

"What?" She was having trouble focusing on what he was saying, but the sound of his voice helped.

"Can you feel it?"

"I think so. Yes, it's coming. Owww—"

Her head reared back, and an avalanche of jagged pain rolled through her abdomen and she pushed. Minutes later, it happened again. And again. Angelina was left shaking and completely drained. She wished she were knocked out or asleep. She wished it were over and done with, one way or another, she just wished it were over.

"Okay," said Guy, "that was perfect. That last one was long and slow, right?"

"I think so," she nodded weakly.

"Okay," he said, "so you know what it feels like now, right? Right?"

"I don't know . . ."

"Long and slow, like pushing on the accelerator in a car. Just ease the throttle up . . ."

"I can't."

"Yes, you can, you can," said Guy urgently. "Breathe through it, ease the throttle up, bear down, then ease it back down. You're doing an incredible job, Angelina. I mean it, you are incredible."

"Th-thanks," she gasped. The pain came again, long and slow. She tried to control it, but it was relentless, expanding and pressing against her insides like a balloon filled with scalding water ready to burst. At its peak, when it crested inside her, when she couldn't stand it any longer, she pushed with all of her might.

"Oh, my God," said Guy. "I can see the top of the head. You hear me, Angelina? I can see it, you're doing it, it's almost over."

Angelina fell back in total desperation. Lights were flashing in her eyes and she felt as if she were going to pass out. She couldn't take any more. That last one was the end, that was all she had left.

"It isn't over," she said. "No, it isn't."

"I can see the head, I'm telling you, just hang on."

"You're lying," she moaned.

Guy grabbed her hand and pushed it down between her legs. "No, I'm not. Feel this?"

Angelina started laughing. "I feel it. I feel it! I feel the baby."

She picked her head up. A tide of strength and will flowed back into her veins. She had to rally herself for the last sprint to the finish line. This little baby was counting on her to bring him into this world and she wasn't going to let him down.

As the next contraction hit, and the next, Angelina fell into a tunnel of agony and had no idea what was on the other side and didn't care anymore where she was or why. Whenever she heard Guy yell, "Push!" she tried to push.

Somewhere she found a rhythm and the power to go on. Nature was in the driver's seat now, and they had to hold on for dear life.

"Owwwww," said Angelina, and put her back into it one last time. Suddenly, she felt an enormous, thundering shudder of release.

"Oh, my Lord Holy God," said Guy. "Yes! I got it. I got it! Holy cripes, it's a boy."

Angelina fell back on the pillow, drenched and gasping for breath. Guy wrapped the baby in a clean towel and held him like a loaf of bread. To Angelina, the room looked to be the wrong shape and misty around the edges.

"How is he?" she asked. "Is he okay? Is he breathing okay?"

Guy pressed his face close to the baby's. An icy chill gripped his spine. "I don't know."

Angelina had the strength to lift her head, not much more. "What? What do you mean you don't know?" she cried, panicked.

"I . . . I can't tell."

Her heart seized, tears spilled from her eyes, and she started sobbing so hard she could hardly catch a breath. "Oh, God. Oh, God, help me, he's not breathing?" she shrieked.

Guy looked at her powerlessly, cradling the still newborn form closer to his chest. "What should I do?"

"Oh, God," Angelina said in wrenching despair, "you have to baptize him."

Her plea hit Guy between the eyes like a rock. "What? I can't."

Angelina was beyond consolation and near hysteria. "Yes, you have to! Please! Baptize my baby!"

"Let me get to the phone!"

Before she knew what had happened, Guy had laid the baby down and escaped through the door.

"Come back!" she screamed.

Instantly, Guy reappeared.

"Wait, I think I got it." A split second later, Guy swiftly but gently grabbed the baby by his ankles, lifted him up, and delivered a firm slap on his bottom.

"E-waaaaaah!"

Angelina started laughing and crying at the same time. The baby, whose little lungs had only required a jump start, was content to just keep howling. Guy managed the cord and laid the baby in Angelina's arms. The reality of her little boy and the sound of his wailing had transported her from the depths of despair to perfect happiness in the blink of an eye.

"Young Dr. Kildare," said Guy with an apologetic smile. "I forgot to smack the baby's behind."

Angelina only had eyes for the new life she held in her hands. "Hi, baby boy. Oh, you're beautiful. Yes, that's right, you just keep crying." She stroked his head and spoke softly to him.

Guy stood at the foot of the bed. He had tears in

his eyes, but he didn't turn or look away; he couldn't have if he'd wanted to because he couldn't take his eyes off her.

"Angelina, I'll be back. I'm just going to try to get Dr. Vitale on the phone."

Angelina gazed at him with an exhausted but peaceful expression. He looked as wiped out as she felt, but he had such a look of relief, accomplishment, and tender affection on his face that she took a deep, calming breath and made sure to take in the moment as completely as she could, to fully imprint the picture of him, so she could keep it in a special place in her mind's eye.

"Tell him thank you. And, Guy . . . thank *you*."

"You're welcome."

As Guy turned and walked out the door, Angelina turned her attention to the infant who lay on her quivering belly under a warm blanket of fluffy terry cloth. His little fist wiggled. Angelina offered him her finger, and he grasped at it with a baby-bird grip. His lips moved and Angelina thought she had never seen anything so delicate in her entire life. He looked alive and beautiful, and she peeked and counted ten fingers and ten toes, then moved him up to her breast and he suckled softly. With his pasted-down hair and tiny, puckered ears, he looked like a little old man. His mouth slipped off her nipple and she held him a little tighter, as much as she dared, and when she did it, she got her first good look at his face.

He looked like his daddy.

Much to Guy's relief, within the half hour, Dr. Vitale arrived, providing much needed moral support and proper medical supervision, just a few minutes ahead of the ambulance. Dr. Fitzpatrick met them at the hospital, and Angelina and the baby were comfortably ensconced in the postnatal ward by mid-afternoon. Johnny escorted Gia and Tina in, and Jerry, Basil, and Pettibone all made it to her bedside later in the day, arriving like the three wise men, bearing gifts, respectively, of flowers, a wonderfully old-fashioned white-on-white paisley bed jacket, and a stuffed mountain lion from the downstairs gift shop. Phil called in on behalf of the Don, who was laid up with a nasty head cold and so was prevented from venturing out in the bad weather. The newborn was soon brought in by the nurse and introduced all around to "his uncles," as Guy received backslapping praise for his performance under fire from every-one and a fine Arturo Fuente cigar from Basil.

As Angelina finally drifted off to sleep, she felt secure in the knowledge that she and her new baby boy were perfectly well cared for and in the company of treasured friends. She would have one hell of a story to tell him about his birthday when he was a little older. She wouldn't have had it any other way.

One month later, they were all gathered together at the baptismal font at Saint Joseph's Church. All of the men from the table were there, and Gia and Gia's friend Mary. Angelina held the baby in her arms. A picture of Frank stood on a small wooden stand by the large baptismal candle.

"Who are the godparents, Angelina?" asked Father DiTucci.

"Joe and Maria, Father."

Joe came forward with his wife, Maria, and took their place next to Angelina. Tina came up silently behind them with Johnny and they stood a few paces back, holding hands.

"What's the baby's name?" asked Father DiTucci.

Joe answered, "Francis Xavier D'Angelo."

"Francis," continued the priest, "what do you ask of the Church of God?"

"To be baptized," replied Joe.

"Receive the sign of the cross upon your forehead and upon your heart."

Father DiTucci made a tiny sign on the baby's forehead and chest, then blessed him and all those assembled.

"Amen," said Joe.

Father DiTucci dabbed his finger and anointed

the baby with oil. "I anoint you with this saving oil in Jesus Christ, our Lord."

"Amen," said Joe.

Father DiTucci took a pinch of salt from a small dish held by the altar boy.

"Francis, receive this salt, learning from it how to relish what is right and good. O God, look upon thy servant Francis, who has now tasted salt as the first nourishment at thy table. Do not leave him hungry. Give to him soul food in abundance that he may be eager in the service of thy name."

Angelina thought about salt. The most fundamental ingredient, it gave flavor, it preserved, it enhanced, it gave an essential foundation to nearly everything you cooked. She must have been to dozens of baptisms, and she had never remembered this part of the ceremony, though it must have been there every time. Maybe you only hear some things when you're ready to listen, she supposed.

"Francis," said Father DiTucci, "are you willing to be baptized?"

"I am," said Joe.

Father DiTucci lifted a cruet and let the water trickle over Francis's head and into the stone bowl over which he was being held. "Francis, *ego te baptizo in nomine Patris, et Filii, et Spiritus Sancti . . .*"

"Amen."

Father DiTucci raised his voice and extended

his arms wide. "Go in peace, Francis, and may the Lord be with you."

"And also with you."

They all responded, "Amen," and Angelina looked over at the picture of Frank, then down at the baby.

His eyes, her lips, his chin, she thought. She missed Frank for part of every day, but now that Francis had arrived, the missing had become less painful and sweeter somehow.

With the baby in her arms, Angelina looked around at her family and friends. They looked as if they were ready for a good meal.

CHAPTER FOURTEEN

Frittatas and High Finance

Life with the baby was so much fun and so much work that it could have been overwhelming for Angelina, given all she'd been through, but instead, each day that passed, she felt more energized. Even though he'd been born a few weeks sooner than expected—and under most unusual circumstances—Francis had been deemed perfectly healthy (and just plain perfect, at least as far as his mother was concerned). It took him a while to start sleeping through the night, but Angelina had never really needed a lot of sleep anyway, except when she was pregnant.

She took to motherhood like mashed potatoes take to gravy and quickly got back into the swing of things with her daily cooking routine. The thing that surprised her most was the impact that having a baby in the house had on her household budget. She breast-fed, so formula or anything along those lines was hardly an issue, but diapers were expensive, baby shampoo and soap and lotion, powders and ointments were expensive, and she seemed to be running through onesies and miniature socks at an alarming rate. And the onset of summer had necessitated the purchase of a whole new tiny wardrobe.

One unexpected benefit was having someone to talk to all day long. Angelina would start talking to Francis, and his head would always turn at the sound of her voice. He'd look at her intently with those warm brown eyes, and when he did, she often had to pause, sigh, and shake her head a little to regather her thoughts. He was the best listener she'd ever met, and she had so much to tell him.

Angelina talked and talked to that little boy, while she was giving him a bath, as she rocked him to sleep at night, when he got up in the morning, or when they were in the kitchen together, he in his rocker swing and she beside Old Reliable. She told him stories about his father, stories about his grandparents, she talked to him about recipes as she was cooking, told him some stories she'd just make up on the spot, and she spent a lot of time reminding him how cute and precious and adorable he was. She figured that there was little risk of his getting a swelled head for at least a couple more months. They even danced to Louis Prima a time or two before bedtime when the mood struck.

Gia came by nearly every day at noon so that Angelina could go shopping, and holding that baby had instantly become Gia's new favorite pastime. Angelina was glad that they all had these first months together in the summertime. They could sit outside and see the neighbors, go for walks with the stroller, or sit out back in lawn chairs and watch the sun go down over the buildings without having to worry too much about bundling up. Angelina had shed most of the baby weight by Francis's fourth month and agreed to a trip down the shore to Beach Haven with Johnny and Tina to get some sun and dip Francis's little toes into the Atlantic surf.

The men had gotten back into the dining routine eagerly, though Johnny's attendance was less regular than before now that Tina had begun experimenting on him a few nights a week in her parents' kitchen (so far with good results). The first communal meal back at Angelina's consisted of medallions of veal, with handmade pecan-stuffed ravioli in a butternut-squash sauce. She made twice as many ravioli as she normally would, correctly suspecting that they'd be ravenously hungry for her cooking.

Like a small child, Jerry was prying open each ravioli with the tip of his knife, then scooping out the stuffing and eating it separately, the way a kid would excavate the cream in the middle of an Oreo cookie. Watching him made Angelina smile. Each of the men had his own little quirks and eating habits—Pettibone concentrated intensely on his plate, hardly ever saying a word as he ate, only expounding on the meal when he'd fully appreciated it and had nearly finished; Don Eddie always took a break halfway through, "to try and make it last"; Phil was a fast eater and always looked sheepishly at his empty plate once he realized that everyone else had a ways to go; Basil was meticulous about preparing perfect bites, making sure to get all the right flavors on each forkful every time; Guy ate precisely until he wasn't hungry anymore, then stopped with perfect discipline, while Johnny cleared his plate like a Zamboni, leaving behind nothing but a pristine white dish. Tonight, every last one of the mountain of ravioli had disappeared before Angelina served up ricotta-cheese-filled, chocolate-chip cannolis with coffee for dessert.

Veal Medallions with Butternut Squash Ravioli

Serves 6 with 8 ravioli each
(48 2-inch ravioli)

INGREDIENTS FOR THE BUTTERNUT
SQUASH SAUCE
One 1-pound butternut squash
1 tablespoon canola oil
2 shallot cloves, minced

½ cup white wine (such as a Sauternes or
  Monbazillac)
2 cups chicken stock
1 tablespoon fresh thyme leaves, minced
1 bay leaf
¼ teaspoon ground allspice
¼ teaspoon ground cloves
3 cardamom pods, ground in a spice mill and
  chaff removed
½ cup heavy cream
Salt and freshly ground black pepper, to taste
2 tablespoons minced fresh basil leaves

INGREDIENTS FOR THE PASTA DOUGH
  4 cups flour
  4 eggs at room temperature
  2 teaspoons olive oil

INGREDIENTS FOR THE RAVIOLI FILLING
  1 cup shelled pecans
  2 to 3 tablespoons extra-virgin olive oil
  ¼ cup golden seedless raisins
  ⅛ teaspoon salt
  1/16 teaspoon black pepper

INGREDIENTS FOR THE VEAL MEDALLIONS
  3 pounds thinly sliced veal, cut into 2-inch
    medallions
  1 cup flour
  Salt and freshly ground black pepper, to taste

1 cup milk
2 to 3 cups fine, dried bread crumbs, as
  needed
4 to 6 eggs as needed for an egg wash
½ cup canola oil, as needed to sauté
1 stick butter, as needed to sauté
2 tablespoons fresh flat-leaf parsley leaves,
  minced

PREPARATION OF THE SQUASH

Early in the day or as many as three days before, preheat the oven to 325°F. Line a baking sheet with heavy-duty aluminum foil and bake the whole squash until a knife pierces the flesh easily, about 1 hour.

Allow to rest until cool enough to handle, then slice the squash open and remove and discard the membrane containing the seeds. Scrape out the pulp and let stand in a colander placed over a pie plate to allow any excess liquid to drain away. Purée until smooth in a food processor or blender. Retrieve 1 cup of pulp. Any extra can be stored in the freezer for a pie or other use.

METHOD FOR THE PASTA

Mound the flour in the center of a clean room-temperature work surface such as a large wooden cutting board. Create a well in the center of the mound. Crack the first egg into the center of the well and add ½ teaspoon of the olive oil. With a fork, gently begin to scramble the mixture within the confines of the well, while integrating the flour from the sides of the well as you carefully beat the egg. Once the first egg is mostly mixed in, shore up the sides of the mound again with flour, maintaining the mounded shape. Repeat the process with the 2nd egg and another ½ teaspoon of olive oil, and again with the 3rd and 4th eggs and remaining olive oil in half-teaspoon increments. Start kneading the dough with your palms, allowing the warmth of your hands to impart elasticity to the dough. Knead until you feel you have created a cohesive mass, for a count of about 400 strokes. Wrap the dough in plastic wrap and allow it to rest for about 30 minutes.

METHOD FOR THE RAVIOLI FILLING AND ASSEMBLY

Place the pecans in a blender and with the blender running, add enough of the olive oil in a slow, thin stream through the feed opening to make a paste. Transfer to a bowl and mix in the raisins. Season to taste with salt and black pepper.

Have a bowl of water handy to moisten and seal the dough. Divide the dough into thirds and work with ⅓ of the dough at a time, keeping the balance wrapped in plastic wrap to prevent it from drying out. Divide the first ⅓ of the dough in half. Use a pasta machine to gradually roll down each of these sections, successively reducing the setting on the machine until it is at its thinnest setting, and lay the sheet of dough onto a floured dough board. Spoon a rounded ½ teaspoon of the filling at 4-inch intervals on the pasta dough. Dip your fingers into the bowl of water and moisten the area surrounding the filling. Cover the filling with the other rolled-out piece of dough and press gently around the filling to seal, being careful not to flatten the filling or tear the dough. Using a pastry or pizza cutter, cut the filled dough into ravioli squares. Remove each ravioli to a floured surface, pressing the edges firmly together as you do so. Cover the ravioli with a clean (non-terry) kitchen towel and set aside for 30 minutes while you begin making the sauce.

METHOD FOR THE BUTTERNUT SQUASH SAUCE

Heat the oil over medium-high heat in a large sauté pan. When it begins to shimmer, add the shallot cloves and cook them until they turn translucent, stirring frequently to prevent burning, about 2 minutes. Deglaze the pan with the wine and allow most of it to evaporate. Then add the chicken stock, thyme, bay leaf, allspice, cloves, and cardamom, and allow the chicken stock to reduce to 1 cup, about 15 minutes. (This is a good time to begin tenderizing the veal.)

Strain the sauce into a large bowl and wipe out the pan. Whisk the pureed squash into the sauce.

Strain again into the pan pushing the squash through the sieve. Add the cream and heat through over medium heat. Season to taste with salt and pepper, cover, and reheat just before service if needed.

METHOD FOR THE VEAL MEDALLIONS

Cover a large cutting board with lengths of plastic wrap, tucking the edges under the board to secure. Lay the veal on the plastic and cover with additional lengths of plastic wrap to help keep the mess down as you tenderize, tucking the edges under in the same way. Use a meat mallet to pound the veal thin. You will have to do this in batches.

(This is a good time to strain and finish up the sauce.)

Mix the flour with salt and pepper, and spread on a flat work surface such as sheets of wax paper. Dip the veal slices in milk to moisten them and dredge them in the flour allowing any excess flour to fall away.

Spread the bread crumbs on a flat work surface. Beat the eggs in a shallow bowl and dip the floured veal in the eggs, then into the bread crumbs to coat, allowing any excess to fall away.

Heat 2 tablespoons of the canola oil over medium heat in a large skillet and melt 2 tablespoons of the butter in it. Sauté both sides of the breaded veal, leaving each side undisturbed for 2 minutes or so to let the coatings integrate into the surface of the meat and to prevent "crusting off." You will need to do this in batches, using 2 tablespoons of butter melted in 2 tablespoons of oil for each batch. Transfer the veal to paper towels to drain as you finish cooking them. Cover them with a large pot lid or aluminum foil to keep them warm. (The covered veal can be stowed for a short while in the oven heated on its "warm" setting.)

COOKING METHOD FOR RAVIOLI

Bring a large shallow pan of water to a boil.

Salt the now boiling water, add the ravioli in batches, reducing the heat and cooking gently just until the dough sets up and the filling is heated through, about 5 minutes, then remove the ravioli with a slotted spoon, transferring them to a utility platter.

PRESENTATION

Place several pieces of veal in the center of each serving plate. Arrange 6 to 8 ravioli around the veal. Spoon about ¼ cup of the butternut squash sauce over the ravioli, and sprinkle each serving with 1 teaspoon minced fresh basil leaves. Sprinkle minced parsley over the veal medallions.

One day shortly after her dining group reconvened, Angelina returned home from a last-minute shopping trip, grabbed the mail from the box, and noticed an envelope stuck in the front door marked CITY OF PHILADELPHIA. She dropped it into her shopping bag along with the rest of the mail as she shifted it to her hip and pulled out her front-door key.

In the rush of relieving Gia of her babysitting duty, unpacking the groceries, and getting the evening meal started for the men, Angelina had forgotten to open the envelope until dinner was well under way. She spied it again on her way past the telephone table and tore it open as she walked back into the dining room. Her audible gasp caused all the men to stop eating and to turn to see what was the matter as she read the yellow notice with the heading DEPARTMENT OF LICENSES AND INSPECTIONS.

It was a cease-and-desist order and notice of a $500 fine. None of the preprinted boxes were checked, but in the bottom Comments section was scrawled *Operating an unlicensed eating establishment.*

For someone who'd never even had so much as a parking ticket, it hit Angelina like a punch in the gut. She wordlessly handed the slip of paper to Basil, who read it and passed it around the table to the others.

Basil hung his head gravely and murmured,

"Bureaucratic entanglement. I should have seen this coming. I blame myself."

Angelina looked up and watched each man's face in turn as he read the paper. She had to fight back the tears welling up in her eyes. Her life had changed so much, and the thought that the magic of her little group might not last forever had been bearing down upon her more and more with each passing day. This notice was yet another unforeseen threat to the emotional bonds that had been forged at her dining table.

They were all silent for a long moment until Jerry said, "We're not an eating establishment. We're family."

Angelina felt helpless and violated, knowing that someone unknown and unseen had been spying on her, maybe even through her windows, maybe over the back fence. Not only was she being watched, but someone had actually gone the nasty extra mile and snitched on her to the authorities.

The men finished the meal mostly in shocked silence. Once they'd gone, Angelina could only clean up, settle Francis down, and take her overpowering sense of defeat to bed and try to get some sleep.

That night, as Angelina lay in bed, she couldn't help but give in to the desperate thought that everything was about to change for the worst. Why was it that no matter what she did, something always seemed to be sneaking up on her, crouching around the corner, waiting until she was at her happiest, then pushing her where she didn't want to go, when she wasn't nearly ready to go? Lying quietly in the middle of the night, her greatest fear snuggled in close and nested next to her, like a coiling serpent of doubt—that she'd used up her last reserves of strength. What if she'd used herself up burying her husband, surviving the loss of her job, cooking day in and day out for those wonderful, kindhearted men, no matter how much she loved doing it, and bringing her child into the world? A tear slipped past her ear and onto the pillow.

God, I miss Frank, she thought. He always, always had her back—they had each other's. And now that she needed him most, especially with the baby . . . her mother used to say, "If you want to make God laugh, tell him your plans." All she had wanted desperately to do was to hang on to the status quo at least until Francis's first birthday. Instead, some horrid city agency was shutting down her "operation," as Don Eddie used to say. She'd have to get a job, there was no other option. She'd have to rely on Gia or some teenager at a day care center to take care of her baby and hope for the best. Good luck and clear sailing just wasn't in the cards for her. She felt as if a noose were curling around her ankles and dragging her down into quicksand.

Off in the nursery, Angelina heard Francis crying. She sat up. She'd get up in the dark, go down the hall, pick him up, and hold him close. She'd kiss him back to sleep and never let on just how low and hopeless she felt. As she crossed the hall, Angelina thought about miracles and happy endings. *They just don't happen,* she thought. *The hand of God doesn't reach down and pull you out of the fire; it just flips you in the pan so you get done evenly on both sides.*

Angelina rode the elevator up to the eleventh floor in the office building where the Department of Licenses and Inspections was housed. Two days after she'd received the legal summons, she'd gotten a call from a woman named Hardy and was given an appointment to come in and "discuss the matter." The woman had seemed stern and unsympathetic over the phone.

Upon further reflection, Angelina had the thought that this Miss Hardy obviously couldn't afford to care about the problems of the insignificant people who were paraded before her. If she did, how would the woman ever be able to get through a single day? Angelina knew that she'd just be another in an endless roll call of faceless people who had consciously, inadvertently, or stupidly run afoul of an indifferent municipal agency, and that depressed her even further, if that was possible.

She had hardly slept a wink for the last four days. It had now been well over a year since Frank died, but she felt his absence more these past few nights than she had even just after the baby had been born. She cooked her way through the daily meals without enthusiasm, going through the motions, and she felt that the men knew it. It showed on the plate. They'd been uncharacteristically somber at the table. No doubt they felt as powerless as she did.

"Mrs. D'Angelo?"

A heavyset woman with swollen ankles called her name, breaking the haze that had surrounded her as she'd quietly sat thinking in the waiting room, which smelled of disinfectant and fusty old magazines. Angelina got up from the cold metal chair. A rip in the cheap green vinyl on the seat scraped against her skirt and pulled a knot in the gray tweed, which made her wince.

Angelina followed the woman, who trundled laboriously around the corner and down an alleyway of cubicles until she left Angelina at the entrance to the office of a severe-looking, unadorned woman who, according to the cheap sign screwed crookedly next to the door frame, was Cordelia Hardy.

Angelina took a deep breath and crossed the threshold. Miss Hardy indicated a chair with a twitch of her left eyebrow, and Angelina took it. She'd prepared her arguments again and again as she'd lain in bed awake, but they all seemed pale, unconvincing, and foolish to her now in this cramped office.

Miss Hardy finished scratching some notes in one folder, then efficiently picked up the next out of her in-box and spread it before her.

Angelina leaned in ever so slightly to try to get an upside-down peek at the papers.

"Mrs. . . . Dangelo, is it?" Miss Hardy had run the name together to make it sound like *danjelo.*

"It's D'Angelo." Angelina immediately regretted having corrected her for fear that they had already gotten off on the wrong foot.

It was as quiet as the inside of a cold oven as Miss Hardy reviewed the facts in the file. She looked up and held out her spindly hand. "Did you bring your check?"

Angelina opened her purse and pulled out the check for $500, which she'd placed right on top for this moment of relinquishment. She felt a pang of humiliation and a bleak sense of despair as she passed it across the desk. Miss Hardy took it with practiced authority. She was clearly used to people handing things over to her.

Angelina cleared her throat. "Miss Hardy, I wanted to ask you about this . . . that it says here, the part about 'cease and desist.' "

Miss Hardy looked up and held the check in front of her, lightly by each end, as if it were something that she were about to eat. She seemed to be enjoying the moment, which made the hair stand up on the back of Angelina's neck.

"You know you're not supposed to be using your house as a diner, don't you, honey?"

Angelina looked down. She thought of the guys, *her* guys. They'd kept her afloat in more ways than just financially. Each of them had earned his place at her table. They valued each other's company. They shared their problems and stories with each other, what their days were like, what they did over the weekend. Instead of dining alone day after day without the pleasure of a good meal shared in good company, they had cheated loneliness and, against all odds, they had become a family; a family that had to be defended. . . .

Angelina heard a quiet ripping sound, a whisper, really.

Miss Hardy had tenderly torn Angelina's check in half. She tore it again in quarters, then slid the pieces toward her across the desk. "Someone's interceded on your behalf. I'm revoking the fine and we'll consider the matter closed. You can go."

Angelina wanted to leave, but she couldn't move. She stared at the remnants of the check. Miss Hardy looked at her kindly, closed the file, and put it aside.

"Who?" said Angelina finally.

"Sister Bartholomew."

Angelina raked her befuddled memory for a match, but came up blank.

Miss Hardy stepped in. "At the Sacred Heart Home. She was my seventh- and eighth-grade teacher. I received a call. . . ."

The Heaven Hotel. So Johnny had told his grandmom, and old Mrs. Cappuccio had taken it upon herself to prove, once again, that nothing got by her, and frail though she might be, she could still be mighty when the need arose. She and the former Maggie O'Healy had saved the day.

"I don't say no to Sister Bartholomew," said Miss Hardy. "I doubt anybody ever has. And, yes, I do have better things to do with my time than to 'bother nice ladies who are just trying to make ends meet.' "

Angelina brushed the torn pieces of paper into her purse, and Miss Hardy stood up to walk her to the door.

"You know, honey," she said, "I wish I could promise you that this kind of thing isn't going to come up again, but I can't. Maybe you should consider getting a regular job."

"I'll . . . I'll think about it," said Angelina, reluctantly accepting that her good fortune might well be only temporary. "Thank you so much," she said, shaking Miss Hardy's hand.

Angelina walked out of the building and onto the street. It seemed like a sunnier day now than it had going in. She'd walked into that office braced for the worst and walked out now with at least the beginnings of her shattered faith restored that good things could happen when they were least expected.

She knew at least one thing for sure—some richly deserving older ladies were about to be on the receiving end of some serious pie.

Angelina was serving breakfast to a full house on a sunny Wednesday in August: Mr. Cupertino, Johnny, Jerry, Don Eddie, Phil, Guy, and Mr. Pettibone were all in attendance. As far as the guys were concerned, the storm clouds had miraculously been lifted as unexpectedly as they had gathered, and much to their relief, it was all clear skies, blueberry waffles, and sunshine again.

Angelina had set four beautiful frittatas on the table, sliced in wedges. She had topped them, in turn, with caramelized shallots and ricotta; grape tomatoes, fresh basil, and mozzarella; bacon and cheddar and broccoli rabe; and roasted garlic and grated Parmigiano-Reggiano. She had laid a cast-iron pan filled with fried potatoes on the table and placed fresh-baked, frosted sweet rolls in a basket in the middle. Everyone had been served his first helpings and was on his way to seconds, and Francis was fed and nestled comfortably in his rocking swing.

"Here you go, everybody, fresh coffee," said Angelina.

One by one, she topped off everyone's cup. She put down the pot and took off her apron, then pulled Frank's chair out at the head of the table and took his seat.

This got everyone's attention. In memory, even at Christmastime, she'd never sat down at the table with them, let alone in this chair; it had become a memorial, a sanctified place of pride and respect. The sounds of eating and sipping and the murmur of light conversation ceased. Angelina leaned her elbows on the table to bring the meeting to order.

"Hey, it got quiet all of a sudden," she said.

They looked at her and she looked back. Nobody spoke.

Angelina glanced up at the ceiling, gathered herself, and took in a quick, sharp breath. "I wanted to talk to you all since we're all here together. I wanted to talk to you about the future."

"What about it?" said Jerry.

Angelina looked at him gratefully, just for breaking their collective silence.

"First, and I think you all know this, that thing with the city scared me half to death. And, truthfully, I've been thinking more about the future since the baby was born. I mean, you kind of have no choice, right? It's not just me and the house to take care of anymore. There's a child here now and I have to be responsible and start thinking about what's going to happen next."

Basil nodded and Pettibone took a tentative sip of coffee.

"Frank and I, whenever we talked about having a baby, we always talked about doing the best for him, sending him to good schools and summer camp and even a good college someday. So, what I'm saying is, I don't think I can keep doing this anymore."

She hesitated. The room was silent and still as they waited for her to continue.

"I have a proposition for you men. A business proposition."

All eyes were on her now.

"What is it?" asked Mr. Pettibone.

"A restaurant. I want to open a restaurant, and I'm asking you all if you want to invest in it. In me."

The room fell quiet again as the reality of what she was asking set in.

"Hmm," said Basil. "That's a big step, Angelina."

"I know."

"What kind of a place are you thinking?" asked Guy.

Angelina brightened a little just talking about the prospect. "A little family place, about forty seats, give or take. I already have it picked out, Scolari's on Tenth. It's been closed for six months. I went to see it, and all of the fixtures are still there in the kitchen. It just needs some tables and chairs and a coat of paint. We could get it going in two, three months, tops."

"Have you ever run a business before,

Angelina?" Don Eddie asked skeptically.

"I've done all of the arithmetic. I know what the food costs, the rent, what to charge, how many seats you have to fill every week. And, look, this here, this is a business. Feeding you men, it's like a business. And truth is, if my father and mother were still alive, I'd be having this talk with them. Instead, I'm having it with you. So, what do you think?"

She was surprised that she seemed to have run out of things to say so soon. The pause that followed was too long for anybody to feel good about.

Basil cleared his throat faintly. "Nobody should really consider doing anything until we've seen the place."

"You'd have to see what kind of shape the place is in before you did anything," Jerry concurred.

Angelina felt as though they had shifted into holding a private conference with one another, from which she had somehow been excluded.

Don Eddie shook his head. "I don't know. The restaurant business can be pretty tough. . . ."

Angelina couldn't tell which way it was going. She couldn't seem to look directly at any of them right now, so she cast her eyes down. Maybe they had to talk about it among themselves, she thought, with her out of the room.

She started to push Frank's chair back away from the table.

"I'm in."

That was an unfamiliar sound.

"What?" said Angelina, looking up.

It was Phil.

Big Phil set his napkin down neatly on the table beside his plate. He pushed back his chair, stood up to his full considerable height, and waited until he had the attention of every person in the room, including the baby.

"I said, 'I'm in.' I have nine grand stashed away for a rainy day, and I'm throwing it all in." He looked at Angelina. "Mrs. D'Angelo, I've eaten in every diner and every restaurant this side of City Hall driving for my uncle, and I have never tasted food as good as you make. Ever. And never had it served by such a lady. It's been an honor for me to eat at your table, and I thank you for the opportunity. I'm in."

Phil sat and Angelina smiled in wonder. Then she glanced at his uncle hopefully. She didn't have to wait long.

"Hey, I never said I wasn't throwin' in," Eddie said as though he'd been deeply wounded by the very idea. "I ate at Scolari's, he couldn't touch your food on his best day."

"Truth be told, Angelina," said Basil, "I've been looking for good investment opportunities since I retired."

Jerry laughed out loud. "Hey, everybody's got to eat."

Mr. Pettibone raised his cup. "This town has never seen the kind of sophisticated fare they'll have at Angelina's place."

Johnny turned to Angelina. He looked worried. "I need to talk to Tina. I want to help, it's just that I'm saving up for the wedding and—"

"Johnny," Angelina cut him off, "I just want your reception to be the first big party at the restaurant. I'll cook up a wedding day feast like you won't believe, with the full family discount."

Johnny grinned. "Consider it booked."

"Then it's settled." Don Eddie got up and patted Phil on the shoulder with pride. "Come on, Philly. We got to go see a guy about the liquor license."

Everyone was on their feet then.

"We should go and see the place," said Basil. "Who can go now?"

"I'll come," said Jerry.

Pettibone checked his watch. "I can stop by after work."

Angelina bounced up out of Frank's chair, and making her way around the table, she kissed them all. She ended up in front of Phil, leaned her head back, reached up, and placed her hands on both sides of his face.

"Boy, for a guy who doesn't say much . . ."

He bent down and she planted a kiss on his forehead, which he shyly accepted before he dutifully helped Don Eddie into his coat.

Angelina gathered up Francis and his things

and they set off with Basil and Jerry to check out the location and tour the new space. When she got home, Guy was sitting on the front steps.

"Hey," he said.

Angelina sat down beside him with Francis asleep in her arms. "Hey, I'm so glad you're here. I was actually going to stop by to see you as soon as the little guy woke up."

"How'd it go?" Guy asked. It was easy to see that he had a lot on his mind, though that never seemed to be an unusual condition for him.

"Really great. They both loved the place, and Jerry has some ideas for sprucing it up, you know, giving it some character. Mr. Cupertino's going to start looking over the papers for me, starting tomorrow."

"I'm glad. Listen, I'm sorry I was so quiet this morning."

"That's okay. I didn't expect that you'd be able to put up any of the money. I know you're not working right now. But I wanted you to be there."

Guy leaned back on his elbows on the step. "I have a little nest egg I've been living off of since I left the seminary. I've really been trying to do some writing."

"That's good. What are you writing?"

"A novel."

"How's it going?"

"Not as well as I would like. I think I have some good characters, but they don't seem to be doing anything. They talk a lot, though."

Angelina thought about that, and the answer seemed obvious to her. "You should put somebody in peril," she said.

"Pardon?"

"Well, maybe if they're just sitting around talking, it's because nobody's sticking their neck out far enough to get into trouble. That's when things usually get interesting."

He sat thinking and she imagined that he might be mentally filing through his protagonists one by one, hanging on to the edge of a cliff by their fingernails, or being trapped in an icy ravine when a big avalanche hit.

"You could be right," he said smiling.

She felt a fleeting sense of triumph in having coaxed that smile out of him, then decided to brave it and give voice to a question that had been drifting around on the fringes of their conversation of late.

"Mind if I ask you something?" said Angelina.

"Go ahead," said Guy.

"The day Francis was born, when I thought he wasn't breathing, why wouldn't you baptize him for me? You must know how to do it."

Guy nodded. "I do. But I wasn't going to accept the idea that he wasn't going to make it. I guess I had faith that, between the two of us, we'd think of something."

"The two of us?"

"Yes."

"You know," said Angelina. "You were really there for us, me and Francis. What I really mean to say is, you were there for me."

"That was probably the best day I've ever had. The best thing I've ever done. I'd do it again in a heartbeat."

Angelina could see the wheels turning. He looked to be having trouble saying what he really wanted to say, so she laughed and said, "Yeah, but let's not, I mean, not anytime soon, right?"

Guy smiled ruefully.

She waited, but it looked as though he was going to let the moment pass. "Guy, I can never pay you back for that day, but I want you to know that, whatever you need, I'll always be here for you."

He met her eyes, and this time he didn't look away. "That's the most important thing in the world to me," he said.

She kissed him on the cheek, and he could feel her warmth and her breath close to his ear before she slowly pulled away. She hugged him with one arm and held the peacefully slumbering baby in the other.

Angelina went into the house.

Guy got up and crossed the street, with peril and things left unsaid on his mind as he made for safer shores.

CHAPTER FIFTEEN

The First Love

Angelina remembered hearing once that the lead-up to the opening of a restaurant was like the lead-up to the opening night of a Broadway play. You have to get investors, ideally the kind who put up the money cheerfully and don't kibitz too much. You need a space that's the right size and sets the right mood. You need a lot of seats. You need the best people that you can find and afford or your run will be short and not so sweet. You have to time it right—open too soon and put out a bad meal or a bum performance, and word of mouth can take you out before the critics get a word in edgewise. But you can't wait too long: every night your lights are off is a night you're not making money. You have to play to your audience: serve caviar and goose-liver pâté to a crowd that's hungry for pizza and beer, and you'll get panned. You have to play to your strengths: if you can sing and dance, put on a musical. If you're going to cook, cook the food you love. And you have to bring your "A" game every time because you'll only ever be as good as your last scene or your last dish.

With Basil's help, Angelina negotiated the lease in short order. He helped to clinch a fire-sale price on the kitchen fixtures, including a serviceable grill top and an otherwise terrific stove that was missing one burner. Of her three ovens, one wouldn't get hotter than one seventy-five, but the walk-in kept things cold and the drains all drained, so, all things considered, she was in business. Don Eddie worked out a sweetheart deal on the liquor license, as promised, and also gave her a list of a few choice suppliers and purveyors of his acquaintance who would be sure to afford her preferred pricing, fast delivery, and excellent credit terms.

Gia and Tina jumped at the chance to babysit Francis, working out a full-time schedule between the two of them in no time flat that freed up Angelina to tend to the million details involved in opening a new restaurant.

Once all the financial details were worked out and the papers spelling out the bachelors' partnership shares in the business were signed, each commensurate with their means and capital contributions, Angelina took possession of the keys to her new establishment. Guy walked the six blocks with her from the small real estate office where the last *t*'s had been crossed and the *i*'s had been dotted on the lease.

Her heels clicked faster and faster on the sidewalk and she was practically skipping by the time they reached the door. She fished the key marked FRONT out of the crinkled white envelope and held it up solemnly at Guy's eye level.

"Maybe you should say something in Latin," she said. "A blessing or something."

He paused thoughtfully. "At a moment like this, there's only one thing to say. *Bovina sancta.*"

"What does it mean?"

" 'Holy cow.' "

Angelina laughed, took in a deep breath, turned the key, and in they went. Dusty streaks of sunlight filtered through the ancient remnants of curtains that hung crookedly in the windows. She'd been in the place before, of course, but now, for the first time, she considered the space with the unambiguously critical eyes, ears, and nose of a proprietor. Guy noticed the sea change immediately.

She walked deeper into the main room with a measured step, as if testing the level, uniformity, and integrity of each board in the hardwood floor. A musty smell was in the air. Angelina bent down and drew her finger across a grimy baseboard. A thin scraping of silt came off, and she rubbed it between thumb and forefinger dubiously, like a seasoned prospector looking for telltale signs of hidden gold. She stood up, brushed her palms together, and put her hands on her hips as she surveyed the space from this secondary vantage.

"Well?" said Guy.

"This place needs a good scrubbing."

"I'm your man," he said gamely.

"Oh, no, I didn't mean you," she replied quickly.

"Believe me, you do. You have no idea." Guy chuckled as he strode to the middle of the room like a clutch-hitter stepping up to the plate. "This is going to be fun."

Sure enough, and to Angelina's unvarnished surprise and pleasure, Guy proved to be nothing less than a marvel at scrubbing, scraping, burnishing, polishing, and sanitizing every square inch of the place. He threw himself into each task with the double discipline and rigor he'd learned in both the Marines and the seminary, as if whipping the restaurant into shape were part military operation and part holy crusade. He found dirt and grease in places she wouldn't have suspected could be reached by the hand of man. He buffed the floor of the dining room to a blinding high-gloss shine. He washed the ceilings. After four days of hard work, every conceivable surface blazed with a spit-polish shine.

Nothing brought Angelina more satisfaction than a sparkling kitchen, and once Guy had finished his shock-and-awe cleaning campaign, you could have served the pope off of the floor and he wouldn't have blinked an eye.

The restaurant also brought out a whole other

side of Jerry that she'd never before seen. He took infinite care in every detail of construction with unwavering concentration and surprising creativity. Angelina discovered that he was a craftsman. Jerry put some beautiful latticework on the windows that faced out onto the street, had a friend in the cement business round out the squared stone steps to look like ascending semicircular platforms, and expanded the lintel to accommodate double wooden doors with brass handles to give the entrance a more august, but welcoming feel. He also recovered a faux electric "gas streetlamp" from a small brownstone he'd renovated up on Delancey Place and installed it near the bottom of the steps, where it shone like a beacon that you could spot from three blocks away.

She caught herself standing captivated and watching him work more than once and chided herself for being as distracted as he was focused.

Angelina frequented the restaurant-supply and overstock places on Arch Street and handpicked every plate, glass, piece of silverware, every bowl, whisk, platter, pot, and copper pan. She found a bargain on an old stand mixer and picked up a pair of classic Waring blenders, two for the price of one. Her chairs and tables came secondhand from a chain store in the Northeast that had recently gone under. She had decided to mix and match styles, which gave the dining room a fun, eclectic feel that was homey and whimsical at the same time.

Douglas Pettibone went antiquing in Lambertville one weekend and brought her back a selection of oil paintings by local artists that he had picked up for pennies on the dollar. He showed her a snapshot of a large, gilt-framed mirror for behind the tiny bar that could be had for a fraction of its original price from an estate sale in Yardley. She authorized him to pick it up the following weekend, and when it was installed by Jerry, it lent the old four-seater bar in the corner an air of old-time Hollywood glamour.

Now that the interior was nearing completion, Angelina turned her attention to the pressing matter of getting food on the plates day in and day out. She'd asked around and found a sous chef named Pepino Della'notte, who had actually worked at Scolari's when it first opened, before the son took it over from the old man. A reliable source had told her that Pepino had been the most talented cook the place had ever seen and had quit, heartbroken, when old Mr. Scolari's son started running the place into the ground, buying commercial soups and sauces, frozen steaks and hamburgers, and putting potato skins with Velveeta and Bac*Os on the appetizer menu.

According to the story, the last straw for Pepino was the day he walked into the kitchen and found them installing a bank of microwave ovens. He'd packed up his knives, turned in his apron, and walked out the door.

Angelina tracked him down through a friend of a friend and invited him to stop by the restaurant around noon the following day. As promised, Pepino walked through the swinging service door to the kitchen at precisely twelve o'clock. He was compact, even small, she thought, but she couldn't help noticing that he navigated the room with a sure familiarity, a kind of grace. His step had a lightness that boded well for smooth movement on the line in front of a stove. He removed his cap and they shook hands. His were calloused and scrupulously clean. She spotted some healed-over but professional-looking scars and burns that spoke eloquently of long, active service with sharp knives in hot places. He had olive skin, gentle, onyx-black eyes that met hers evenly, and dark hair with streaks of gray.

"You must be Pepino," Angelina said warmly.

He nodded.

"Would you like to sit and have a cup of coffee?"

He shrugged.

She poured two steaming mugs, they sat, and after a few cordial pleasantries, Angelina began to describe to him the kind of food she wanted to cook. She had a storehouse of great recipes in her notebooks and binders and explained her ideas for keeping the menu fresh and exciting by changing it up week to week. To begin with, she would focus on tried-and-true dishes that she loved to make and which she knew would turn a profit. She had a petite filet mignon planned, which she would rotate with different sauces, but she would keep lobster and lump crabmeat confined to supporting roles with fresh pasta, in ravioli and in sauces, rather than serving up whole Maine lobsters at "market price." Her Chicken Cacciatore de Provence was an upscale twist on a farmhouse classic that paired her love of exotic mushrooms, sun-dried tomatoes, and fresh herbs with eminently affordable cuts of chicken. She wanted to serve a Spiral Stuffed Pork Loin in a savory reduction with yam patties and fresh garden peas, in season, which lent itself to a marvelous visual presentation and tasted like Thanksgiving dinner all on one plate.

Angelina had an encyclopedia's worth of soups and bisques that were sure to become specialties of the house, starters of unexpected flavor and surprising complexity that she would use to set the stage for the rest of the meal. For desserts, she'd keep it simple to begin with, serving the kinds of cakes and pies that her bachelors had always loved, maybe with some nice homemade ice creams and gelati and an artisanal-cheese plate on offer.

Pepino listened to her plans quietly but attentively. She'd started off slowly, fully aware that this was the first time she had ever shared her ideas with an experienced culinary professional, a man who had most likely spent his entire adult life working in commercial kitchens.

She suddenly found herself wanting his approval and felt a surge of confidence each time he nodded in agreement. They had just finished off their second cups of coffee when Angelina popped the question:

"Have you had lunch, Pepino? Would you like to make us something to eat?"

His eyes were so dark that they seemed to catch a different light whenever he moved his head even slightly, so she couldn't be quite sure if the gleam came from amusement, his acceptance of her politely but pointedly proffered challenge, or simply a trick of the light. With the presence and dignity of a toreador, he rose, took off his jacket, and draped it neatly over the back of his chair.

Pepino took his time making his way over to the walk-in, where Angelina had stocked assorted proteins, herbs, butter, onions, carrots, and a few more sundry essentials. She saw him slip his hand unobtrusively to the undersides of the counters as he went. When he returned to the big cutting board with his supplies, he stroked the inlaid wooden slab in a way that reminded her of the way she touched her child's head one last time before he dropped off to sleep. Pepino indicated the chef's knife lying beside the board.

"May I use this, miss?"

"Sure."

He had barely washed his hands and started his *mise en place* when his face suddenly split into a big smile. "It's just . . . so clean!"

He laughed and Angelina joined in. Pepino seemed to relax then and talked as he worked, mostly about the old days at Scolari's. He didn't talk about the people so much, but about little details, cook's things, things specific to this kitchen, such as the slightly-off height of the grill, how long the fryer took to heat up properly, which racks to keep mushrooms on in the fridge so they stayed cool and dry; how he'd always liked to come in early before deliveries to check how the cleaner did the night before, make sure nothing was missed, to write his prep lists in a quiet room, to think; then once he'd seen what was delivered fresh, to plan a soup of the day, poach fat cloves of garlic slowly in olive oil for dipping at the table, blanch tomatoes, sear off his meats, build his sauces for that night's service.

As he talked, Pepino roughly diced a concasse into a stainless steel bowl, deftly peeling and deseeding three small, vine-ripened tomatoes in a blink of an eye, leaving them to marinate in extra-virgin olive oil with some brunoised carrot, parsley, and garlic. He heated butter and oil in a pan and let it come up to a foam while he quickly rinsed a dozen shrimp. He dropped the vegetables into the pan and let them cook down with a beaker of white wine while he delicately deveined the backs and bellies of the shrimp, leaving the heads undisturbed. He set a second pan on low heat, poured a light coating of olive oil and rubbed the pan with a large clove of garlic; he browned four large, bias-cut slices from a baguette. and left them to gently brown in the oil. He added a whisper of salt to his sauce, a generous grind of black pepper, saffron, a pinch of cayenne, and a dash of brown sugar. He laid the shrimp into the sauce, turned them and let them finish, then quickly pulled them out to a side plate at the precisely pink moment of doneness. He mounted his improvised beurre blanc with a knob of butter, plated the fried bread, laid on the shrimp and fragrant sauce, which he left unsieved and rustic, and sprinkled chopped scallions and parsley over everything.

Angelina poured two glasses from the remainder of the wine he'd used in the sauce, an acidic, wonderfully dry *Gavi di Gavi* from Piedmont, and they touched glasses before diving in. The shrimp were fresh and perfectly cooked. They ate them shells and all, sucked the sweet meat of the heads with relish, then wiped every last drop of the sauce from their plates with the crostini, which were beautifully crisp on the outside and moist and lacy on the inside.

When they finished, Angelina formally asked Pepino if he would like to come work with her.

"Yes, miss. I would like to. Very much."

Pepino recommended his nephews to Angelina —Tomas, as dishwasher, prep cook, and general utility man in the kitchen, and Michael, who could tend the bar and fill in as needed just about anywhere else. In addition, Angelina hired two waitresses, Peggy and Lisa. Peggy was older and more experienced and had been in the business for twenty years. Lisa had a great smile, was fresh out of school, seemed to have a great way with people and was eager to learn. Lastly, Angelina found a hostess who lived right around the corner from the restaurant, Mrs. Fielding, who had worked at the old Bellevue-Stratford and agreed to come out of retirement, partly because she had lately been looking for a way to fill her days, but mostly because she and Angelina hit it off like old comrades right away.

A week before the planned opening, Angelina was in the kitchen working out the finishing touches on a dish of sweetbreads with artichokes and Tuscan white beans when Jerry popped into the kitchen with two giant lemonades and a large paper shopping bag in tow.

"Hey, Chef," he said. "Remember when you told me you needed a clock in here?"

"Hey there," said Angelina brightly. "I keep forgetting to pick one up even though I keep looking up at the same blank space on the wall fifty times a day."

"Guess what I got. Look at this." He reached into the bag and took out a big, round, institutional-looking, old clock, with a white face and the plainest possible black numbers and hands.

"Nice. That'll do the trick."

"But guess where I got it from."

"Where?"

"It came from Saint Teresa's."

"No way."

"Yeah, really. I found it in the basement at Saint Joe's with some other stuff. It used to hang up in the library, it's marked on the back with Magic Marker. When I used to get detention in third grade, this was the slowest-moving clock in the world. I'm telling you, this thing ticked, like, once an hour."

"There's nothing wrong with that clock," said Angelina. "It's just that juvenile delinquents can't tell time."

"True. Here, I got you some lemonade." Jerry put a big plastic cup next to her on the counter.

"Thank you."

"I'm gonna go get a ladder and stick this baby up on the wall for you."

"Nice work!" Angelina called after him.

Jerry disappeared into the dining room and reappeared with an aluminum folding ladder. Angelina starting heating grapeseed oil in a sauté pan to sear her veal, while Jerry positioned the ladder under the exposed wiring for the clock fixture high up on the wall.

Angelina's focus was entirely on the oil in the pan. She wanted to start cooking when the oil was shimmering, but before the smoking point. It was just a matter of watching and practiced waiting.

"Whoa!"

Angelina looked up, startled. One of the legs of Jerry's ladder had slipped on an errant slick spot on the floor. He neatly jumped down in time without hurting himself, but the ladder clattered noisily to the floor. Angelina's hand slipped and she yelped when she burned her thumb on the edge of the blazing-hot pan.

Jerry was at her side in an instant. "Quick, let me see."

"Dammit!" Tears sprang up immediately. The burn was right on the edge of her palm, at the sensitive little web of skin where the base of the thumb joins the hand. "Don't touch it!" she cried.

"It's okay, hold on a minute."

Jerry flipped the lid off her lemonade and popped an ice cube into his mouth. He took her by the hand, pressed his lips tenderly into her palm, then moved his mouth gently against the spot.

He seemed to know just how and when to draw the warming liquid back in and when to allow the coolness of the ice to seep through and soothe the pain. In seconds, the cool kiss of it sent a thrill of relief into her hand, up her arm, to the back of her neck, and into her cheeks. She shuddered a little as the stinging ache ebbed and subsided.

"Oh."

Jerry looked up. "Does that help?"

"Yes," she said, exhaling. "That's better. I don't think it's too bad."

He brushed a tear away from her cheek. "You okay?"

"Yes. Thanks."

Just then, Gia walked in with little Francis bundled in her arms and saw the ladder sprawled sideways on the floor, an oily pan smoking and spattering on the stove, and Angelina and Jerry standing close in the middle of the kitchen holding hands, gazing into each other's eyes.

She cleared her throat authoritatively, but tried to do it without sounding too judgmental.

They both turned their heads in her direction. Jerry released Angelina's hand and starting scooping some ice cubes into a side towel.

"Oh, hi, Gia," said Jerry.

"Hi, Ma."

"Everything okay in here?" asked Gia.

Jerry handed the towel to Angelina, and she wrapped it gingerly around her hand.

"The ladder fell and I burned my hand. Jerry was just putting some ice on it for me." Angelina felt her cheeks coloring.

"Uh-huh."

"It's an old trick my mother taught me," said Jerry. "It works pretty well."

"I feel much better already," said Angelina helpfully.

Gia paused for a few seconds with the unmistakable air of a mother who has seen it all before. "Well, Francis and I went out for a walk and thought we'd stop by to see how it was going in here," she said finally.

"It's going good," said Jerry.

"It's going great," said Angelina, suddenly feeling like his echo. "Let me clean up and put something on this burn, then I'll make us a little lunch."

"Okay," said Gia. "We'll go sit at a table and wait outside."

Jerry moved over and picked up the ladder. "You do that and I'll just finish putting up this clock."

Gia took a turn around the room like a beat cop, past Angelina, who busied herself in her purse looking for Neosporin and a Band-Aid, and stopped briefly to give the once-over to Jerry, who gave her his most innocent and affable-looking smile in return.

Gia backed out of the door slowly with the baby nestled in her arms. "As long as nobody gets hurt, that's all that matters."

On a sunny Saturday in October, a small crowd was gathered on the pavement at the site of the old Scolari's on Tenth. Angelina was there, Johnny and Tina, Mamma Gia with little Francis in her arms, Don Eddie and Big Phil, Jerry and Guy, Mr. Cupertino and Mr. Pettibone; it was a family affair.

Jerry had jury-rigged a mechanism for the unveiling. Big swatches of cloth covered both the awning and the classic, hand-carved sign that Angelina had commissioned, which hung from a wrought-iron armature above their heads. Angelina held the end of the rip cord in her hand.

"Is everybody here?" asked Basil.

"We're here," said Tina, after a quick head count.

Angelina took a step forward. "First, I want to say a few words. This is the first day of the new restaurant, and it couldn't have happened without all of you. I wanted you all to be here to see the new name."

"It's got to be Angelina's," said Johnny.

Jerry gave him a friendly shot in the arm. "Come on, John, don't guess, you'll ruin it."

"Sorry," said Johnny.

"So," said Angelina, "please come for dinner as often as you can, tell your friends, tell strangers, tell everybody, starting tonight. And . . ."

"Come on, Aunt Angelina, please," said Tina. "I can't wait anymore!"

Angelina smiled and raised both hands over her head. "Okay, here goes."

She pulled on the cord and the drapes sprung

from their places dramatically and fluttered to the ground, revealing the awning and the sign, both lettered in gold on a field of forest green. The establishment's new name now stood proudly for all to see:

Il Primo Amore

They all clapped and cheered and Angelina glowed.

"It's so pretty," said Tina.

"*Il Primo Amore,*" said Basil, and tried his hand at an Italian accent when he did. "Why'd you pick that name, Angelina?"

"It's an old Italian saying: *Il primo amore che non dimenticate mai.* 'The first love you never forget.' "

Guy moved a step closer to her. "So you named it after Frank."

"And Francis," said Angelina, "and food, cooking for all of you. Cooking for my family and for you all will always be the most special to me. In fact, let's face it, it's really one and the same thing."

Gia handed Angelina the baby and she waved them all inside.

"Come on in, everybody," said Angelina. "I have some coffee and soda and sandwiches waiting. Then I have to get busy. We've got a full house tonight."

• • •

The first three weeks were nothing but hard work and kinks that needed to be ironed out, from seating charts to turning the tables quickly enough, to ovens that ran hot and cold, and all of the other endless minutiae that have to be taken into consideration simply to muscle a nice plate of food on the table. Angelina had sensibly tried to keep the menu simple to start with, but she and Pepino still had their hands full until they learned to work as a unit. Pepino had a razor-sharp focus and an unerring instinct for the sweet spot in every one of Angelina's recipes. *Overcooked* and *underdone* were not words that existed in his culinary vocabulary.

The biggest—and best—problem they had was keeping up with demand. They built up a reliable crowd almost overnight and word of mouth, which was kind, bordering on enthusiastic, spread quickly. It became a rarity when at least one person at a table of new customers didn't casually mention to Peggy or Lisa that so-and-so had sent them, or that they had felt compelled to come in to "see what all of the fuss was about."

Gia willingly and happily took charge on the home front, with Tina filling in the gaps, and before too long they, Angelina, and Francis had achieved a reliable balance of home life in relation to work life that at least showed a promise of relative normalcy for the foreseeable future.

Angelina kept Il Primo Amore closed on Sundays and Mondays and for lunches, but the business they did at dinner during the week and especially on Fridays and Saturdays was enough to make their start out of the gate look encouraging. The Don and Phil were regulars, as was Mr. Cupertino, and as investors, they all had special house accounts that took the sting out of eating out almost every night.

One Sunday in mid-November, Angelina and Francis were enjoying a lazy morning at home when Mr. Pettibone called.

"Angelina," he said, "I hate to intrude on your day off, but do you think I could stop by for a few minutes later this morning? There's something I need to consult with you about." He seemed uncharacteristically stressed.

"Sure, Douglas, of course. What is it?"

"I'll explain when I see you." He hung up without saying good-bye.

Angelina's curiosity was most definitely piqued.

Douglas arrived, quite out of breath, about twenty minutes later. He came in, took off his coat, and made sure to say a formal "Hello" to Francis. He was dressed in jeans and a knotted, old fisherman's sweater.

"Douglas, I don't think I have ever seen you wearing a pair of blue jeans," said Angelina.

He looked at her in deadly earnest and said, "These are my cooking clothes."

The story unfolded in a blur. In a nutshell, Pettibone had a date coming to his apartment that very evening, and he didn't know what to make for dinner.

"So, here is my predicament. This is a person I think I like very much, who seems to really enjoy good food, and, to be honest, I may have . . . exaggerated my cooking skills a bit."

"A bit?"

"Maybe," he said tensely, "a bit."

The only time Angelina could ever remember being this nervous about a meal was the first time she cooked just for Frank.

"I'll go upstairs and get my book," said Angelina, snapping into action. "Meet me in the kitchen." When she reached the top of the stairs, she called down, "What's her name?"

Mr. Pettibone hadn't heard her clearly and he came to the foot of the steps. "Excuse me?"

"What is your date's name?"

"Oh," he said bashfully, "Leslie."

"Well, let's make sure we give Leslie a night to remember."

Angelina brewed a pot of tea, and after a few minutes' intense discussion, they spread out at the big kitchen table and set to work outlining his campaign. She wanted to design a menu for him that was technically achievable, that she thought was harmonious and balanced, full of provocative tastes and textures, without being too showy, and for which he still had time to shop and to cook.

It immediately became apparent that the man knew his way around a cookbook. He took notes and asked smart questions and made a couple of insightful suggestions to a few of her recipes that Angelina noted in the margins for later.

She decided to start them off with a Sweet Corn Bisque with Crab "Soufflé." The puréed texture of this deeply penetrating soup gave it a rich, suede-smooth mouth-feel, and the stack of jumbo lump crabmeat mounded in the center, warm and bound together with a whisper of mayonnaise and coriander, told someone immediately that you were excited they came.

The main course would be center-cut Filet Mignon in a Grand Marnier Reduction, with Chestnut Mashed Potatoes and Green Beans Amandine. Romantic encounters had been preceded by bold yet classically inspired meals like this since Casanova's day. She advised Pettibone in no uncertain terms that the steaks needed to be done just to the brink of medium-rare, then finished with butter and allowed to carry-over cook their last five minutes for the best results.

Dessert would be a delicate Flan with Sauternes Caramel, a velvety, infused custard that finished with a rapturous, dulcet swirl of caramel on the tongue. Mr. Pettibone seemed most sure of himself when it came to desserts, but he was nervous about the soup and the reduction sauce for the filets. Angelina checked her larder and found that she had the ingredients for the soup at hand, so they decided that they would prepare it in advance together, and she also agreed to take him through a dry run on her method for the sauce before he left.

Angelina quickly concluded that if Mr. Pettibone had overstated his cooking abilities, it couldn't have been by much. As they assembled the soup and rehearsed the Grand Marnier reduction to their mutual satisfaction, Angelina could see that Pettibone had that innate, unerring sense of proportion, temperature, and timing that truly fine cooking required. When he sautéed a shallot, he waited until it was perfectly translucent and soft before he disturbed it. When he added spices, Angelina could see that his "dash" was exactly the same every time and precisely equivalent to two of his "pinches."

"Hey, Douglas, you're actually really good at this," said Angelina admiringly as he swirled his last, perfectly calibrated measure of cayenne pepper into the pot on the stove.

"I have credible skills, and normally I'd say that I'm more than comfortable in the kitchen. But I've never seen anybody put together a menu the way that you do, Angelina. The way your courses follow and build on one another, I've learned so much from you. I've had flavors at your table that pay off during dessert that were started way back at the soup course. When I first started coming here, it was like some sort of drug. And your sauces, my goodness, your sauces . . ."

Pettibone went on and on, and near the end of their session he confided a secret to her, a secret that he had shared with very few people in his life. Angelina hatched a plan on the spot that would soon allow her to reveal his secret to everybody she knew.

By the time they had finished talking, the soup was done to perfection, and Douglas seemed like his old relaxed and suavely assured self again.

"These choices are inspired, Angelina," he said as he folded her notes into his pocket. "Thank you so much. You saved the day."

She saw him to the door, the soup safely tucked away in Tupperware in a shopping bag in his hands.

"Let me know how Leslie likes everything, Douglas."

"I promise I will."

"And, oh, make sure you start the flan as soon as you get home so it has time to chill."

"Got it," he said, and sailed off down the street. Angelina closed the door, and stood beguiled by the thought of imagining the proper Mr. Pettibone falling in love.

And, she had to admit, he had her thinking about romance again.

Flan with Sauternes Caramel

....

Serves 6

INGREDIENTS
¾ cup sugar (½ cup for the caramel and
    ¼ for the custard)
¼ cup Sauternes or Monbazillac wine
⅜ teaspoon ground cinnamon
1 cup condensed milk
½ cup evaporated milk
½ cup whole milk
1 teaspoon vanilla extract
3 egg yolks

EQUIPMENT
6 individual-size, lightly buttered flan tins or
    custard cups (these should have a ½-cup
    capacity and be about 3 inches in diameter)

METHOD
Preheat the oven to 325°F.

Spread ½ cup of the sugar in an even layer in a medium heavy-bottomed saucepan. Evenly pour the Sauternes onto the sugar. (Have a tray of ice water ready into which you will be able to immerse the pot to stop the cooking.) To chill the custard cups, prepare a second roasting pan or baking dish filled with ice water so that the level rises halfway up the sides of the custard cups.

(This will also serve as your bain-marie baking vessel.) Stand the empty cups in this pan. Stir the sugar and wine over medium heat, stirring constantly until you don't see any cloudiness or sugar crystals. Do not let the syrup boil *until* you see that the sugar has dissolved. You may have to remove the pot from the heat periodically to keep it from boiling before the syrup is clear. Once the sugar has entirely dissolved, do not stir again (as this will leave crystallized streaks in the syrup). Cover the pot, increase the heat to medium high, and once it begins to boil, cook covered for 2 minutes. Remove the lid and continue to cook until you see that the syrup is beginning to darken. When it becomes deep amber, remove the pot to the bowl of ice water you have standing by. Working quickly (and carefully due to the extreme heat of the hot sugar), immediately spoon a teaspoon of the caramel into each custard cup and use the tip of the spoon to swirl the strands in a random pattern to coat the sides of the custard cups. Sprinkle a pinch of cinnamon ($\frac{1}{16}$ teaspoon) onto the bottom of each cup and place them back into the roasting pan of ice water.

Pour the condensed milk, evaporated milk, and milk into a separate medium heavy-bottomed saucepan and add the vanilla. Over medium-low heat slowly bring to a boil, then remove from the heat and let cool to room temperature. In a large bowl, whisk the egg yolks until no streaks remain and they turn lemon yellow, then gradually add the remaining ¼ cup sugar, whipping constantly until you see another change in color. Create a liaison by incorporating half of the milk mixture, 1 tablespoon at a time, into the egg-yolk mixture, whisking continuously as you go. (This will equalize the temperature to prevent the eggs from curdling.)

Pour even amounts of the custard into the caramel-coated custard cups and place them into a roasting pan. Prepare a bain-marie by adding hot water to the pan so that the water level is halfway up the sides of the flan tins, taking care to avoid splashing any water into them. Bake the custard in the oven until a butter knife inserted in the center comes out clean, about 90 minutes. Carefully remove the custard cups from the bain-marie, allow to cool to room temperature, then refrigerate for at least 4 hours before serving.

PRESENTATION

Just before serving, remove the custard cups from the refrigerator and allow them to warm up a little. Loosen the edges of each with a butter knife, then invert each custard from the molds onto chilled dessert dishes.

———

Sweet Corn Bisque with Crab "Soufflé"

Serves 6

INGREDIENTS FOR THE BISQUE
  2 tablespoons butter
  2 tablespoons canola oil
  1 large white onion, chopped
  3 stalks celery, chopped
  2 quarts chicken stock
  1 large sprig fresh tarragon
  2 bay leaves
  ½ teaspoon Spanish paprika
  ¼ teaspoon cayenne
  1 teaspoon curry powder
  1 teaspoon salt
  ½ teaspoon ground black pepper
  1 cup white rice
  2 pounds frozen sweet corn
  1 fresh lemon, micro-zested and juiced
  2 tablespoons minced fresh basil leaves

INGREDIENTS FOR THE CRAB "SOUFFLÉ"
  4 tablespoons mayonnaise
  ½ teaspoon ground coriander
  1 large sprig fresh thyme, leaves stripped off
    and minced
  1 large sprig fresh oregano, leaves stripped
    off and minced
  1 pound fully-cooked lump crabmeat, picked
    over for shells

Salt and freshly ground black pepper, to taste
1 teaspoon Old Bay Seasoning
1 tablespoon minced fresh garlic chives

METHOD FOR THE BISQUE

In a large pot, melt the butter in the oil over medium-high heat and add the onion and celery, stirring frequently until the onion turns translucent. Add the chicken stock, tarragon, bay leaves, paprika, cayenne, curry powder, salt, pepper, rice, corn, and 1 cup of water and return to a boil. Reduce the heat, cover, and let simmer 20 minutes, undisturbed. Remove from the heat and let stand another 5 minutes before removing the lid of the pot. Uncover the pot, stir to loosen the rice, and return to medium heat and cook until the corn is very soft, and all flavors are integrated, another 10 minutes or so. Discard the tarragon sprig and the bay leaves. Remove from the heat and purée right in the pot with an immersion blender, adding water if necessary to achieve the consistency of a thick soup. Season to taste with salt and pepper and cover to keep warm over low heat.

METHOD FOR THE CRAB "SOUFFLÉ"

In a medium mixing bowl, combine the mayonnaise, coriander, thyme, and oregano. Gently fold in the crabmeat while trying to avoid breaking up the lumps of crab. Season to taste with salt and pepper.

PRESENTATION

Ladle the soup into wide bowls. Scoop a rounded tablespoon of the crab mixture into the center of the soup and sprinkle with a little Old Bay Seasoning and top with a pinch of garlic chives and lemon zest. Drizzle 1 to 2 teaspoons of lemon juice and sprinkle 1 teaspoon minced basil over the surface of the soup.

———

Filet Mignon in a Grand Marnier Reduction with Chestnut Mashed Potatoes and Green Beans Amandine

Serves 4

INGREDIENTS FOR THE STEAK AND SAUCE
Four 4-to-6-ounce beef filet mignon steaks
Salt and freshly ground black pepper, to taste
2 tablespoons dried savory, ground to a
   powder with a mortar and pestle
5 tablespoons unsalted butter, cut into cubes
1 tablespoon olive oil (not extra-virgin)
1 shallot clove, minced
2 garlic cloves, minced
½ cup Grand Marnier liqueur
1 cup beef stock
2 bay leaves

INGREDIENTS FOR THE GREEN BEANS
AMANDINE
2 tablespoons butter
½ cup blanched, sliced almonds
1 pound fresh green beans, trimmed and cut
Salt and freshly ground black pepper, to taste

INGREDIENTS FOR THE CHESTNUT MASHED
POTATOES
4 large potatoes, peeled, cut into 1-inch
cubes, and placed in a pot of enough water
to cover
4 tablespoons butter
½ cup jar packed chestnuts (such as Haddon
House brand), minced, plus 4 left whole for
garnish
1 cup heavy cream
Salt and freshly ground black pepper, to taste

METHOD FOR THE STEAKS
Rinse the steaks and pat them dry with paper
towels. Season to taste with salt and pepper, and
rub the savory into all surfaces of the meat. Let sit
while you cook the sauce and vegetables.

Just before service, preheat the grill or grill pan
over medium-high heat.

Place the steaks on the grill or grill pan and
place approximately 1 teaspoon butter on top of
each filet. Grill the steaks for about 5 minutes
leaving undisturbed to let the seasonings integrate

into the surface of the meat. Flip the steaks and place another teaspoon of butter on other side of each steak and grill undisturbed in the same way.

Let rest for 5 minutes while you reheat the sauce.

METHOD FOR THE GREEN BEANS AMANDINE

In a large sauté pan, melt the butter over medium heat and cook the almonds for about 5 minutes until the butter emits a slightly nutty fragrance. Transfer them to a small bowl, cover, and keep warm. (Use this same sauté pan to begin cooking the steak sauce.)

Once the potatoes are cooked, steam the green beans until tender but still bright green, about 5 minutes.

Stir the almonds into the steamed green beans and season to taste with salt and pepper. Cover and keep warm.

METHOD FOR THE GRAND MARNIER
REDUCTION (SAUCE)

In the same sauté pan in which you cooked the almonds, heat the olive oil over medium-high heat and sauté the shallots and garlic until the shallots turn translucent, stirring frequently to keep them from burning, 2 to 3 minutes.

Deglaze the pan with the Grand Marnier and let most of it boil off, about 3 minutes.

Add the beef stock and the bay leaves and

allow the liquid to reduce by half, about 8 to 10 minutes.

(Now would be a good time to begin boiling the potatoes.)

Strain the sauce, return it to the pot, and cover to keep it warm.

(Return to drain the potatoes.)

While the steaks are resting, gently reheat the sauce without further cooking it, remove it from the heat, and gradually whisk in the remaining 2 tablespoons of cubed butter, allowing each addition to melt before adding the next. Season the sauce to taste with salt and pepper.

METHOD FOR THE CHESTNUT MASHED POTATOES

Boil the potatoes until tender, about 10 minutes. (Attend to the sauce while they're cooking.) Preheat the oven to its "warm" setting (175°F to 200°F).

Drain the potatoes well, add the butter to the pot to allow it to melt. Add the chestnuts to the pot, cover, and keep warm (while you begin steaming the green beans).

Mash the potatoes and chestnuts together by hand, then add the cream and whip with an electric beater. Season to taste with salt and pepper, cover, and place in the oven to keep warm.

(Begin grilling the meat once the vegetables are done.)

PRESENTATION

Spoon some sauce into the center of each serving plate and place a steak on it. Spoon some chestnut mashed potatoes around the steak encircled by green beans amandine. Garnish with a whole chestnut.

———

CHAPTER SIXTEEN

Crullers, Champagne, and Croquembouche

On the day of his wedding, Johnny Cappuccio rose early, at six o'clock. The house was empty and quiet, as it had been ever since his grandmother had gone to the Sacred Heart Home, but he had grown used to the solitude. Johnny had never minded bringing her meals, or helping her up and down the stairs, but he took comfort in knowing that she was safe and well looked after, that she didn't have to worry about whether he'd be there for her at a moment's notice when she needed help or, worse for her, worry that she was ever keeping him from being somewhere else that a young man ought to be.

The house, which had been his home as long as he could remember, had been paid off long ago by Johnny's grandfather, and Mrs. Cappuccio had the deed transferred into Johnny's name as soon as she decided to move to Sacred Heart.

"Johnny, I'm a little old lady and I'm not gonna last forever," she'd said. "You're a man now, and you're a good boy, and I want you to have the house. You'd be getting it anyway. Now it's settled. One day you're going to want to get married, and I don't want you and your bride worrying about having a roof over your heads. You'll thank me that day."

"Grandmom . . . ," Johnny had said, feeling the color coming into his face, "I . . . don't know what to say."

"You can say thank you today, too, you know."

He'd given her a grateful hug and she'd simply gone back to making him his favorite breakfast, bacon with hard-fried eggs and thick slices of fried Italian bread with syrup.

Jerry, Guy, and Basil had thrown a bachelor party for Johnny two nights before, with his pals from the car shop and a few other single guys from the neighborhood. They all met at the Red Rooster Tavern, shot pool, drank pitchers of Ballantine, and ate roast pork sandwiches with provolone and peppers.

Johnny wasn't much of a drinker. He liked to knock back a beer or two once in a while, though, and he appreciated having the chance to talk to the others about life in general and married life in particular.

Around 1:00 a.m., before they called it a night, Jerry, Johnny, and Guy found themselves standing at the bar over three shots of John Jameson's. They all raised their glasses in a toast.

"To love," said Guy.

"To love," said Jerry and Johnny, knocking back their whiskeys in unison.

"Johnny," called Basil, standing by the pool table, vigorously chalking a cue and puffing on a Macanudo Double Corona. "C'mere, boy, I want to show you how to sink the nine ball on the break."

"See you guys," said Johnny, and trotted off for a lesson from the master.

Guy and Jerry leaned against the bar and stood in silence while the jukebox played "Desperado." They sipped at their beers and watched Johnny and Basil shoot pool.

Guy broke the silence. "Hey, Jerry, think you'll ever get married?"

"Maybe. I really don't know. All told, my parents had a very sad marriage. To tell you the truth, I don't know if it's in the cards for me or not. You have to put a lot on the line when you get married. If you don't put your head on the chopping block, you don't get it chopped off, right?"

They nodded in unison.

"How about you?"

"I really don't know either," said Guy.

They were quiet again, each lost in his own thoughts as they drained the last of their mugs.

"Well, I'm going to head out," said Guy, shaking Jerry's hand.

"See you Saturday. Big day."

"It is." Guy threw a twenty down on the bar and waved good-night to Basil and Johnny.

"Hey, Jerry," said Guy as he was leaving.

"Yeah?"

"If you do decide to stick your neck out, let me know."

"You'll be the first," said Jerry.

Early on Saturday, with the wedding not scheduled till five o'clock, Johnny decided to go for a walk around the neighborhood one last time as a single man.

He left the house and walked through the cool sunshine to the corner park where he had spotted Tina for the first time, when she was seventeen and he was twenty. Since then, he'd never looked at another girl, and he'd never looked at that park the same way again.

As he walked down past Saint Joseph's, he remembered how he used to sneak a peek at her in church. He thought back to the first time that he had perfectly timed it so that they ended up walking out of mass together and had continued on down the steps and all the way to the steps in front of her house, which was in the opposite direction from his. The first time hadn't been the last.

Johnny stopped in at Toscani's Bakery and ordered two French crullers. Tina had worked the counter one summer, and Johnny made sure he stopped by and ordered the same thing every day until she went back to school. She noticed all right, and more often than not, he'd find an extra cruller or a chocolate éclair in his bag.

He walked for another hour, and the neighborhood was full of memories of Tina, memories of Tina and him and of things that reminded him of Tina. When it was getting late and he walked past Angelina's house on his way back, he realized that it was when he'd started going to Mrs. D'Angelo's for his meals that something had come over the two of them. It was as if somebody had whispered "Yes" in both of their ears at the same time.

He got home, made sure his bag was packed for their trip to the Poconos, and put on his tux. At three o'clock, Jerry, his best man, similarly attired, rapped on the door to pick him up.

Johnny had been thinking about it all day, and he could hardly wait until he and Tina were married.

And so they were.

When the pictures were taken after the service, Tina arranged for a special photo to be taken of Don Eddie, Mr. Pettibone, Basil, Johnny, Phil, Jerry, and Guy, the four tallest in the back, three down in the front, all beaming like proud uncles in their best suits and biggest smiles. She later had the picture framed with a simple brass plate affixed to the front that read THE BACHELORS' CLUB, as a thank-you to Angelina, who hung it up in her kitchen at home next to Old Reliable.

The reception was held at the big room next door to the restaurant, a nice open space that the landlord rented out for parties and catered affairs. With easy access to the kitchen through Il Primo's dining room, service went on like clockwork. Angelina had hired a couple of extra waitresses and busboys for the evening, since a little over sixty people were expected. They began to filter in around six thirty, helped themselves to drinks and champagne, and nibbled at the crudités and antipasto, the platters of imported cheeses and warming trays of hot hors d'oeuvres that Angelina had strategically laid out around the room. A friend of Tina's who had graduated from the University of the Arts carved an ice sculpture of two doves, which Angelina surrounded with mounds and mounds of chilled shrimp, at Jerry's request.

He'd given Angelina an amazingly detailed account of seeing a "mountain of shrimp" for the first time at a family wedding when he was a little kid. His father had told him that it meant good luck for the bride and groom, and Jerry spoke so fondly of the memory that Angelina decided that she'd have to try to re-create it especially for him.

Tina and Johnny had hired a DJ instead of a live band, although they had paid for a violinist to wander during dinner. It wasn't a big crowd, but everyone who had been invited was either a good friend or family to the bride and groom, so the crowd all wished them the very best, which is how a wedding reception should be.

The sit-down meal had started at seven, with Wine-Poached Bay Scallop Tartlets, delicate tiny scallops bound with a light cheese sauce in pastry, the perfect opening bite to go with the champagne toast.

Pepino and Tomas were plating the salad course, a traditional Spinach and Bacon Salad with a Warm Honey and Balsamic Dressing, when Angelina stopped for a quick look over Pepino's shoulder.

"How's our new pastry chef doing, Pepino?"

"Looking good, Chef. The cream puffs look beautiful, like nothing I've ever seen before. *Magnifico!*"

Just then, Basil stuck his head in the kitchen. "Angelina," he called, "you have to come out for a minute. They're doing the toast."

"Coming!" she cried, untying her long, blue apron and hurrying to the dining room.

The party was in full swing. Johnny and Tina sat blissfully aglow at the head table, flanked by Tina's maid of honor, Alicia; her parents, Joe and Maria; Mrs. Cappuccio; Father DiTucci; and Sister Bartholomew, who reminded Angelina more than anyone else of Harry Truman in a nun's habit, with a campaigning politician's charm to boot.

At the table closest to the front, Mamma Gia sat beside Guy, who was holding Francis on his lap. Angelina blew them all a kiss as she hurried by. Don Eddie rose to his feet and came around the table to Angelina with two glasses of champagne in his hands.

"Don Eddie, happy wedding day!" she said as she kissed him and took a glass.

Eddie clearly had a little glow on himself. "Happy, happy, Angelina," he said loudly. "It's a beautiful place and a beautiful bride. What a day, huh?"

"That was so nice of you to spring for the champagne."

He waved off her thanks modestly. "It's nothing, they're good kids. Sometimes I get lucky and get a good deal. Was four crates enough?"

Angelina laughed. "Twenty-four cases of champagne for sixty people? That's about four bottles per person. Yeah, I think four crates was enough."

Basil caught Jerry's attention and pointed to Angelina, giving him the high sign and letting him know that Basil had succeeded in prying her out of the kitchen. Jerry took his fork and started tapping the side of his water glass, then everybody started clinking and shouts rang out for Johnny to kiss his bride, which he cheerfully did.

Jerry called for quiet. "Okay, everybody, listen up. First off, let's give thanks. Thanks to God for the beautiful weather, and thanks for the chance to be here together with Johnny and Tina on their big day. Father DiTucci?"

Father DiTucci got up and led them in the Lord's Prayer, then blessed those gathered, as well as the newlyweds, before turning the floor back over to the best man.

"Thanks, Father," said Jerry. "My dad, rest in peace, used to tell me that the secret to a good marriage is a sense of humor and a short memory. He didn't have either one, but that's another story."

That got a nice laugh.

"I had a bunch of thoughts I wrote down about marriage, but I don't think I'm going to share them, because I think I figured something out looking at Johnny and Tina today at the church. One thing that even I can tell, just by the way they look at each other, is that they'll always take care of one another. And that's all that counts. Good times come and hard times eventually go away, but as long as you take care of each other, nothing can stop you. And nothing ever will." Jerry raised his glass. "And if you ever need backup, we'll all be here for you. To Johnny and Tina! *Salute!*"

Cheers and applause, glassware chimed, Tina blushed and squeezed Johnny's hand, and the first wave of Don Eddie's ocean of champagne disappeared in a tide of good wishes.

Angelina ran to the table, kissed the bride and groom, hugged the best man, and ran back toward the kitchen. The DJ played "Cherish" by the Association, and Johnny and Tina got up for their first dance.

Guy had handed the baby off to Gia, and he and Basil got up at the same time to congratulate Jerry on a job well done.

"Very nice, young man," said Basil, "very nice."

Guy patted Jerry on the back and they shook hands. "I think you got it just right," said Guy.

"Thanks," said Jerry. "I did have a bunch of stuff written down—jokes mostly. But that just kind of came to me and it felt right, so I went with it."

"They'll remember that one," said Basil. "Came from the heart."

Jerry drank from his champagne flute and watched Angelina cross the room and reenter the kitchen. "Angelina looks great, doesn't she?" he said, then added quickly, "I guess I haven't seen her in a while. You guys either, for that matter."

"They kind of busted up that old gang of ours, didn't they?" said Guy.

"How's she doing with the baby?" asked Jerry.

"Very well," said Basil. "He's growing like a weed."

"Does she mention me at all?" said Jerry.

Guy took a sip from his glass. Basil looked at them both. Guy looked as if he wanted to be someplace else, and Jerry looked like a school kid waiting to get a bad test paper handed back to him.

"Um, sure," said Basil. "Just the other day, she asked me if I knew what you've been up to."

"I've been busy," Jerry said a touch too casually. "But it must be nice for you two, being right across the street and all."

Basil rolled his finger around the rim of his glass. It made a little ringing sound.

"I guess you're over there all the time," Jerry said to Guy.

Guy looked at Basil and shifted on his feet. "Not so much. I mean, not really."

"Jerry, you should drop by more often," offered Basil. "She's doing a wonderful job with the restaurant. And I'm sure she'd like to see more of you."

"I should go and see her," said Jerry, as if thinking aloud. "I mean, what am I waiting for, an engraved invitation? It's just that she's so busy with this place and with Francis, I'd hate to intrude."

"You definitely wouldn't be intruding," Basil reassured him, then discreetly nudged his nephew.

"Definitely not," Guy added, as he finished off his drink.

Jerry laughed. "Listen to me, I sound like a

teenager. I'm going to go and see if Gia wants to dance. Catch you later."

As Jerry walked off, Basil gave Guy a sphinx-like look.

"What?" asked Guy.

Basil just shook his head and went in search of a dance partner of his own.

As Lisa and Peggy were efficiently picking up salad plates and disappearing, then reappearing, through the swinging kitchen doors, Angelina was sweating the count, which had split almost evenly among the three entrées: Gorgonzola Beef Tenderloin in a Barolo Reduction, Toasted-Nut Chicken Breasts with Dried-Fruit Wild Rice and Amaretto Sauce, and Pistachio-Crusted Salmon with a Cointreau Glaze and Cranberries. Everybody was getting Vegetables Julienne, and the steak and the fish were accompanied by a Gnocchi Soufflé.

"The gnocchi dough is perfect, Pepino," Angelina said. "How're we doing on the salmon?"

"Searing off the last of it, Chef," called Pepino. "Steaks are done, chicken's done. We're right on time, miss."

They cranked for the next forty minutes and knocked out sixty-plus plates that were each as pretty as a picture on a cookbook cover. Angelina turned her head when the music suddenly got louder. Basil stood in the open doorway calling her name. She could see by the look on his face that he had his dancing shoes on.

"Angelina, my darling, may I have this dance?"

She laughed. "Can't, I'm busy!"

Pepino gave her a nudge toward the door. "Go on, miss. Everything's nearly done here. You can come back when we plate dessert. Go out and have a dance."

"You sure?" asked Angelina.

"Positive, Chef," Pepino said with a grin. "Go!"

"Okay. Thanks, Pepino."

Angelina wiped her hands, took off her apron, and followed Basil through the door. She felt self-conscious for all of two seconds out among the guests in her chef's jacket, but relaxed as soon as the music played and Basil took her for a turn around the floor. He really was a good dancer.

"One dance," she said, smiling. "Then I have to get back into my kitchen."

"How does it feel to say 'my kitchen' as a professional chef?" he asked as they swayed together in time.

"Feels great. You know, I don't think I ever would have made it this far without you all. You guys have been so great, especially when it came to buying everything for the baby. That day Jerry took me to pick out the crib and clothes and everything else, and told me that you all chipped in, I could have cried . . . I still might."

Basil raised an eyebrow, but when Angelina rested her head on his shoulder, he couldn't seem to say a word.

Dottie chose that moment to stumble by, with her fourth glass of champagne in hand, and grabbed Angelina by the shoulder. "Angelina! Why are you dancing with this old man? You should be dancing with somebody young and handsome!"

Basil pretended outrage and Angelina pulled him closer. "Dottie, who could be more handsome than your brother? Basil, take me in your arms!"

Dottie laughed, having already set her sights on another target, and went reeling happily away. Basil and Angelina continued dancing.

"That is the first time you have ever called me Basil."

"Well, we're business partners now," said Angelina, "so if it's okay with you . . ."

"It most certainly is. I wouldn't have it any other way. Listen, by the way, Dottie and I were wondering, what are your plans for the Christmas holidays?"

Angelina looked out at the other couples on the floor. "I'm hoping we'll be busy right up till Christmas week. We're taking a lot of reservations. Then I plan to spend as much time as possible with Francis."

"Why don't you come to us on Christmas Day? Dottie and I would love to host you and Francis," said Basil.

"And Guy?"

"He may be there, too."

"Thanks," she said. "But I don't know. I might just stay home with the baby, on my own—be by ourselves, peace and quiet."

Basil frowned. "Angelina, that doesn't sound like you at all."

"I'll let you know, okay? I need to think about it."

The song came to an end and Basil dipped her gracefully. As she was thanking him for the dance, she saw Pepino's face in the window of the kitchen door trying to catch her eye.

"Wait," she said suddenly, signaling back with a thumbs-up sign. "I have to make an announcement."

Angelina grabbed the microphone from the DJ and moved to the middle of the dance floor and waved Johnny and Tina over to her side.

"If I could have everyone's attention, please! I know we still have a lot of eating to do—"

"And drinking!" said Jerry.

"And I hope you liked the food . . . ," said Angelina.

The big round of applause confirmed it.

"Now I'd like to bring out my gift to the bride and groom for you all of you to see. And I also have a little surprise to share with you all."

It got quieter at the mention of a surprise. Angelina had their attention.

"I didn't want to let anyone know until today, but Il Primo Amore has taken on our first-ever pastry chef. He was never able to pursue *his* first love because he had to take care of his mother when he finished school, but he studied baking in France at Le Cordon Bleu school in *Paris*. He is a *maître pâtissier*, a master at his craft, and he's amazing. He's the one who made tonight's cake, which I think you'll agree is spectacular, and we give it with all our love to Johnny and Tina!"

A fanfare played, followed by a grand march, and the waitresses swung open the doors.

Douglas Pettibone, dressed in whites and wearing a pastry chef's toque at a rakish angle, wheeled out the most elaborate, astonishing monument of pastry that anyone in the room had ever seen. It was a monumental *croquembouche*, a classically French, intricately crafted tower of individual profiteroles, each thinly crusted with hard-crack sugar, filled with pastry cream, bound together with luscious, glistening strands of caramel and chocolate into a conical, colorful Christmas-tree shape that rose proudly high over the heads of the delighted newlyweds. *Chef de Pâtisserie* Pettibone had covered his *pièce montée* with a lustrous white-chocolate coating decorated with delicate, individually constructed marzipan roses and dusted ever so lightly in twenty-four-karat gold.

Johnny strode to the center of the room and heartily shook Mr. Pettibone's hand. When Tina recovered from the shock, she rushed over and hugged him tightly. Pettibone bowed and discreetly presented them both with a tiny, single-layered fruitcake with white frosting and a bride and groom on top, to stash away until their first anniversary. "For tradition's sake and for luck," he whispered.

Douglas Pettibone received the first standing ovation of his life, and as the music came up, everybody clapped and danced and sang along to a rousing chorus of *"Finiculì, Finiculà!"*

Angelina had to practically yell in Pettibone's ear, "Well, your secret's out."

"I know, and thank you, Angelina. It's a dream come true."

"I thought we might see Leslie here tonight . . ."

Pettibone took Angelina by the shoulders, turned her, and pointed through the raucous crowd in the direction of a slim, dashing, undeniably handsome, middle-aged gentleman in a tasteful black Savile Row tux with a bold, green plaid cummerbund.

"I'll introduce you formally later," he said. "I promise. He's desperate to meet you."

Angelina threw her arms Pettibone's neck and kissed him on both cheeks. "Douglas, I'm so happy for you. Hey, you never told me, how did you two make out with the big dinner?"

Pettibone smiled a smile that was angelic and devilish at the same time.

"It was the meal that sealed the deal!"

Gorgonzola Beef Tenderloin in a Barolo Reduction

Serves 6

INGREDIENTS FOR THE BAROLO
REDUCTION (SAUCE)
4 tablespoons unsalted butter (2 tablespoons
to sauté and 2 tablespoons cubed and kept
cold, to finish the sauce)
2 shallot cloves, minced
2 large garlic cloves, lightly crushed and
minced
1 large sprig fresh oregano, leaves stripped
off and chopped
1 ½ cups Barolo wine (such as Sordo 2007,
Pio Cesare 2004, or Renato Ratti 2004)
2 bay leaves
1½ cups beef stock
Salt and freshly ground black pepper, to taste

INGREDIENTS FOR THE MEAT
Six 4-to-6-ounce beef filet mignon steaks
Salt and freshly ground black pepper, to taste
2 tablespoons (about 1 ounce) Gorgonzola
cheese (such as Mountain Piccante,
Galbani, Klin, Lodigiani, or Mauri) cut into 6
sections

METHOD FOR THE SAUCE

In a large sauté pan, melt 2 tablespoons of the butter over medium heat. Add the shallots, garlic cloves, and oregano and cook until the shallots turn translucent, about 2 to 3 minutes, stirring frequently to prevent burning. Deglaze the pan with the Barolo, add the bay leaves, and let reduce by two-thirds, about 8 minutes. Add the bay leaves and beef stock and let reduce again by two-thirds. Remove from the heat, cover, and keep warm while you grill the steaks.

Just before service, reheat the sauce and strain. Remove from the heat and whisk in the remaining 2 tablespoons of cold cubed butter, a little at a time, letting each addition melt before adding the next. Adjust the seasoning to taste with salt and pepper.

METHOD FOR THE STEAKS

Preheat the oven to 400°F, and heat a grill pan over medium-high heat, or a grill to High. Season the steaks with salt and pepper, and sear undisturbed to begin caramelization and to prevent tearing of the flesh, about 4 minutes on each side. Continue to cook until cooked to your desired level of doneness, paying attention to creating desirable "grill marks." For medium-rare/medium, this will be to an internal temperature of 112°F to 115°F as measured with a meat thermometer, about 7 minutes per side (depending on the thickness of the steak). Transfer to a baking sheet and cut small slits in the top surface of the steaks, tucking the Gorgonzola cheese into the slits. Place in the oven and let the cheese melt, for about 2 minutes but no more than 5 minutes. Remove from the oven and let rest while you finish the sauce.

PRESENTATION
Spoon 2 tablespoons of the Barolo reduction into the center of each serving plate and place a steak on top of the sauce.

Pistachio-Crusted Salmon with a Cointreau Glaze and Cranberries

Serves 4

INGREDIENTS FOR THE CRANBERRIES
   1 fresh lemon, zested and juiced
   1 tablespoon sugar
   ½ cup Craisins (dried cranberries)

INGREDIENTS FOR THE SALMON
   Four 4-to-6-ounce salmon fillets
   Salt and freshly ground black pepper, to taste
   3 tablespoons canola oil
   2 shallot cloves, minced
   1 cup dry white wine
   1 fresh lemon, micro-zested and juiced

¼ cup Cointreau liqueur (you can use the 50 ml airplane-size bottle)

½ cup shelled pistachios, rubbed in a clean towel to remove covering, toasted for 5 minutes in a 250°F oven, and crushed in a plastic bag with a rolling pin

ACCOMPANIMENT
Scalloped Potatoes
Fresh Steamed Asparagus with Lemon Butter

METHOD FOR THE CRANBERRIES
Add 3 tablespoons water, the lemon juice, and the sugar to a saucepot. Bring to a boil over medium heat. Add the cranberries and lemon zest and return to a boil. Turn off the heat, cover, and let stand for about 10 minutes. Remove the pot from the stove and allow to cool to room temperature.

METHOD FOR THE FISH
Season the salmon with salt and pepper, rubbing the seasonings into the flesh. In a medium skillet, heat 1 tablespoon of the canola oil over medium heat. Add the shallots and sauté until they turn translucent, stirring frequently to prevent burning, about 1 minute. Transfer the shallots briefly to a utility plate. Increase the heat to medium high and add the remaining canola oil to the pan. When the oil begins to shimmer, sear the salmon with the skin side up, leaving the fish undisturbed for 3 or 4 minutes to allow caramelization to begin. This

will prevent any tearing of the flesh or "crusting off" of the seasonings. Flip the fish to sear the other side in the same way. After 2 minutes, pour ¼ cup of the wine into the pan. Cook briefly (about 2 more minutes) to allow the flavors to integrate, then transfer the salmon fillets to a platter, drizzle the lemon juice over them, and cover to keep warm and to let carryover cook.

Return the shallots to the pan and add the remaining wine, allowing the liquids to reduce to ½ cup over medium-high heat, about 3 to 5 minutes, monitoring to prevent burning. Strain the liquid, wipe out the pan, and return the juices to the skillet. Add the liqueur and allow to further thicken to a approximately ¼ cup of glaze, about 2 more minutes.

PRESENTATION
Place a fillet in the center of each serving plate, spoon two or three teaspoons of the warm glaze over the entire surface of each fish fillet, and sprinkle each with 1 to 2 tablespoons toasted pistachios, covering all of the top surface. Place a tablespoon of the cranberries next to the fish and top with a pinch of lemon zest. Serve with scalloped potatoes and 3 or 4 asparagus spears as an accompaniment. For a treat serve with a French white wine. Try a Grand Cru burgundy such as Corton-Charlemagne, Louis Jadot 2005.

Toasted-Nut Chicken Breasts with Dried-Fruit Wild Rice and Amaretto Sauce

Serves 6

INGREDIENTS FOR THE DRIED-FRUIT
WILD RICE
2½ cups low-sodium chicken stock
1½ cups wild-rice mix (such as a blend of
long-grain brown, sweet brown, whole-grain
black, etc.), briefly soaked in 3 to 5 changes
of enough cold water to cover and rinsed
with clear water through a fine-mesh strainer
¾ cup mixed dried fruits (apricots, apples,
pears, plums, and/or currants, such as
Woodstock Farms brand unsulfured), cut
into ¼-inch pieces
1 tablespoon unsalted butter
1½ teaspoons salt
½ cup cashews lightly crushed (place them in
a plastic bag and crush with a rolling pin)

INGREDIENTS FOR THE CHICKEN
1 cup dry-roasted walnuts (about 4 ounces),
such as Emerald brand
½ cup millet or sorghum flour
Six 6-ounce boneless, skinless chicken
breasts
Salt and freshly ground black pepper, to taste

2 eggs, beaten
½ cup milk
2 to 4 tablespoons canola oil, as needed to
  sauté
3 to 6 tablespoons unsalted butter, as needed
  to sauté
Juice of 1 fresh lime

INGREDIENTS FOR THE AMARETTO SAUCE
  1 tablespoon canola oil
  1 shallot clove, minced
  ½ cup Amaretto di Saronno liqueur
    (100 ml or 2 airplane-size bottles)
  1½ cups low-sodium chicken stock
  ¼ cup dry-roasted almonds (about 3 ounces),
    crushed, such as Blue Diamond or Emerald
    brand
  2 tablespoons cold unsalted butter, cut into
    cubes
  Salt and freshly ground black pepper, to taste

METHOD FOR THE DRIED-FRUIT WILD RICE
Bring the stock plus 1¼ cups water to a boil in a
medium saucepot. Stir in the rice, dried fruit,
butter, and salt. Return to a boil, reduce the heat to
low, cover, and cook undisturbed for 50 minutes.

  Remove from the heat and let stand for 5
minutes, then stir in the crushed cashews.

METHOD FOR THE TOASTED-NUT CHICKEN

Through the feed opening of a running blender or food processor, add the walnuts and the millet flour and chop them finely. Set aside briefly.

Lay plastic wrap over a large cutting board, tucking the edges under the board to secure it. Season both sides of the chicken breasts with salt and pepper and place them in a single layer on the plastic wrap. Cover the seasoned chicken with another layer of plastic wrap, tucking the edges under in the same way to keep the mess down while you tenderize them. Pound the chicken with a meat mallet to integrate the seasonings into the surface of the chicken.

Spread the flour/nut combination in a shallow pie plate or on a clean, flat work surface. Whisk together the eggs and milk, using the mixture to moisten each piece of chicken before coating them with the flour/nuts.

Preheat the oven to 350°F. In a large sauté pan, melt 2 tablespoons of the butter in 1 table-spoon oil over medium-high heat and sauté the coated chicken, curved side down first, leaving undisturbed for the first 4 minutes or so to allow the coating to integrate into the surface of the flesh and to prevent "crusting off." Melt another tablespoon of butter in a tablespoon of oil and flip the chicken breasts, cooking the other side in the same way. (You will probably have to sauté the chicken in batches.) Place the pieces of chicken into a roasting pan or onto a baking sheet. Bake in the oven until the flesh is fork tender and no longer pink, about 25 to 35 minutes.

METHOD FOR THE AMARETTO SAUCE

Make the sauce in the same pan in which you sautéed the chicken. Heat the oil over medium-high heat until it shimmers and cook the shallot until it turns translucent, stirring frequently to prevent burning, about 1 minute. Deglaze the pan with the amaretto, allowing most of it to evaporate, about 3 minutes. Then, add the chicken stock and allow it to reduce by half, about 5 minutes. Remove this sauce from the heat, strain it, and return it to the pan with the almonds, letting it reduce over medium heat to about ½ cup.

Remove the pan from the heat and use a small whisk or fork to gradually whisk the butter into the sauce, allowing each addition to melt before whisking in the next. Season to taste with salt and pepper.

PRESENTATION

Spoon ¾ cup rice into the center of each serving plate. Top with a chicken breast, spoon some sauce with almonds over it, and drizzle 1 teaspoon lime juice over each piece of chicken.

———

CHAPTER SEVENTEEN

Christmas Day Delivery

There was no Feast of the Seven Fishes that Christmas Eve. It would be a quiet holiday this year, not for a lack of festive spirit or reverence for the occasion, but because everyone seemed to have other plans. Pettibone had gone to Leslie's; Don Eddie and Phil went to visit the Don's older sister, Ronnie, who was getting on and lived in a nice house in the suburbs; Johnny and Tina had invited Joe and Maria, Gia, and Mrs. C over for spaghetti and meatballs. They had invited Angelina and Francis, of course, but Angelina had decided to spend the last four days before Christmas exclusively with her son. The holiday fell on Thursday, so she closed Il Primo that Tuesday and got their tree up and decorated and all of her Christmas shopping done under the wire by Wednesday morning.

Angelina's gift to herself was to spend every waking minute with her little boy. She promised the family that she and the baby would come for a visit after dinner on Christmas Day, to open presents and such, but she keenly felt the need to play Santa on her own, maybe drink a mimosa toast to Frank, relax, play Christmas carols on the hi-fi, and celebrate with Francis. The best idea, it seemed to her, was to quit rushing after the future as if it were trying to get away from her and, for just one day, stop and think about what the future had to offer instead.

Basil had spent the day shopping for stocking stuffers and came home at twilight on Christmas Eve to an empty house, except for a note from Dottie letting him know that she had gone to pick up a ham for dinner and that Guy had gone over to the National. Basil put his hat and coat back on and decided to wander over to the diner for a nice piece of cake.

He had been worried about Guy for the last few weeks. He had gotten quieter and hadn't been hanging around the house much. Whenever Basil asked him about it, he'd sigh or say that he'd been writing at the library or had gone for a long walk. So this, Basil decided, might be his chance to get to the bottom of it.

When he walked into the National, the place was uncharacteristically quiet, seeing as it was Christmas Eve. He scanned the booths and saw Guy sitting at the counter in front of a napkin holder decorated with plastic holly, nursing a cup of coffee. Basil hung his jacket and hat on the coat rack.

"There you are," said Basil, and clapped Guy on the shoulder as he took a seat beside him.

"Hey," said Guy.

The waitress behind the counter dropped a menu in front of Basil. He opened it and scanned it with feigned interest.

"I haven't seen you around very much these days," said Basil.

Guy shrugged. "I've been spending a lot of time in the library—"

"—and walking, I know."

Guy took a sip from his cup, but it had long gone cold. He pushed it away and signaled to the waitress.

"This is a funny place to be spending Christmas Eve," said Basil, replacing his menu in the little spiral rack.

"I just wanted to sit and think for a while."

The waitress came over and tipped hot coffee into Guy's cup.

Basil nodded to her. "I'll have a cup of coffee and a piece of that Bundt cake, please, miss."

"Sure," she said, and scuttled off.

Basil clasped his hands together professorially. "Sitting and thinking, eh? We have chairs at the house."

"I thought I'd pick up a pie, too."

"Now you're talking. So, what are you sitting and thinking about?"

"Christmas, I guess. Baby Jesus. The future."

"Ah," said Basil as his cake arrived, "speaking of the future, I think you should try to get Angelina to come over for dinner tomorrow. Maybe you could stop by in the early afternoon and invite her. I already asked, but she might not turn down a face-to-face invitation from you on Christmas Day when she's home all alone with the baby."

Guy turned and looked at him. "She's going to be all alone on Christmas?"

Basil took a forkful of his cake. "I don't think it's a good idea either."

Guy went quiet and thoughtful, the way he so often did.

Basil pushed the cake aside. It was a little dry for his taste, but the coffee was strong and piping hot.

"You like Angelina, don't you?"

Guy seemed to perk up at the mention of her name. "A lot. Basil, I've never known anyone like her. She's mostly what I've been sitting here thinking about."

"So . . ."

Guy's mouth drew itself into a thin line of frustration. "But, I feel a pull, too. A pull back to the life I left behind. Being with her, especially the day her baby was born . . . I never told you, but, at first, we thought there was something wrong with the baby, that he wasn't breathing. She asked me to baptize him."

"Did you?" asked Basil, surprised.

For an instant, Guy was back in Angelina's bedroom on that day, hearing her call out to him. "No. I didn't have to. He was fine. But I could see how important it was to her. How important the condition of his soul was to her."

Basil nodded; these were big issues that Guy was grappling with, and they were especially resonant tonight of all nights.

"Some men might not like seeing a woman, a widow, with a new baby," Basil said, then sipped.

"That's not it. Not even close. I just feel like I have more questions than answers in my head. I am attracted to Angelina and I think that helping to deliver her baby was the most moving and powerful thing I have ever experienced. But I have questions—questions about faith, and about myself. About where I belong, where I need to be so that I can do the most good. Maybe she deserves somebody who's not questioning everything all the time. Somebody who will be there just for her, on her terms."

Basil decided the time had come to speak frankly. "Guy, maybe what she deserves is a good man with a good heart who can be with her and love her and her child. Terms? They can always be negotiated. If you want my honest opinion, she needs to move on, and you need to move on. But nothing can happen until somebody makes a move. You need to make a choice, Guy. If you don't, somebody might beat you to it."

Guy nodded solemnly, knowing that Basil was right.

Their waitress came by with a white cardboard pie box tied with string and placed it down in front of Guy with the check.

"By the way. I was offered a job."

Basil looked shocked, then tried not to. "Really?"

"Yeah. At a paper out in Bucks County, doing some writing and editing. Pretty good money, too, considering it's not a big paper. All those hours at the library dusting off my writing skills might be paying off."

"Are you going take it?"

Guy laughed, since he knew what kind of a response his answer was going to get. "I haven't decided."

Basil had to laugh, too. "Oh, and while we're talking about money," he said, "I have a question for you. At the wedding, Angelina mentioned to me that Jerry took her shopping for a crib and all the baby things and thanked us all for pitching in the money. I didn't say anything to her, but I never put in any money, did you?"

"No. Jerry never asked me."

"Me neither," said Basil. "I asked the others if they chipped in, but he didn't ask any of them either."

"So, Jerry did it all on his own and paid for everything?"

401

"I guess so."

Basil shook a little sugar into his cup and stirred it with the wrong end of his spoon.

Guy looked at the door and back at Basil, as though he'd just heard the bell ring and seen somebody he knew unexpectedly come in. A change seemed to come over him, something clicked, as if he'd just solved the toughest clue in a tricky crossword puzzle.

Without warning, Guy stood up and threw some money on the counter. "I have to go. I have something I have to do."

Basil looked up, startled. "When are you coming home?"

"I'm not sure." Guy put on his coat and picked up his pie box.

Basil turned on his stool to face Guy head-on. "Guy, if you'll take some advice from an older man, let me just say that someday, somehow, you are going to have to make up your mind."

Guy put his hand on Basil's shoulder and looked him right in the eye. "Know what? I think I just did. Merry Christmas!"

Christmas morning came bright and clear, and Angelina could hear the church bells ringing off in the distance. She had bundled Francis up and had taken him to midnight mass the night before, which was her favorite mass of the year. The church always looked so marvelous, and all of the altar boys got the chance to participate at one time in their bright red cassocks and white gowns, and the singing was the most enthusiastic of the entire calendar year, by far. Francis slept right through the whole thing.

They woke up and had a little breakfast together, then Angelina carried him into the living room and his eyes opened wide when he saw the colors and shapes and sizes of all the boxes and packages that she had stayed up to lay under the tree the night before. They opened a few and saved some for later. She wanted to make the day last.

Angelina'd had a dream about Frank early Christmas morning, which surprised her. She hadn't had one for a month or two, even though she thought of him at least a few times every day, most often whenever she looked at Francis.

In her dream, Francis was older, about five she guessed, and he and Frank were down in the basement. They were building a child's writing desk together, just in time for the start of first grade. Frank was teaching Francis how to hold a hammer and tap in a nail, how to drive it in straight and evenly. She watched them work for a while, then said to Frank, "I didn't know you guys were down here."

Frank said, "Sure. It's nice down here. I'll be down here if you need me."

"Isn't he beautiful?" she said.

"What'd you expect? He's ours."

That's when she woke up.

Angelina and Francis watched *Miracle on 34th Street*, which Angelina was seeing for the hundredth time and Francis, the first. She cried at the scene when Kris Kringle spoke Dutch to the little orphan girl, and Francis cried when it was time for lunch. She fed him Gerber's and Cheerios, and she had a grilled-cheese-and-tomato sandwich. Angelina had absolutely nothing planned for dinner, which was a situation she hadn't found herself in for ages, and she found it strangely liberating. She figured that she would throw something simple together later in the day, then pack up around sixish with the baby and head to Tina and Johnny's down the street for a yuletide visit with Francis's grandma and the folks.

Bing Crosby was crooning in the background as they were sitting on the floor in the early afternoon, opening the last of the packages, when the doorbell rang.

Angelina looked up, and through the curtains she could just make out the shape of a man, carrying a box of some kind in his hands.

She sat up and wondered if Basil had sent poor Guy to her house on another mercy mission. Or maybe it was Basil himself, coming to invite her over one last time.

"Oh, my goodness, who could that be?" she whispered to Francis. "It could be Santa coming back for more cookies! Come on, let's go see."

She scooped him up in her arms, and they rushed over and opened the door.

"Jerry! What are you doing here?"

Jerry looked around, pretending he was checking that he'd come to the right address. He had a wrapped present under each arm, and in his hands he held a large, covered Pyrex dish. He smiled and one of the packages started to slip. Angelina maneuvered a free hand and helped shove it back under his arm.

"It's Christmas! Um, so I decided to come and see you. And the baby."

Angelina just smiled back and waited for him to continue.

"I was talking to a mutual friend of ours . . . and I heard you two were over here all by yourselves on Christmas Day. And I had some presents for you anyway, so . . . here I am!"

Angelina laughed. "Come on in," Angelina said. "Francis, look who's here!"

Jerry came in and dropped the presents on the couch from under his arms one at a time, then turned to face Angelina. "I'd have been here sooner, but . . ." He sheepishly held up the Pyrex.

"What's in the dish?" asked Angelina, genuinely curious.

"I didn't think you should have to cook on Christmas Day, so I made something."

If he had wanted to, Jerry could have knocked Angelina over with a string of tinsel.

"*You* made?"

"Yeah. Don't be scared."

Suddenly, she couldn't wait to get a peek under the lid. "What is it?"

"*Stracotto*. Italian Pot Roast. I found my mom's recipe and I've been cooking since early this morning. Came out pretty good. I think."

Angelina shifted Francis into the crook of her arm and leaned in as Jerry lifted the lid to show her. She looked inside, breathed in deeply, tasted the sauce with her finger, then started to laugh.

"What's so funny?"

"You made this?" she asked in wide-eyed disbelief.

"Yeah."

"It's *perfect*."

"You don't have to act so surprised."

Now all three of them were laughing. They shifted their respective loads, and Angelina ended up with the dish and Jerry ended up with the baby. She stood there for a long moment, watching him make faces at Francis, and looked him over thoroughly, up and down and up again.

"Thank you very much for the *stracotto*," said Angelina. "I just don't know what to say. I am so glad you came over. Look at you. You look different somehow."

He just shrugged, took off his jacket and took

Francis over to the couch. Angelina shook her head and looked back at him over her shoulder again as she took the dish into the kitchen. A minute later, she returned carrying a bottle of red and two glasses.

"Let's celebrate," Angelina said.

"Celebrate what?"

"Christmas. And you know what? I'm pretty sure this is the first time you've ever been here on your own. For a visit, I mean."

Jerry thought for a minute. "No. Really?"

Angelina smiled. "I'm pretty sure." She popped the cork and poured.

Jerry sat on the sofa with Francis settled comfortably in his lap. They looked nice together, thought Angelina, like old pals. She sat next to them. Their glasses sounded a clear, crystal-sweet note when they touched them together and both said "Merry Christmas," simultaneously.

"You want to open your presents?" asked Jerry.

"No, I just want to sit here for a minute." Then, after a few seconds of silence, finally, it dawned on her.

"That's it."

"That's what?"

"The tie. You're wearing a tie."

Jerry was as nonchalant as he could be, and acted as if they'd both only just noticed it at the same time. "Oh, this? How about that? I came from church, is all."

"Oh, from church? Really?"

He grinned. "Come on, it's Christmas! And I know you've got this thing about ties, so . . ."

"I'm just saying, it's a very nice tie. How about some music?"

Jerry lifted the baby to face him and gave him a little wiggle. "Whaddya say, Francis? How about some music?"

Just outside and across the street, Guy closed the front door behind him. He'd just said his good-byes to Basil and Dottie, who were both genuinely happy for him and the decision he had made. Guy stopped and looked toward Angelina's house, where he could see in through the front window. He saw Francis bobbing up and down and laughing, and the top of Jerry's head.

He pulled the scarf up around his priestly collar, tipped his steamer trunk back on its wheels, and rolled off toward the bus stop. Guy wasn't very good at taking advice, but he was pretty good at giving it—and he was glad to see that Jerry had taken his.

Inside, Angelina put her favorite Christmas record on the turntable, the one she had been saving for last, Nat King Cole's *The Christmas Song*. The record spun and she dropped the needle. Lush strains of piano and strings played, and that silky, sweet voice started singing, *"Chestnuts roasting on an open fire . . ."*

Angelina turned and stood still and looked at Jerry, who had come right to her door on Christmas Day, who had cooked her dinner, and was sitting on her couch playing with her baby boy. Wearing a tie.

She hardly knew what to think.

It was like falling asleep next to the tree and waking up on Christmas morning. You never knew what you might see once you opened your eyes.

Angelina went back to the sofa and sat down. She kissed Francis on the head, but didn't take him out of Jerry's lap.

It would be just perfect, she thought, if snow started falling gently outside the window.

Oh, look, there it goes.

Stracotto *(Italian Pot Roast)*

Serves 6 to 8

INGREDIENTS
   3-to-4-pound beef round or rump roast
   3 large garlic cloves, lightly crushed and
      sliced in half lengthwise
   1 teaspoon dried oregano
   1 teaspoon dried thyme
   ½ teaspoon dried rosemary
   ½ teaspoon salt

¼ teaspoon ground black pepper

2 tablespoons canola oil

1 large white onion, diced

2 cups white mushrooms, cleaned, trimmed, and quartered

1½ cups dry red wine

2 large carrots, peeled and cut into 1-inch slices

1 celery stalk, cut into 1-inch pieces

2 bay leaves

2 tablespoons tomato paste

2 cups beef stock

One 29-to-32-ounce can whole plum tomatoes

½ teaspoon celery seed

½ teaspoon fennel seed

6 medium potatoes (about 1½ to 2 pounds)

2 tablespoons unsalted cold butter, cubed

2 tablespoons fresh flat-leaf parsley leaves, minced

METHOD

Rinse the roast to remove impurities and pat dry with paper towels. Make slits in the meat and firmly insert the garlic cloves. Mix together the oregano, thyme, rosemary, salt, and black pepper and, using a mortar and pestle, pulverize to a powder. Rub the herb mixture into the meat.

Heat one tablespoon of the oil over medium-high heat in a sauté pan that is 4-quarts or larger.

When the oil begins to shimmer, sear the meat on all sides, leaving each side undisturbed for about 3 minutes to allow the seasonings to integrate into the surface of the meat and to prevent the flesh from tearing. When the roast has been browned on all sides, temporarily transfer it to a utility platter.

Add the remaining oil to the same pan over medium heat. When it begins to shimmer, sauté the onion until it turns translucent, stirring frequently to prevent burning, about 2 minutes. Add the mushrooms and sauté them until they give up their juices, about 7 minutes. Deglaze the pan with ½ cup of the red wine and allow most of it to evaporate. Then, add the carrots, celery, and bay leaves, and stir in the tomato paste. Add the beef stock, tomatoes, celery seed, fennel seed, and the rest of the wine and bring to a boil over medium-high heat. Return the meat to the pan, reduce the heat to medium low, cover, and let cook slowly until the meat is fork tender, but still intact, about 2 to 2½ hours.

In the last 20 minutes of cooking time, peel the potatoes and slice them into ¼-inch-thick slices into the pot. Cover and cook until tender.

Remove the meat to a platter. Discard the bay leaves and, using a slotted spoon, transfer the carrots, celery, tomatoes, and potatoes to the same platter. Cover to keep warm and let rest.

Pour the cooking liquids into a clear heatproof

container, such as a Pyrex measuring container, and refresh the pan. Spoon or pour off any layer of fat that forms at the top of the cooking juices and strain what remains back into the pan to make a sauce. Over medium-high heat, reduce the juices to about 1 cup of liquid, about 5 to 8 minutes. Just before serving, remove the sauce from the heat and gradually whisk in the butter, allowing each addition to melt before adding the next. Season to taste with salt and pepper.

PRESENTATION

Slice the roast into ¾-to-1-inch-thick slices using a sharp knife. Spoon about ½ cup potatoes into the center of each serving plate and top with a slice of meat and some carrots and celery. Spoon some of the sauce over and sprinkle with parsley leaves.

INDEX OF RECIPES

365 Filet Mignon in a Grand Marnier Reduction
with Chestnut Mashed Potatoes and
Green Beans Amandine
387 Gorgonzola Beef Tenderloin in a Barolo
Reduction
389 Pistachio-Crusted Salmon with a Cointreau
Glaze and Cranberries
392 Toasted-Nut Chicken Breasts with
Dried-Fruit Wild Rice and Amaretto
Sauce
409 *Stracotto* (Italian Pot Roast)

ACKNOWLEDGMENTS

The authors would like to thank Lucinda Blumenfeld, Tricia Boczkowski, Kate Dresser, Stephen Boldt, Ayelet Gruenspecht, Dana Sloan, and Alexandra Lewis for working to make this book a reality. Virginia would like to acknowledge the tutelage and guidance of the professional chefs she's worked with over the years, especially David, George & George, and Robert. She sends her thanks to her godmothers and grandmothers for having generously shared their extensive culinary knowledge and expertise with a little girl eager to learn to cook. Our appreciation is also extended to Michel Richard, Cat Cora, Paula Deen, and Ming Tsai.

Readers Group Guide

Introduction

When Angelina finds herself suddenly widowed and jobless, she picks herself up the best way she knows how—by cooking. Her culinary pursuits catch the attention of retiree Basil, who has just moved in across the street from Angelina. Basil makes Angelina an offer she can't refuse: he'll pay her handsomely in return for preparing most of his meals. Angelina jumps at the chance to make some money doing what she loves, and soon expands her list of clientele to seven hungry bachelors. This disparate but charming group of men forms a protective circle around Angelina —providing her with a new kind of family.

Topics and Questions for Discussion

1. In the beginning of the novel, Angelina states ". . . cooking was not just about food. It was about character." (p. 10) What does she mean by this statement? How is it true throughout the book? How does food define her character?

2. Angelina is furious when Amy tries to pass off a store-bought cake as her own. Why does this anger her so much? How would you have reacted?

3. Family and community are extremely important to the characters in this novel. "In South Philly, the organizing principles were family, church, and neighborhood, in that order." (p. 56) What are the "organizing principles" in your life? Are they similar to Angelina's?

4. Angelina turns to her passion for cooking as therapy after her husband dies. Do you have a hobby that has helped you through a tough time?

5. Basil is the one who initially proposes that Angelina cook for him. Were you surprised at his rather unique request?

6. Angelina learns to cook from her mother and other family members, and she in turn teaches Tina. Do you have any family cooking traditions? How did you learn to cook?

7. Think of your own relationship with food and cooking. Are there particular meals that elicit memories or strong emotional responses? What is your favorite "comfort food"?

8. Angelina and Guy pay a spontaneous visit to a fortune-teller, who tells them "You may hold a new life in your hands." (p. 204) What did you think she meant by that? Do you believe in fortune-telling?

9. Two momentous events happen on Christmas Eve: Johnny proposes to Tina and Angelina discovers she is pregnant! Which surprised you more? What did you think of Johnny's proposal?

10. Basil tells Angelina about a book he has read, *Cyrano de Bergerac*. (pp. 241) Of its heroine he says, "So, by not choosing, she made her choice." (p. 242) Do you see any parallels between *Cyrano de Bergerac* and *Angelina's Bachelors*?

11. Look back over the chapter titles, which often include the names of food dishes and clever plays on words. Which is your favorite? Why?

12. When Angelina is in labor, she thinks, "The only way to get to the other side of anything is to go through it." (p. 297) Do you agree? How is this evident in the novel?

13. *Angelina's Bachelors* features strong, independent women, such as Angelina, Gia, and

Mrs. Cappuccio. Think about the gender roles in this novel. How are they traditional and how are they unconventional?

14. Compare and contrast Guy and Jerry. Which one do you think is a better match for Angelina? Who would you pick for her?

15. Angelina names her restaurant Il Primo Amore, after the Italian saying meaning "The first love you never forget." If you were to open a restaurant, what would you name it?

Enhance Your Book Club

1. Have everyone in your group make a recipe from the book to bring to your meeting—make sure to coordinate main dishes and sides! Or gather in the kitchen and make a meal together.

2. Angelina's tight-knit community frequently brings food to neighbors in times of trouble. Make an extra dish and take it to a neighbor or friend, or donate food and/or your time to a local food pantry or soup kitchen.

3. Angelina loves cooking to the music of Louis Prima. You can pick up his Greatest Hits

CD for under $10 online, or download a few tracks to get a feel for his exuberant and eclectic style—make sure to listen to his hit song "Angelina"!

4. Angelina and Guy visit a fortune-teller for fun one night. As a group visit a local fortune-teller, or use Tarot playing cards and an online guide to tell one another's fortune yourselves.

5. Basil wants to "experience the artistic side of life" in his retirement. Reread his "bucket list" on page 100 (reading epic poetry, going to museums, listening to opera, etc.), and pick one to do with your group. Do you have your own "bucket list"?

A Conversation with Brian O'Reilly

You collaborated with your wife, Virginia, for this novel. Tell us about your partnership. Did you come up with all the recipes? How did you choose which to include?

Angelina's Bachelors was a true partnership. Roughly, the division of labor between Virginia and me fell along the lines that I was primarily responsible for the writing, she for the recipes, but there was a lot of crossover, particularly since she provides much-needed feminine perspective. It's probably fair to say that first and foremost I write for her—she reads everything before anyone else, usually as the chapters are being written, and I rely on her judgment implicitly. Her critiques and suggestions are inevitably spot-on. Her input was invaluable (as you might expect) in crafting the scene in which Angelina gives birth, for instance, and in charting the course of the complex and shifting relationship between Guy, Jerry, and Angelina. The name "Angelina" was Virginia's suggestion. In terms of the recipes, I often request a recipe for an element I feel I need from a literary or plotting standpoint (". . . the most incredible cake ever made, please—and work Frangelico in there somehow"; or "an irresistible, seductive

423

three-course dinner for two"; "oh, and a lasagna that changes a man's life forever . . ."), that sort of thing; Virginia makes them a reality. If I'm not looking for something specific, she just goes off and comes up with something wonderful and surprising that surpasses my wildest expectations (Aubergine Napoleons, anyone?). She's created a recipe for virtually everything mentioned in the book, and we chose which to use based on what made the most impact in context.

Who does the cooking in your house, you or your wife?

We're pretty much a cooking household, and I think we have complementary skill sets. When I'm in-house writing, I like doing the day-to-day cooking—my favorite thing is to stick my head in the refrigerator, see what we have on hand, and throw together omelets for breakfast, or an interesting pasta or salad dish for lunch; I like to sauté and roast for dinner, with maybe a hearty soup or stew (I love single-pot meals) and a giant, seasonal salad thrown in for good measure. (We rely on tomato sauce—red gravy to some—with sausages and meatballs, cooked faithfully every Monday, to fill in the gaps.) Virginia is a skilled baker (thus, my sad addiction to pie) and, I'd say, is more of a fine cook than I am. She now has vast experience in researching, testing, and creating chef-level recipes, having written for *Dinner: Impossible*, two published cookbooks, and for *Angelina's Bachelors*. She knows how to build mother sauces, what pairings work best classically, and so forth. I'm more of an improviser in the kitchen. Once, we received a gift of lobster tails for Christmas, and I just backed out of the kitchen slowly and let her go to work. Most memorable—open-face lobster-and-mascarpone raviolis made with handmade pasta sheets in a champagne lobster sauce.

Angelina learns many of her cooking skills from her mother. Who taught you how to cook?

My mother always made sure we had big family dinners at home, so I grew up in that tradition. I like to say that I really started to learn how to cook from Emeril Lagasse; I was obsessed with *Emeril Live* when it first started and I would watch what he made one day, then try my hand at re-creating his dishes for dinner the next (his garlic soup was a revelation). Virginia and I are both fortunate to have worked with fantastic chefs during the run of *Dinner: Impossible* and throughout the writing of two cookbooks, and that was a full-blown cooking education in and of itself. Virginia has been cooking since she was little; the story about making butter from whipping cream is a real-life experience from her childhood. She's always researching and studying and picking up new techniques (Michel Richard has been an ongoing inspiration for her). In the end, I think you learn the most from doing—once you start cooking real food day in and day out for your family and friends, you're on your way.

Do you have a favorite dish or comfort food you turn to during difficult times?

Good days and bad, we always try to make sure we eat well. Good food brings you right to back to your center, even if you're feeling assailed on all sides. Spaghetti alla carbonara, fish and chips, bangers and mash, deviled eggs, duck cassoulet, lemon meringue pie, even a good bagel with lox and cream cheese (and maybe a little red onion . . . couple of capers . . .), all fit the bill. Virginia makes a tuna melt with fresh albacore tuna steaks that can cure a rainy day—and her shrimp cocktail . . . oh, my.

One note along these lines—make soup. If you can chop vegetables and boil water, you can learn to make soul-satisfying soups in practically no time at all. Get your hands on an immersion blender and get started right away. There is simply nothing that compares with homemade soup.

Your characters are well developed and have original quirks—they feel like they could be real neighbors. Are any of them based on people you know?

I would say that the characters in *Angelina's Bachelors* are more amalgamations of people I've known, informed by real-life events, but not so much based on real individuals. Partly, the character of Don Eddie is inspired by stories I've heard over the years from my mom and dad about a guy named Blinky who lived across the driveway from my grandmother outside of Philadelphia. He was legendarily known as a "fight fixer" but had a soft spot for my mother's family. I kept some of the more colorful elements (the cases of champagne at Johnny and Tina's wedding is based on a real story from my parents' wedding), and took out the scarier ones. Virginia contributed many anecdotes, such as those about a priest she knew who left the clergy for a while and who, upon his return, was very open in his sermons about some of the experiences he'd had as a lay person that ultimately enriched his ability to minister to his congregation. We both have the deepest affection for the character of Basil Cupertino, the quasi-confirmed-bachelor uncle, loosely based on a number of professorial and genteel older gentlemen we've observed and admired over the years.

You seem very familiar with Italian culture and the neighborhoods of South Philly. Are you Italian? From Philadelphia?

I went to school in Philadelphia and I've had friends and acquaintances from South Philly. It's a place with a deep "people" culture. People who grew up in South Philadelphia seem to intrinsically know something about one another, even if they've never met. I've never lived there, but I think it's a very human place, where the values of family, loyalty, and neighborhood are front and center. It always struck me as an interesting place to be from. At the heart of it, there's the food. Red gravy seems to flow through everybody's veins in South Philly from birth. Food is taken seriously there. Philadelphia is a world-class city in many ways and under-appreciated, perhaps because it is eclipsed by its proximity to New York and Washington, D.C. It has so much history and culture to offer. It's an appealing setting because the history that's important isn't just the colonial history of Independence Hall, but the kind of history that the funeral director Mr. DiGregorio prides himself in knowing, how families are intertwined—the history that impacts our daily lives and how we live those lives. The culture is not just the "culture" of the Philadelphia Orchestra, it is the culture of ancestry that, in a setting like South

Philly, you can practically taste. For lovers of food and cooking, the 9th Street Italian Market is as real as you can get. A visit there makes you want to be an Italian. Choosing this particular setting was a very conscious choice because of its natural fit with the story line.

This is your first novel. What inspired you to move from cookbook to novel format? How was the writing process for Angelina's Bachelors *different from that of* Mission: Cook! *and* Impossible to Easy?

Writing *Angelina's Bachelors* was an exercise in pure pleasure. The novel was inspired by a story my wife told me about a woman she knew of, an older widow who cooked for gentlemen in similar circumstances. The idea grabbed me right out of the box; it seemed wonderfully old-fashioned and had limitless possibilities for the exploration of character through the prism of cooking and food. The cookbooks were fun to write and, as I said, intensely educational, but my aspiration has always been to write fiction—hopefully, we're off to a good start!

You are the creator and executive producer of Food Network's Dinner: Impossible. *What inspired you to create the show?*

Dinner: Impossible came about some time after I had met Robert Irvine. I'd had it in mind for a while to pursue the idea of creating a Food Network show and Robert had amazing credentials. I also thought he had some compelling personal attributes that were ready-made for TV. We tried a couple of different formats that didn't work, but once I got to know him better and heard some of his stories of cooking under fire (for instance, throwing together a last minute bash for the 2005 Oscar ceremony), we went with the idea of essentially putting him into "impossible" cooking situations (in an authentic colonial kitchen without electricity, in an ice hotel in sub-freezing temperatures, on a deserted island . . .), and watching what happens as he tries to cook his way out of them. I think he's a remarkable chef.

Can you tell us about any projects you're currently working on? Do you have plans for a sequel?

On the TV front, I'm working on a developing a couple of projects for PBS that have more to do with politics (another passion of mine) than

430

cooking. We've just about completed work on a second novel. Don't want to give out too many details, but it's another "Novel with Food," and features a strong female central character who, you're probably not shocked to learn, is also an excellent cook. Beyond that, still have a few surprises in store.

Angelina's Bachelors seems like it would lend itself well to a movie format, such as books-turned-movies like Julie & Julia *and* Eat Pray Love. *Do you envision a movie for your novel? If so, who would you cast?*

We actually talk about a possible film version of *Angelina's Bachelors* quite a bit. The name that most often comes up for Angelina is Marisa Tomei; for Basil, Alan Arkin, which would be a dream come true. The mental image we have of Jerry is Dermot Mulroney from *My Best Friend's Wedding*, and, as a *Boston Legal* fan, I can't get Mark Valley (Brad Chase) out of my head as Guy. We're huge Alan Rickman fans and I think he'd make an indelible Douglas Pettibone. For Don Eddie? We like Ernest Borgnine (and not just because he's Mermaid Man!).

Center Point Publishing
600 Brooks Road • PO Box 1
Thorndike ME 04986-0001 USA

(207) 568-3717

US & Canada:
1 800 929-9108
www.centerpointlargeprint.com